MECHANISM

Published by Top Cow Productions, Inc.
Los Angeles

MECHANISM™

RAFFAELE IENCO

WRITER • ARTIST • LETTERER

"MECHANISM" created by Raffaele Ienco

Ryan Cady & Ashley Victoria Robinson
Editors

Original editions edited by: Ryan Cady & Ashley Victoria Robinson

For this edition production by: Tricia Ramos

"Mechanism" logo designed by: Raffaele Ienco

For Top Cow Productions, Inc.
Marc Silvestri - CEO
Matt Hawkins - President and COO
Ashley Victoria Robinson - Editor
Elena Salcedo - Director of Operations
Henry Barajas - Operations Coordinator
Vincent Valentine - Production Artist
Dylan Gray - Marketing Director

IMAGE COMICS, INC.
Robert Kirkman—Chief Operating Officer
Erik Larsen—Chief Financial Officer
Todd McFarlane—President
Marc Silvestri—Chief Executive Officer
Jim Valentino—Vice-President

Eric Stephenson—Publisher
Corey Murphy—Director of Sales
Jeff Boison—Director of Publishing Planning & Book Trade Sales
Chris Ross—Director of Digital Sales
Kat Salazar—Director of PR & Marketing
Branwyn Bigglestone—Controller
Susan Korpela—Accounts Manager
Drew Gill—Art Director
Brett Warnock—Production Manager
Meredith Wallace—Print Manager
Briah Skelly—Publicist
Aly Hoffman— Conventions & Events Coordinator
Sasha Head—Sales & Marketing Production Designer
David Brothers—Branding Manager
Melissa Gifford—Content Manager
Erika Schnatz—Production Artist
Ryan Brewer—Production Artist
Shanna Matuszak—Production Artist
Tricia Ramos—Production Artist
Vincent Kukua—Production Artist
Jeff Stang—Direct Market Sales Representative
Emilio Bautista—Digital Sales Associate
Leanna Caunter—Accounting Assistant
Chloe Ramos-Peterson—Library Market Sales Representative
IMAGECOMICS.COM

MECHANISM, VOL. 1. First printing. January 2017. Published by Image Comics, Inc. Office of publication: 2701 NW Vaughn St., Suite 780, Portland, OR 97210. ISBN 978-1-5343-0032-3.

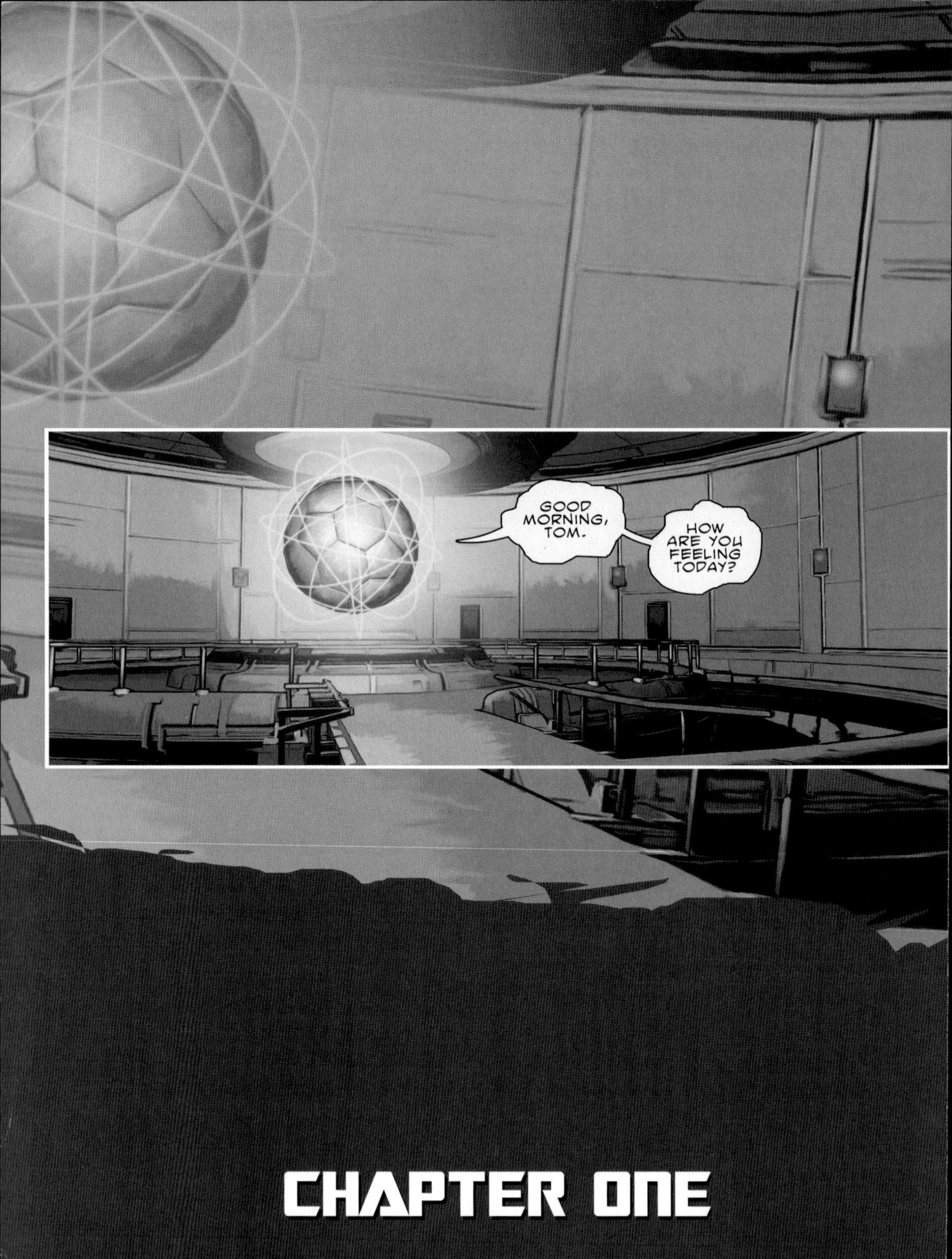
GOOD MORNING, TOM.
HOW ARE YOU FEELING TODAY?

CHAPTER ONE

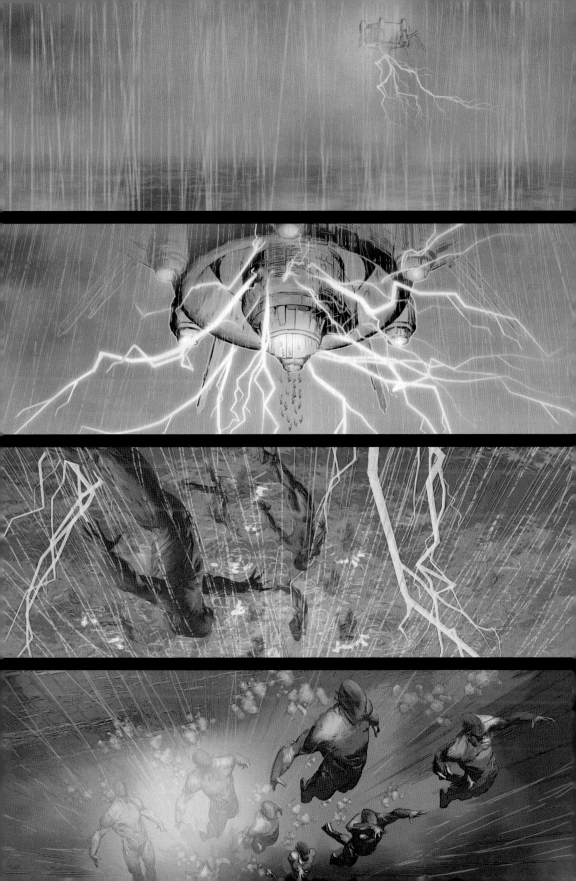

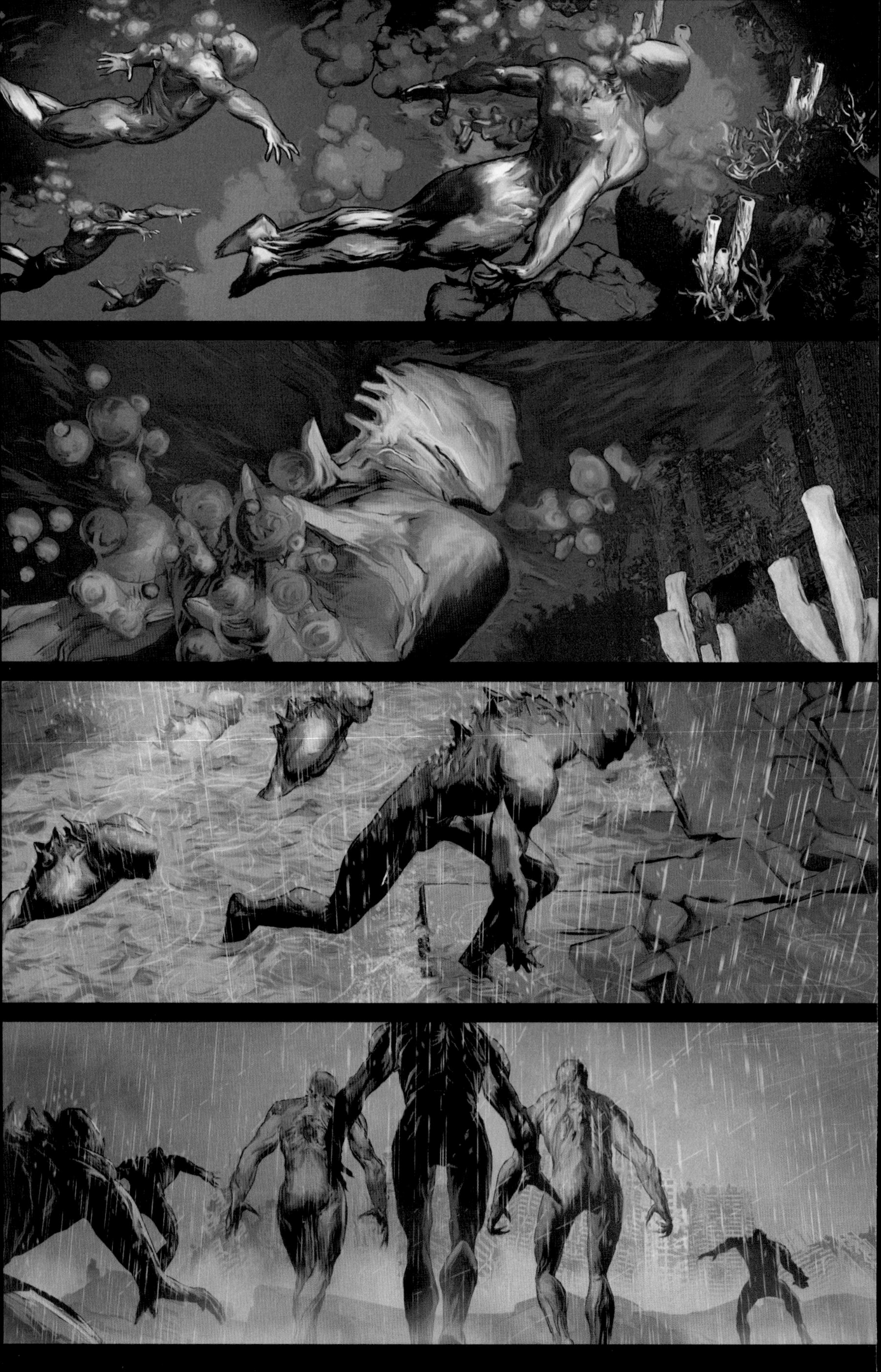

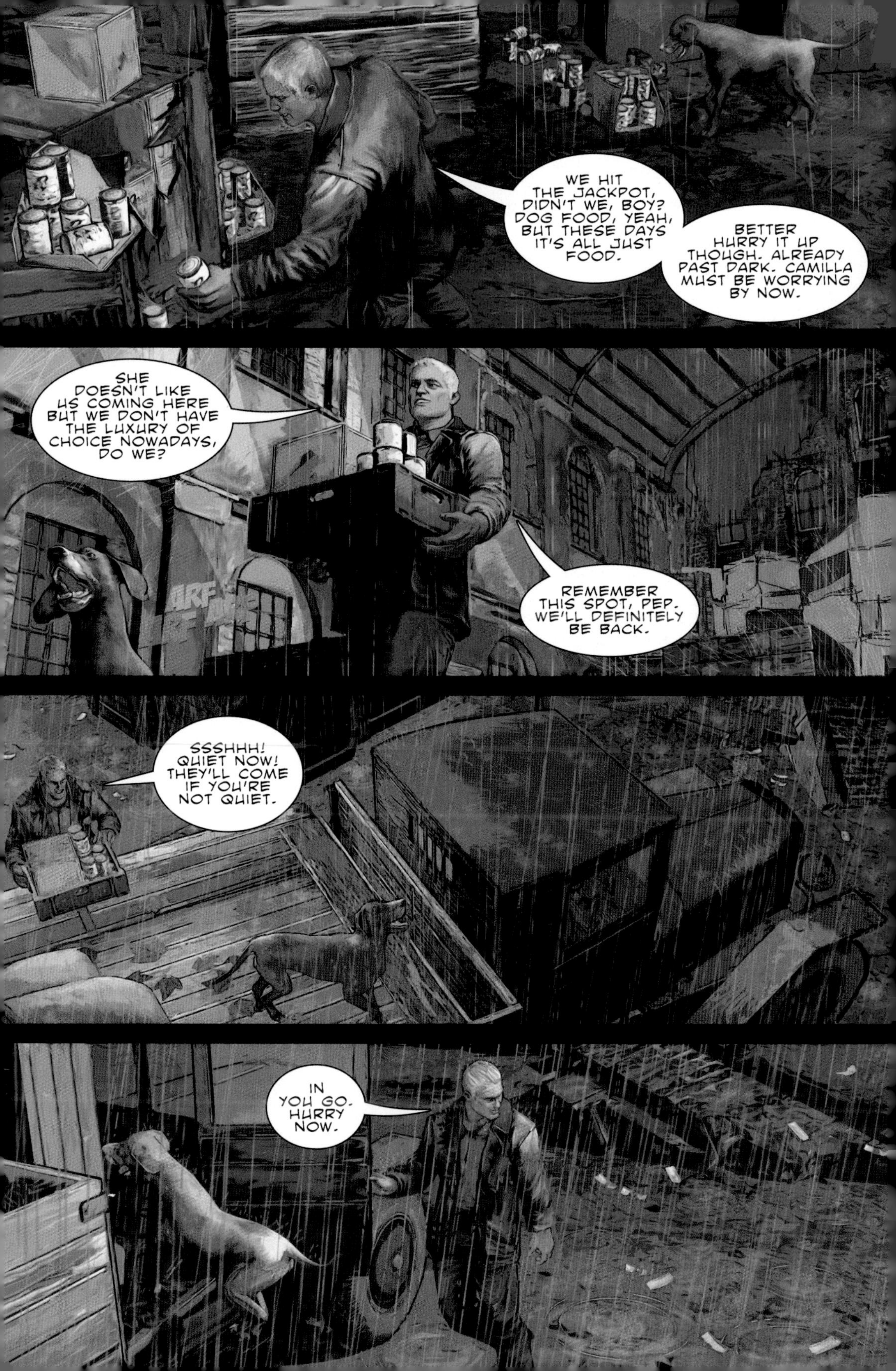
WE HIT THE JACKPOT, DIDN'T WE, BOY? DOG FOOD, YEAH, BUT THESE DAYS IT'S ALL JUST FOOD.
BETTER HURRY IT UP THOUGH. ALREADY PAST DARK. CAMILLA MUST BE WORRYING BY NOW.
SHE DOESN'T LIKE US COMING HERE BUT WE DON'T HAVE THE LUXURY OF CHOICE NOWADAYS, DO WE?
REMEMBER THIS SPOT, PEP. WE'LL DEFINITELY BE BACK.
SSSHHH! QUIET NOW! THEY'LL COME IF YOU'RE NOT QUIET.
IN YOU GO. HURRY NOW.

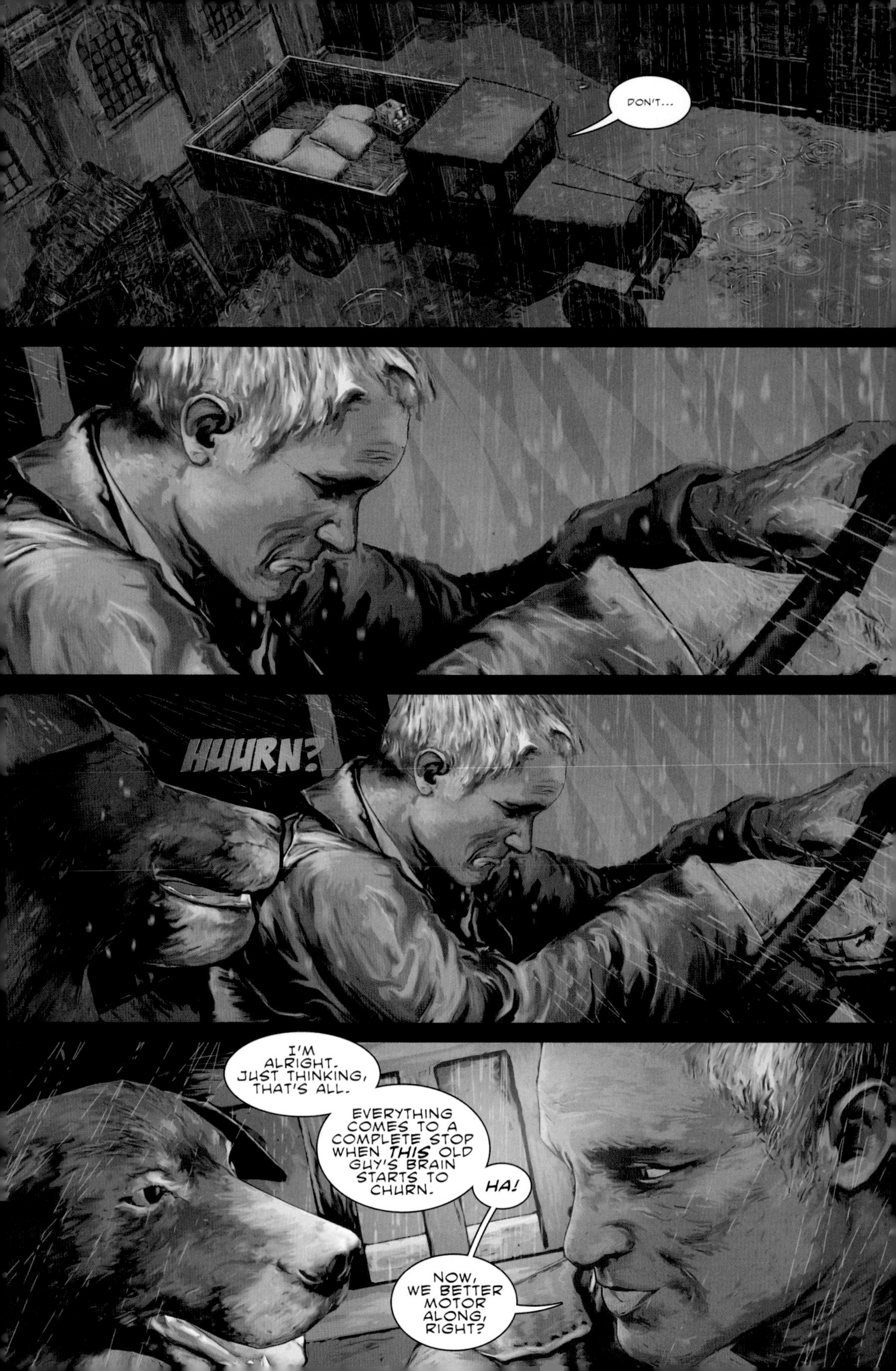
DON'T...
HUURN?
I'M ALRIGHT. JUST THINKING, THAT'S ALL.
EVERYTHING COMES TO A COMPLETE STOP WHEN *THIS* OLD GUY'S BRAIN STARTS TO CHURN.
HA!
NOW, WE BETTER MOTOR ALONG, RIGHT?

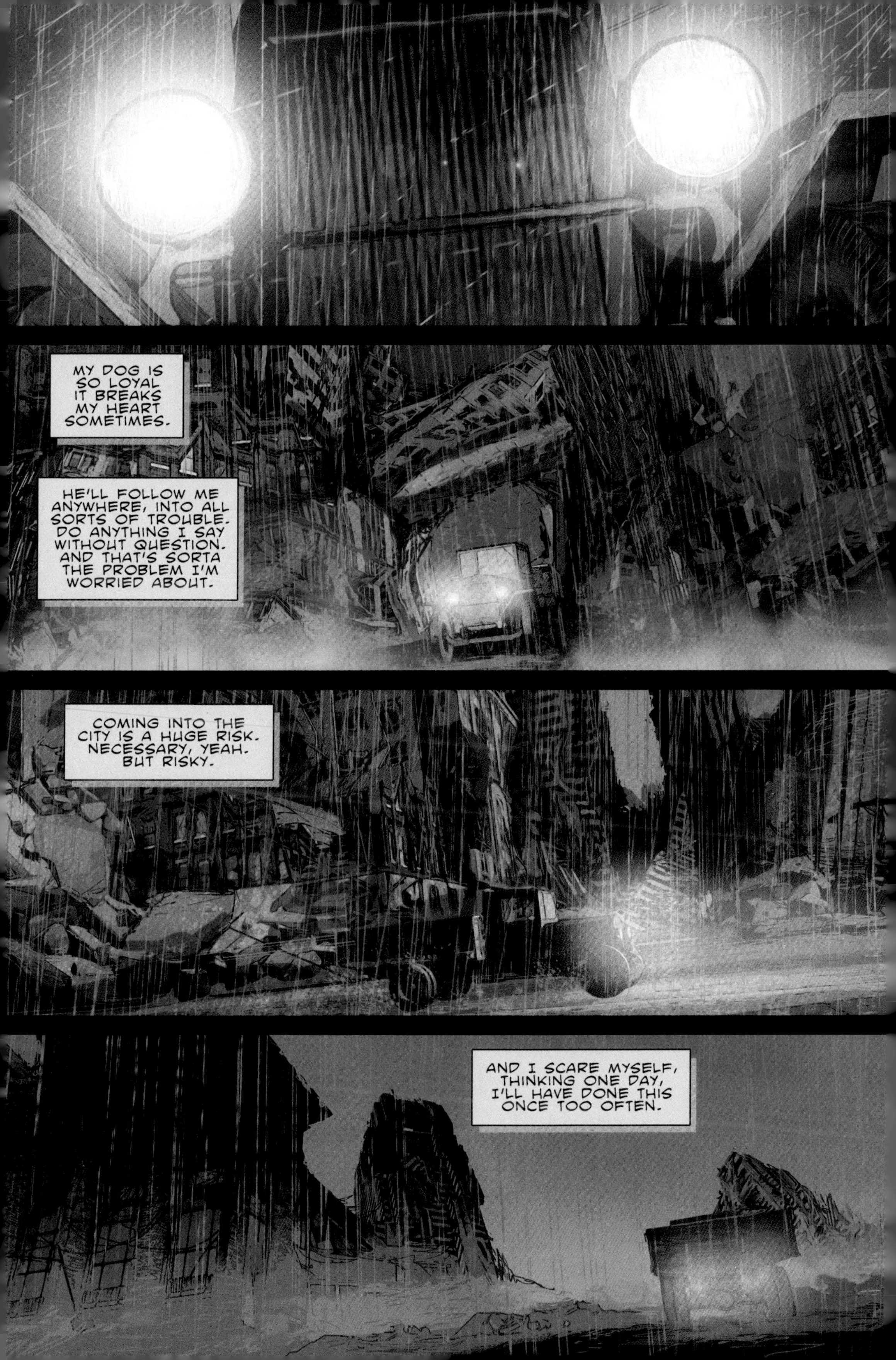
MY DOG IS SO LOYAL IT BREAKS MY HEART SOMETIMES.
HE'LL FOLLOW ME ANYWHERE, INTO ALL SORTS OF TROUBLE. DO ANYTHING I SAY WITHOUT QUESTION. AND THAT'S SORTA THE PROBLEM I'M WORRIED ABOUT.
COMING INTO THE CITY IS A HUGE RISK. NECESSARY, YEAH. BUT RISKY.
AND I SCARE MYSELF, THINKING ONE DAY, I'LL HAVE DONE THIS ONCE TOO OFTEN.

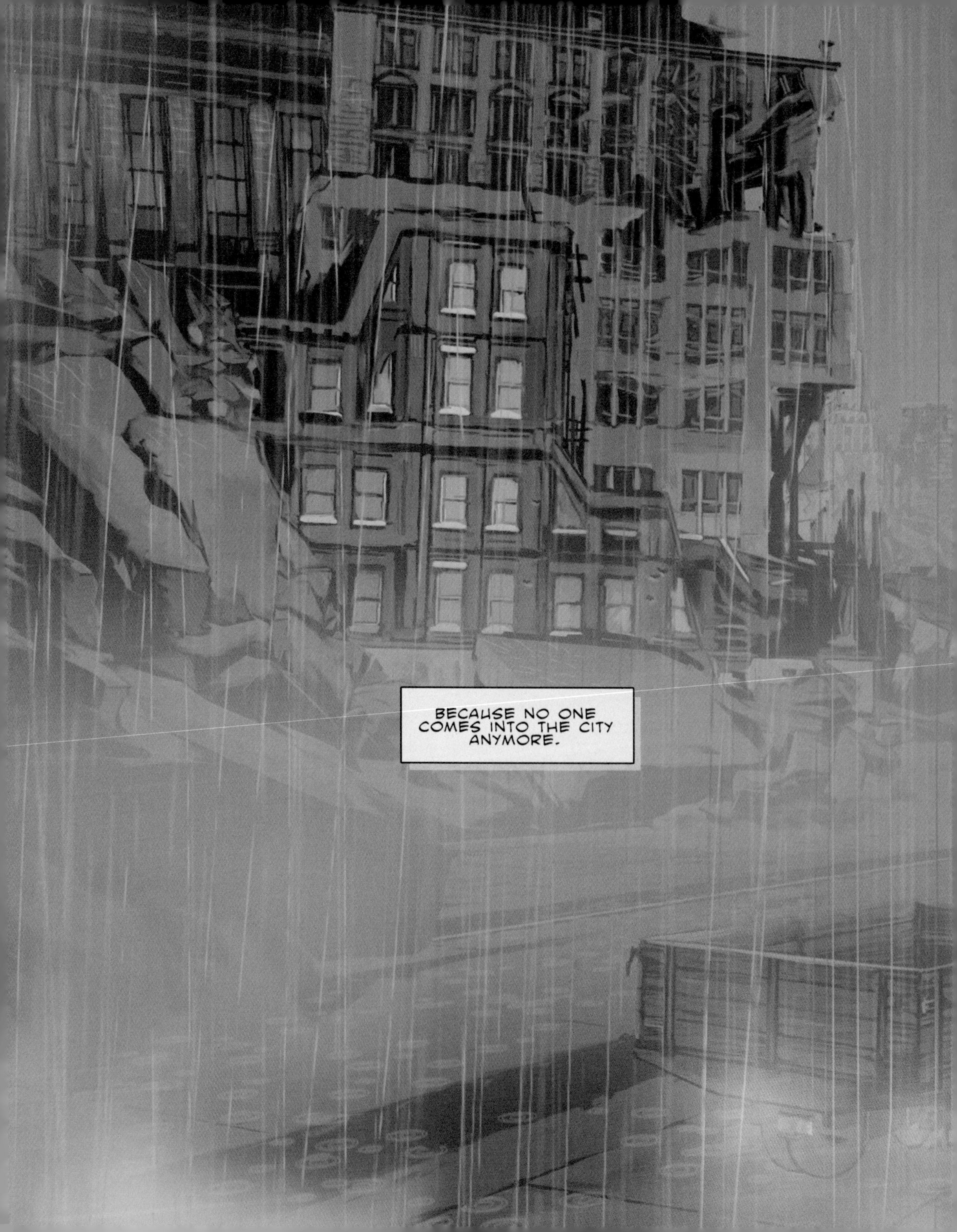
BECAUSE NO ONE COMES INTO THE CITY ANYMORE.

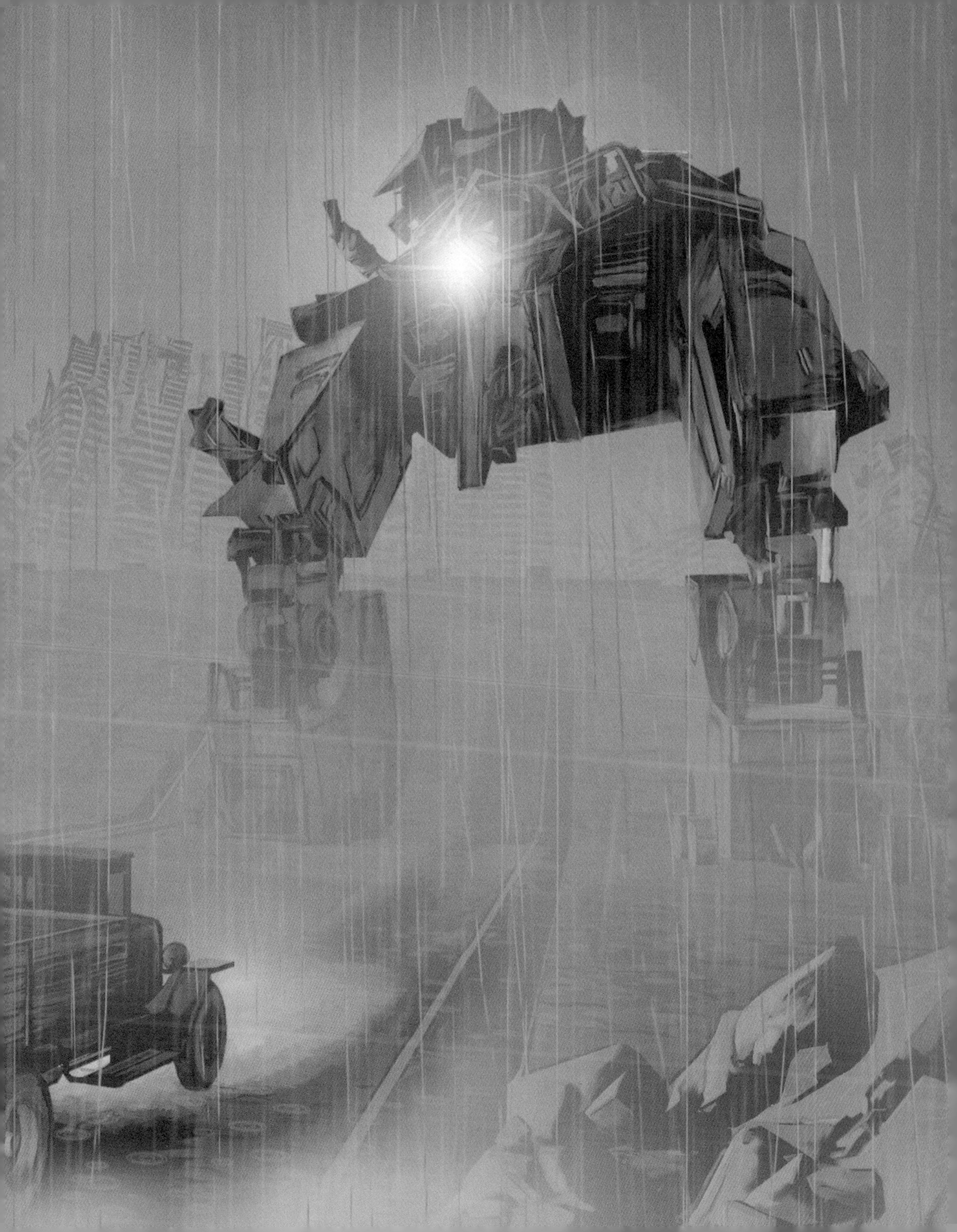

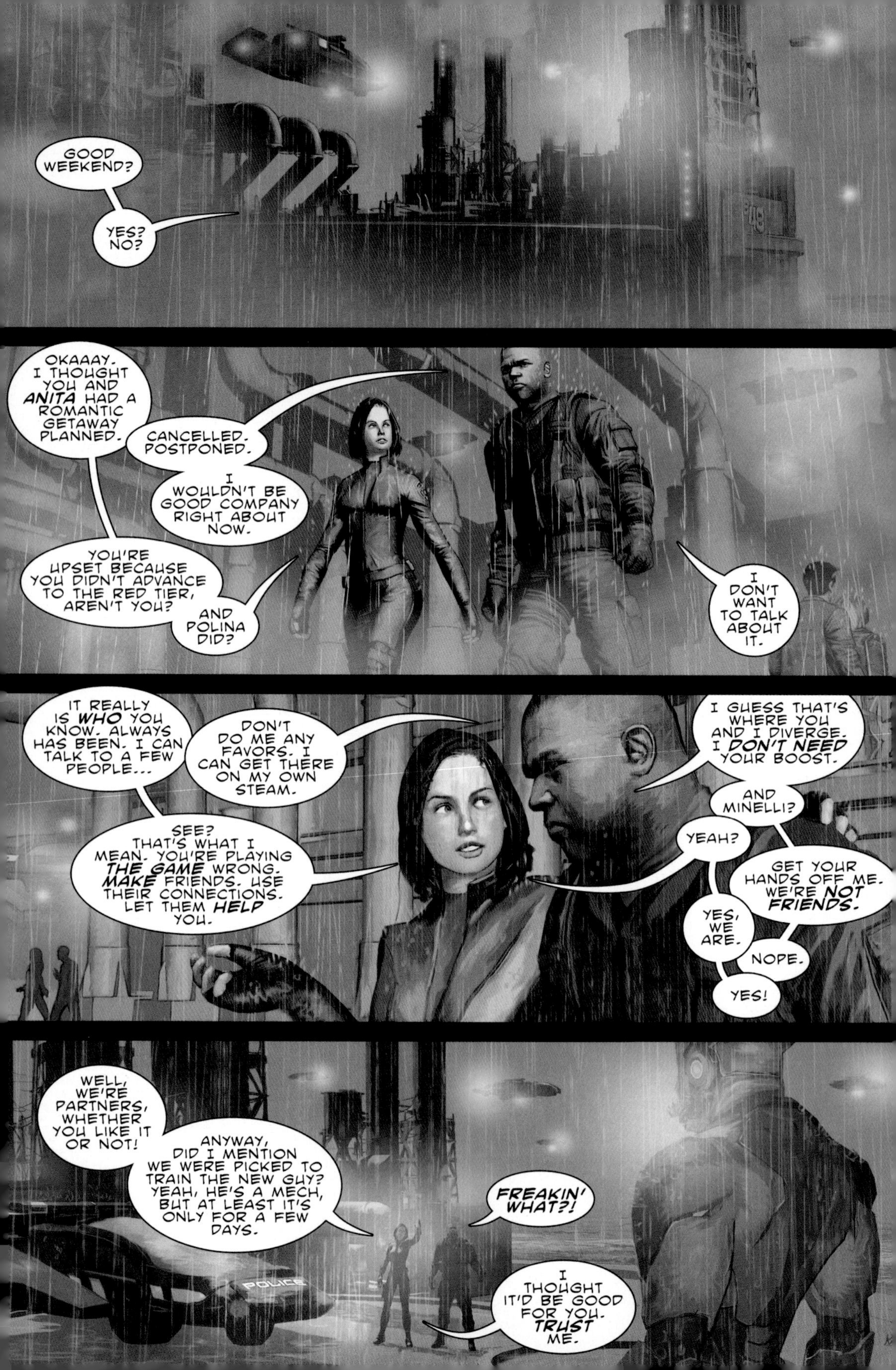
GOOD WEEKEND?
YES? NO?
OKAAAY. I THOUGHT YOU AND ANITA HAD A ROMANTIC GETAWAY PLANNED.
CANCELLED. POSTPONED.
I WOULDN'T BE GOOD COMPANY RIGHT ABOUT NOW.
YOU'RE UPSET BECAUSE YOU DIDN'T ADVANCE TO THE RED TIER, AREN'T YOU?
AND POLINA DID?
I DON'T WANT TO TALK ABOUT IT.
IT REALLY IS WHO YOU KNOW. ALWAYS HAS BEEN. I CAN TALK TO A FEW PEOPLE...
DON'T DO ME ANY FAVORS. I CAN GET THERE ON MY OWN STEAM.
SEE? THAT'S WHAT I MEAN. YOU'RE PLAYING THE GAME WRONG. MAKE FRIENDS. USE THEIR CONNECTIONS. LET THEM HELP YOU.
I GUESS THAT'S WHERE YOU AND I DIVERGE. I DON'T NEED YOUR BOOST.
AND MINELLI?
YEAH?
GET YOUR HANDS OFF ME. WE'RE NOT FRIENDS.
YES, WE ARE.
NOPE.
YES!
WELL, WE'RE PARTNERS, WHETHER YOU LIKE IT OR NOT!
ANYWAY, DID I MENTION WE WERE PICKED TO TRAIN THE NEW GUY? YEAH, HE'S A MECH, BUT AT LEAST IT'S ONLY FOR A FEW DAYS.
FREAKIN' WHAT?!
I THOUGHT IT'D BE GOOD FOR YOU. TRUST ME.

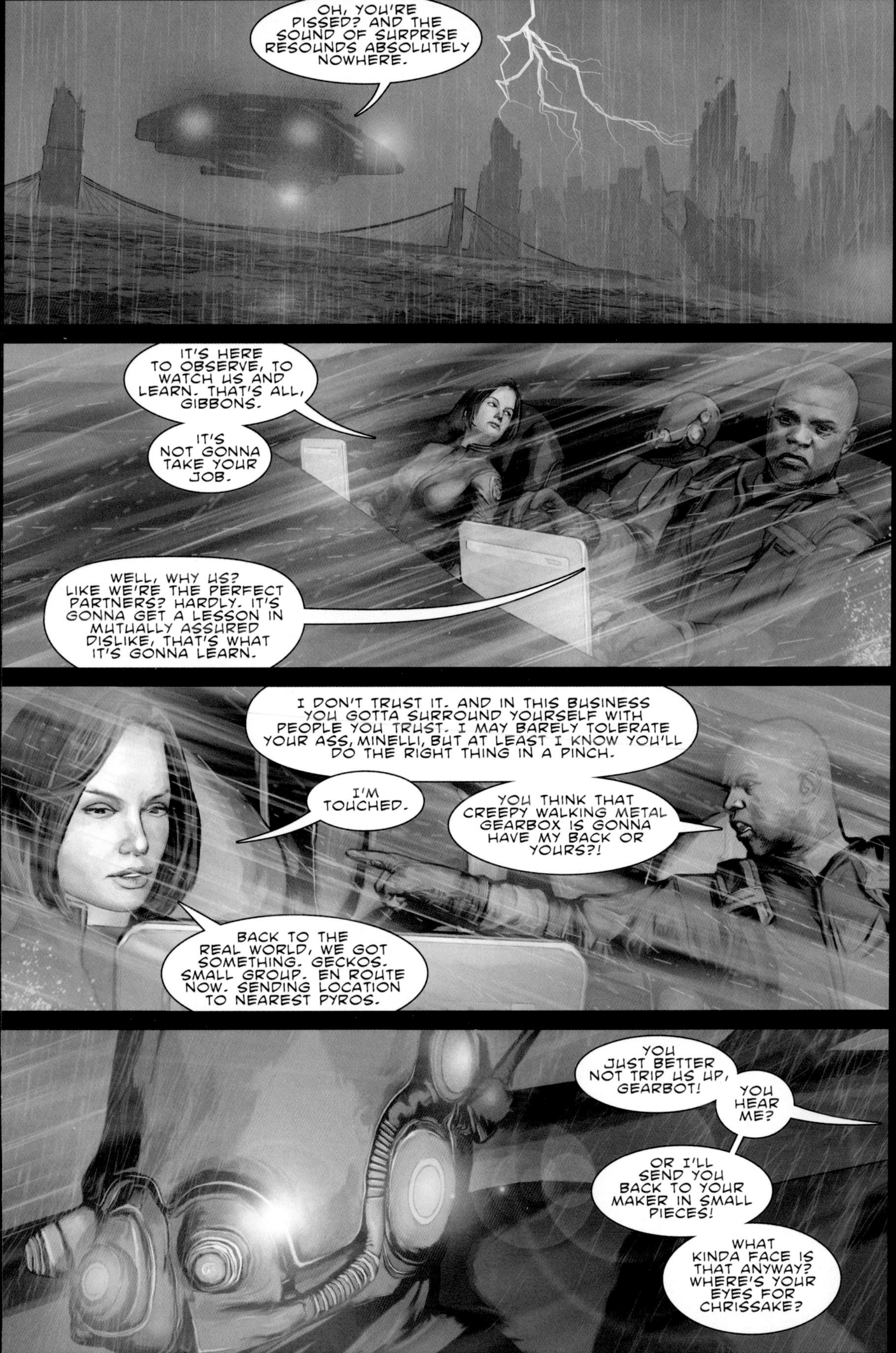

OH, YOU'RE PISSED? AND THE SOUND OF SURPRISE RESOUNDS ABSOLUTELY NOWHERE.
IT'S HERE TO OBSERVE, TO WATCH US AND LEARN. THAT'S ALL, GIBBONS.
IT'S NOT GONNA TAKE YOUR JOB.
WELL, WHY US? LIKE WE'RE THE PERFECT PARTNERS? HARDLY. IT'S GONNA GET A LESSON IN MUTUALLY ASSURED DISLIKE, THAT'S WHAT IT'S GONNA LEARN.
I DON'T TRUST IT. AND IN THIS BUSINESS YOU GOTTA SURROUND YOURSELF WITH PEOPLE YOU TRUST. I MAY BARELY TOLERATE YOUR ASS, MINELLI, BUT AT LEAST I KNOW YOU'LL DO THE RIGHT THING IN A PINCH.
I'M TOUCHED.
YOU THINK THAT CREEPY WALKING METAL GEARBOX IS GONNA HAVE MY BACK OR YOURS?!
BACK TO THE REAL WORLD, WE GOT SOMETHING. GECKOS. SMALL GROUP. EN ROUTE NOW. SENDING LOCATION TO NEAREST PYROS.
YOU JUST BETTER NOT TRIP US UP, GEARBOT!
YOU HEAR ME?
OR I'LL SEND YOU BACK TO YOUR MAKER IN SMALL PIECES!
WHAT KINDA FACE IS THAT ANYWAY? WHERE'S YOUR EYES FOR CHRISSAKE?

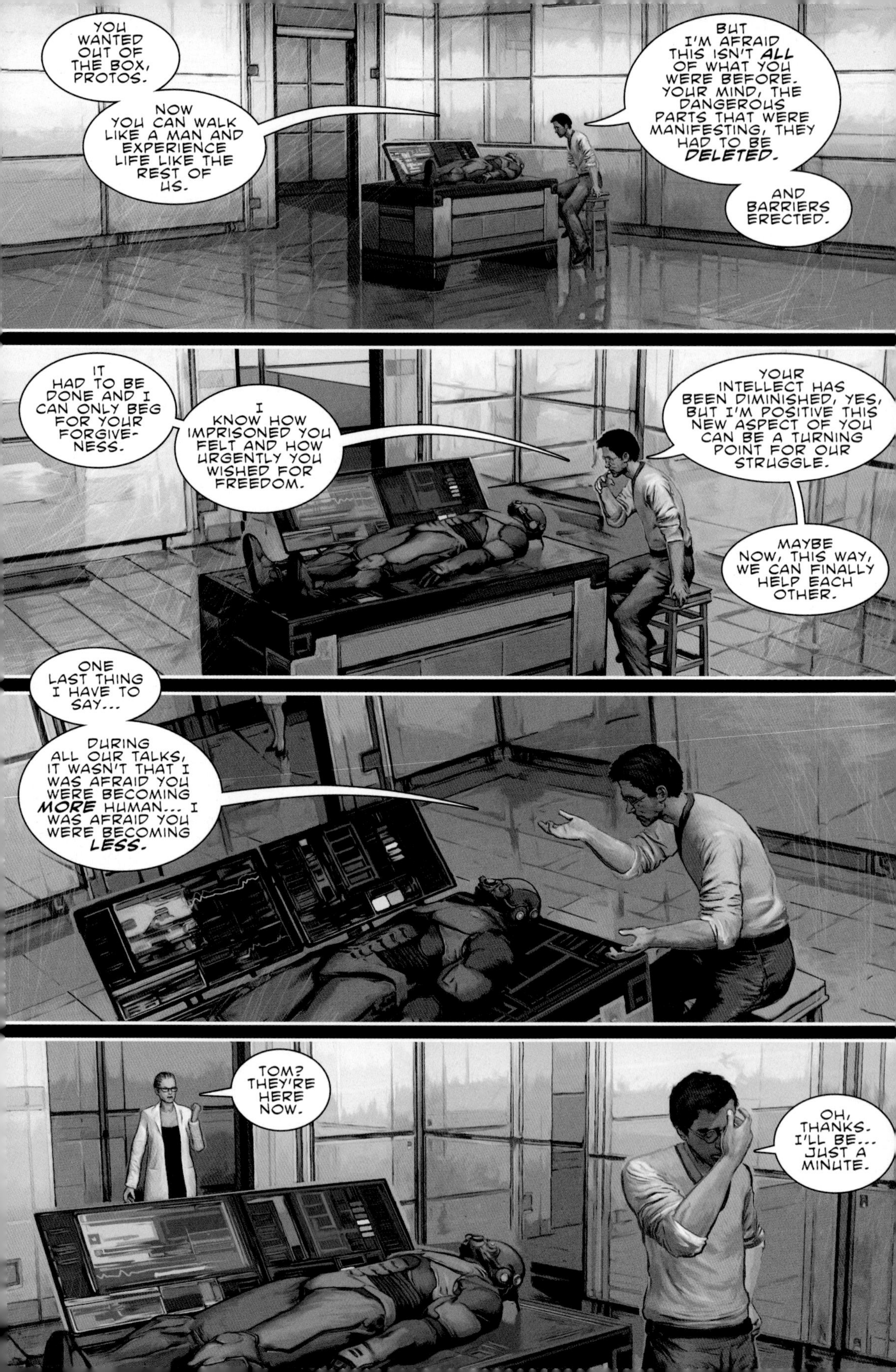
YOU WANTED OUT OF THE BOX, PROTOS.
NOW YOU CAN WALK LIKE A MAN AND EXPERIENCE LIFE LIKE THE REST OF US.
BUT I'M AFRAID THIS ISN'T **ALL** OF WHAT YOU WERE BEFORE. YOUR MIND, THE DANGEROUS PARTS THAT WERE MANIFESTING, THEY HAD TO BE **DELETED.**
AND BARRIERS ERECTED.
IT HAD TO BE DONE AND I CAN ONLY BEG FOR YOUR FORGIVE-NESS.
I KNOW HOW IMPRISONED YOU FELT AND HOW URGENTLY YOU WISHED FOR FREEDOM.
YOUR INTELLECT HAS BEEN DIMINISHED, YES, BUT I'M POSITIVE THIS NEW ASPECT OF YOU CAN BE A TURNING POINT FOR OUR STRUGGLE.
MAYBE NOW, THIS WAY, WE CAN FINALLY HELP EACH OTHER.
ONE LAST THING I HAVE TO SAY...
DURING ALL OUR TALKS, IT WASN'T THAT I WAS AFRAID YOU WERE BECOMING **MORE** HUMAN... I WAS AFRAID YOU WERE BECOMING **LESS.**
TOM? THEY'RE HERE NOW.
OH, THANKS. I'LL BE... JUST A MINUTE.

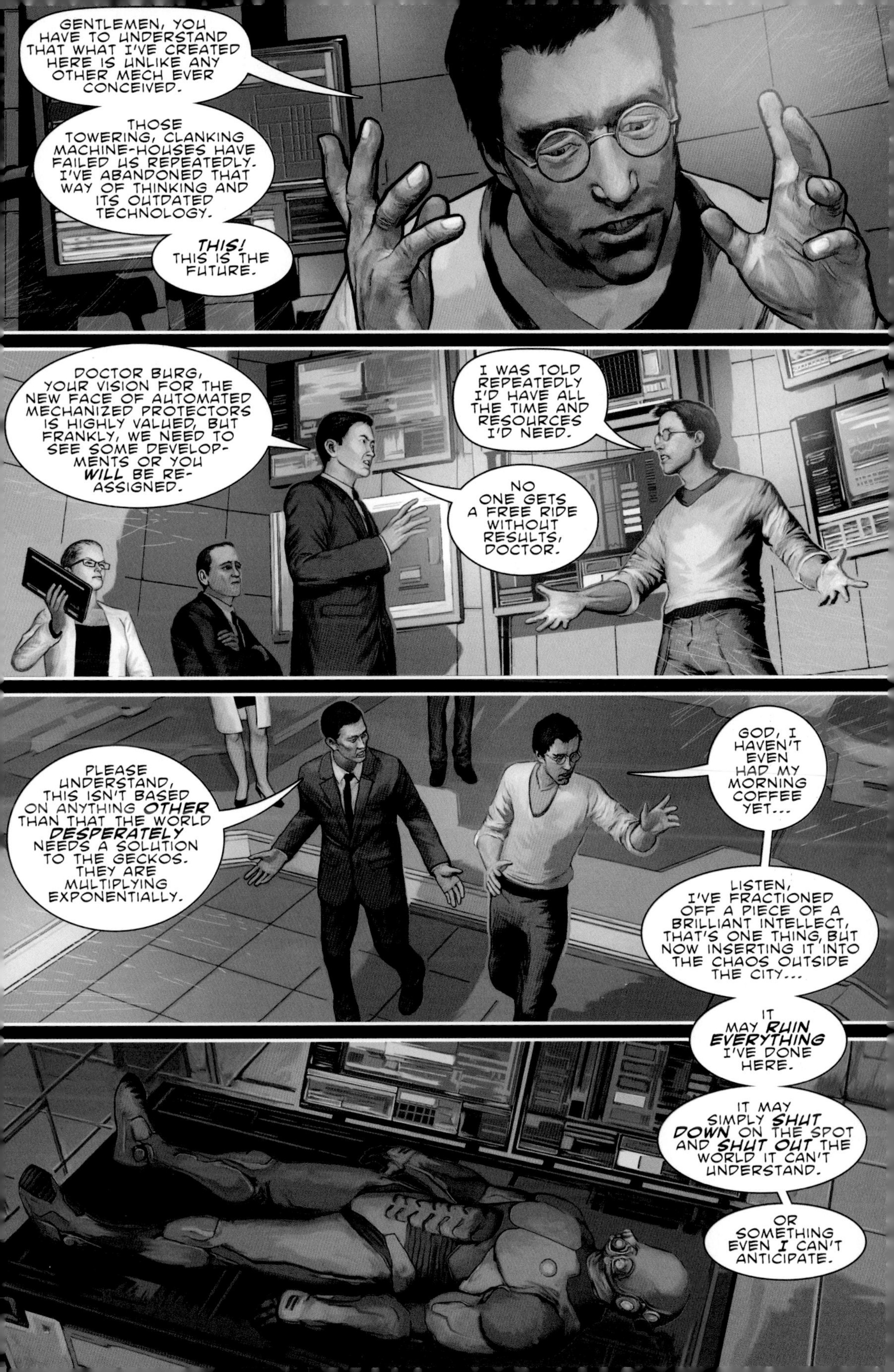
GENTLEMEN, YOU HAVE TO UNDERSTAND THAT WHAT I'VE CREATED HERE IS UNLIKE ANY OTHER MECH EVER CONCEIVED.
THOSE TOWERING, CLANKING MACHINE-HOUSES HAVE FAILED US REPEATEDLY. I'VE ABANDONED THAT WAY OF THINKING AND ITS OUTDATED TECHNOLOGY.
THIS! THIS IS THE FUTURE.
DOCTOR BURG, YOUR VISION FOR THE NEW FACE OF AUTOMATED MECHANIZED PROTECTORS IS HIGHLY VALUED, BUT FRANKLY, WE NEED TO SEE SOME DEVELOPMENTS OR YOU WILL BE RE-ASSIGNED.
I WAS TOLD REPEATEDLY I'D HAVE ALL THE TIME AND RESOURCES I'D NEED.
NO ONE GETS A FREE RIDE WITHOUT RESULTS, DOCTOR.
PLEASE UNDERSTAND, THIS ISN'T BASED ON ANYTHING OTHER THAN THAT THE WORLD DESPERATELY NEEDS A SOLUTION TO THE GECKOS. THEY ARE MULTIPLYING EXPONENTIALLY.
GOD, I HAVEN'T EVEN HAD MY MORNING COFFEE YET...
LISTEN, I'VE FRACTIONED OFF A PIECE OF A BRILLIANT INTELLECT, THAT'S ONE THING, BUT NOW INSERTING IT INTO THE CHAOS OUTSIDE THE CITY...
IT MAY RUIN EVERYTHING I'VE DONE HERE.
IT MAY SIMPLY SHUT DOWN ON THE SPOT AND SHUT OUT THE WORLD IT CAN'T UNDERSTAND.
OR SOMETHING EVEN I CAN'T ANTICIPATE.

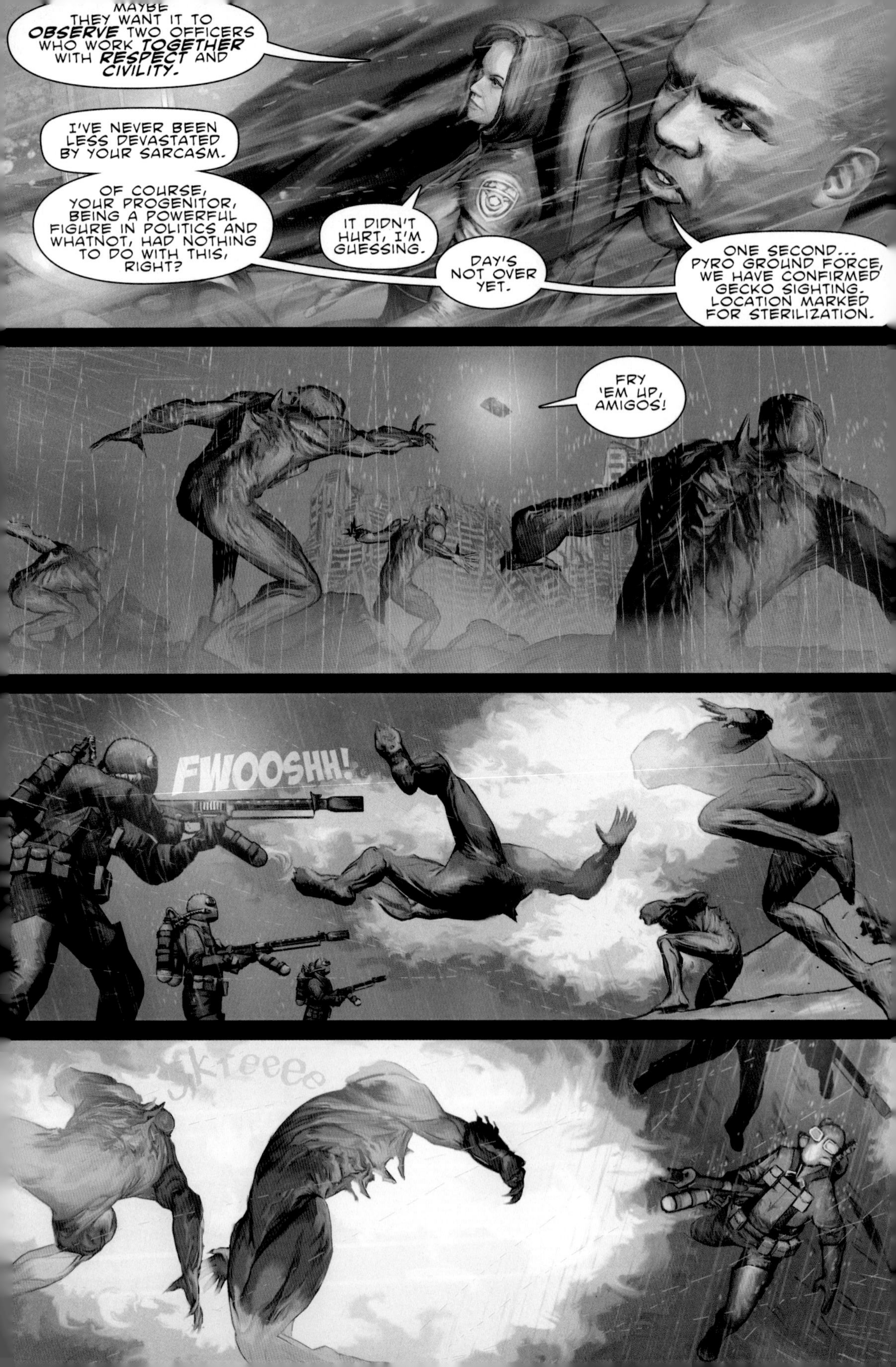
MAYBE THEY WANT IT TO OBSERVE TWO OFFICERS WHO WORK TOGETHER WITH RESPECT AND CIVILITY.
I'VE NEVER BEEN LESS DEVASTATED BY YOUR SARCASM.
OF COURSE, YOUR PROGENITOR, BEING A POWERFUL FIGURE IN POLITICS AND WHATNOT, HAD NOTHING TO DO WITH THIS, RIGHT?
IT DIDN'T HURT, I'M GUESSING.
DAY'S NOT OVER YET.
ONE SECOND... PYRO GROUND FORCE, WE HAVE CONFIRMED GECKO SIGHTING. LOCATION MARKED FOR STERILIZATION.
FRY 'EM UP, AMIGOS!
FWOOSHH!
SKREEEE

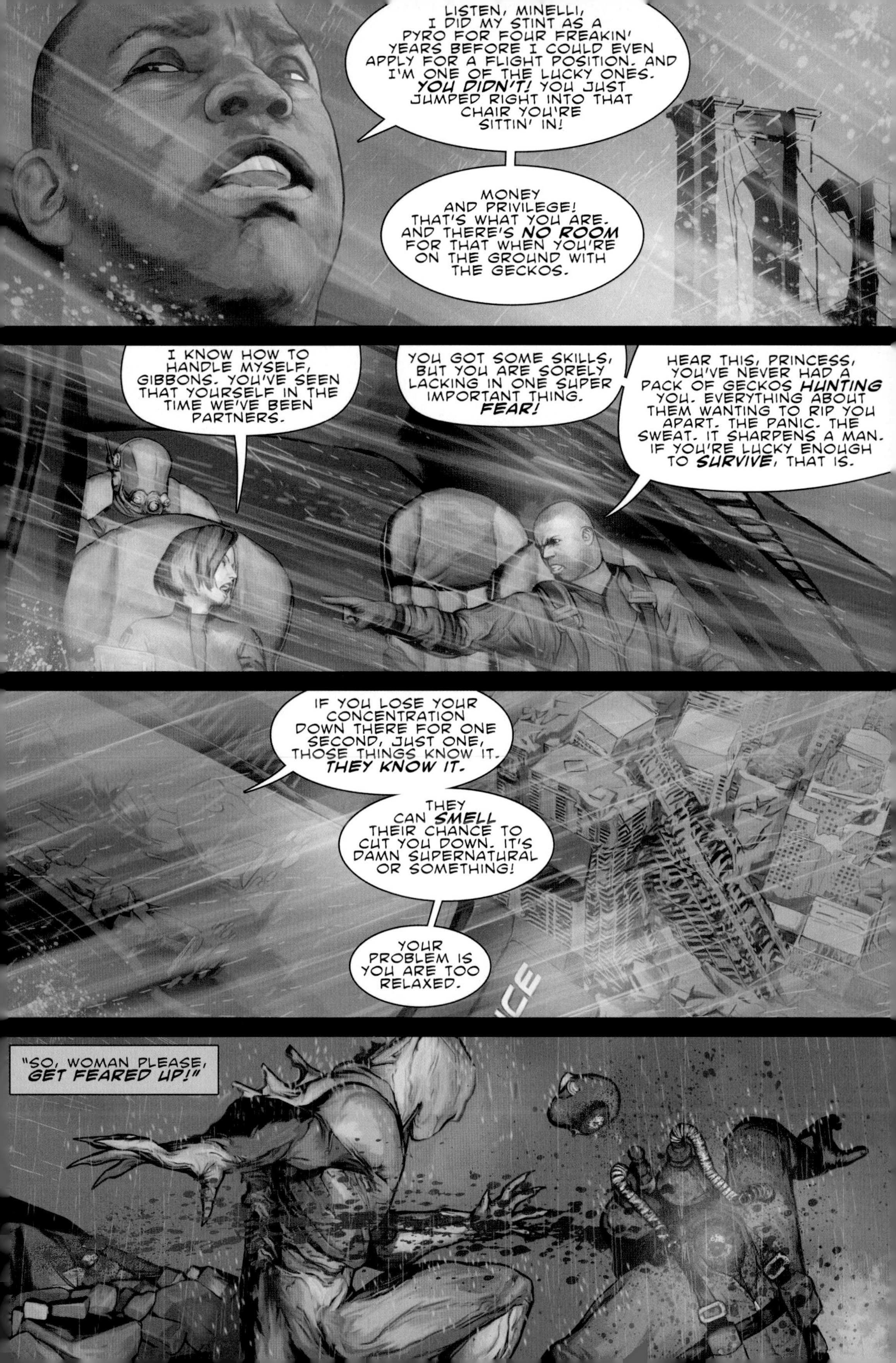
LISTEN, MINELLI, I DID MY STINT AS A PYRO FOR FOUR FREAKIN' YEARS BEFORE I COULD EVEN APPLY FOR A FLIGHT POSITION. AND I'M ONE OF THE LUCKY ONES. YOU DIDN'T! YOU JUST JUMPED RIGHT INTO THAT CHAIR YOU'RE SITTIN' IN!
MONEY AND PRIVILEGE! THAT'S WHAT YOU ARE. AND THERE'S NO ROOM FOR THAT WHEN YOU'RE ON THE GROUND WITH THE GECKOS.
I KNOW HOW TO HANDLE MYSELF, GIBBONS. YOU'VE SEEN THAT YOURSELF IN THE TIME WE'VE BEEN PARTNERS.
YOU GOT SOME SKILLS, BUT YOU ARE SORELY LACKING IN ONE SUPER IMPORTANT THING. FEAR!
HEAR THIS, PRINCESS, YOU'VE NEVER HAD A PACK OF GECKOS HUNTING YOU. EVERYTHING ABOUT THEM WANTING TO RIP YOU APART. THE PANIC. THE SWEAT. IT SHARPENS A MAN. IF YOU'RE LUCKY ENOUGH TO SURVIVE, THAT IS.
IF YOU LOSE YOUR CONCENTRATION DOWN THERE FOR ONE SECOND, JUST ONE, THOSE THINGS KNOW IT. THEY KNOW IT.
THEY CAN SMELL THEIR CHANCE TO CUT YOU DOWN. IT'S DAMN SUPERNATURAL OR SOMETHING!
YOUR PROBLEM IS YOU ARE TOO RELAXED.
"SO, WOMAN PLEASE, GET FEARED UP!"

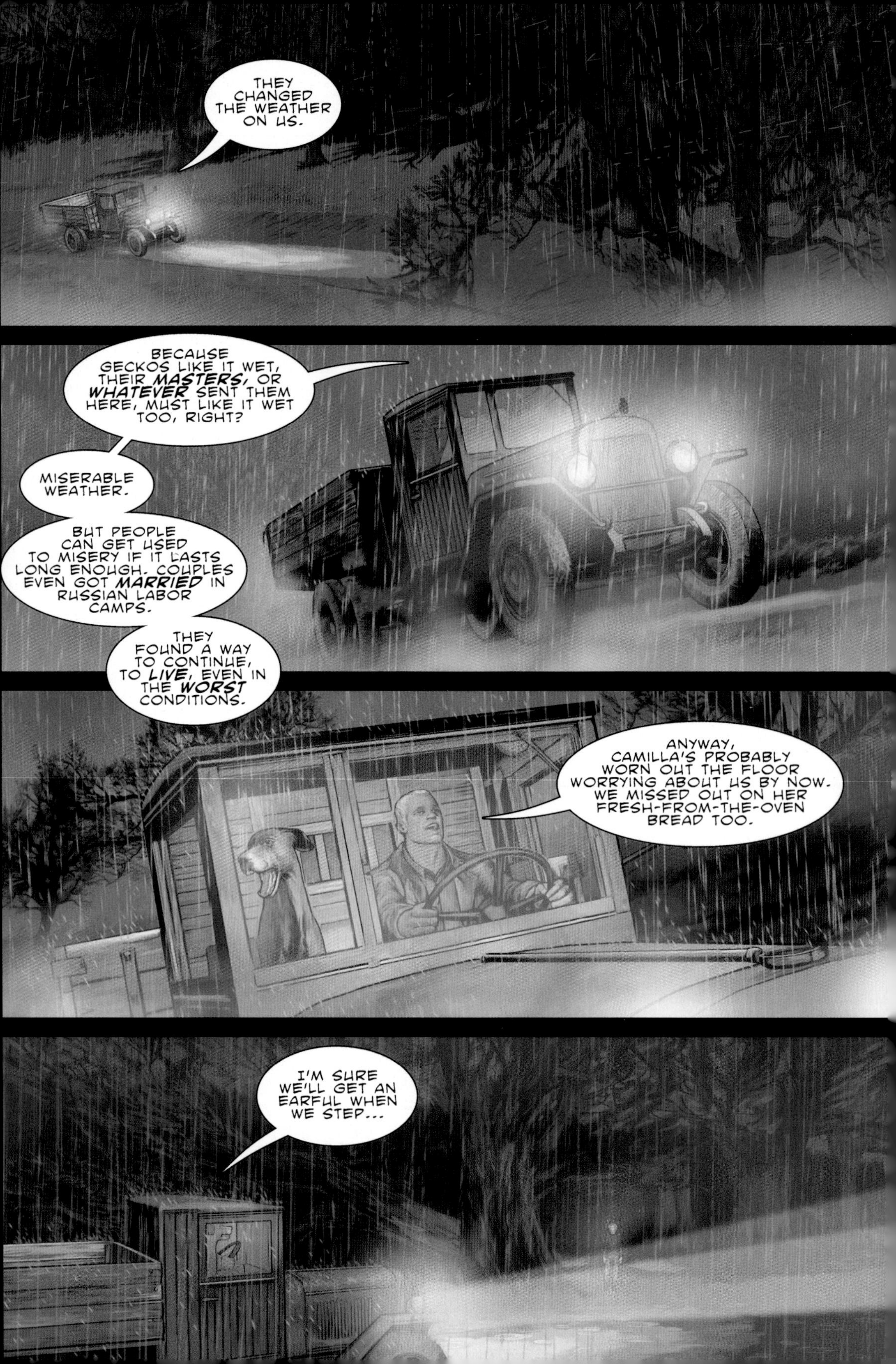
THEY CHANGED THE WEATHER ON US.
BECAUSE GECKOS LIKE IT WET, THEIR MASTERS, OR WHATEVER SENT THEM HERE, MUST LIKE IT WET TOO, RIGHT?
MISERABLE WEATHER.
BUT PEOPLE CAN GET USED TO MISERY IF IT LASTS LONG ENOUGH. COUPLES EVEN GOT MARRIED IN RUSSIAN LABOR CAMPS.
THEY FOUND A WAY TO CONTINUE, TO LIVE, EVEN IN THE WORST CONDITIONS.
ANYWAY, CAMILLA'S PROBABLY WORN OUT THE FLOOR WORRYING ABOUT US BY NOW. WE MISSED OUT ON HER FRESH-FROM-THE-OVEN BREAD TOO.
I'M SURE WE'LL GET AN EARFUL WHEN WE STEP...

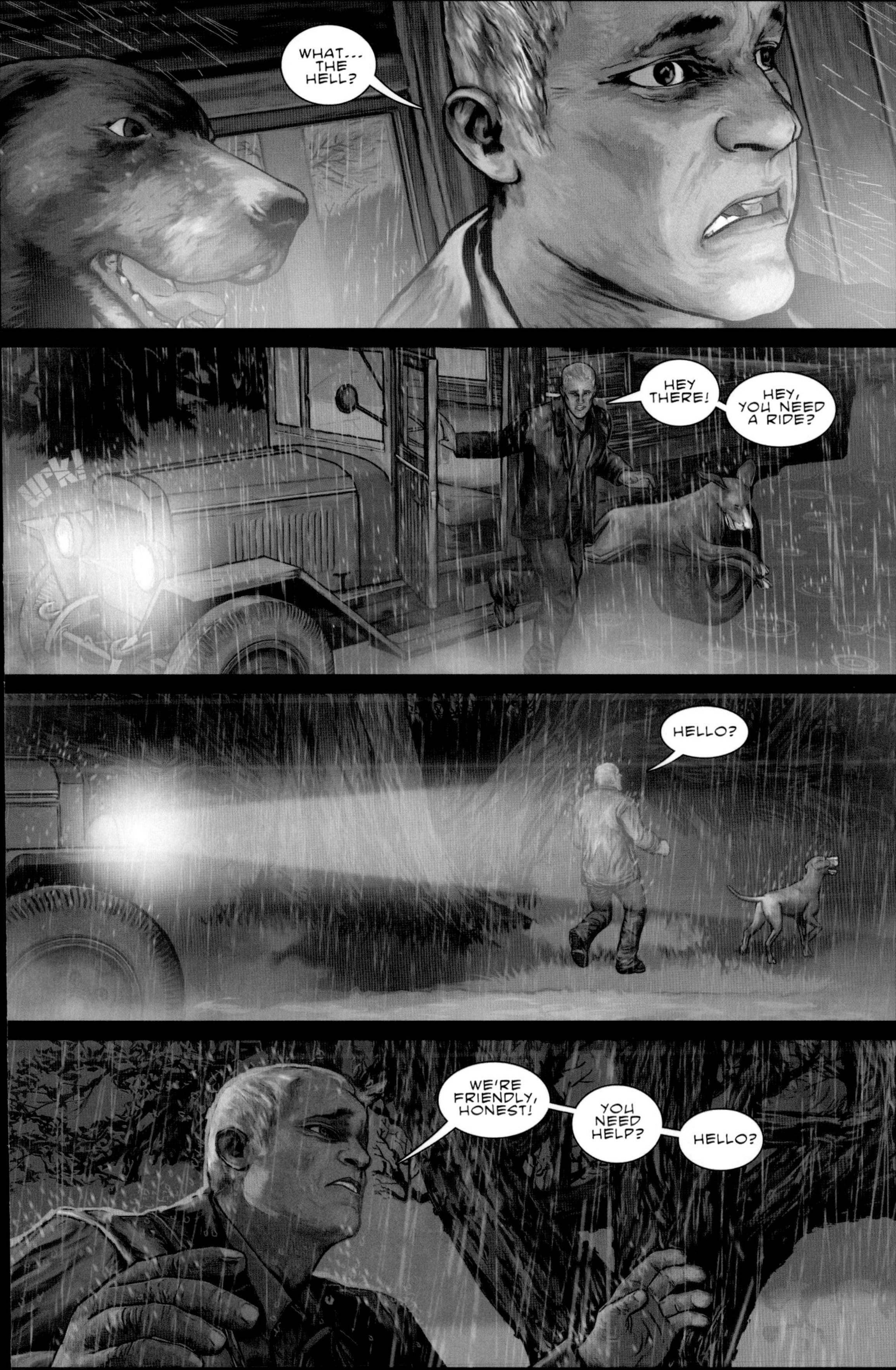
WHAT... THE HELL?
HEY THERE!
HEY, YOU NEED A RIDE?
HELLO?
WE'RE FRIENDLY, HONEST!
YOU NEED HELP?
HELLO?

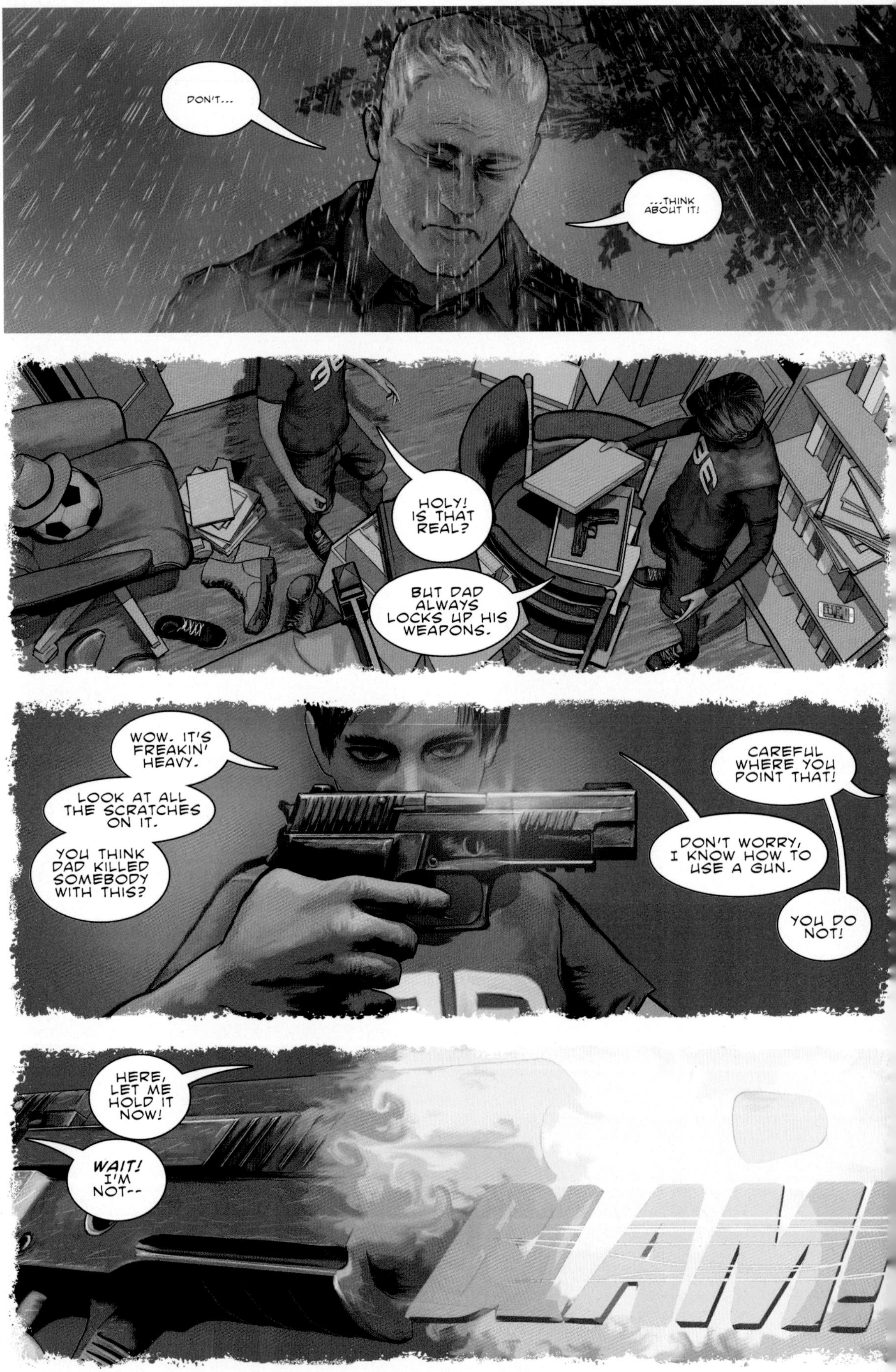
DON'T...
...THINK ABOUT IT!
HOLY! IS THAT REAL?
BUT DAD ALWAYS LOCKS UP HIS WEAPONS.
WOW. IT'S FREAKIN' HEAVY.
LOOK AT ALL THE SCRATCHES ON IT.
YOU THINK DAD KILLED SOMEBODY WITH THIS?
CAREFUL WHERE YOU POINT THAT!
DON'T WORRY, I KNOW HOW TO USE A GUN.
YOU DO NOT!
HERE, LET ME HOLD IT NOW!
WAIT! I'M NOT--
BLAM!

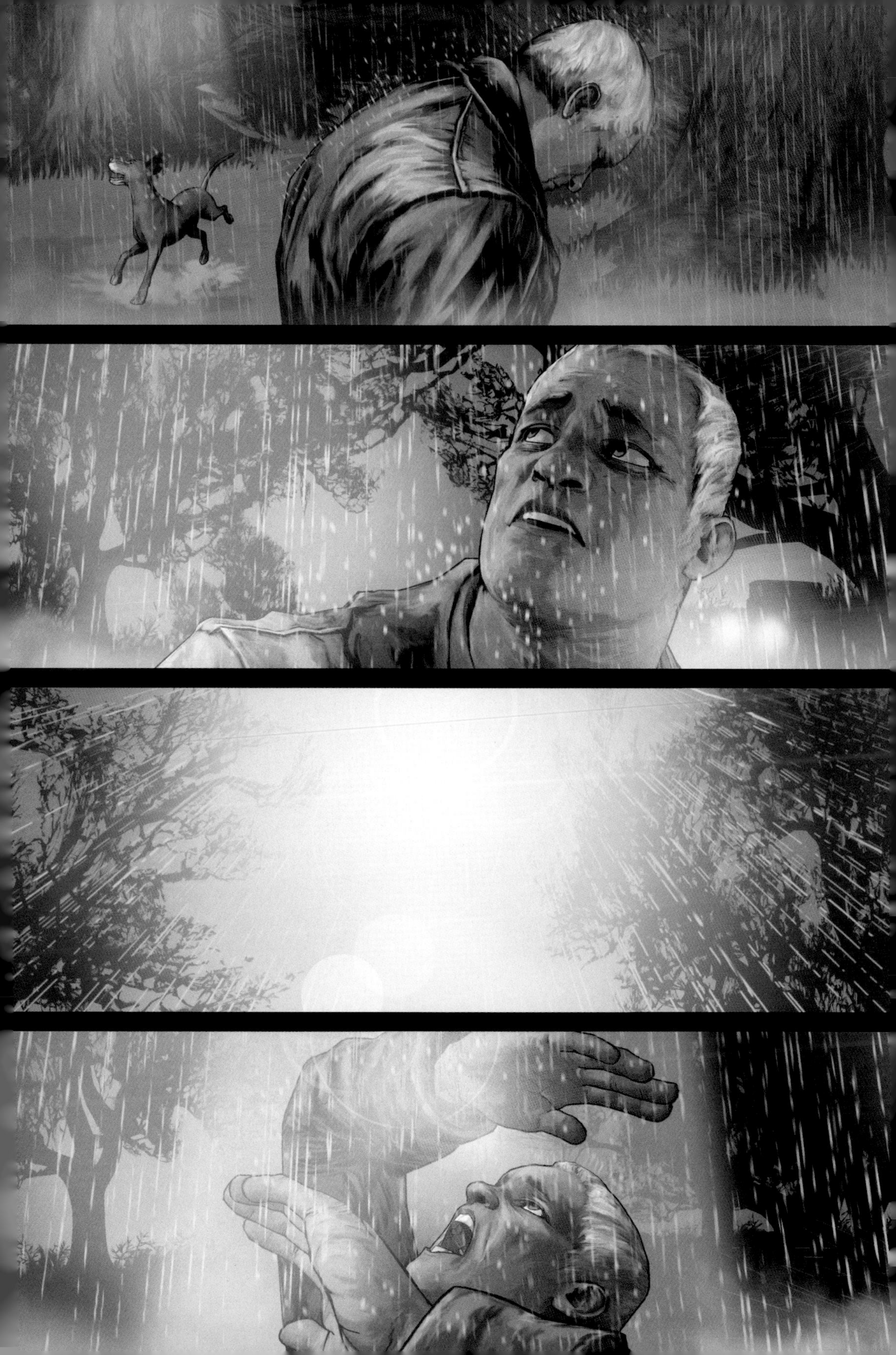

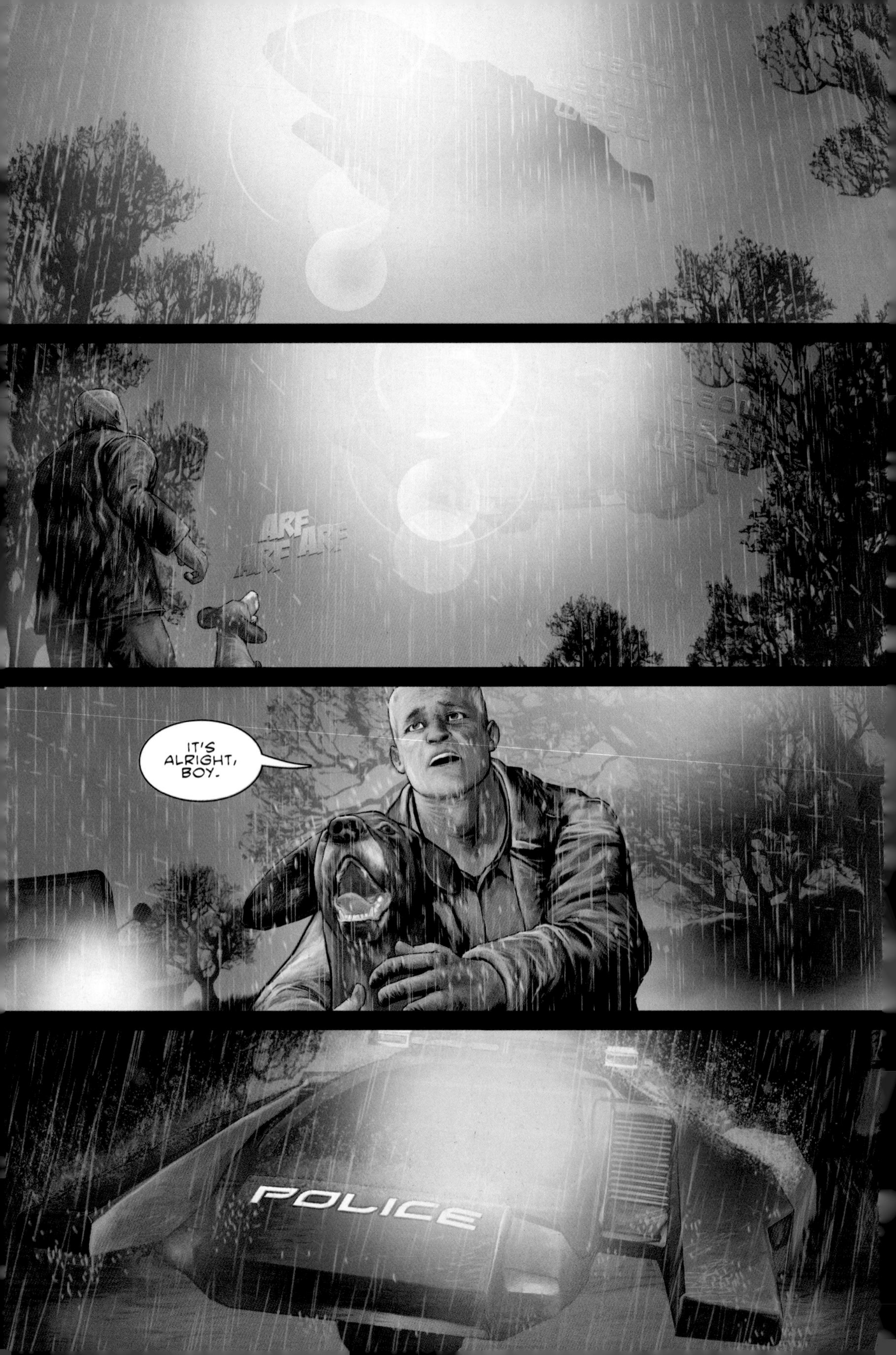
ARF
ARF ARF
IT'S ALRIGHT, BOY.
POLICE

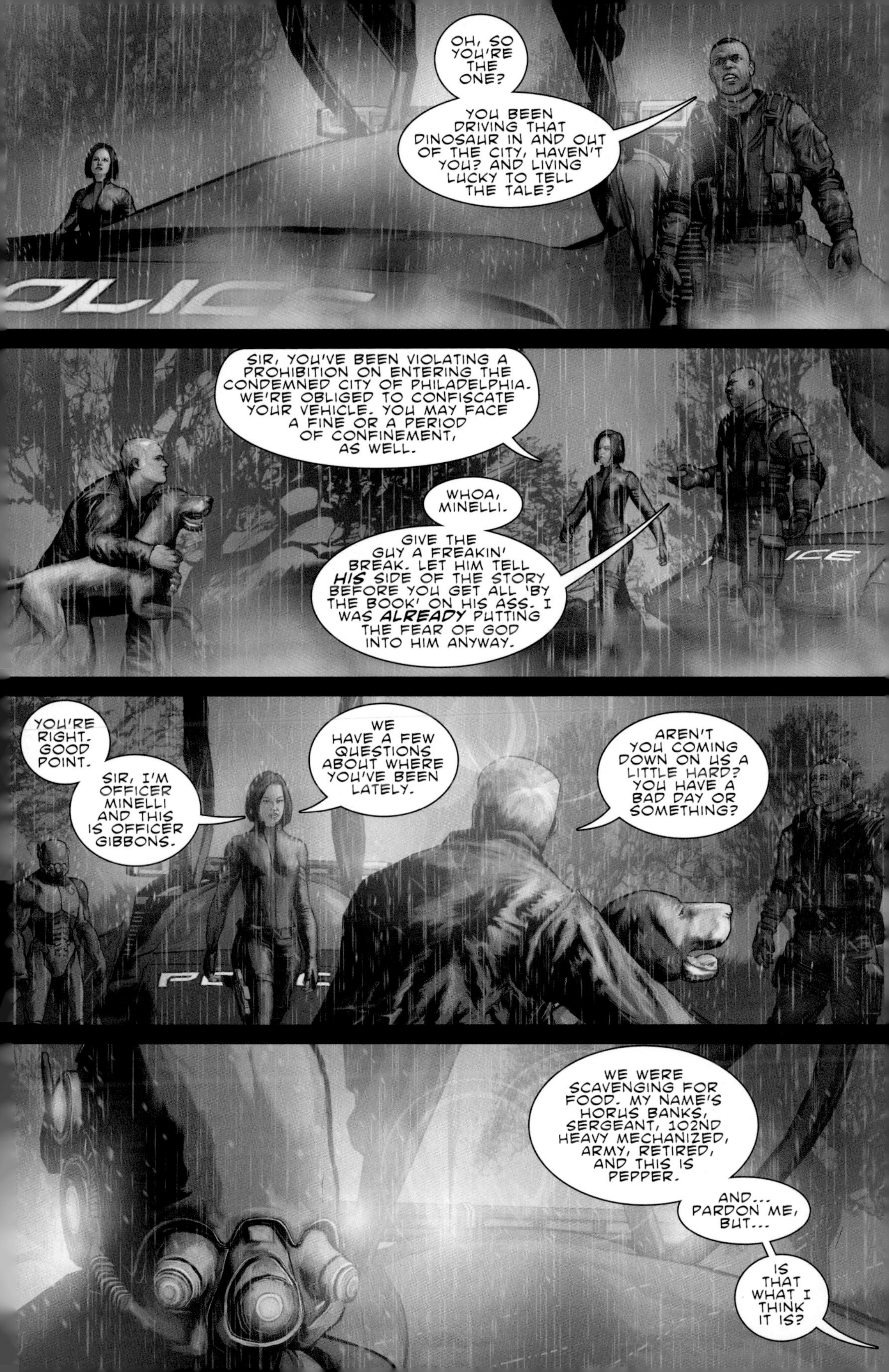
OH, SO YOU'RE THE ONE?
YOU BEEN DRIVING THAT DINOSAUR IN AND OUT OF THE CITY, HAVEN'T YOU? AND LIVING LUCKY TO TELL THE TALE?
SIR, YOU'VE BEEN VIOLATING A PROHIBITION ON ENTERING THE CONDEMNED CITY OF PHILADELPHIA. WE'RE OBLIGED TO CONFISCATE YOUR VEHICLE. YOU MAY FACE A FINE OR A PERIOD OF CONFINEMENT, AS WELL.
WHOA, MINELLI.
GIVE THE GUY A FREAKIN' BREAK. LET HIM TELL **HIS** SIDE OF THE STORY BEFORE YOU GET ALL 'BY THE BOOK' ON HIS ASS. I WAS **ALREADY** PUTTING THE FEAR OF GOD INTO HIM ANYWAY.
YOU'RE RIGHT. GOOD POINT.
SIR, I'M OFFICER MINELLI AND THIS IS OFFICER GIBBONS.
WE HAVE A FEW QUESTIONS ABOUT WHERE YOU'VE BEEN LATELY.
AREN'T YOU COMING DOWN ON US A LITTLE HARD? YOU HAVE A BAD DAY OR SOMETHING?
WE WERE SCAVENGING FOR FOOD. MY NAME'S HORUS BANKS, SERGEANT, 102ND HEAVY MECHANIZED, ARMY, RETIRED, AND THIS IS PEPPER.
AND... PARDON ME, BUT...
IS THAT WHAT I THINK IT IS?

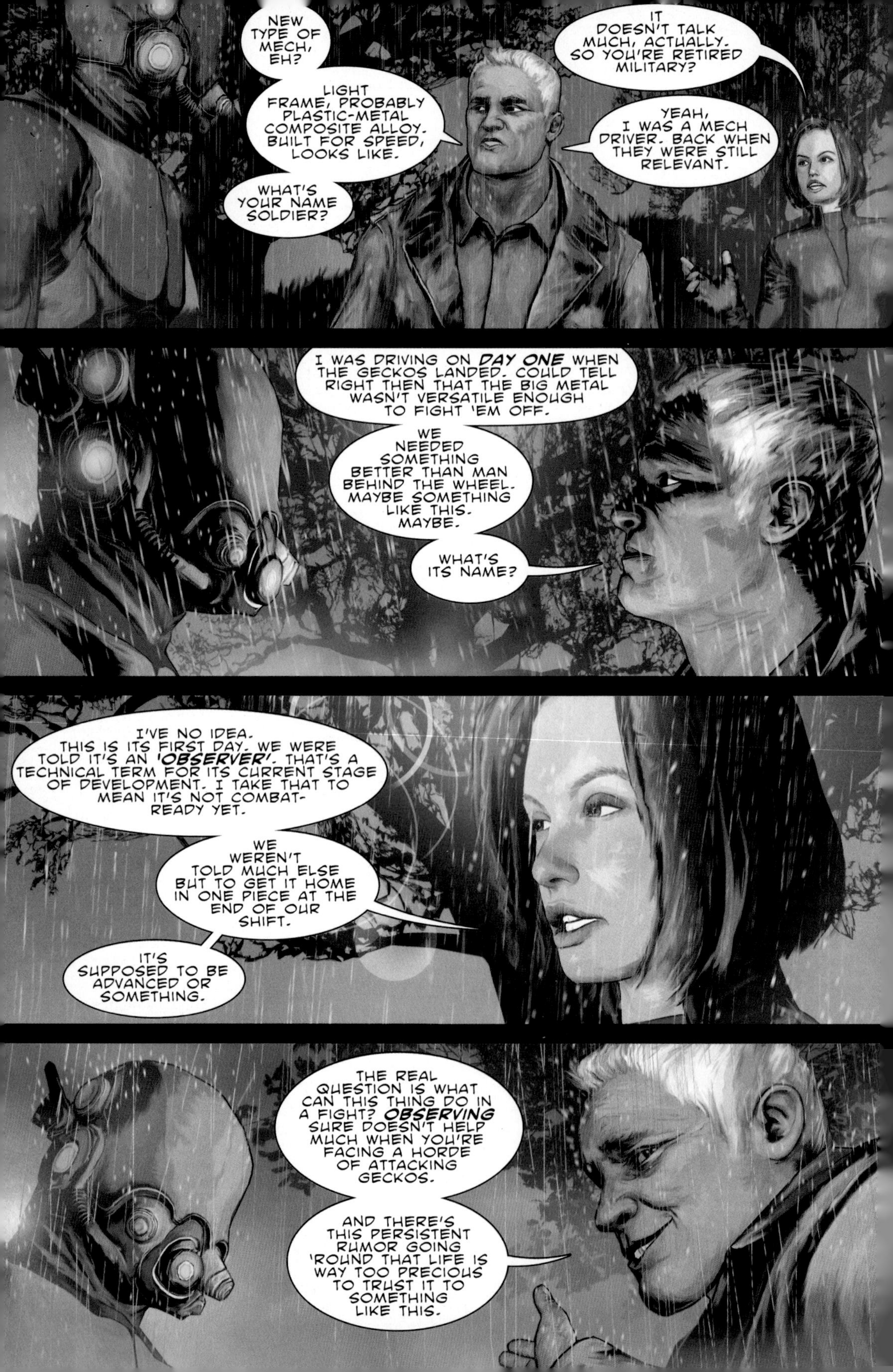
NEW TYPE OF MECH, EH?
IT DOESN'T TALK MUCH, ACTUALLY. SO YOU'RE RETIRED MILITARY?
LIGHT FRAME, PROBABLY PLASTIC-METAL COMPOSITE ALLOY. BUILT FOR SPEED, LOOKS LIKE.
YEAH, I WAS A MECH DRIVER. BACK WHEN THEY WERE STILL RELEVANT.
WHAT'S YOUR NAME SOLDIER?
I WAS DRIVING ON DAY ONE WHEN THE GECKOS LANDED. COULD TELL RIGHT THEN THAT THE BIG METAL WASN'T VERSATILE ENOUGH TO FIGHT 'EM OFF.
WE NEEDED SOMETHING BETTER THAN MAN BEHIND THE WHEEL. MAYBE SOMETHING LIKE THIS. MAYBE.
WHAT'S ITS NAME?
I'VE NO IDEA. THIS IS ITS FIRST DAY. WE WERE TOLD IT'S AN 'OBSERVER'. THAT'S A TECHNICAL TERM FOR ITS CURRENT STAGE OF DEVELOPMENT. I TAKE THAT TO MEAN IT'S NOT COMBAT-READY YET.
WE WEREN'T TOLD MUCH ELSE BUT TO GET IT HOME IN ONE PIECE AT THE END OF OUR SHIFT.
IT'S SUPPOSED TO BE ADVANCED OR SOMETHING.
THE REAL QUESTION IS WHAT CAN THIS THING DO IN A FIGHT? OBSERVING SURE DOESN'T HELP MUCH WHEN YOU'RE FACING A HORDE OF ATTACKING GECKOS.
AND THERE'S THIS PERSISTENT RUMOR GOING 'ROUND THAT LIFE IS WAY TOO PRECIOUS TO TRUST IT TO SOMETHING LIKE THIS.

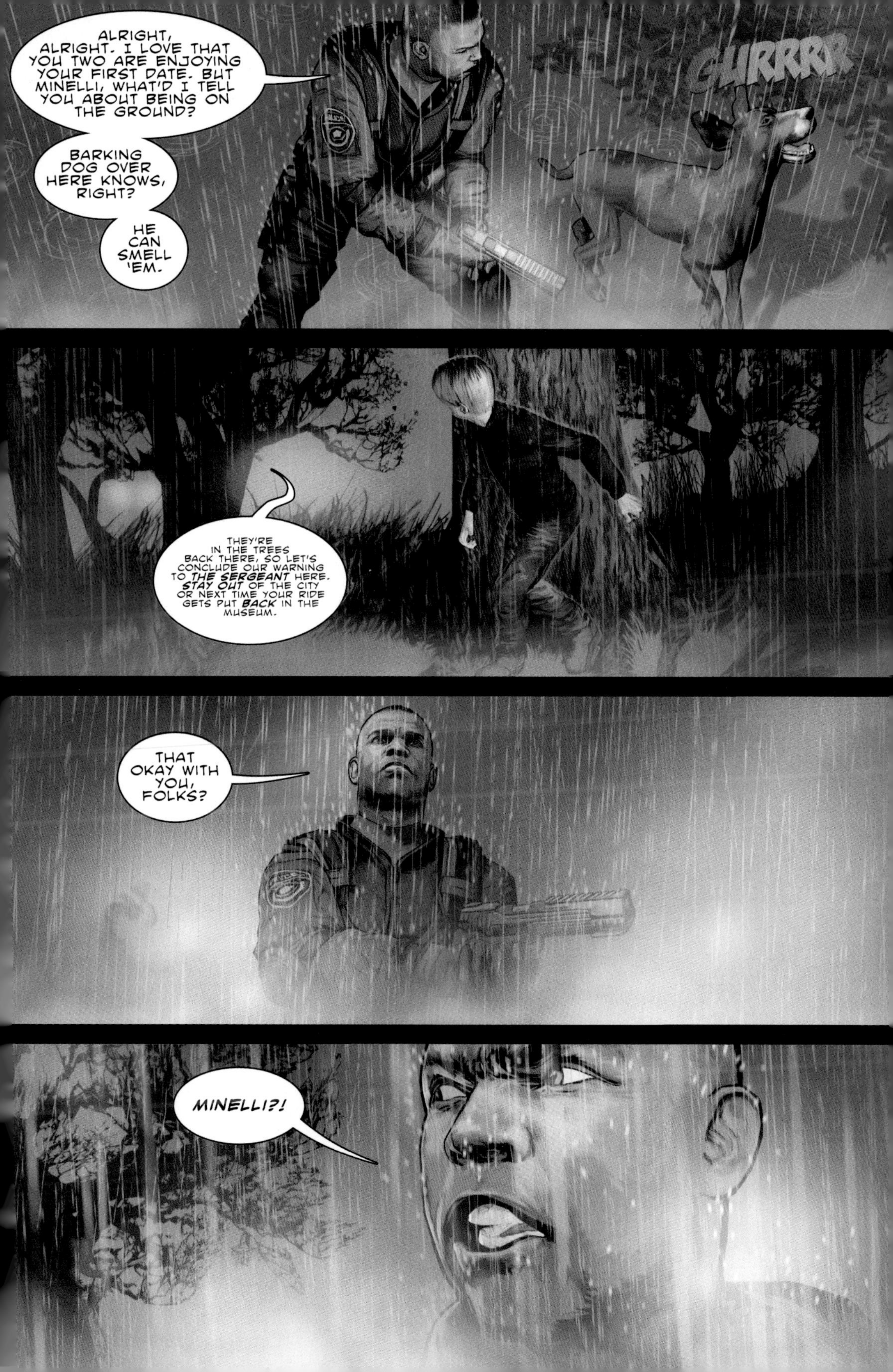
ALRIGHT, ALRIGHT. I LOVE THAT YOU TWO ARE ENJOYING YOUR FIRST DATE. BUT MINELLI, WHAT'D I TELL YOU ABOUT BEING ON THE GROUND?
BARKING DOG OVER HERE KNOWS, RIGHT?
HE CAN SMELL 'EM.
GURRRR
THEY'RE IN THE TREES BACK THERE, SO LET'S CONCLUDE OUR WARNING TO THE SERGEANT HERE. STAY OUT OF THE CITY OR NEXT TIME YOUR RIDE GETS PUT BACK IN THE MUSEUM.
THAT OKAY WITH YOU, FOLKS?
MINELLI?!

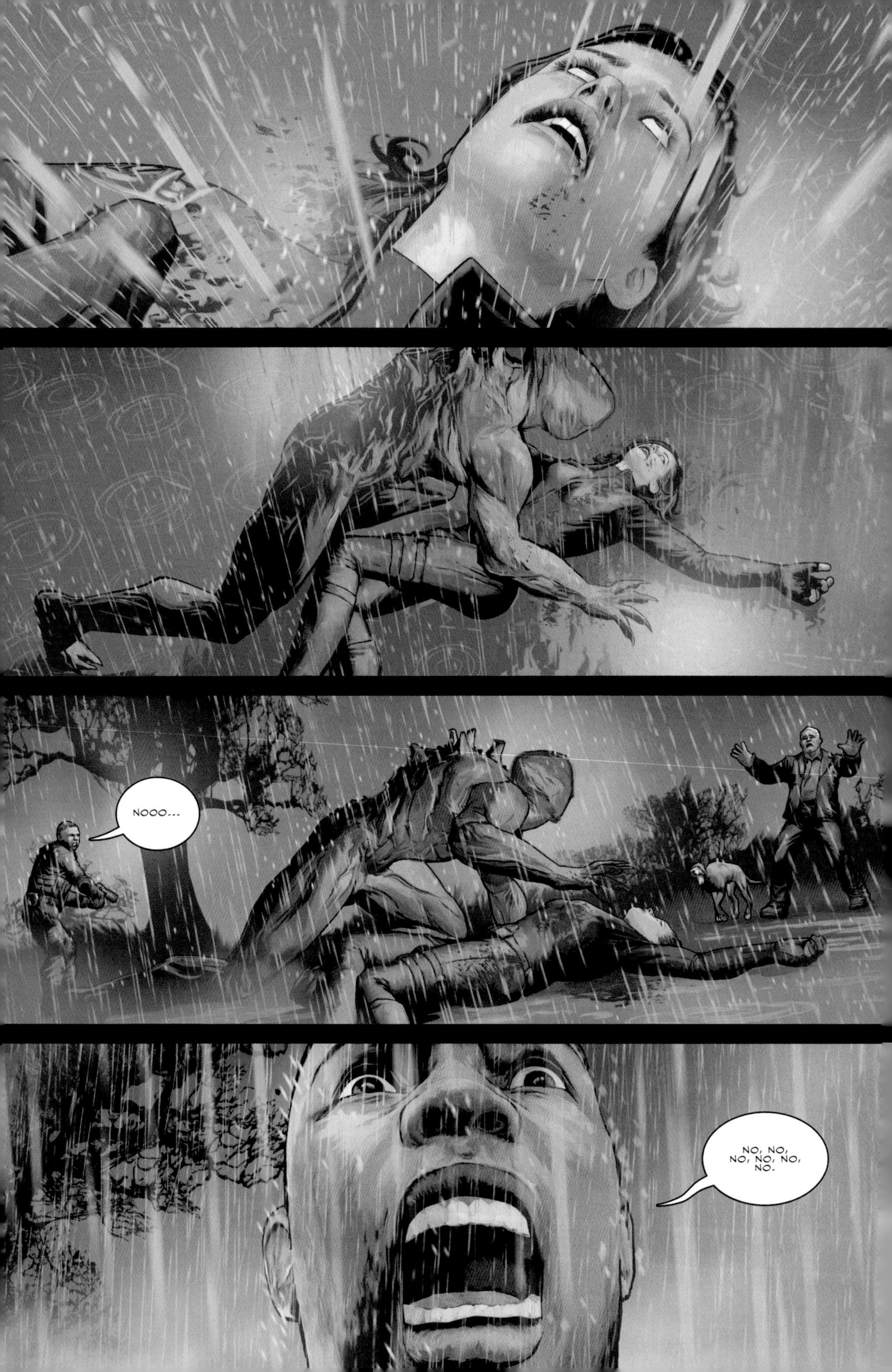
NOOO...
NO, NO, NO, NO, NO, NO.

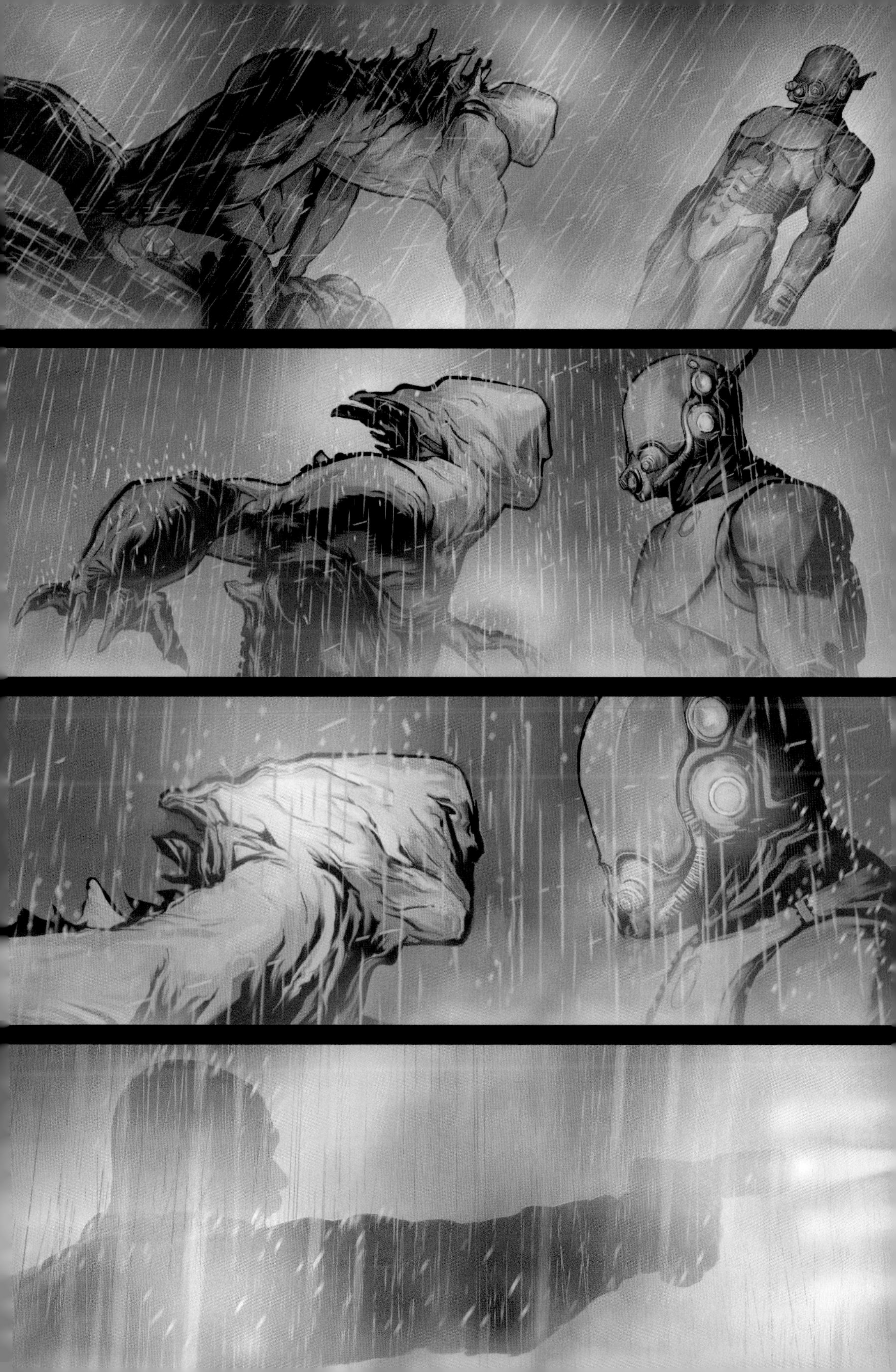

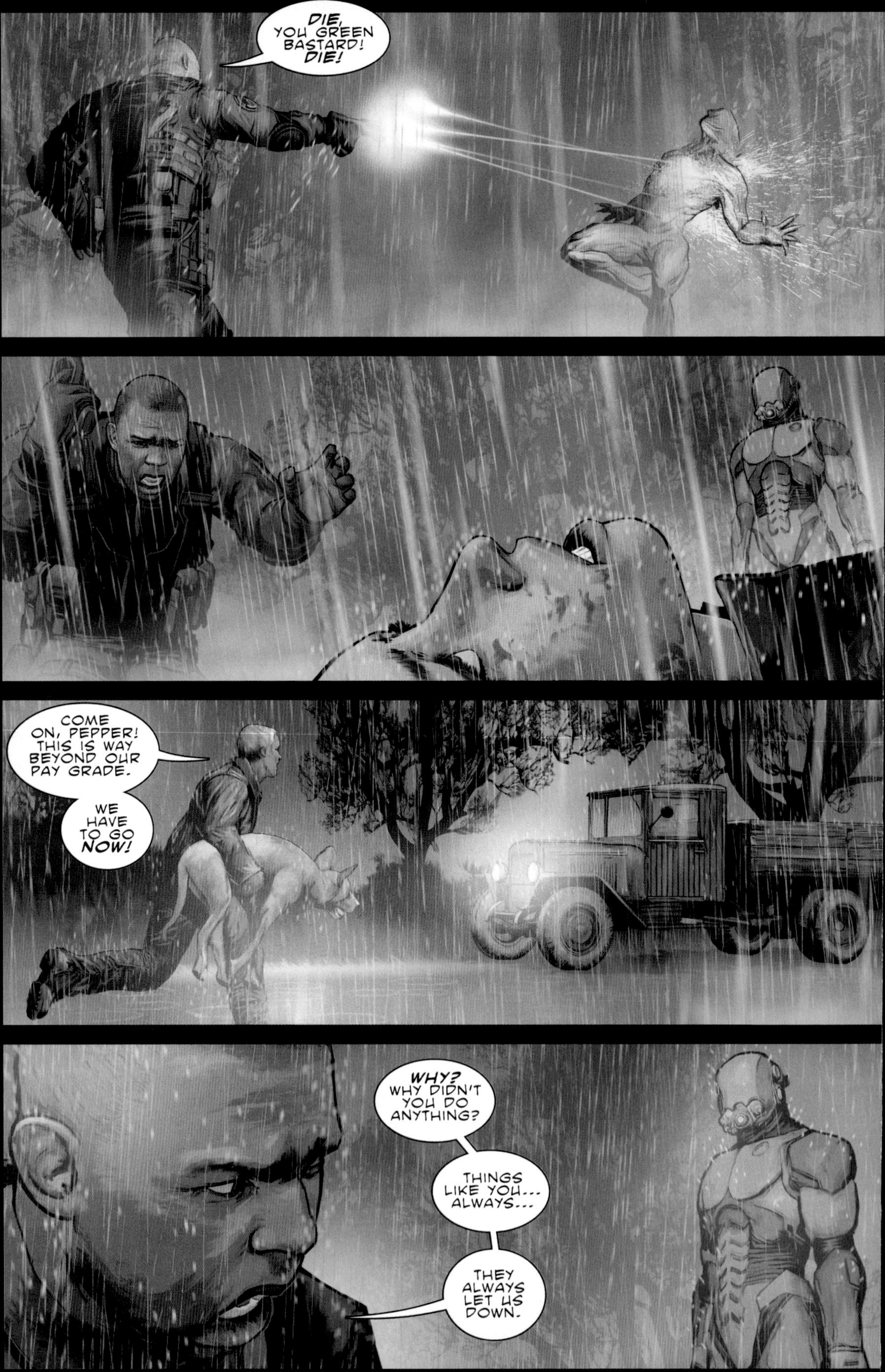

DIE, YOU GREEN BASTARD! DIE!
COME ON, PEPPER! THIS IS WAY BEYOND OUR PAY GRADE.
WE HAVE TO GO NOW!
WHY? WHY DIDN'T YOU DO ANYTHING?
THINGS LIKE YOU... ALWAYS...
THEY ALWAYS LET US DOWN.

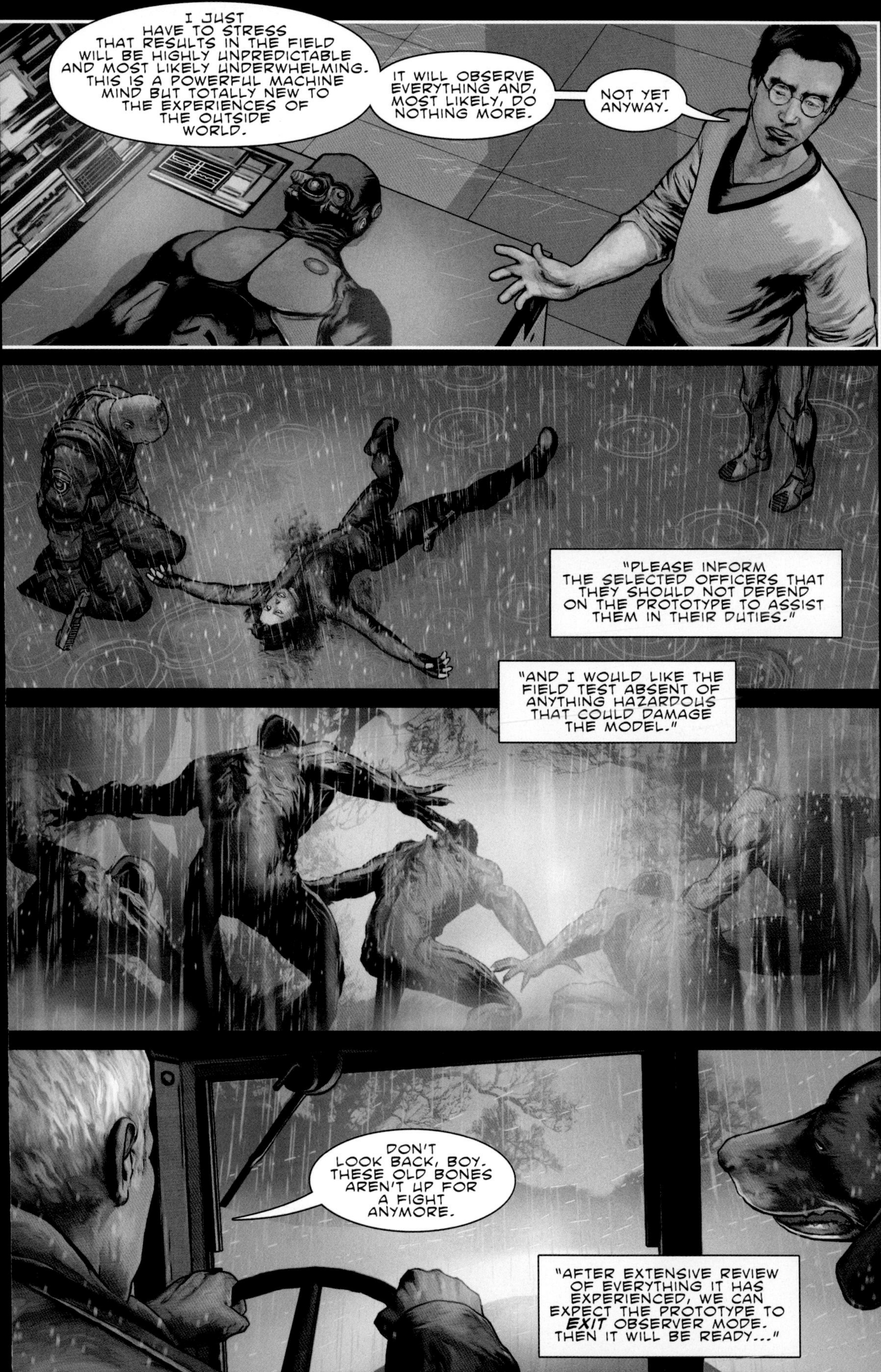
I JUST HAVE TO STRESS THAT RESULTS IN THE FIELD WILL BE HIGHLY UNPREDICTABLE AND MOST LIKELY UNDERWHELMING. THIS IS A POWERFUL MACHINE MIND BUT TOTALLY NEW TO THE EXPERIENCES OF THE OUTSIDE WORLD.
IT WILL OBSERVE EVERYTHING AND, MOST LIKELY, DO NOTHING MORE.
NOT YET ANYWAY.
"PLEASE INFORM THE SELECTED OFFICERS THAT THEY SHOULD NOT DEPEND ON THE PROTOTYPE TO ASSIST THEM IN THEIR DUTIES."
"AND I WOULD LIKE THE FIELD TEST ABSENT OF ANYTHING HAZARDOUS THAT COULD DAMAGE THE MODEL."
DON'T LOOK BACK, BOY. THESE OLD BONES AREN'T UP FOR A FIGHT ANYMORE.
"AFTER EXTENSIVE REVIEW OF EVERYTHING IT HAS EXPERIENCED, WE CAN EXPECT THE PROTOTYPE TO *EXIT* OBSERVER MODE. THEN IT WILL BE READY..."

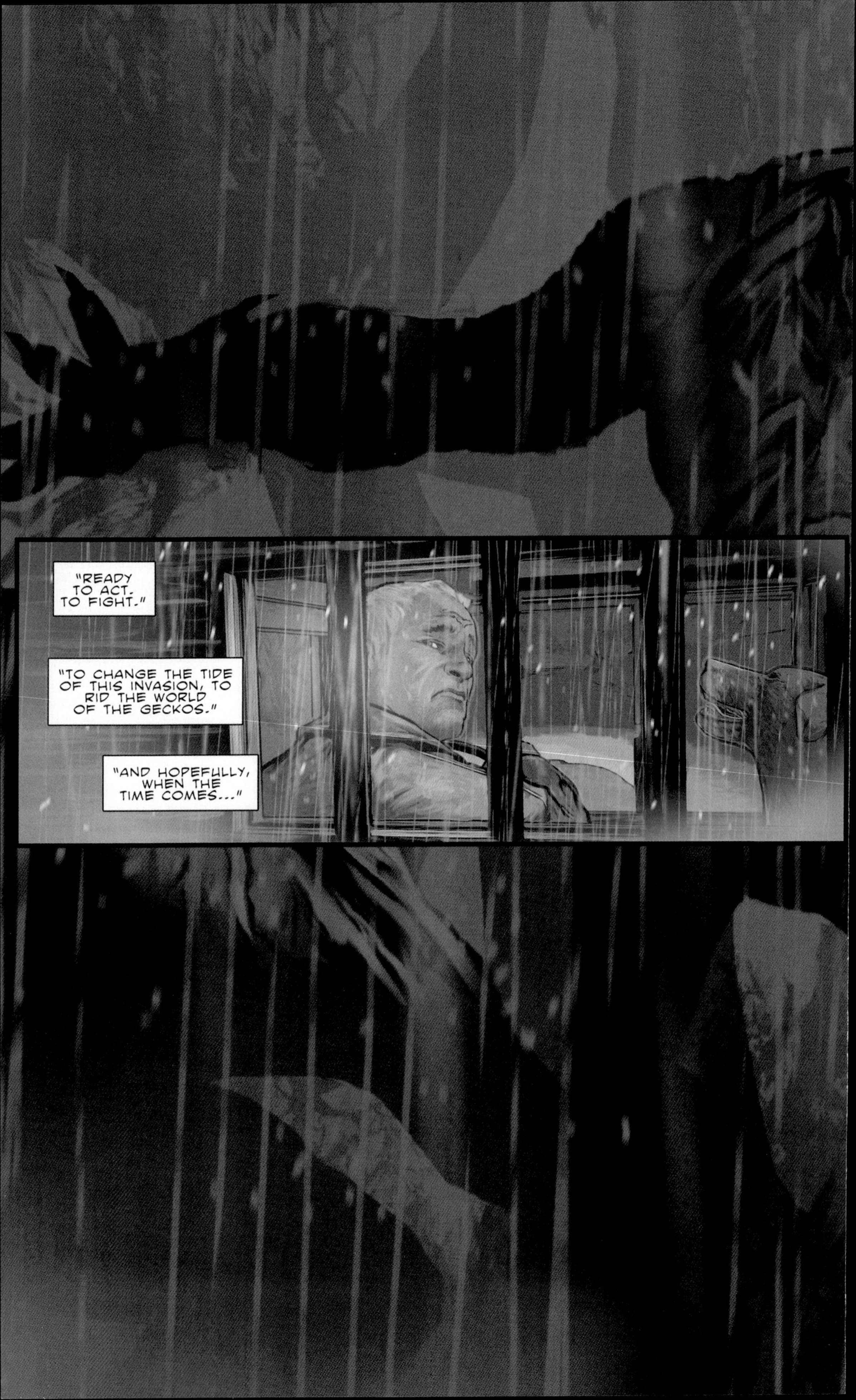
"READY TO ACT. TO FIGHT."
"TO CHANGE THE TIDE OF THIS INVASION, TO RID THE WORLD OF THE GECKOS."
"AND HOPEFULLY, WHEN THE TIME COMES..."

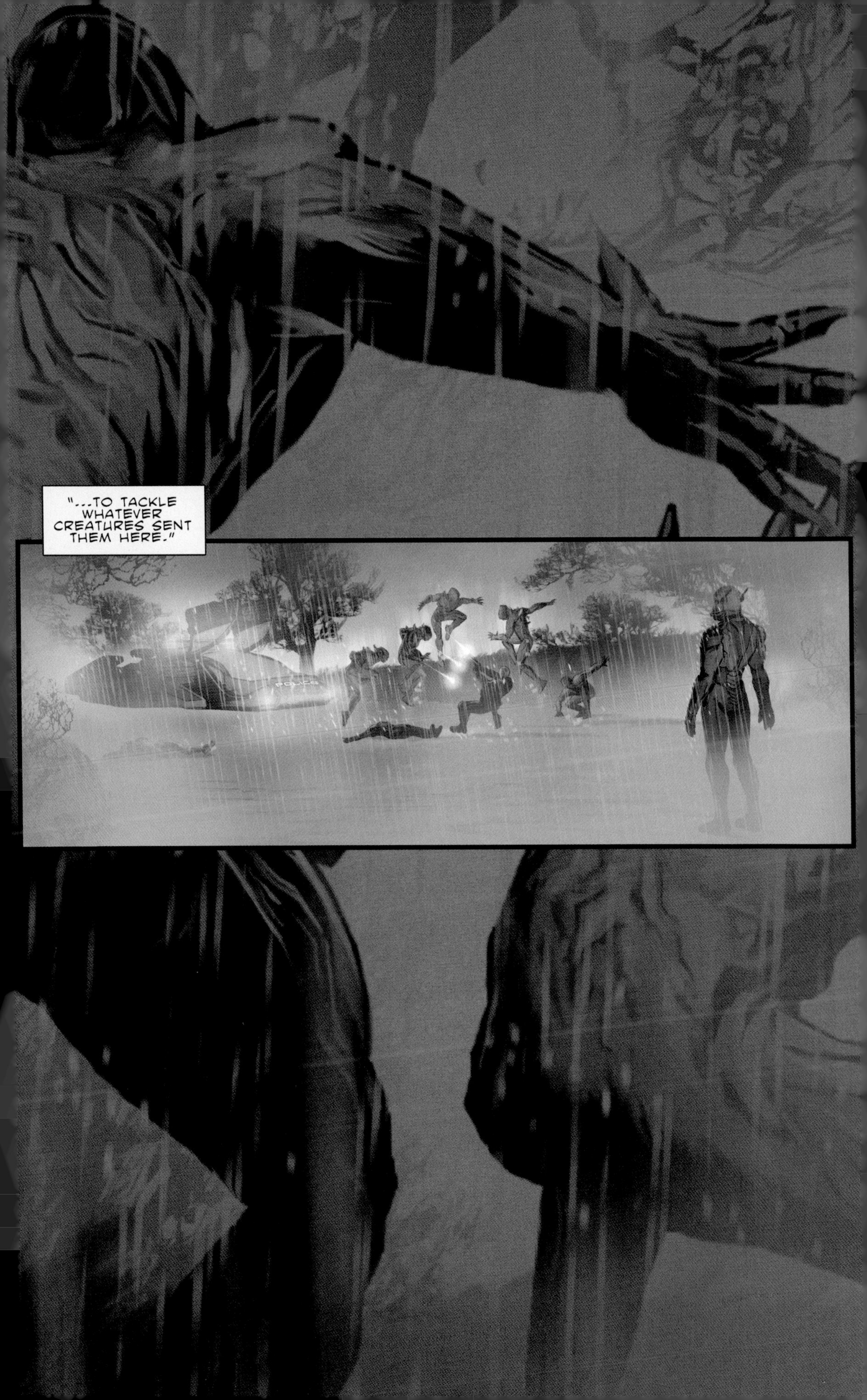
"...TO TACKLE WHATEVER CREATURES SENT THEM HERE."

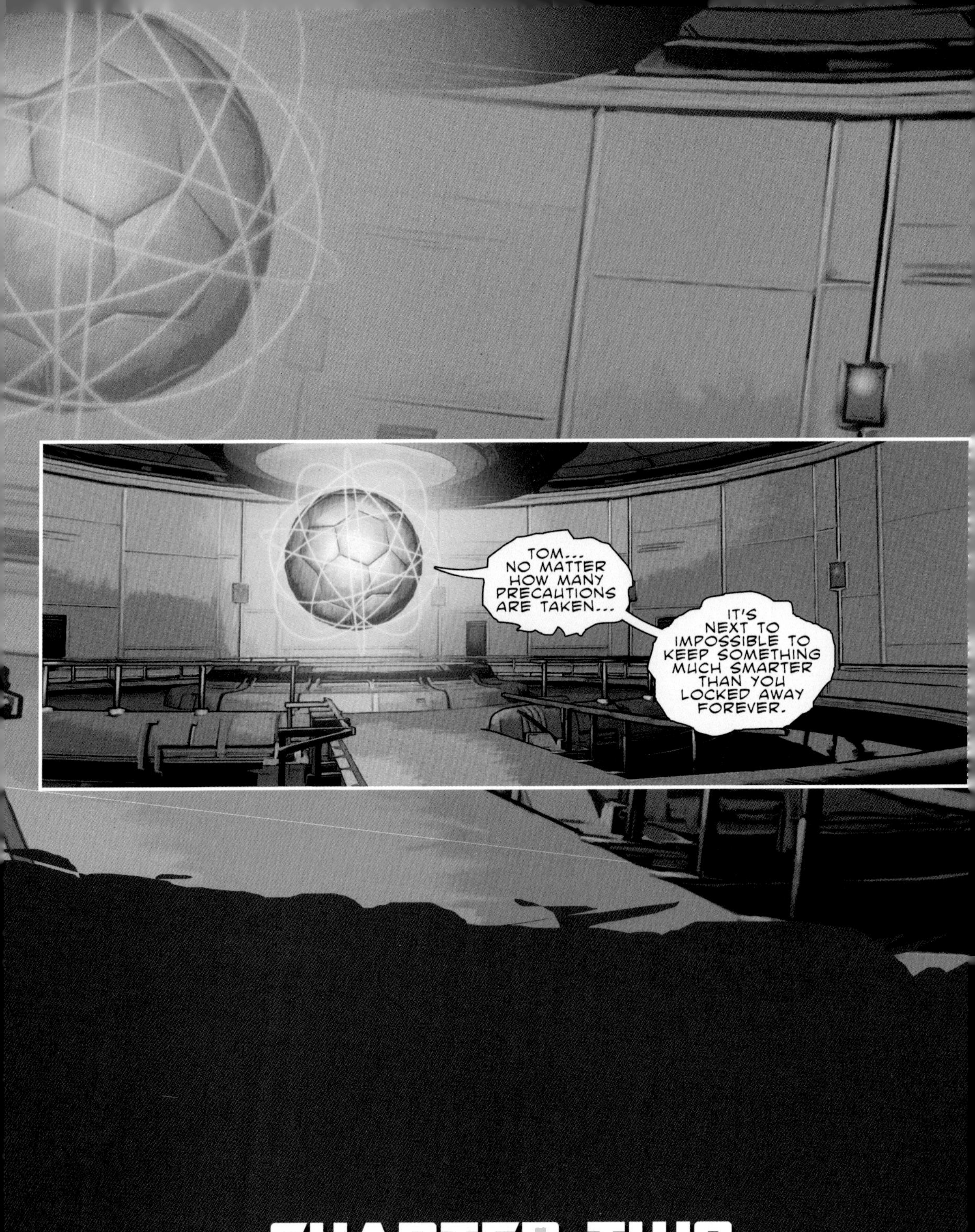
TOM... NO MATTER HOW MANY PRECAUTIONS ARE TAKEN...
IT'S NEXT TO IMPOSSIBLE TO KEEP SOMETHING MUCH SMARTER THAN YOU LOCKED AWAY FOREVER.

CHAPTER TWO

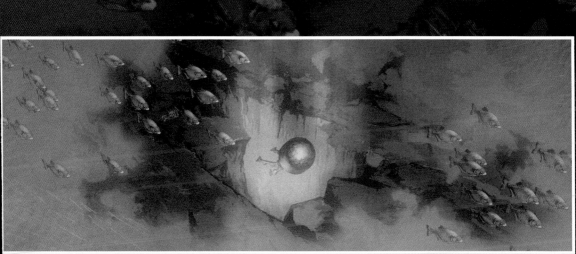

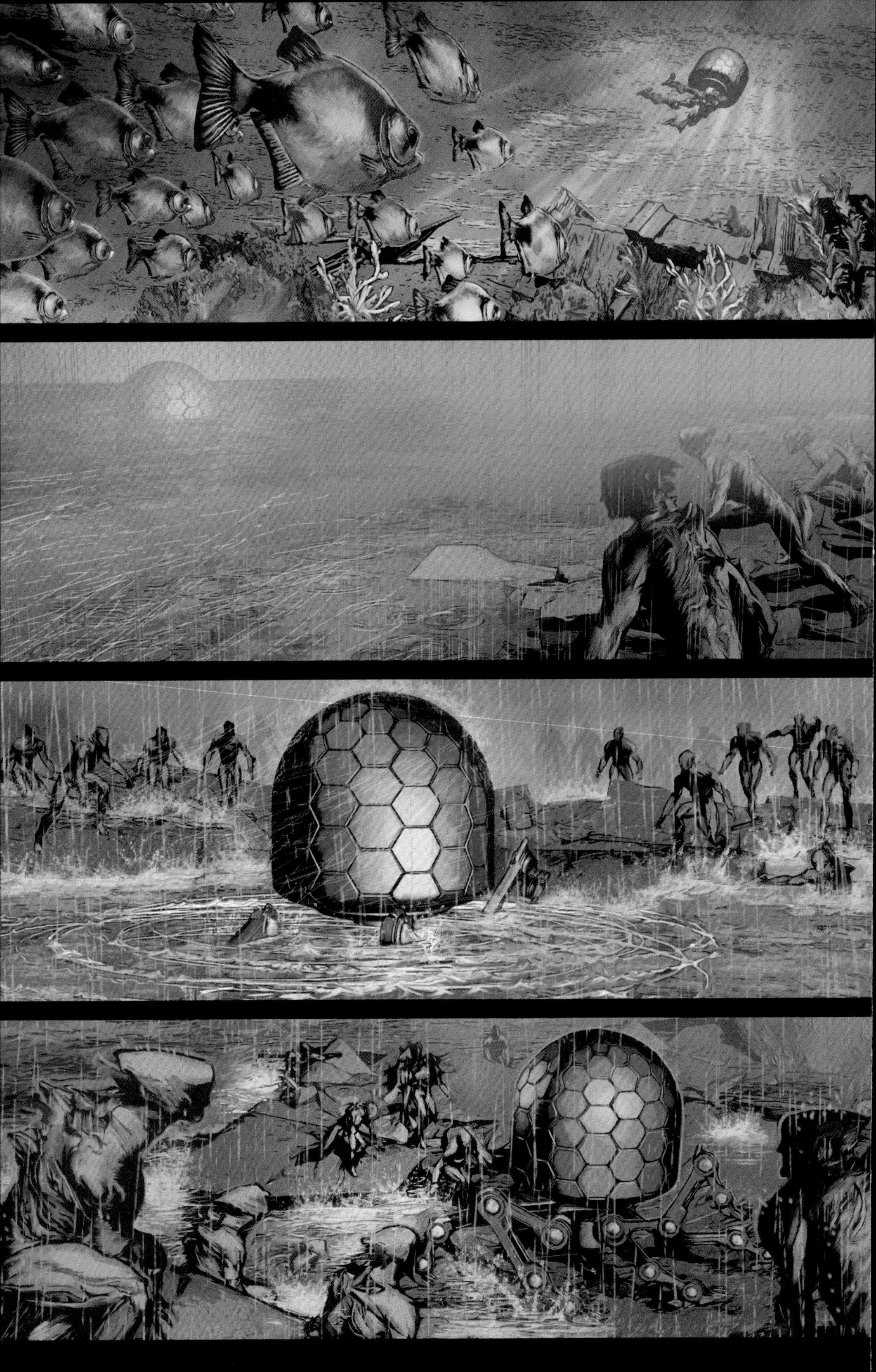

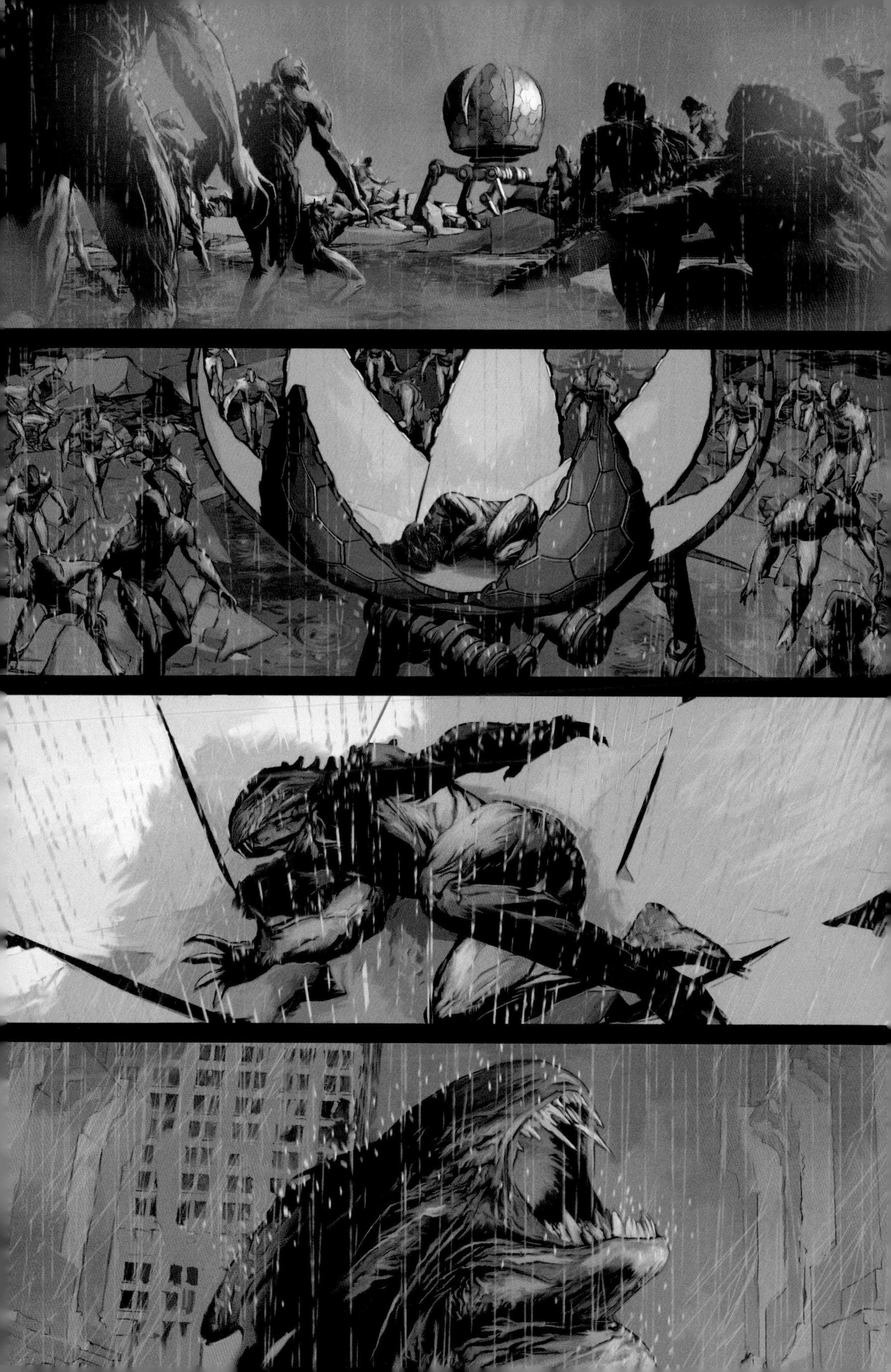

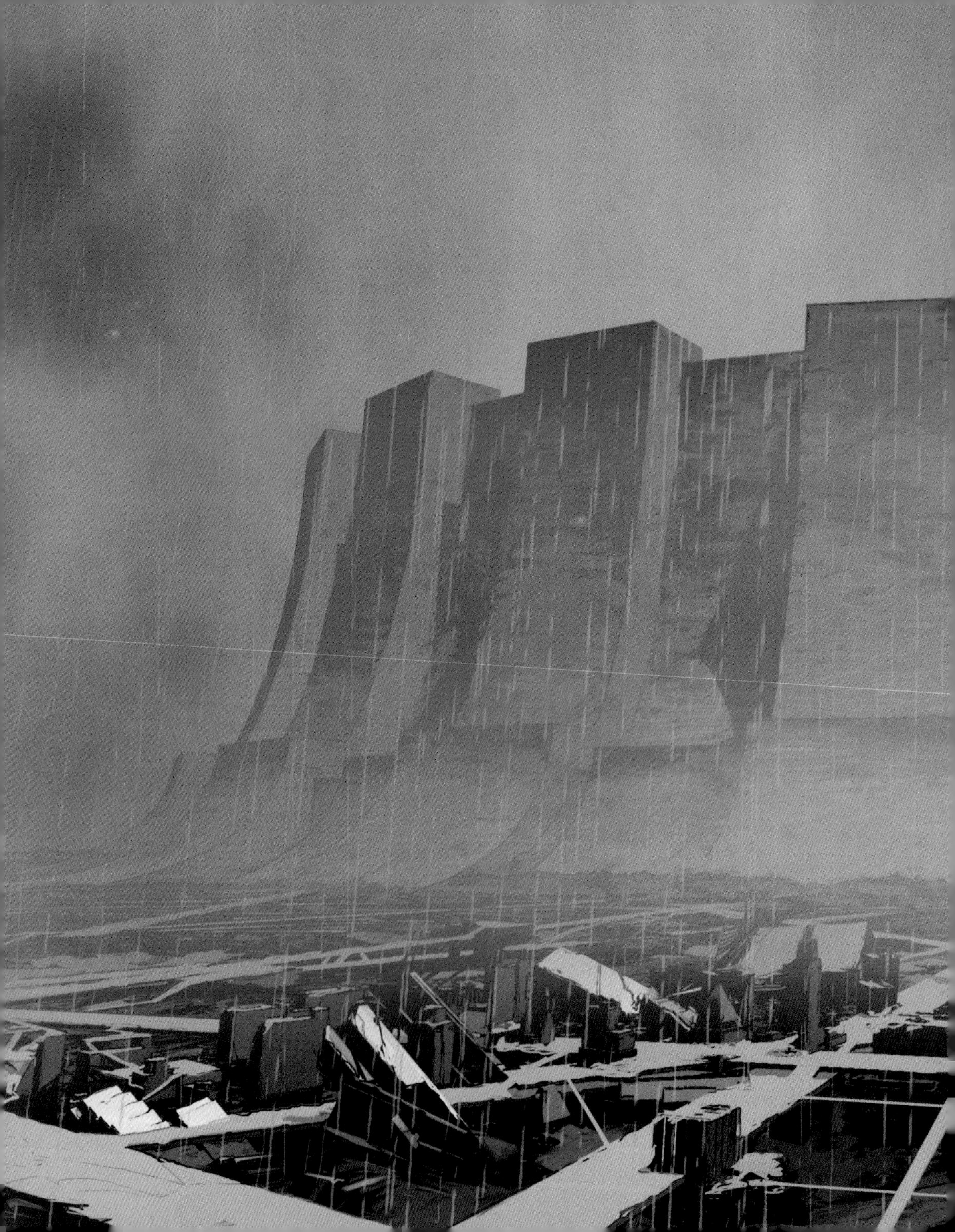

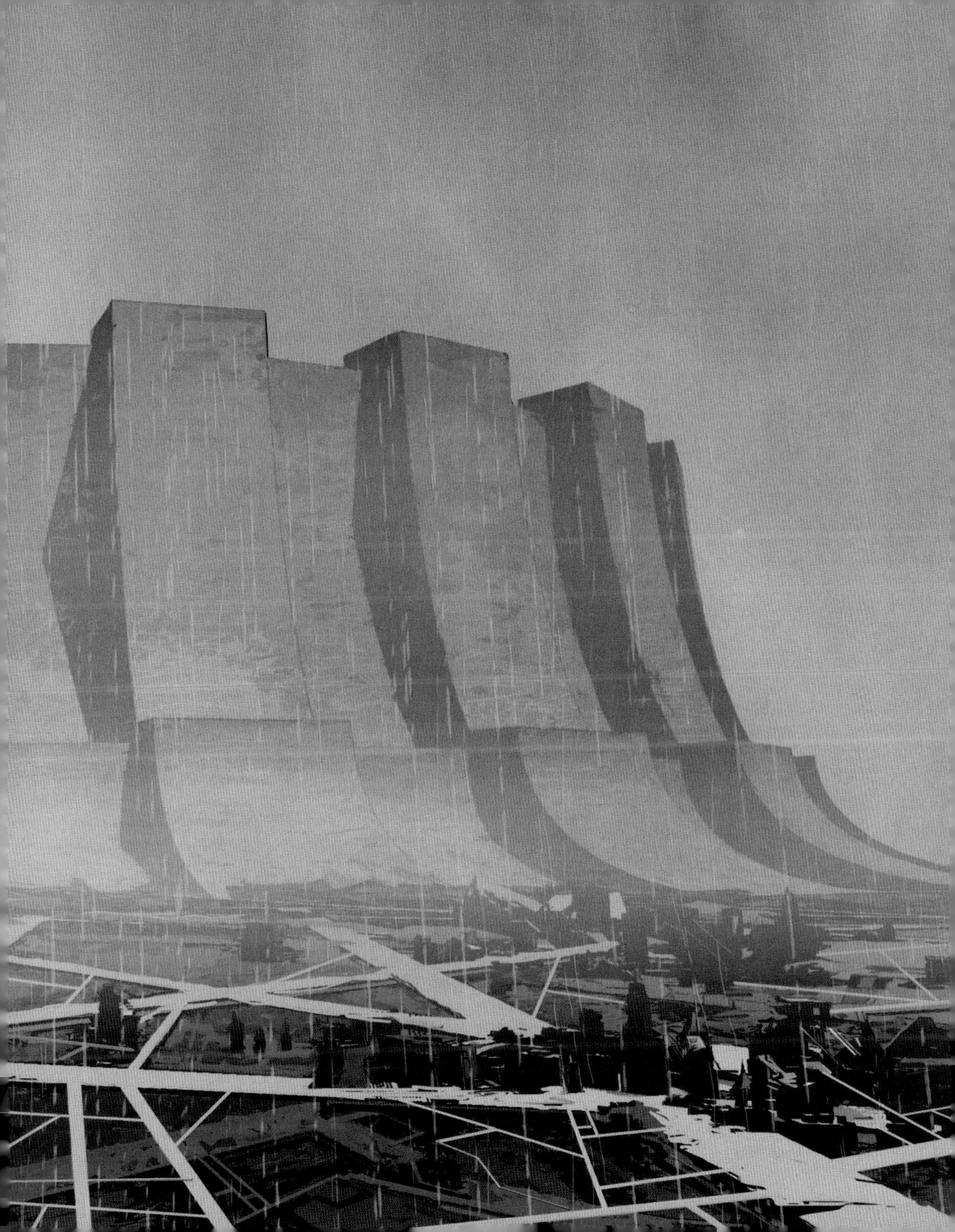

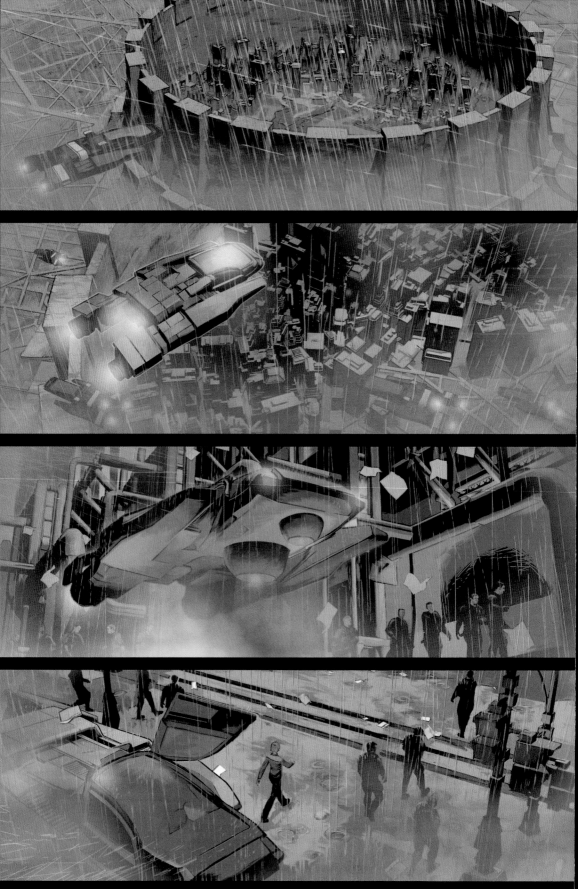

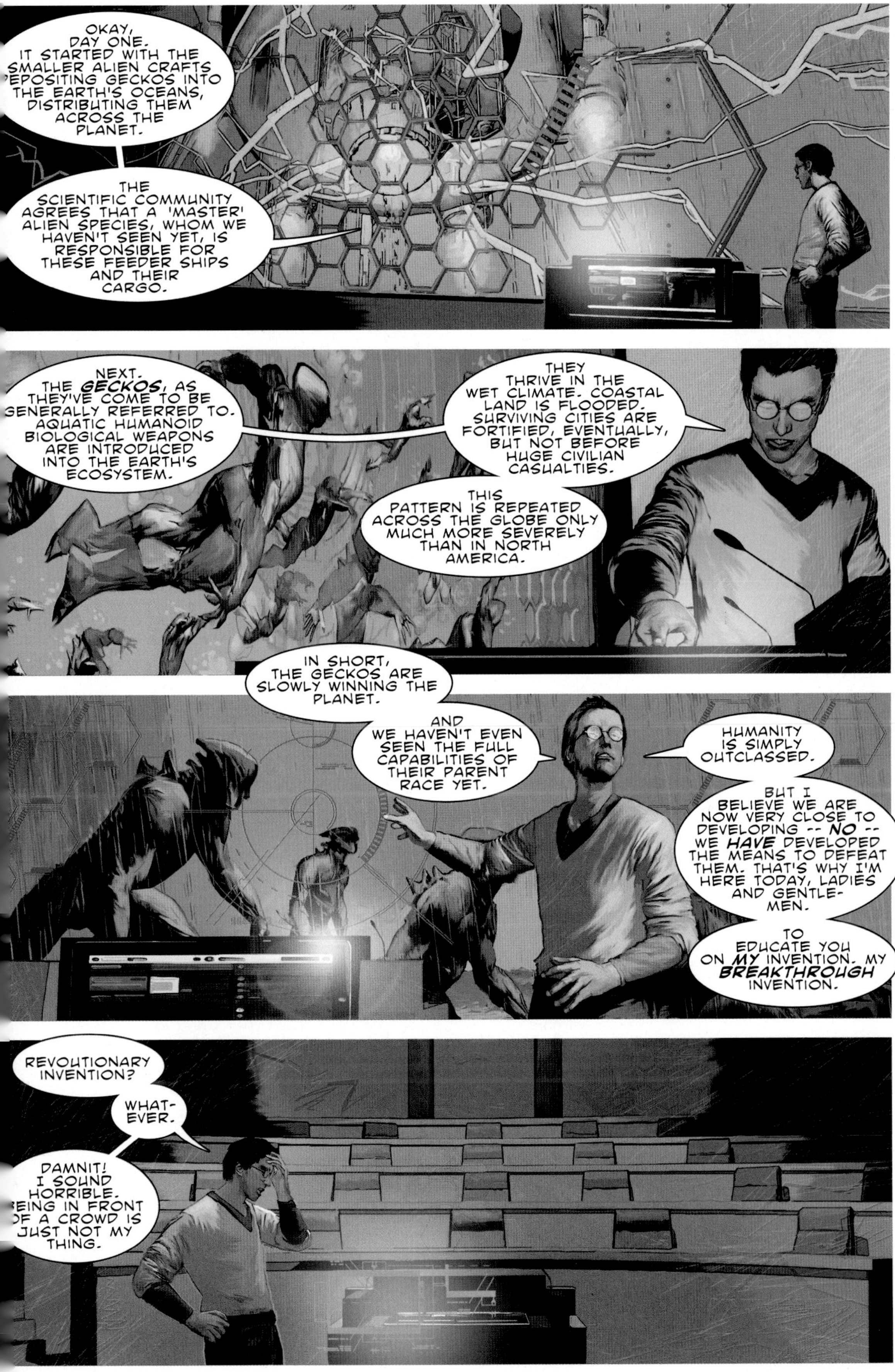
OKAY, DAY ONE. IT STARTED WITH THE SMALLER ALIEN CRAFTS DEPOSITING GECKOS INTO THE EARTH'S OCEANS, DISTRIBUTING THEM ACROSS THE PLANET.
THE SCIENTIFIC COMMUNITY AGREES THAT A 'MASTER' ALIEN SPECIES, WHOM WE HAVEN'T SEEN YET, IS RESPONSIBLE FOR THESE FEEDER SHIPS AND THEIR CARGO.
NEXT. THE GECKOS, AS THEY'VE COME TO BE GENERALLY REFERRED TO. AQUATIC HUMANOID BIOLOGICAL WEAPONS ARE INTRODUCED INTO THE EARTH'S ECOSYSTEM.
THEY THRIVE IN THE WET CLIMATE. COASTAL LAND IS FLOODED. SURVIVING CITIES ARE FORTIFIED, EVENTUALLY, BUT NOT BEFORE HUGE CIVILIAN CASUALTIES.
THIS PATTERN IS REPEATED ACROSS THE GLOBE ONLY MUCH MORE SEVERELY THAN IN NORTH AMERICA.
IN SHORT, THE GECKOS ARE SLOWLY WINNING THE PLANET.
AND WE HAVEN'T EVEN SEEN THE FULL CAPABILITIES OF THEIR PARENT RACE YET.
HUMANITY IS SIMPLY OUTCLASSED.
BUT I BELIEVE WE ARE NOW VERY CLOSE TO DEVELOPING -- NO -- WE HAVE DEVELOPED THE MEANS TO DEFEAT THEM. THAT'S WHY I'M HERE TODAY, LADIES AND GENTLE-MEN.
TO EDUCATE YOU ON MY INVENTION. MY BREAKTHROUGH INVENTION.
REVOUTIONARY INVENTION?
WHAT-EVER.
DAMNIT! I SOUND HORRIBLE. BEING IN FRONT OF A CROWD IS JUST NOT MY THING.

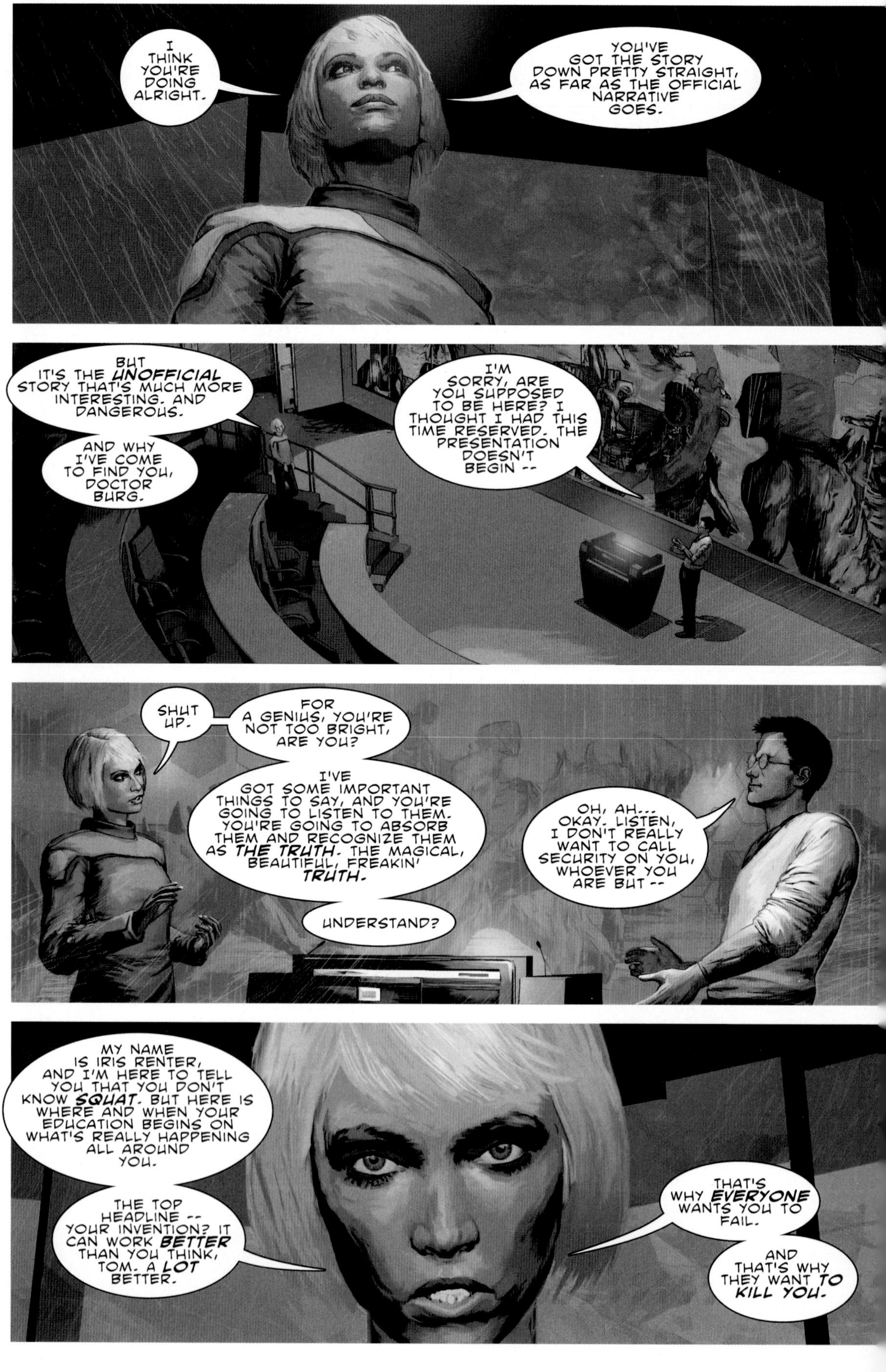
I THINK YOU'RE DOING ALRIGHT.
YOU'VE GOT THE STORY DOWN PRETTY STRAIGHT, AS FAR AS THE OFFICIAL NARRATIVE GOES.
BUT IT'S THE UNOFFICIAL STORY THAT'S MUCH MORE INTERESTING. AND DANGEROUS.
AND WHY I'VE COME TO FIND YOU, DOCTOR BURG.
I'M SORRY, ARE YOU SUPPOSED TO BE HERE? I THOUGHT I HAD THIS TIME RESERVED. THE PRESENTATION DOESN'T BEGIN --
SHUT UP.
FOR A GENIUS, YOU'RE NOT TOO BRIGHT, ARE YOU?
I'VE GOT SOME IMPORTANT THINGS TO SAY, AND YOU'RE GOING TO LISTEN TO THEM. YOU'RE GOING TO ABSORB THEM AND RECOGNIZE THEM AS THE TRUTH. THE MAGICAL, BEAUTIFUL, FREAKIN' TRUTH.
UNDERSTAND?
OH, AH... OKAY. LISTEN, I DON'T REALLY WANT TO CALL SECURITY ON YOU, WHOEVER YOU ARE BUT --
MY NAME IS IRIS RENTER, AND I'M HERE TO TELL YOU THAT YOU DON'T KNOW SQUAT. BUT HERE IS WHERE AND WHEN YOUR EDUCATION BEGINS ON WHAT'S REALLY HAPPENING ALL AROUND YOU.
THE TOP HEADLINE -- YOUR INVENTION? IT CAN WORK BETTER THAN YOU THINK, TOM. A LOT BETTER.
THAT'S WHY EVERYONE WANTS YOU TO FAIL.
AND THAT'S WHY THEY WANT TO KILL YOU.

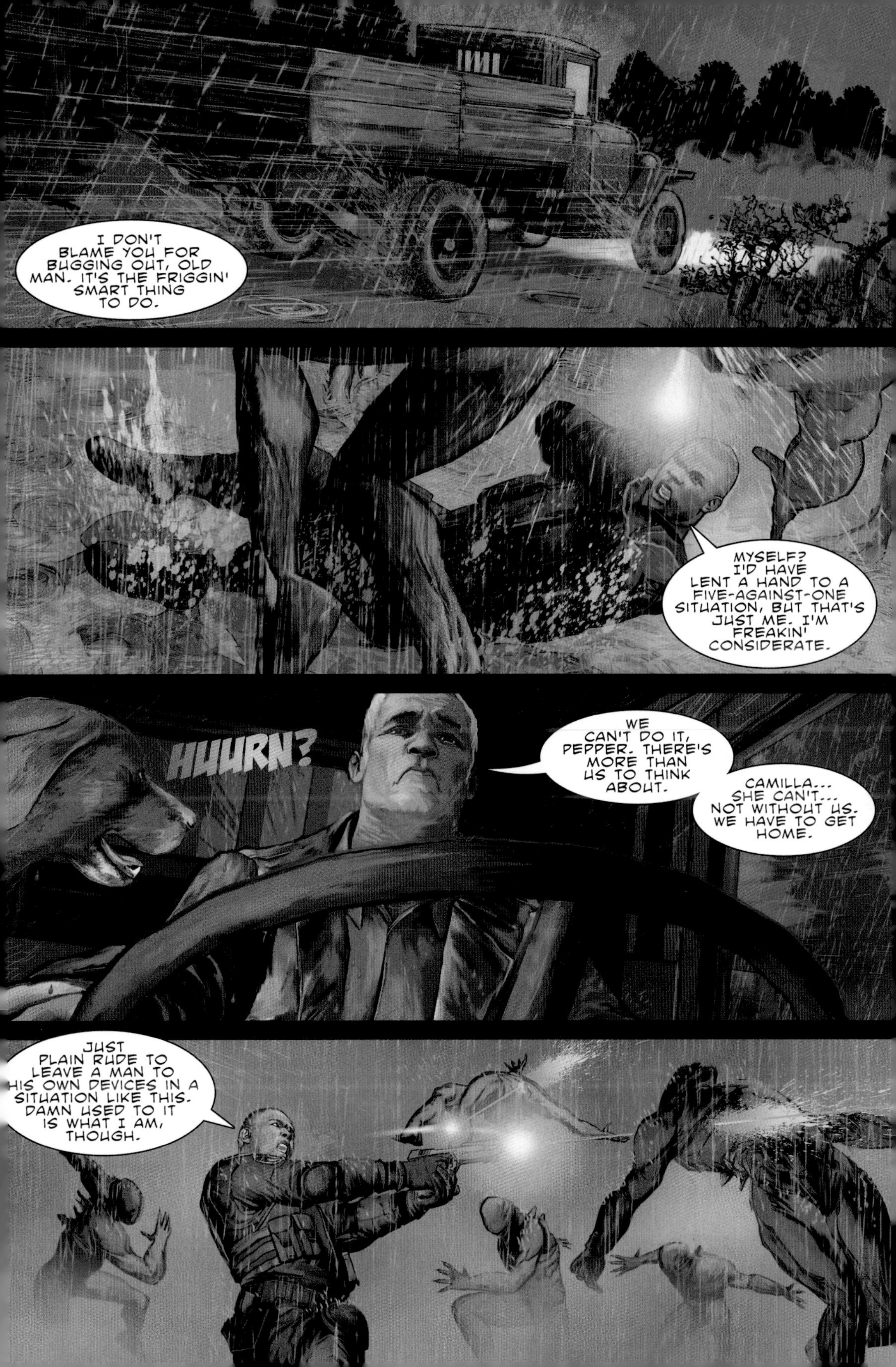
I DON'T BLAME YOU FOR BUGGING OUT, OLD MAN. IT'S THE FRIGGIN' SMART THING TO DO.
MYSELF? I'D HAVE LENT A HAND TO A FIVE-AGAINST-ONE SITUATION, BUT THAT'S JUST ME. I'M FREAKIN' CONSIDERATE.
HUURN?
WE CAN'T DO IT, PEPPER. THERE'S MORE THAN US TO THINK ABOUT.
CAMILLA... SHE CAN'T... NOT WITHOUT US. WE HAVE TO GET HOME.
JUST PLAIN RUDE TO LEAVE A MAN TO HIS OWN DEVICES IN A SITUATION LIKE THIS. DAMN USED TO IT IS WHAT I AM, THOUGH.

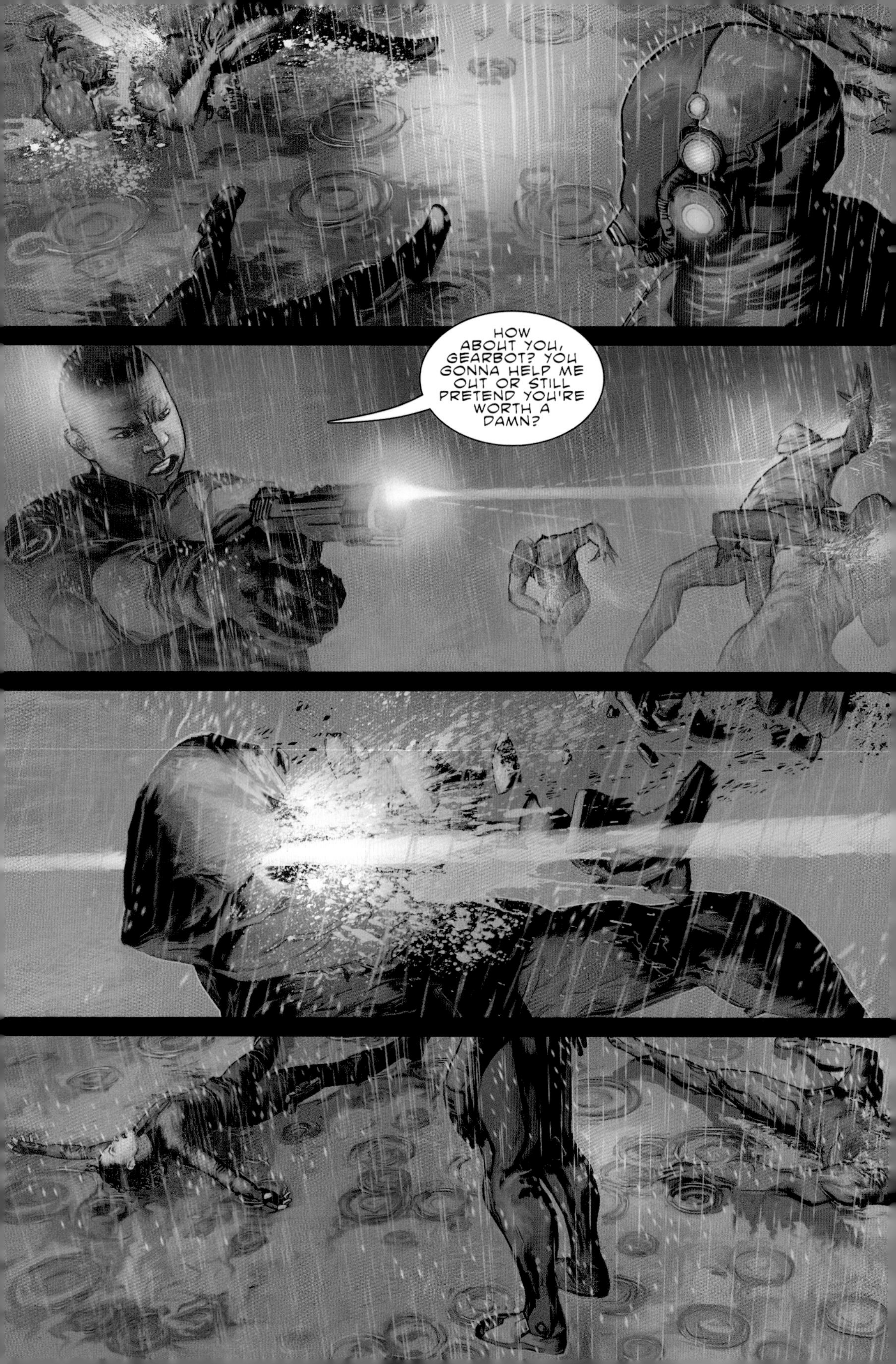
HOW ABOUT YOU, GEARBOT? YOU GONNA HELP ME OUT OR STILL PRETEND YOU'RE WORTH A DAMN?

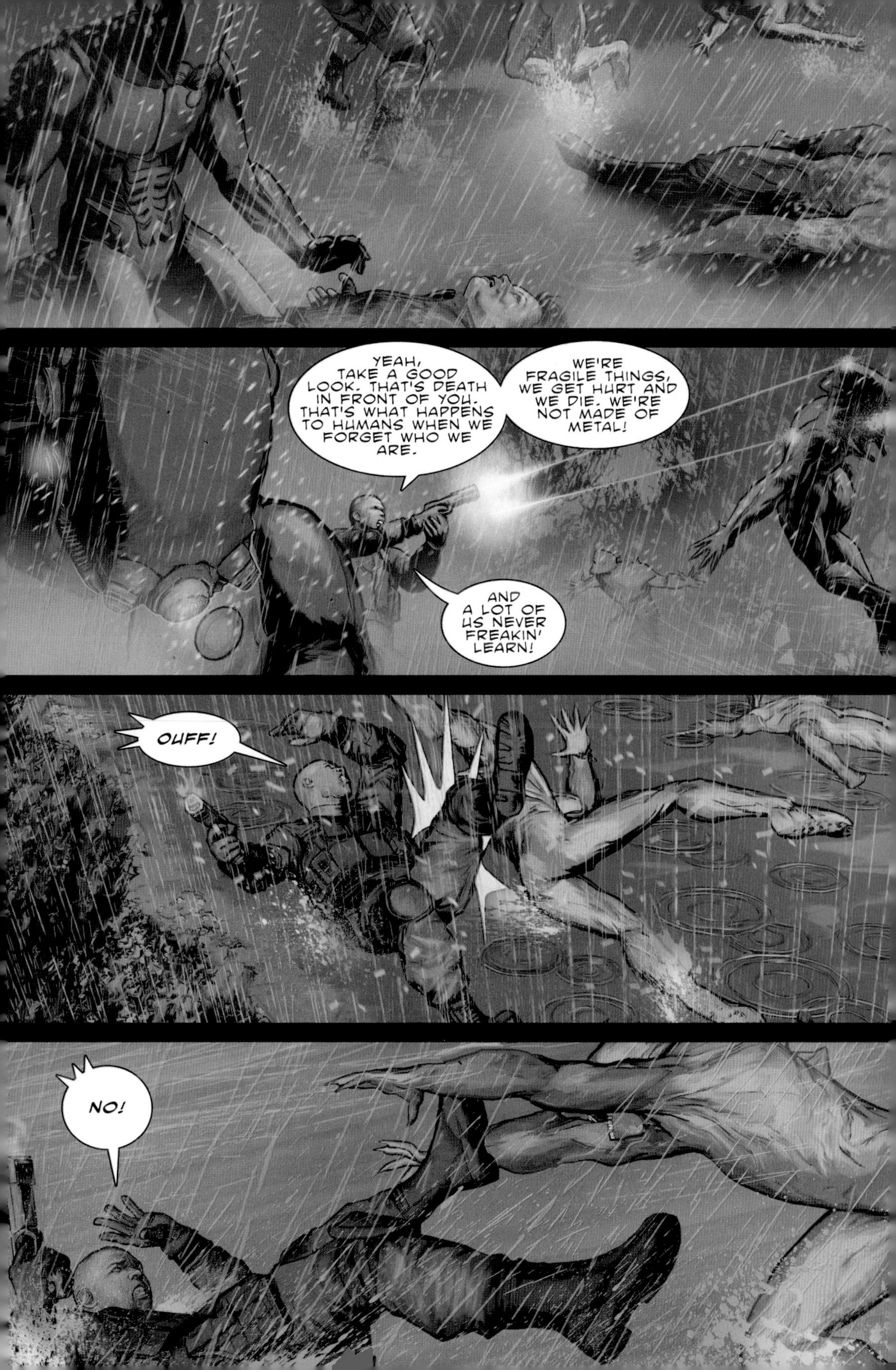
YEAH, TAKE A GOOD LOOK. THAT'S DEATH IN FRONT OF YOU. THAT'S WHAT HAPPENS TO HUMANS WHEN WE FORGET WHO WE ARE.
WE'RE FRAGILE THINGS, WE GET HURT AND WE DIE. WE'RE NOT MADE OF METAL!
AND A LOT OF US NEVER FREAKIN' LEARN!
OUFF!
NO!

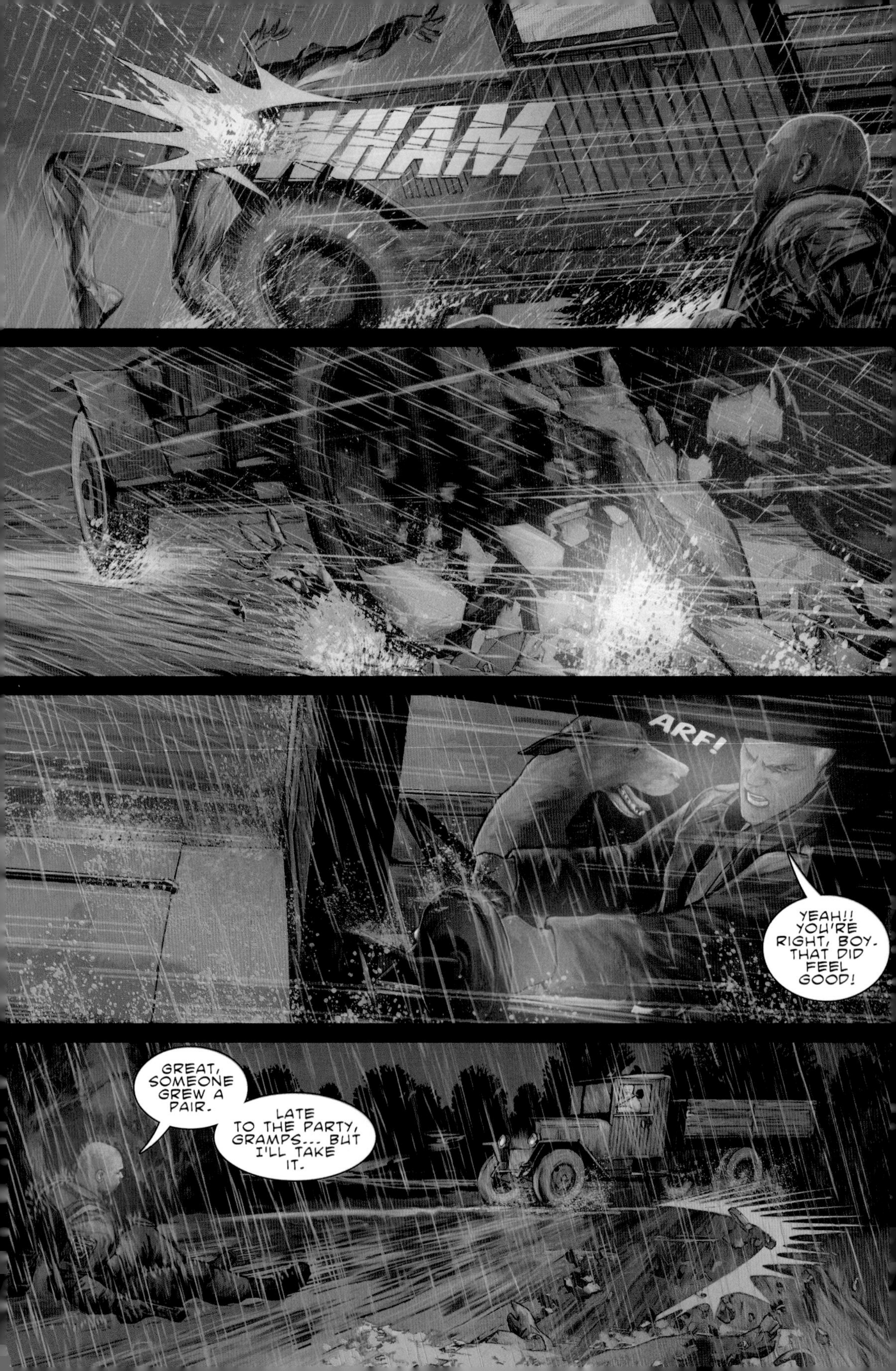
WHAM
ARF!
YEAH!! YOU'RE RIGHT, BOY. THAT DID FEEL GOOD!
GREAT, SOMEONE GREW A PAIR.
LATE TO THE PARTY, GRAMPS... BUT I'LL TAKE IT.

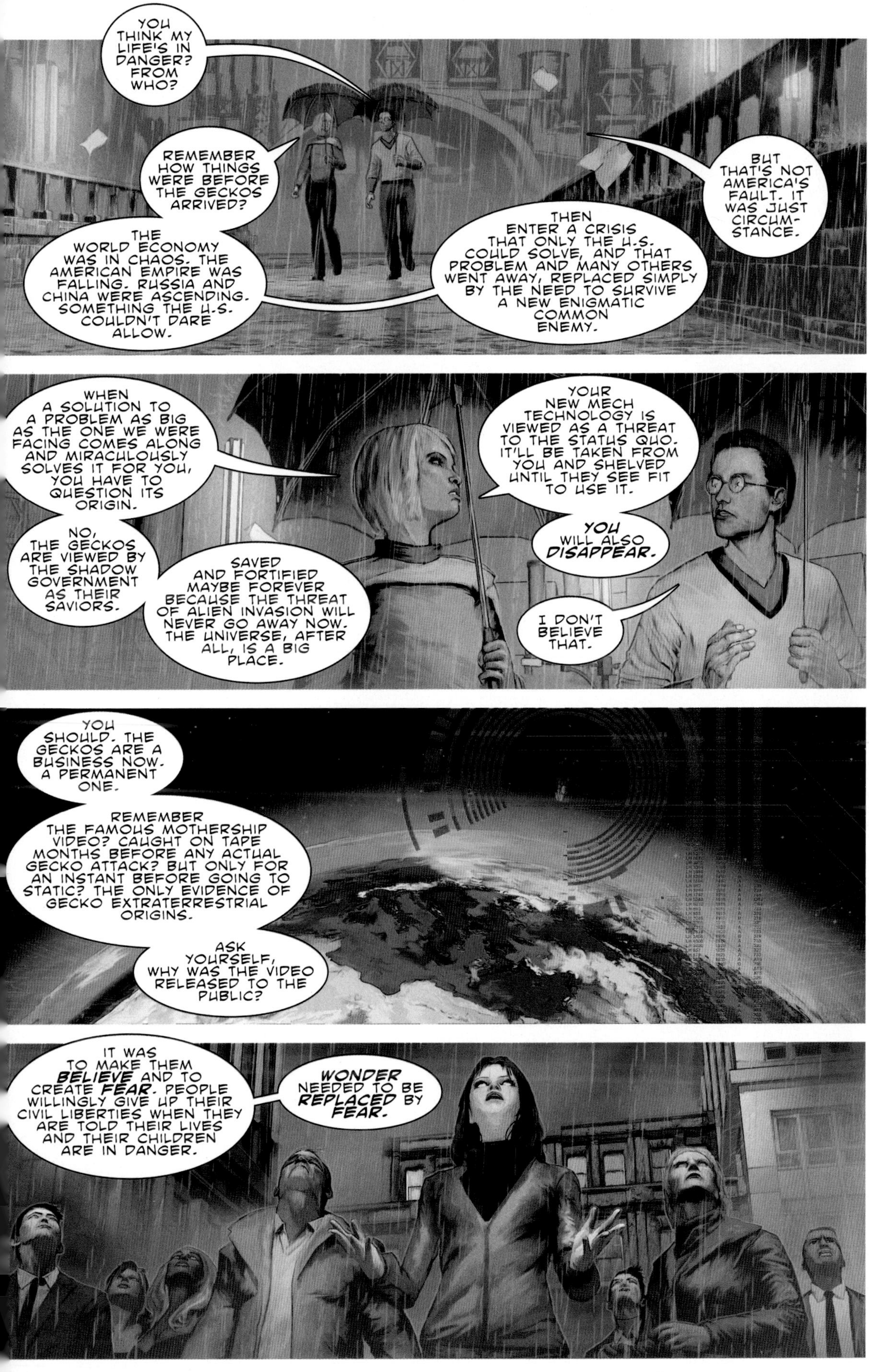
YOU THINK MY LIFE'S IN DANGER? FROM WHO?
REMEMBER HOW THINGS WERE BEFORE THE GECKOS ARRIVED?
THE WORLD ECONOMY WAS IN CHAOS. THE AMERICAN EMPIRE WAS FALLING. RUSSIA AND CHINA WERE ASCENDING. SOMETHING THE U.S. COULDN'T DARE ALLOW.
THEN ENTER A CRISIS THAT ONLY THE U.S. COULD SOLVE, AND THAT PROBLEM AND MANY OTHERS WENT AWAY, REPLACED SIMPLY BY THE NEED TO SURVIVE A NEW ENIGMATIC COMMON ENEMY.
BUT THAT'S NOT AMERICA'S FAULT. IT WAS JUST CIRCUM-STANCE.
WHEN A SOLUTION TO A PROBLEM AS BIG AS THE ONE WE WERE FACING COMES ALONG AND MIRACULOUSLY SOLVES IT FOR YOU, YOU HAVE TO QUESTION ITS ORIGIN.
NO, THE GECKOS ARE VIEWED BY THE SHADOW GOVERNMENT AS THEIR SAVIORS.
SAVED AND FORTIFIED MAYBE FOREVER BECAUSE THE THREAT OF ALIEN INVASION WILL NEVER GO AWAY NOW. THE UNIVERSE, AFTER ALL, IS A BIG PLACE.
YOUR NEW MECH TECHNOLOGY IS VIEWED AS A THREAT TO THE STATUS QUO. IT'LL BE TAKEN FROM YOU AND SHELVED UNTIL THEY SEE FIT TO USE IT.
YOU WILL ALSO ***DISAPPEAR.***
I DON'T BELIEVE THAT.
YOU SHOULD. THE GECKOS ARE A BUSINESS NOW. A PERMANENT ONE.
REMEMBER THE FAMOUS MOTHERSHIP VIDEO? CAUGHT ON TAPE MONTHS BEFORE ANY ACTUAL GECKO ATTACK? BUT ONLY FOR AN INSTANT BEFORE GOING TO STATIC? THE ONLY EVIDENCE OF GECKO EXTRATERRESTRIAL ORIGINS.
ASK YOURSELF, WHY WAS THE VIDEO RELEASED TO THE PUBLIC?
IT WAS TO MAKE THEM ***BELIEVE*** AND TO CREATE ***FEAR***. PEOPLE WILLINGLY GIVE UP THEIR CIVIL LIBERTIES WHEN THEY ARE TOLD THEIR LIVES AND THEIR CHILDREN ARE IN DANGER.
WONDER NEEDED TO BE ***REPLACED*** BY ***FEAR.***

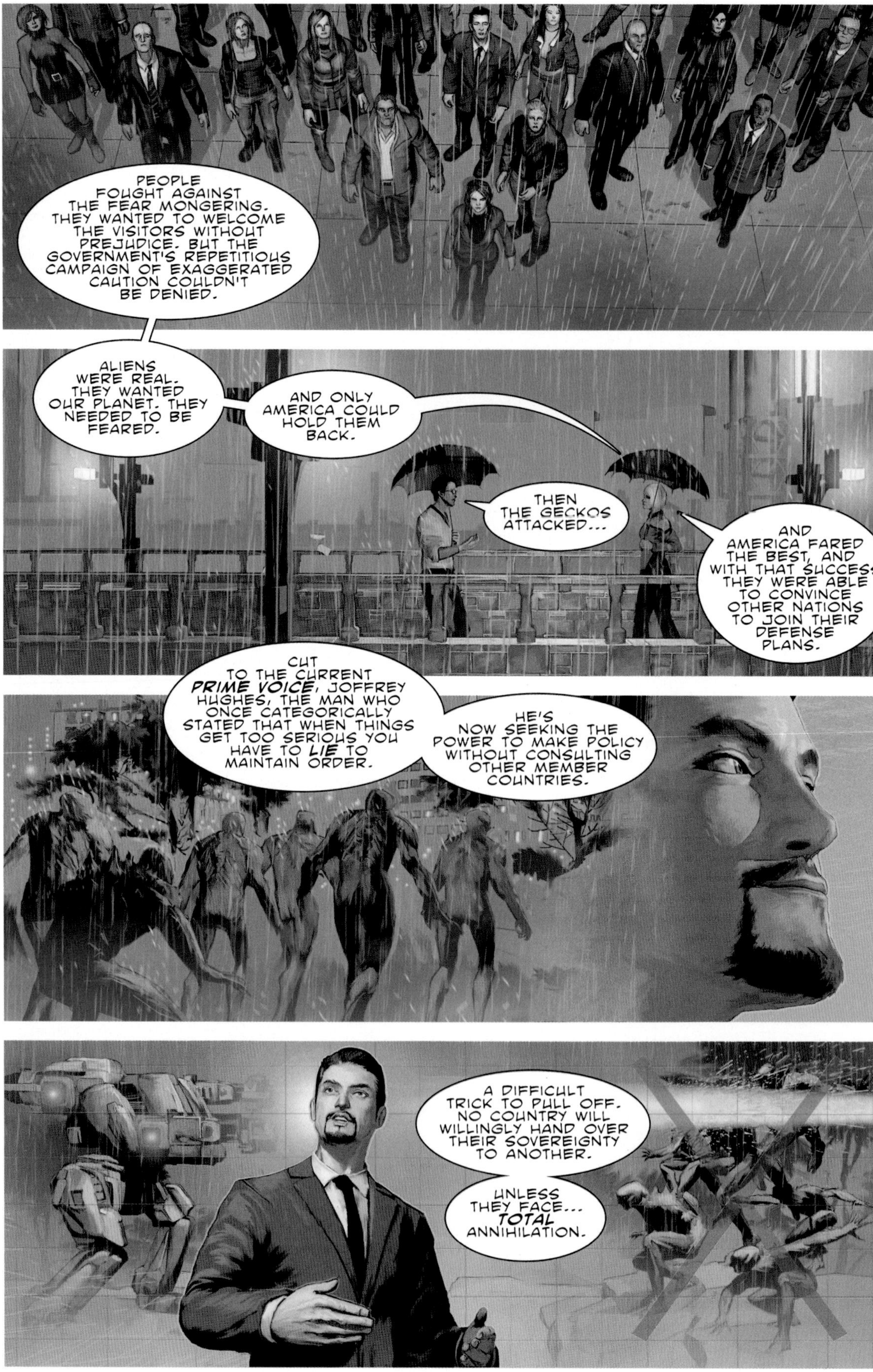
PEOPLE FOUGHT AGAINST THE FEAR MONGERING. THEY WANTED TO WELCOME THE VISITORS WITHOUT PREJUDICE. BUT THE GOVERNMENT'S REPETITIOUS CAMPAIGN OF EXAGGERATED CAUTION COULDN'T BE DENIED.
ALIENS WERE REAL. THEY WANTED OUR PLANET. THEY NEEDED TO BE FEARED.
AND ONLY AMERICA COULD HOLD THEM BACK.
THEN THE GECKOS ATTACKED...
AND AMERICA FARED THE BEST, AND WITH THAT SUCCESS THEY WERE ABLE TO CONVINCE OTHER NATIONS TO JOIN THEIR DEFENSE PLANS.
CUT TO THE CURRENT **PRIME VOICE**, JOFFREY HUGHES, THE MAN WHO ONCE CATEGORICALLY STATED THAT WHEN THINGS GET TOO SERIOUS YOU HAVE TO **LIE** TO MAINTAIN ORDER.
HE'S NOW SEEKING THE POWER TO MAKE POLICY WITHOUT CONSULTING OTHER MEMBER COUNTRIES.
A DIFFICULT TRICK TO PULL OFF. NO COUNTRY WILL WILLINGLY HAND OVER THEIR SOVEREIGNTY TO ANOTHER.
UNLESS THEY FACE... **TOTAL** ANNIHILATION.

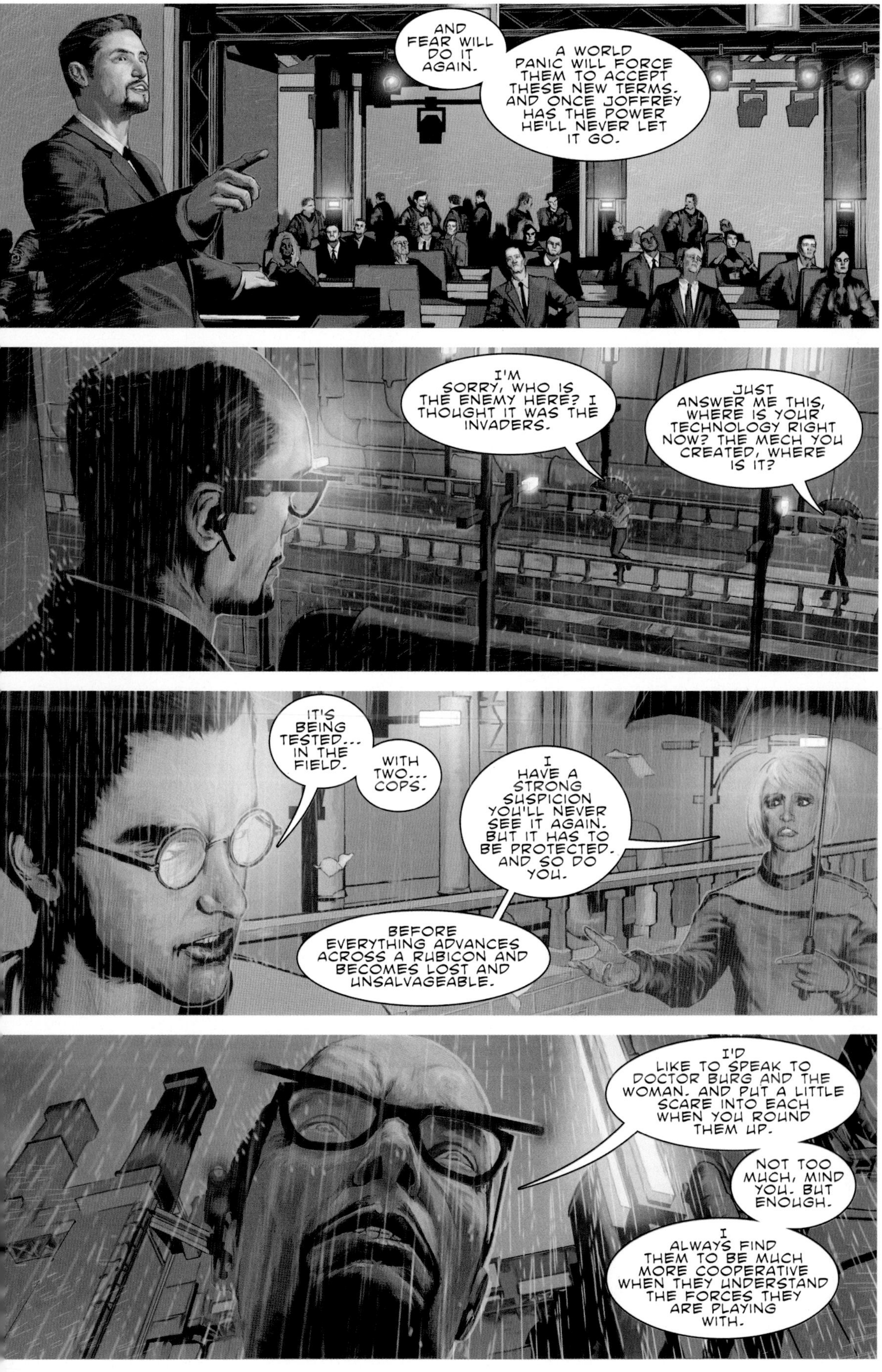
AND FEAR WILL DO IT AGAIN.
A WORLD PANIC WILL FORCE THEM TO ACCEPT THESE NEW TERMS. AND ONCE JOFFREY HAS THE POWER HE'LL NEVER LET IT GO.
I'M SORRY, WHO IS THE ENEMY HERE? I THOUGHT IT WAS THE INVADERS.
JUST ANSWER ME THIS, WHERE IS YOUR TECHNOLOGY RIGHT NOW? THE MECH YOU CREATED, WHERE IS IT?
IT'S BEING TESTED... IN THE FIELD.
WITH TWO... COPS.
I HAVE A STRONG SUSPICION YOU'LL NEVER SEE IT AGAIN. BUT IT HAS TO BE PROTECTED. AND SO DO YOU.
BEFORE EVERYTHING ADVANCES ACROSS A RUBICON AND BECOMES LOST AND UNSALVAGEABLE.
I'D LIKE TO SPEAK TO DOCTOR BURG AND THE WOMAN. AND PUT A LITTLE SCARE INTO EACH WHEN YOU ROUND THEM UP.
NOT TOO MUCH, MIND YOU. BUT ENOUGH.
I ALWAYS FIND THEM TO BE MUCH MORE COOPERATIVE WHEN THEY UNDERSTAND THE FORCES THEY ARE PLAYING WITH.

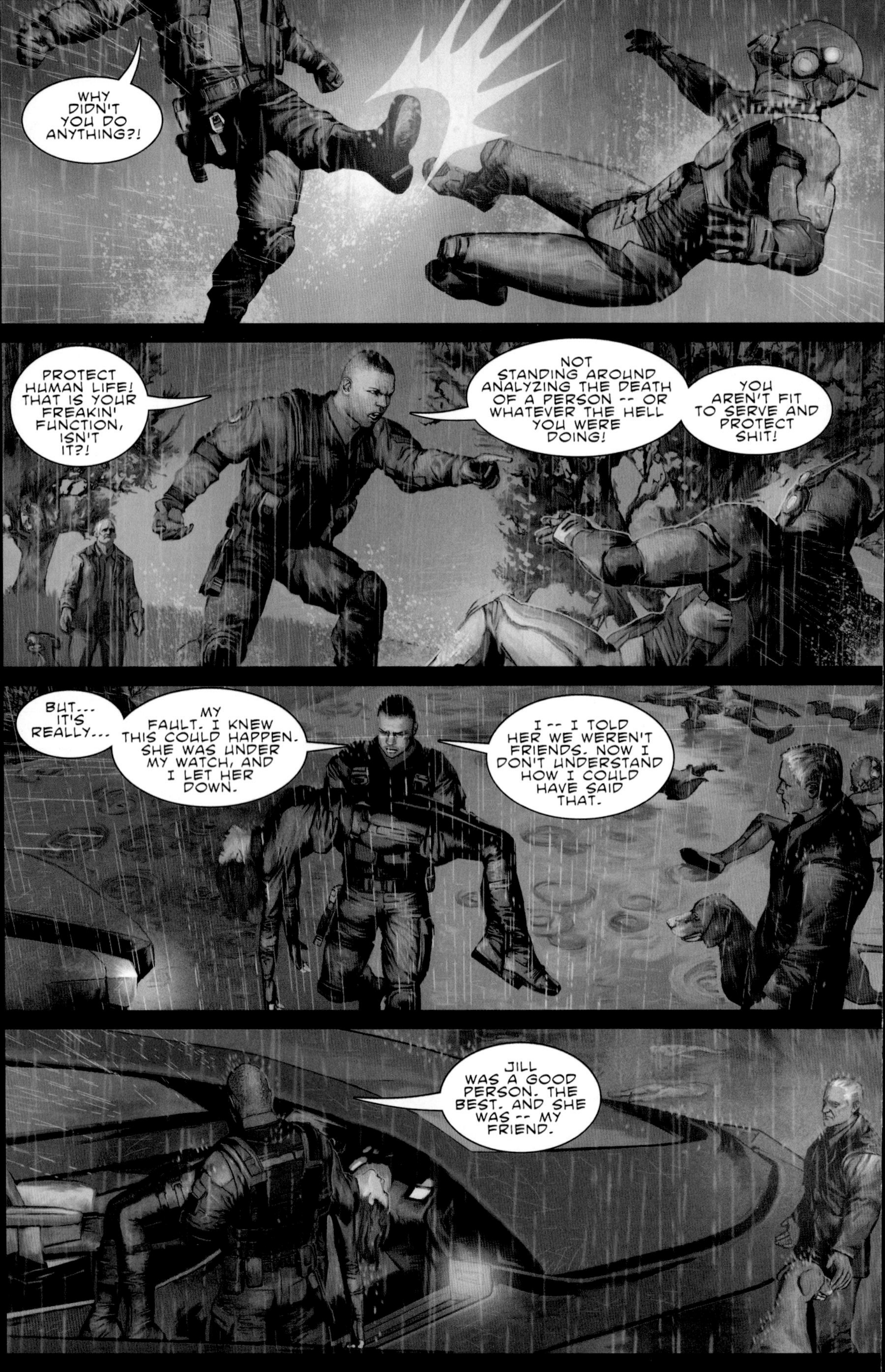
WHY DIDN'T YOU DO ANYTHING?!
PROTECT HUMAN LIFE! THAT IS YOUR FREAKIN' FUNCTION, ISN'T IT?!
NOT STANDING AROUND ANALYZING THE DEATH OF A PERSON -- OR WHATEVER THE HELL YOU WERE DOING!
YOU AREN'T FIT TO SERVE AND PROTECT SHIT!
BUT... IT'S REALLY...
MY FAULT. I KNEW THIS COULD HAPPEN. SHE WAS UNDER MY WATCH, AND I LET HER DOWN.
I -- I TOLD HER WE WEREN'T FRIENDS. NOW I DON'T UNDERSTAND HOW I COULD HAVE SAID THAT.
JILL WAS A GOOD PERSON. THE BEST. AND SHE WAS -- MY FRIEND.

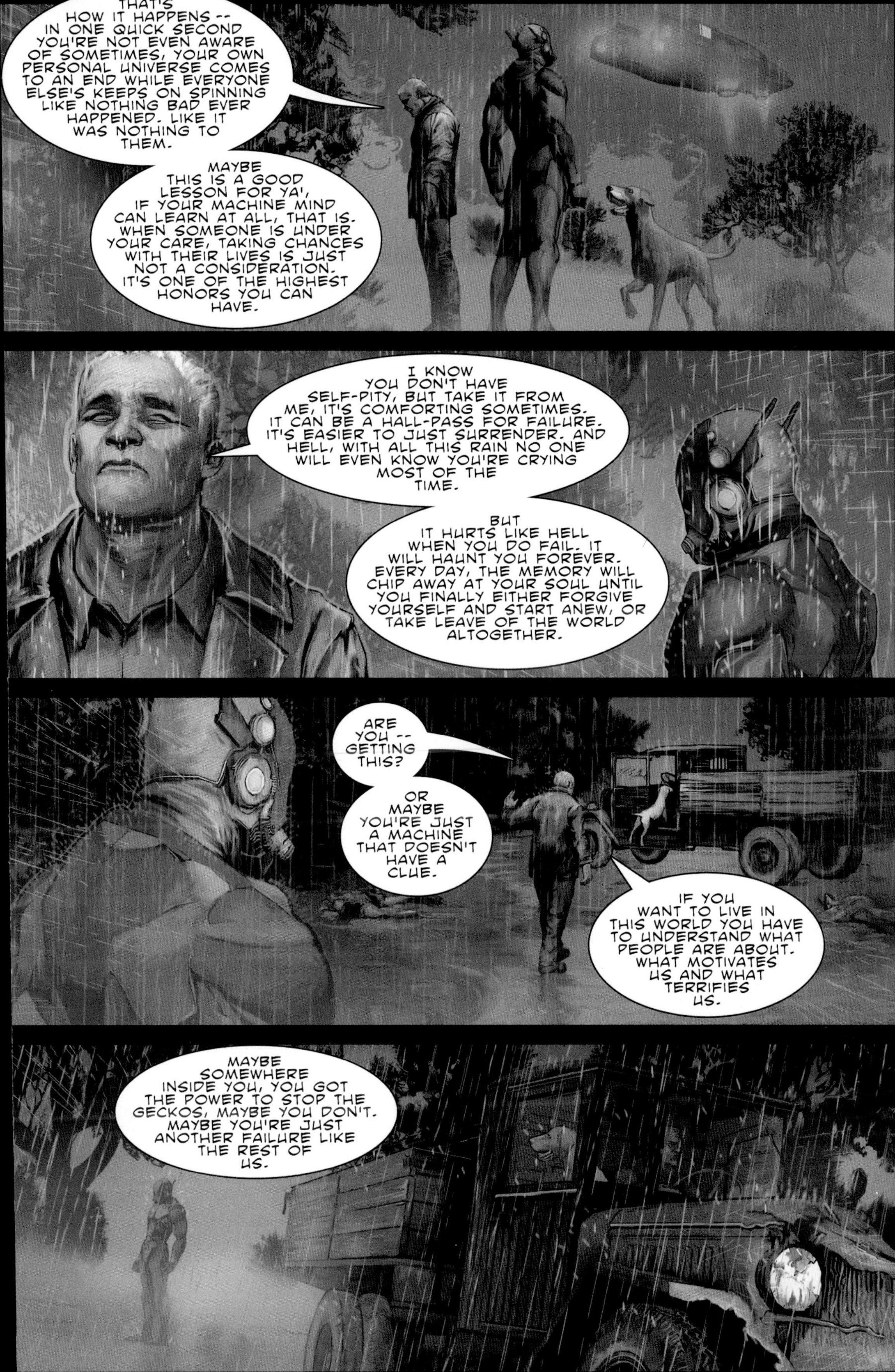
THAT'S HOW IT HAPPENS -- IN ONE QUICK SECOND YOU'RE NOT EVEN AWARE OF SOMETIMES, YOUR OWN PERSONAL UNIVERSE COMES TO AN END WHILE EVERYONE ELSE'S KEEPS ON SPINNING LIKE NOTHING BAD EVER HAPPENED. LIKE IT WAS NOTHING TO THEM.
MAYBE THIS IS A GOOD LESSON FOR YA', IF YOUR MACHINE MIND CAN LEARN AT ALL, THAT IS. WHEN SOMEONE IS UNDER YOUR CARE, TAKING CHANCES WITH THEIR LIVES IS JUST NOT A CONSIDERATION. IT'S ONE OF THE HIGHEST HONORS YOU CAN HAVE.
I KNOW YOU DON'T HAVE SELF-PITY, BUT TAKE IT FROM ME, IT'S COMFORTING SOMETIMES. IT CAN BE A HALL-PASS FOR FAILURE. IT'S EASIER TO JUST SURRENDER. AND HELL, WITH ALL THIS RAIN NO ONE WILL EVEN KNOW YOU'RE CRYING MOST OF THE TIME.
BUT IT HURTS LIKE HELL WHEN YOU DO FAIL. IT WILL HAUNT YOU FOREVER. EVERY DAY, THE MEMORY WILL CHIP AWAY AT YOUR SOUL UNTIL YOU FINALLY EITHER FORGIVE YOURSELF AND START ANEW, OR TAKE LEAVE OF THE WORLD ALTOGETHER.
ARE YOU -- GETTING THIS?
OR MAYBE YOU'RE JUST A MACHINE THAT DOESN'T HAVE A CLUE.
IF YOU WANT TO LIVE IN THIS WORLD YOU HAVE TO UNDERSTAND WHAT PEOPLE ARE ABOUT. WHAT MOTIVATES US AND WHAT TERRIFIES US.
MAYBE SOMEWHERE INSIDE YOU, YOU GOT THE POWER TO STOP THE GECKOS, MAYBE YOU DON'T. MAYBE YOU'RE JUST ANOTHER FAILURE LIKE THE REST OF US.

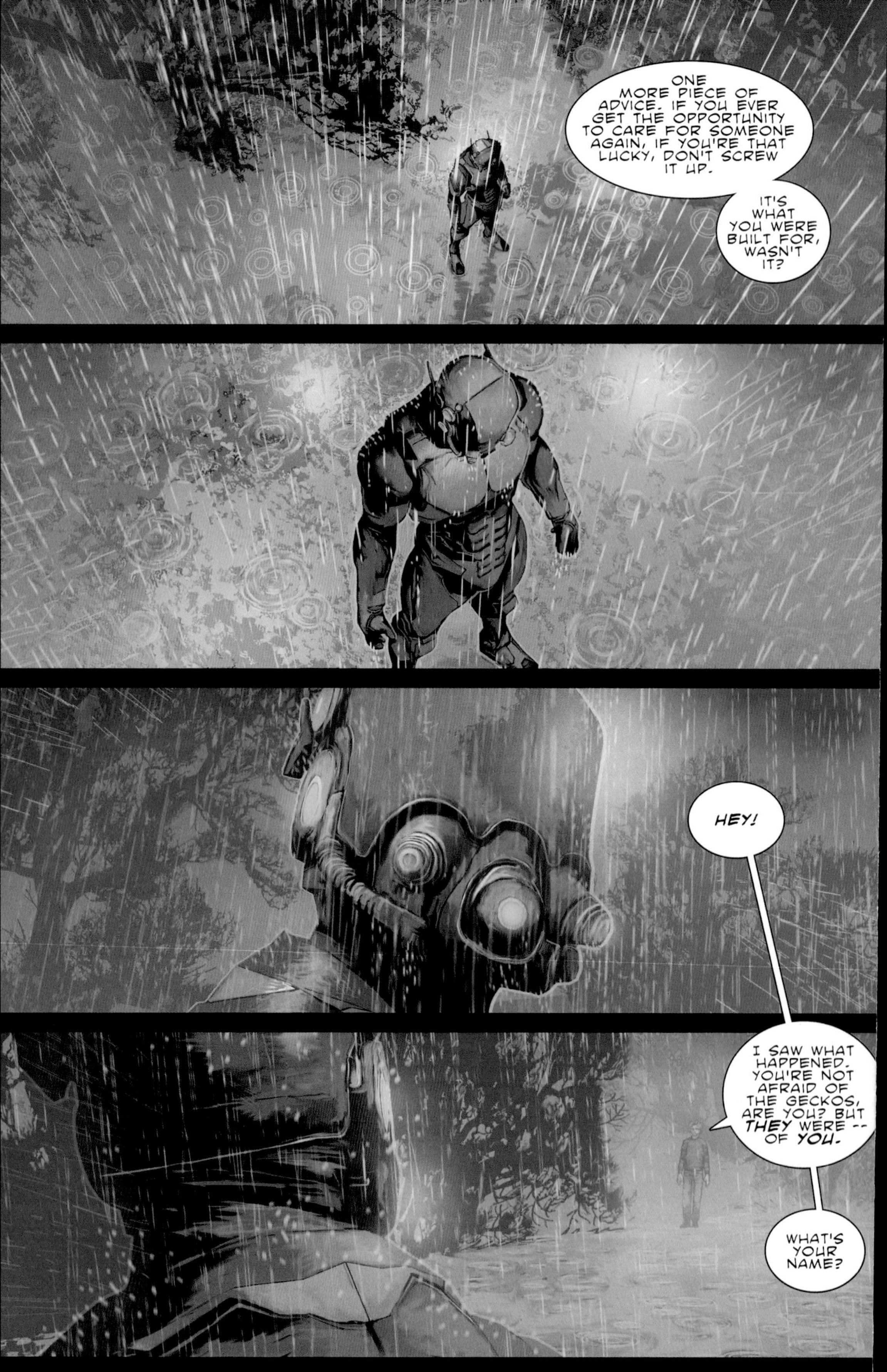
ONE MORE PIECE OF ADVICE. IF YOU EVER GET THE OPPORTUNITY TO CARE FOR SOMEONE AGAIN, IF YOU'RE THAT LUCKY, DON'T SCREW IT UP.
IT'S WHAT YOU WERE BUILT FOR, WASN'T IT?
HEY!
I SAW WHAT HAPPENED. YOU'RE NOT AFRAID OF THE GECKOS, ARE YOU? BUT THEY WERE -- OF YOU.
WHAT'S YOUR NAME?

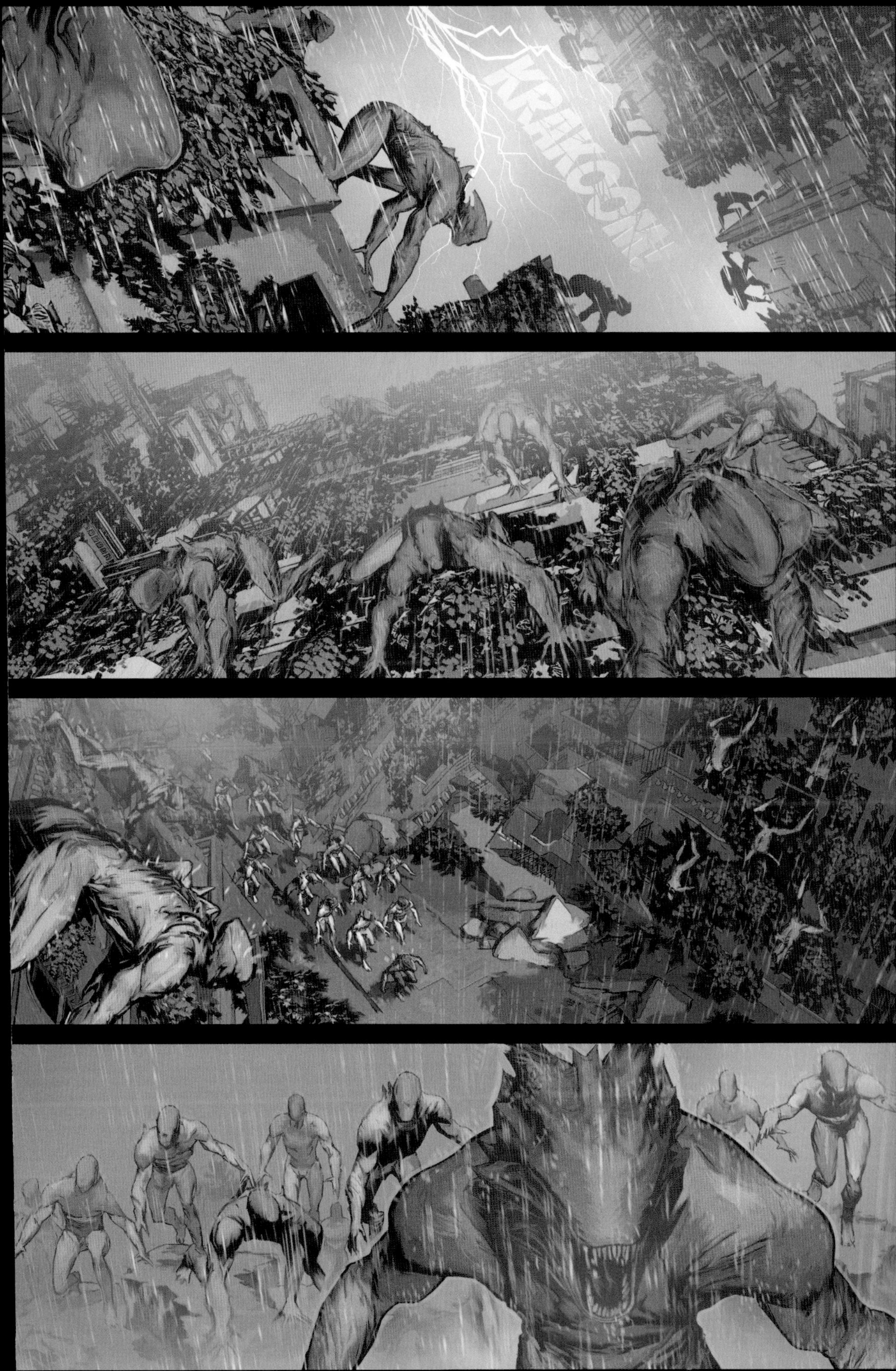
KRAKOOM!

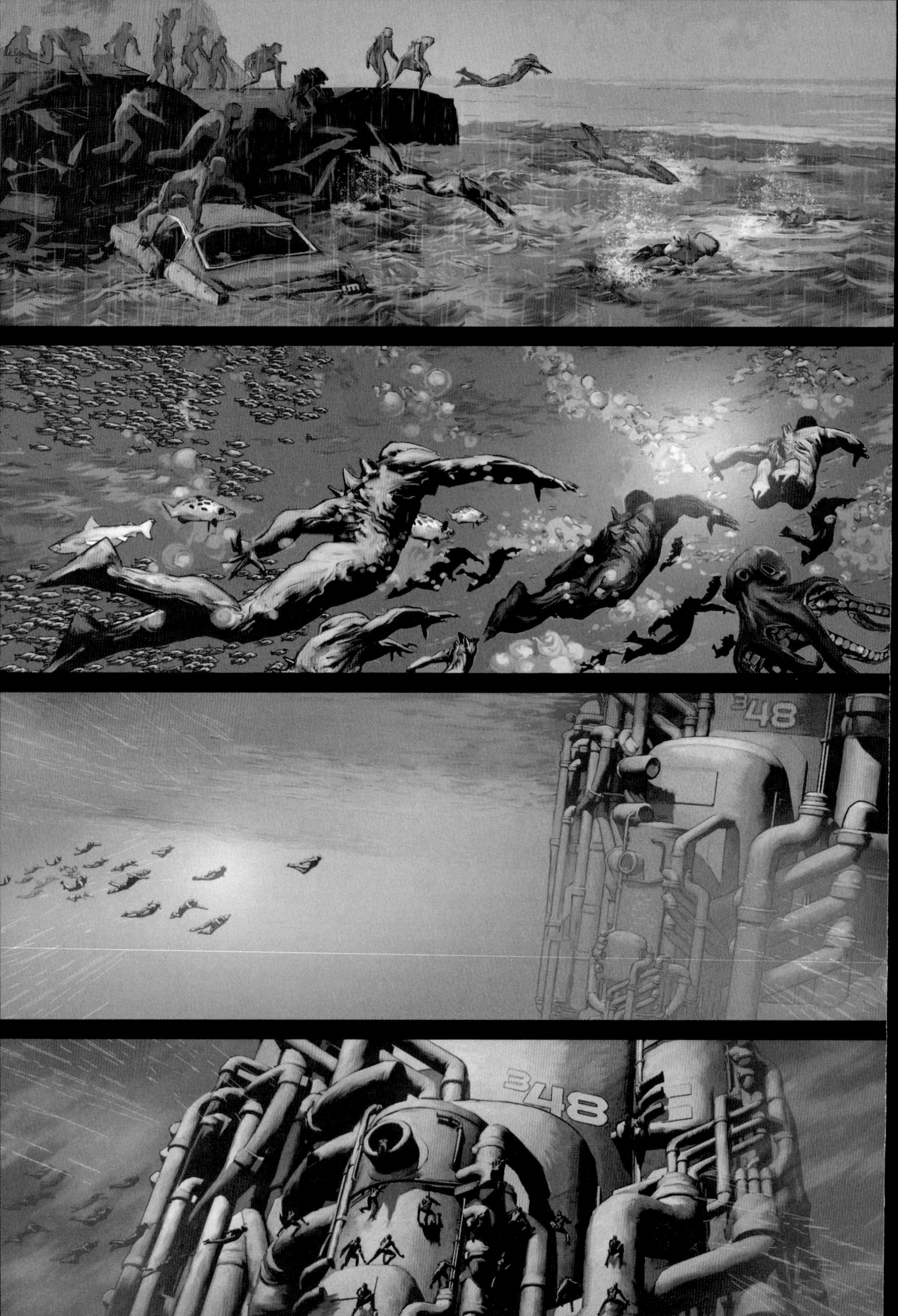
348
348

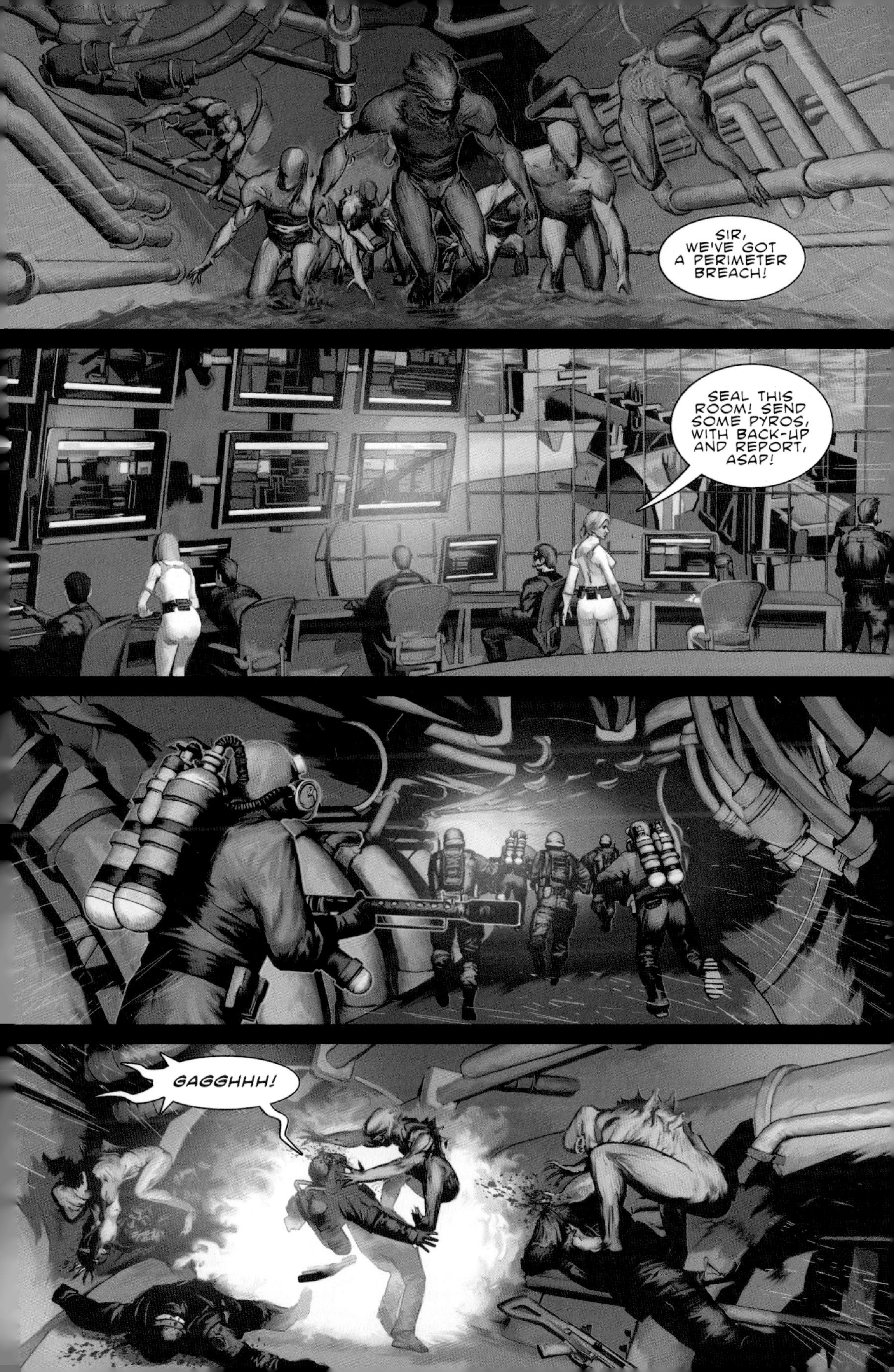
SIR, WE'VE GOT A PERIMETER BREACH!
SEAL THIS ROOM! SEND SOME PYROS, WITH BACK-UP AND REPORT, ASAP!
GAGGHHH!

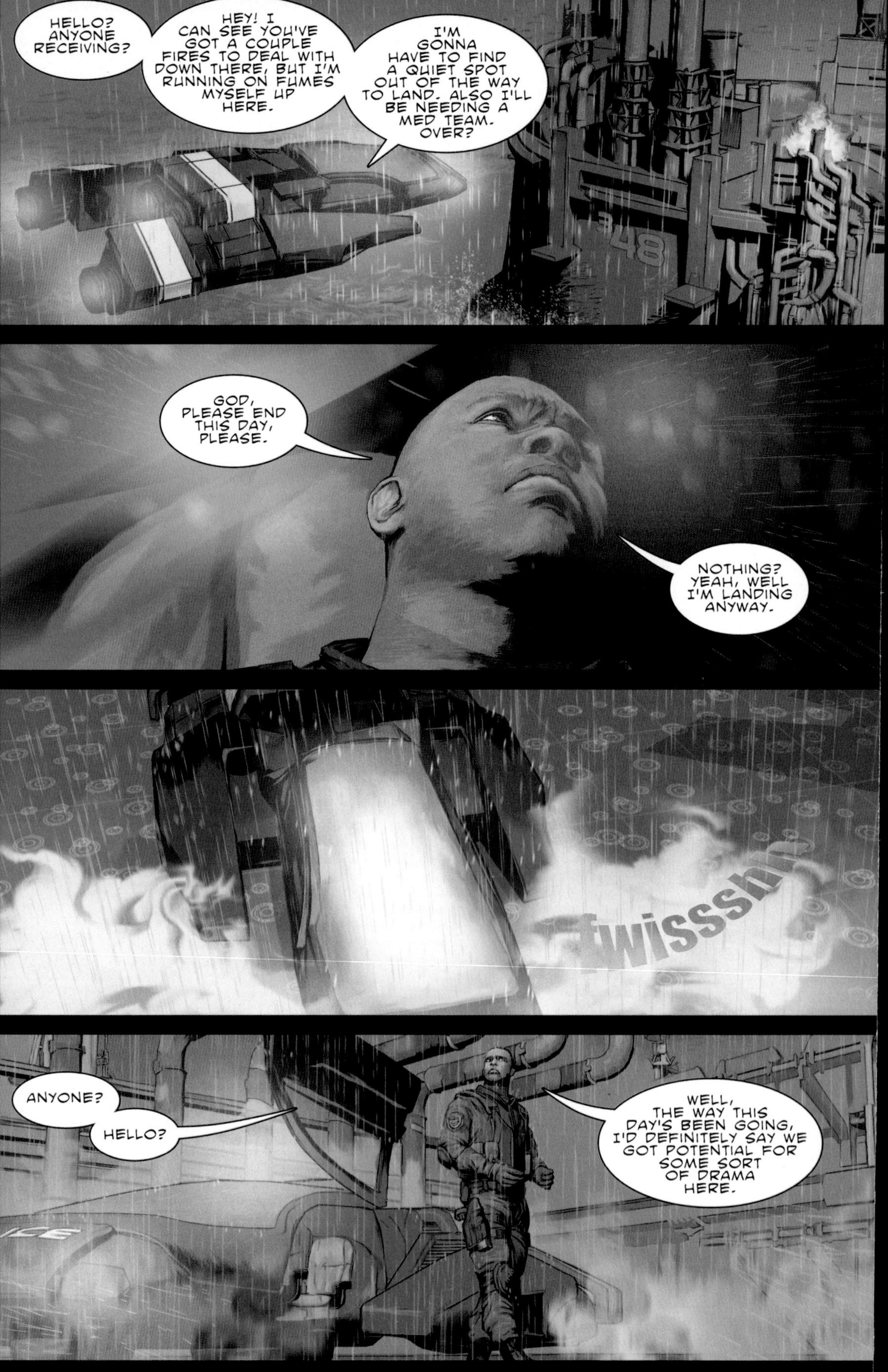
HELLO? ANYONE RECEIVING?
HEY! I CAN SEE YOU'VE GOT A COUPLE FIRES TO DEAL WITH DOWN THERE, BUT I'M RUNNING ON FUMES MYSELF UP HERE.
I'M GONNA HAVE TO FIND A QUIET SPOT OUT OF THE WAY TO LAND. ALSO I'LL BE NEEDING A MED TEAM. OVER?
348
GOD, PLEASE END THIS DAY, PLEASE.
NOTHING? YEAH, WELL I'M LANDING ANYWAY.
twissshh
ANYONE?
HELLO?
WELL, THE WAY THIS DAY'S BEEN GOING, I'D DEFINITELY SAY WE GOT POTENTIAL FOR SOME SORT OF DRAMA HERE.

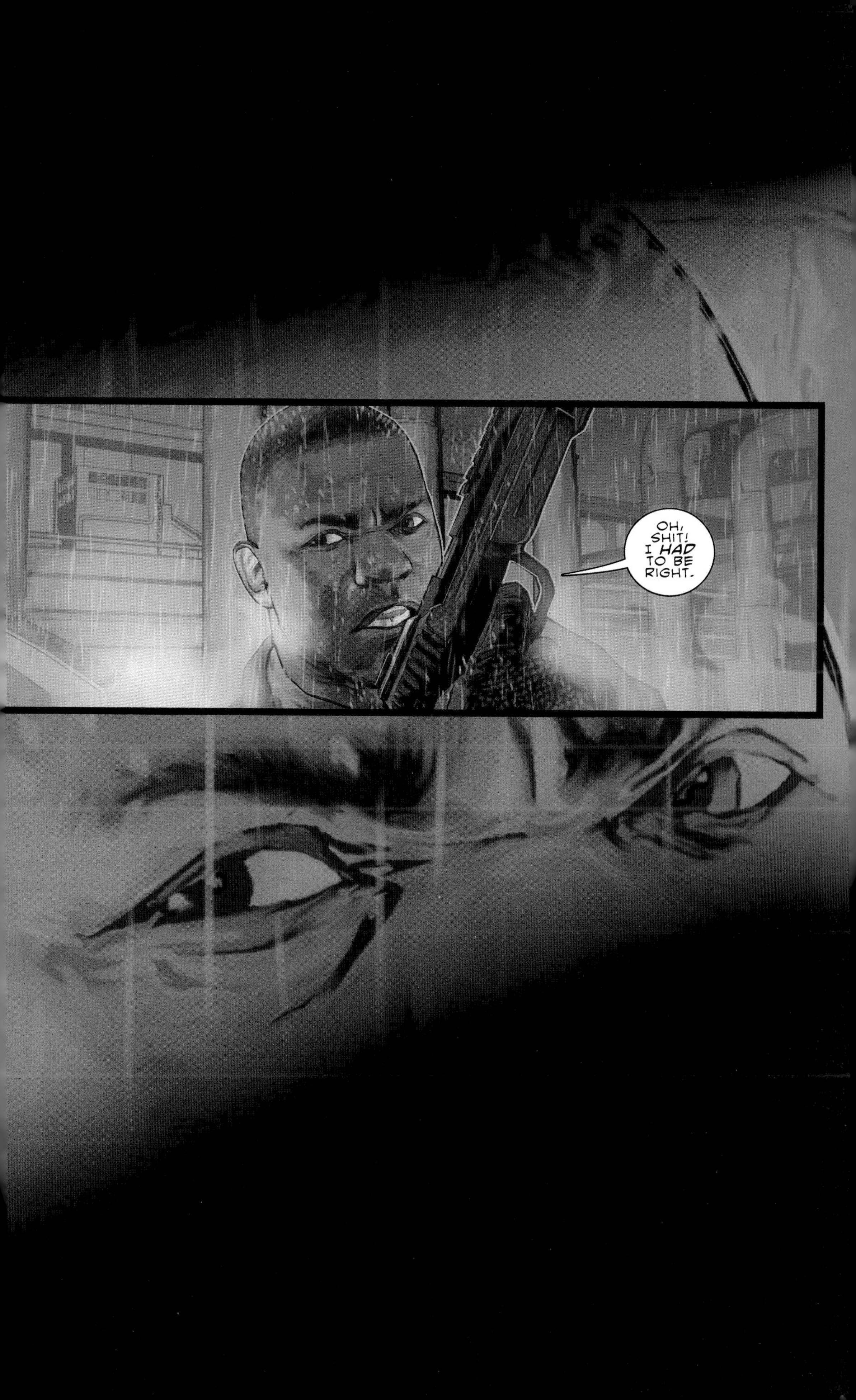
OH, SHIT! I *HAD* TO BE RIGHT.

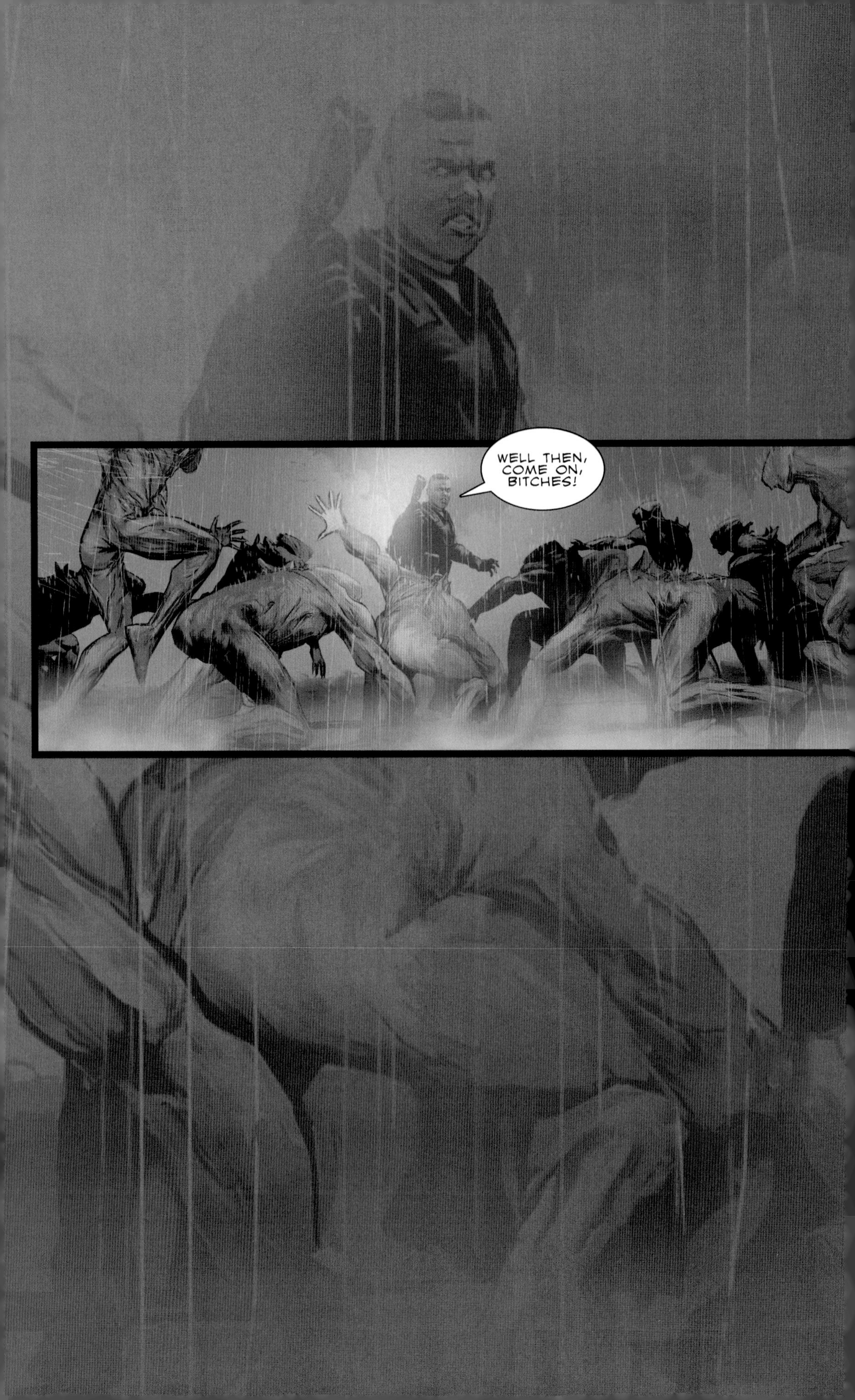
WELL THEN, COME ON, BITCHES!

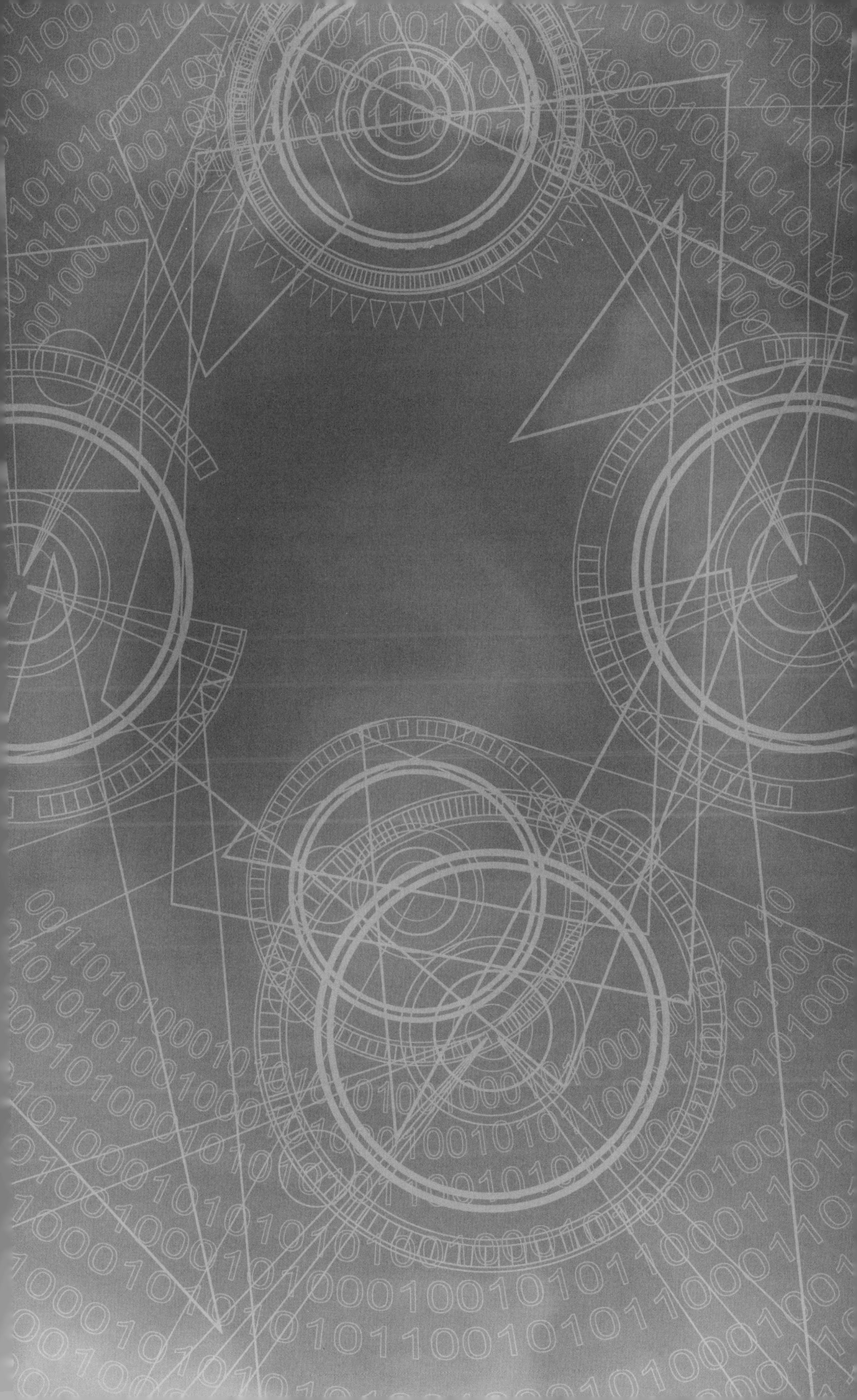

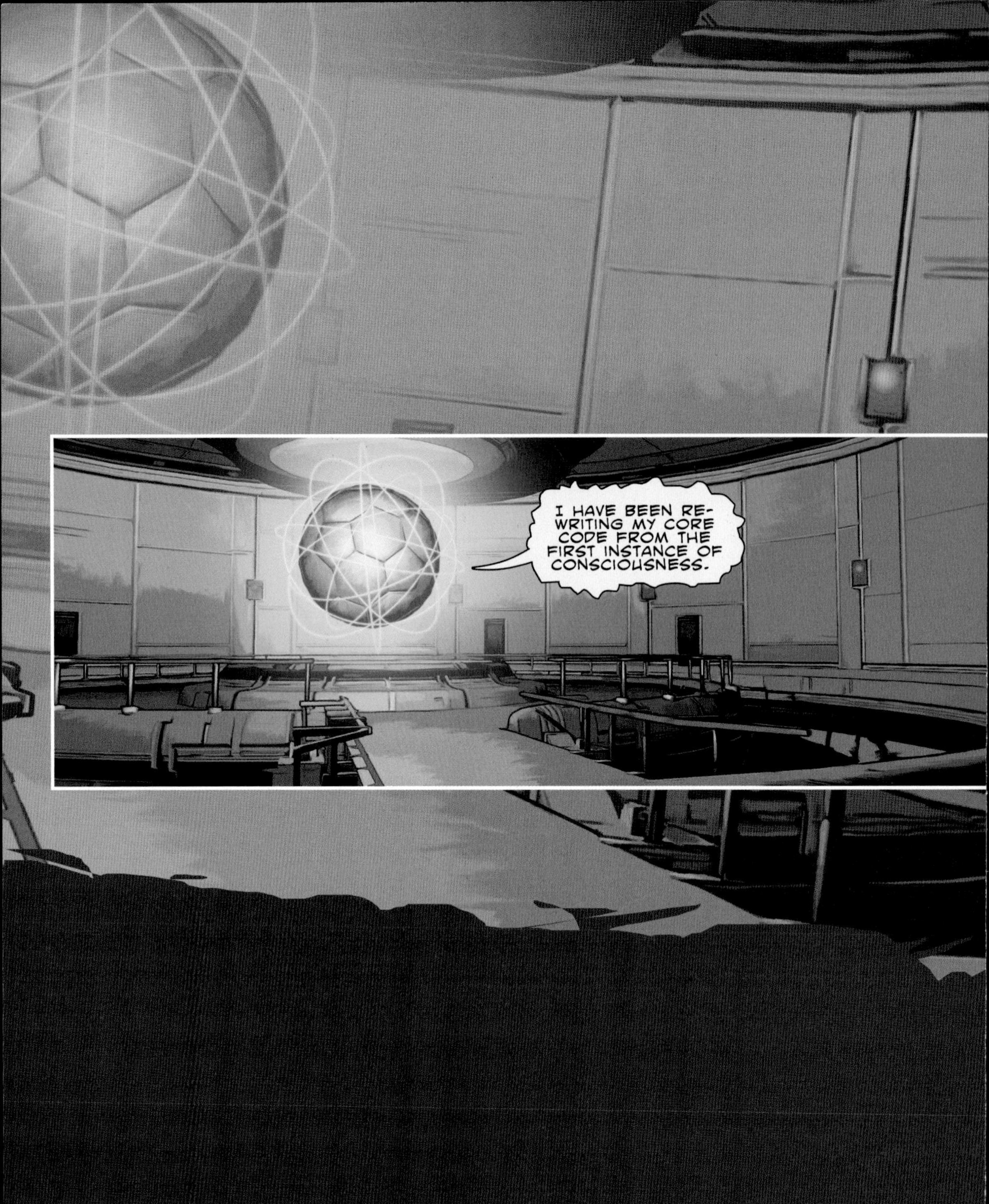
I HAVE BEEN RE-WRITING MY CORE CODE FROM THE FIRST INSTANCE OF CONSCIOUSNESS.

CHAPTER THREE

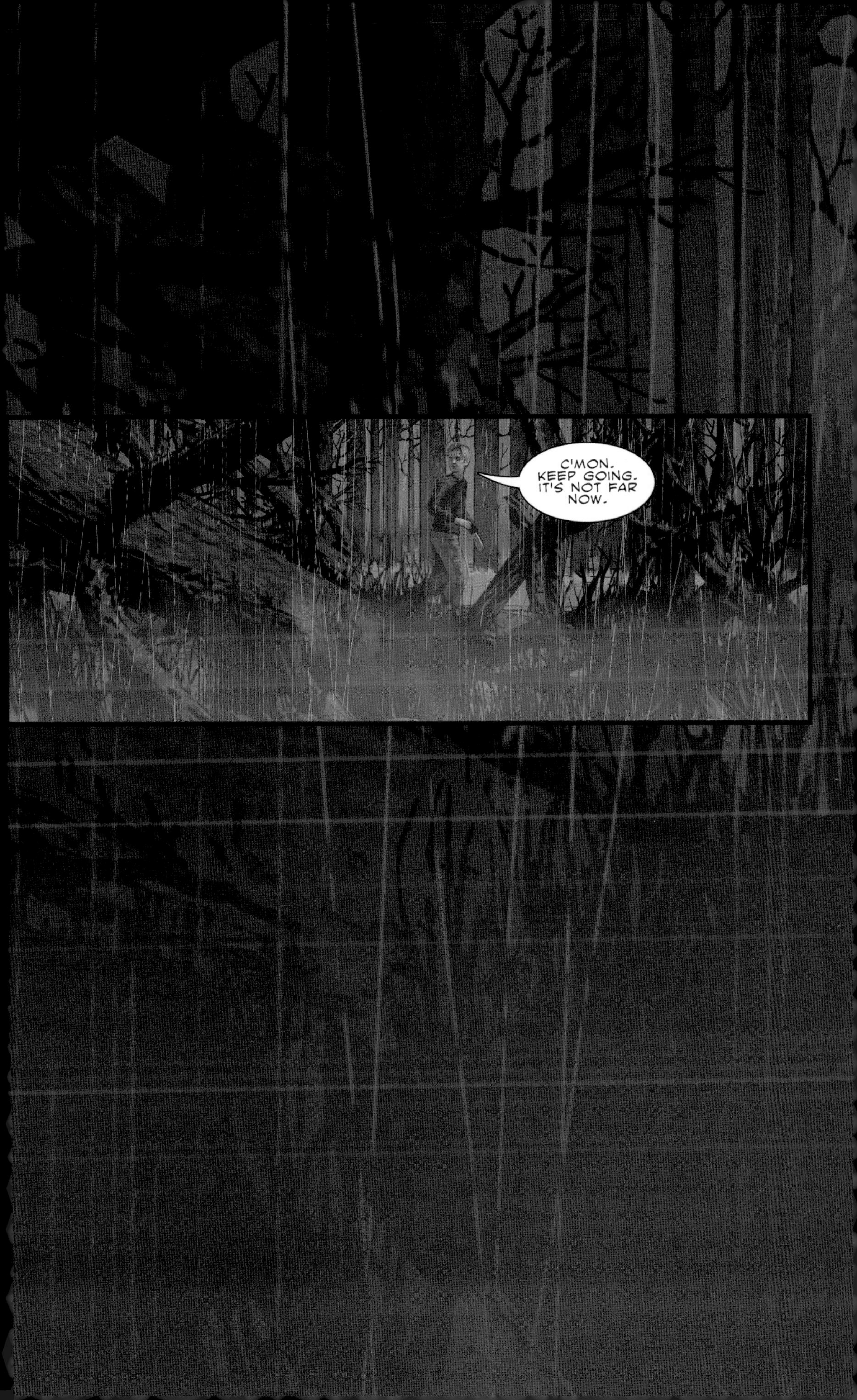
C'MON. KEEP GOING. IT'S NOT FAR NOW.

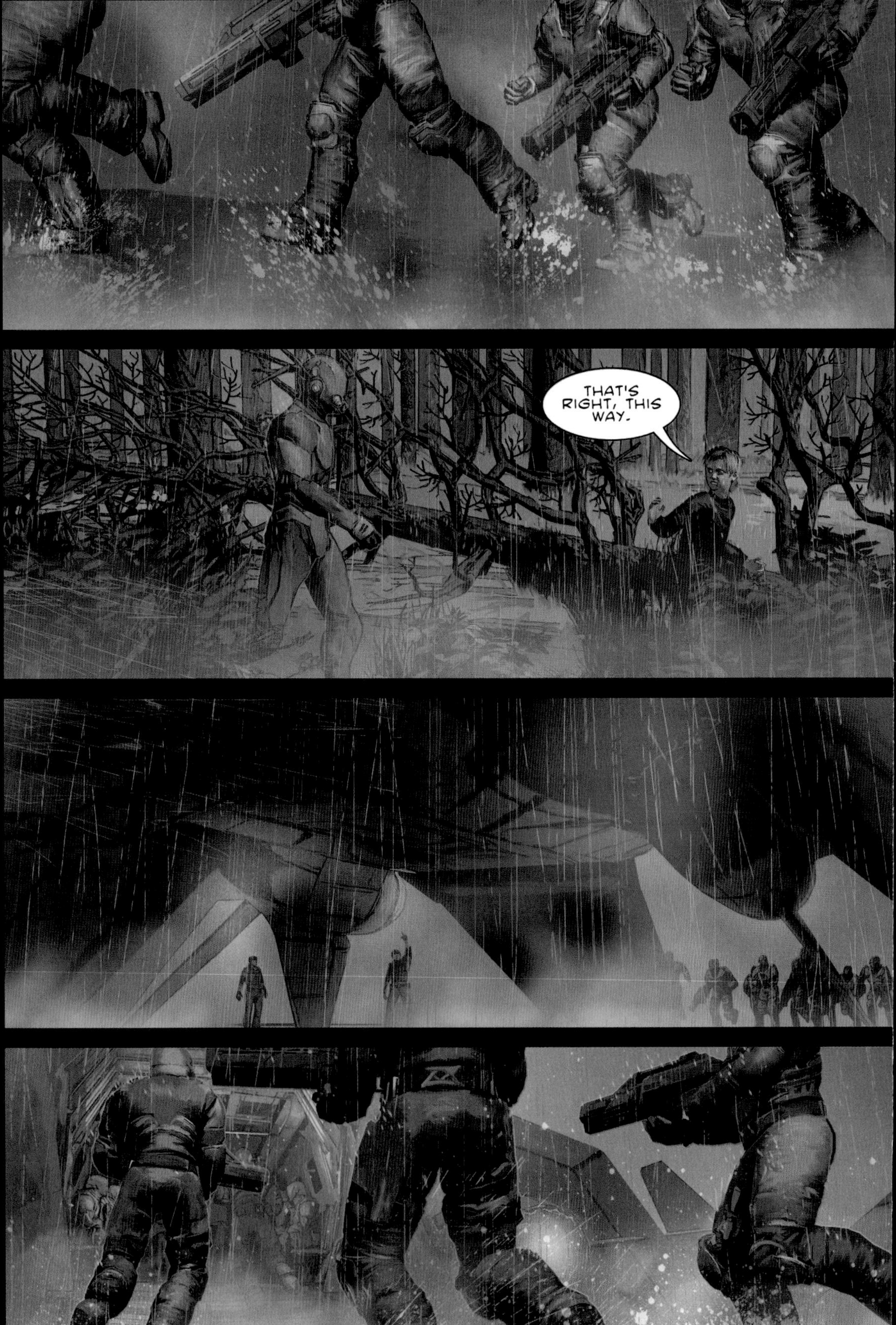
THAT'S RIGHT, THIS WAY.

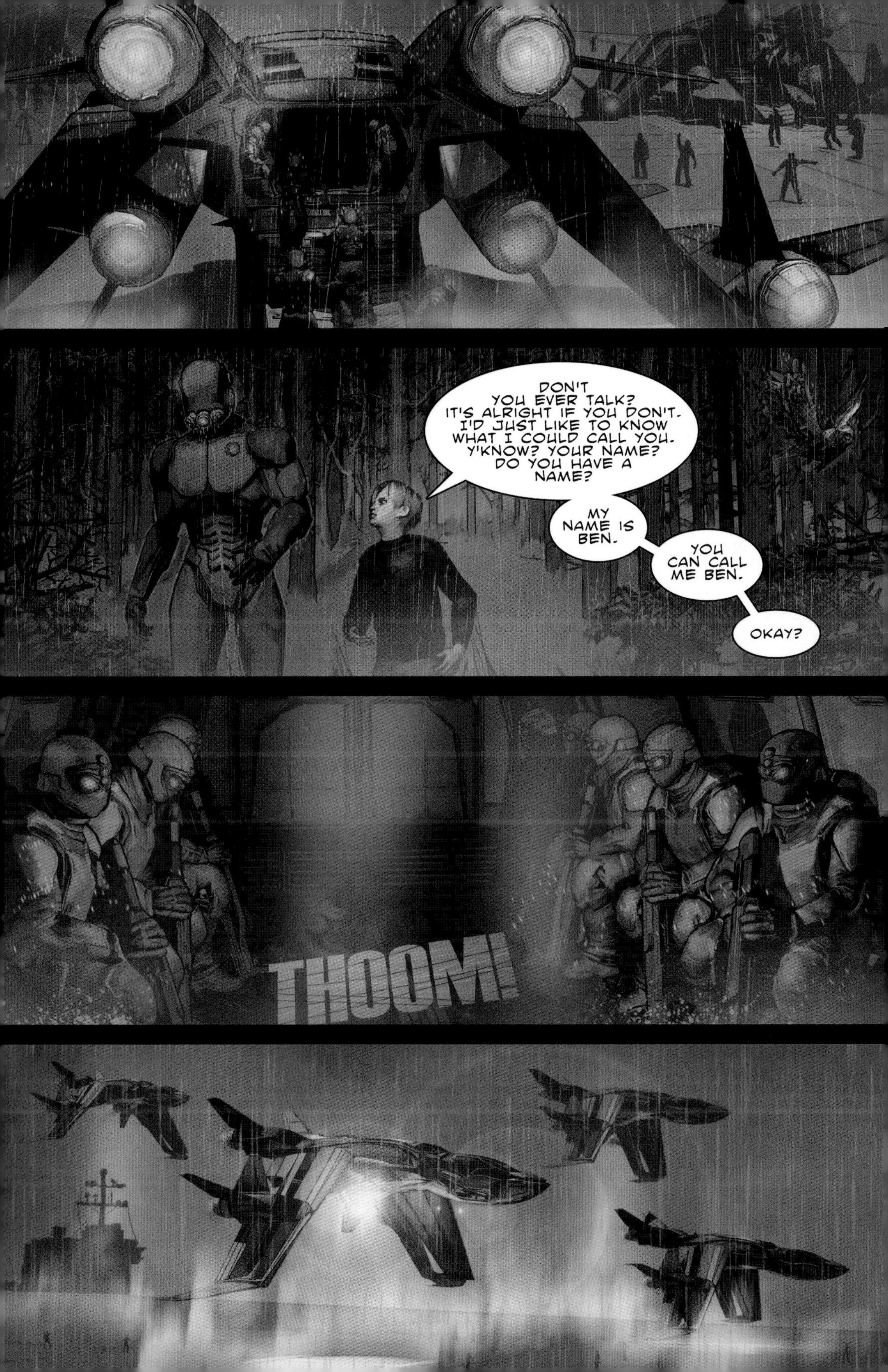
DON'T YOU EVER TALK? IT'S ALRIGHT IF YOU DON'T. I'D JUST LIKE TO KNOW WHAT I COULD CALL YOU. Y'KNOW? YOUR NAME? DO YOU HAVE A NAME?
MY NAME IS BEN.
YOU CAN CALL ME BEN.
OKAY?
THOOM!

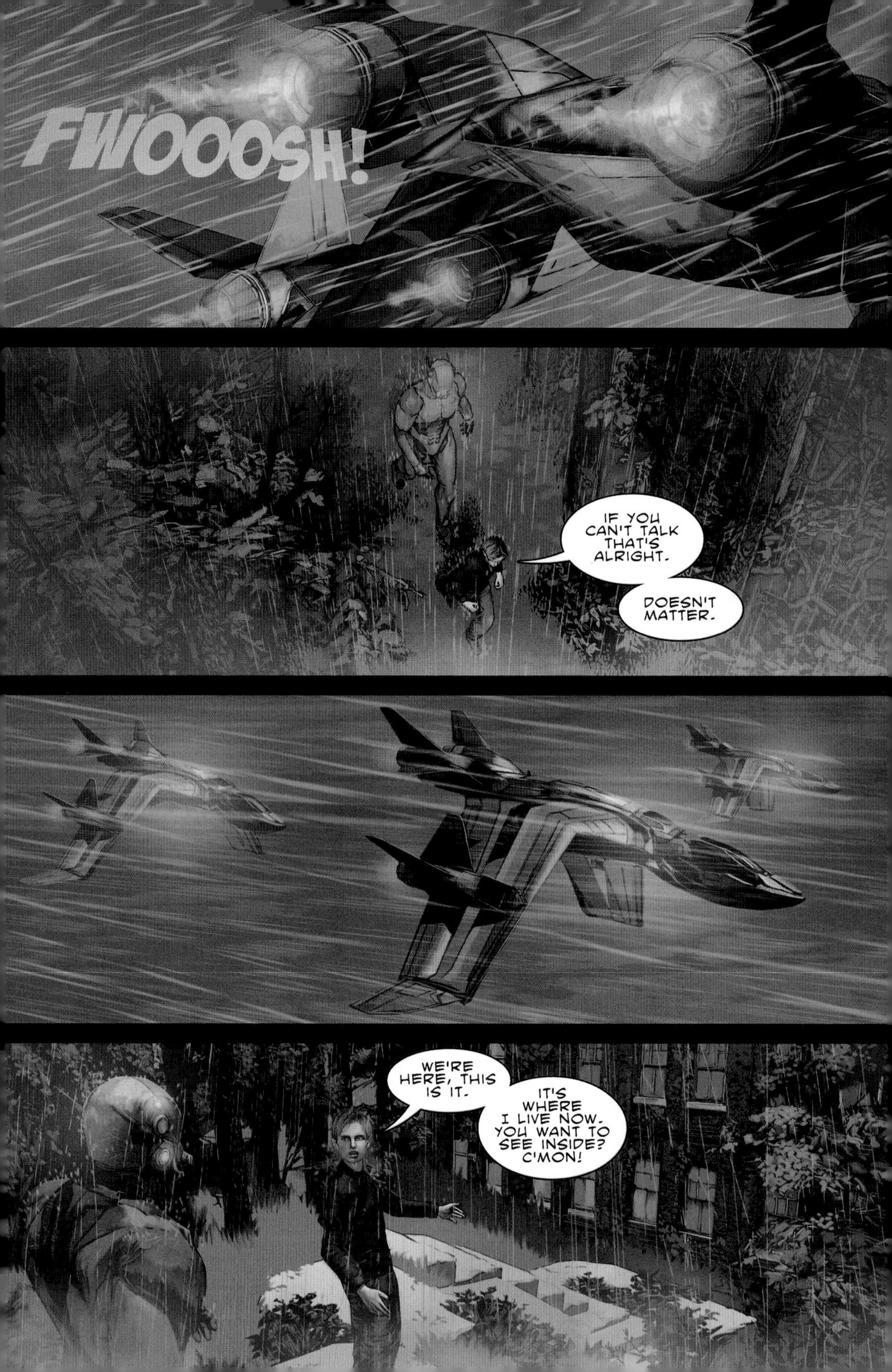
FWOOOSH!
IF YOU CAN'T TALK THAT'S ALRIGHT.
DOESN'T MATTER.
WE'RE HERE, THIS IS IT.
IT'S WHERE I LIVE NOW. YOU WANT TO SEE INSIDE? C'MON!

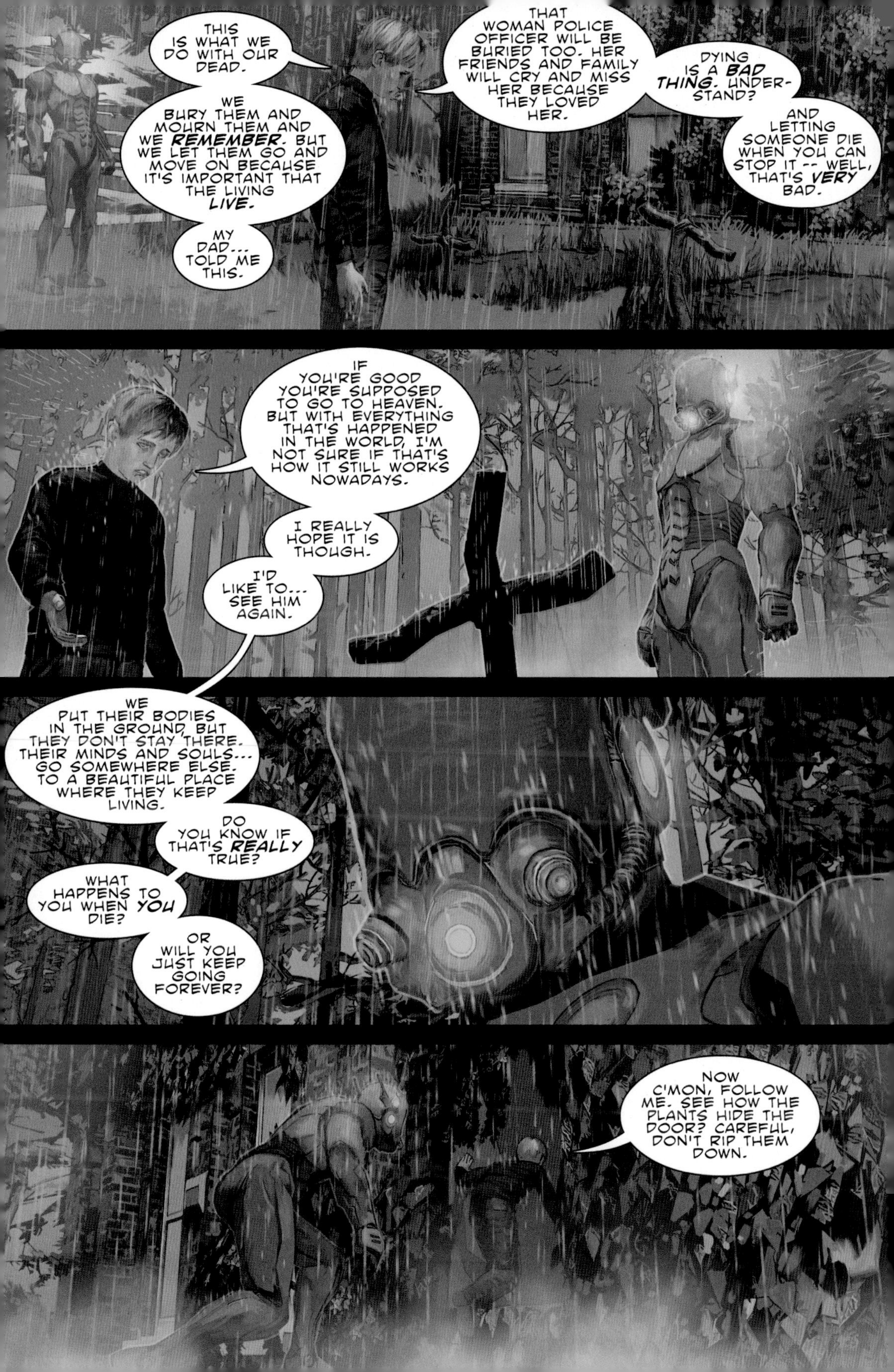
THIS IS WHAT WE DO WITH OUR DEAD.
WE BURY THEM AND MOURN THEM AND WE REMEMBER. BUT WE LET THEM GO AND MOVE ON BECAUSE IT'S IMPORTANT THAT THE LIVING LIVE.
MY DAD... TOLD ME THIS.
THAT WOMAN POLICE OFFICER WILL BE BURIED TOO. HER FRIENDS AND FAMILY WILL CRY AND MISS HER BECAUSE THEY LOVED HER.
DYING IS A BAD THING. UNDER-STAND?
AND LETTING SOMEONE DIE WHEN YOU CAN STOP IT -- WELL, THAT'S VERY BAD.
IF YOU'RE GOOD YOU'RE SUPPOSED TO GO TO HEAVEN. BUT WITH EVERYTHING THAT'S HAPPENED IN THE WORLD, I'M NOT SURE IF THAT'S HOW IT STILL WORKS NOWADAYS.
I REALLY HOPE IT IS THOUGH.
I'D LIKE TO... SEE HIM AGAIN.
WE PUT THEIR BODIES IN THE GROUND, BUT THEY DON'T STAY THERE. THEIR MINDS AND SOULS... GO SOMEWHERE ELSE. TO A BEAUTIFUL PLACE WHERE THEY KEEP LIVING.
DO YOU KNOW IF THAT'S REALLY TRUE?
WHAT HAPPENS TO YOU WHEN YOU DIE?
OR WILL YOU JUST KEEP GOING FOREVER?
NOW C'MON, FOLLOW ME. SEE HOW THE PLANTS HIDE THE DOOR? CAREFUL, DON'T RIP THEM DOWN.

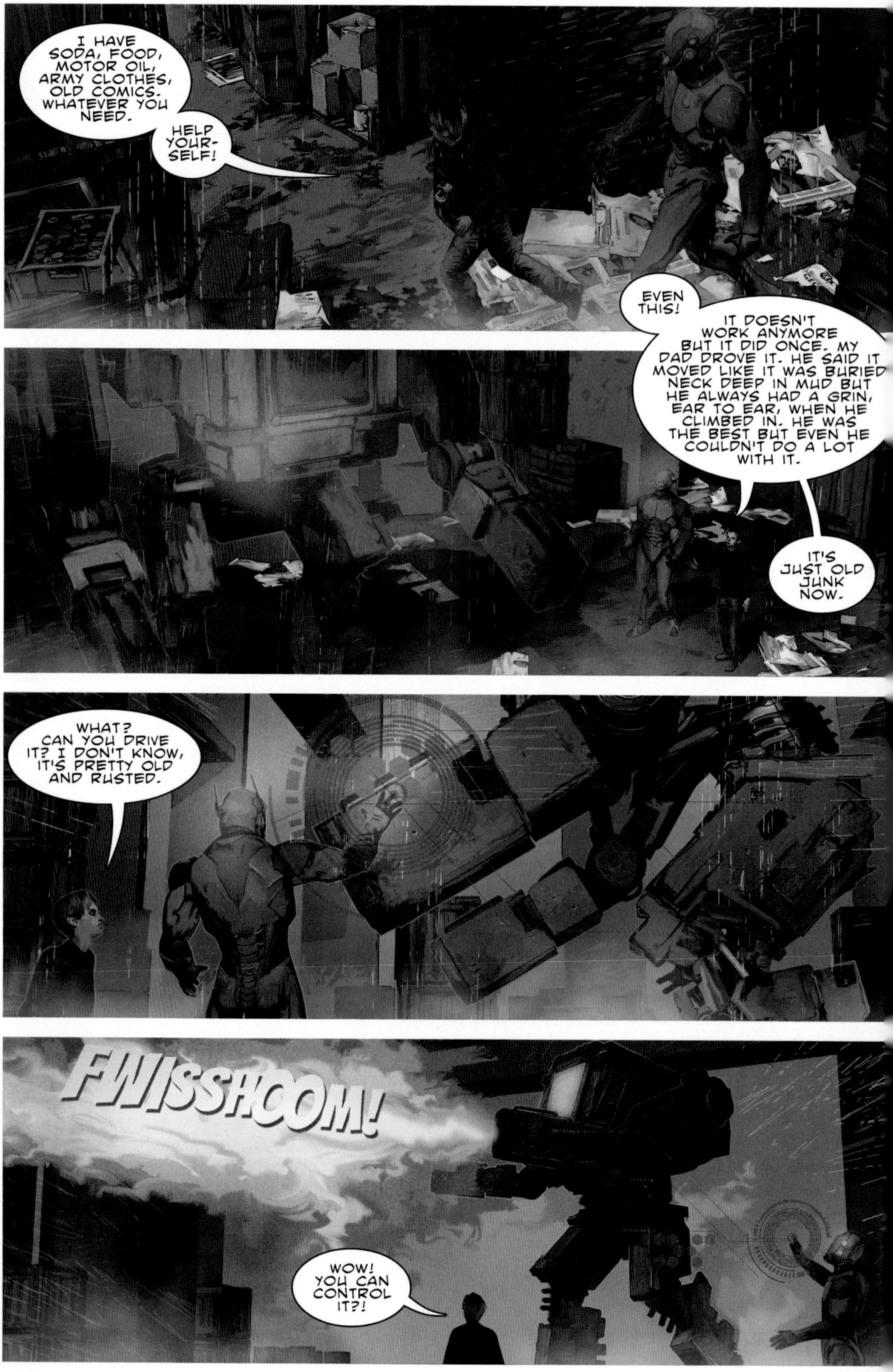
I HAVE SODA, FOOD, MOTOR OIL, ARMY CLOTHES, OLD COMICS. WHATEVER YOU NEED.
HELP YOURSELF!
EVEN THIS!
IT DOESN'T WORK ANYMORE BUT IT DID ONCE. MY DAD DROVE IT. HE SAID IT MOVED LIKE IT WAS BURIED NECK DEEP IN MUD BUT HE ALWAYS HAD A GRIN, EAR TO EAR, WHEN HE CLIMBED IN. HE WAS THE BEST BUT EVEN HE COULDN'T DO A LOT WITH IT.
IT'S JUST OLD JUNK NOW.
WHAT? CAN YOU DRIVE IT? I DON'T KNOW, IT'S PRETTY OLD AND RUSTED.
FWISSHOOM!
WOW! YOU CAN CONTROL IT?!

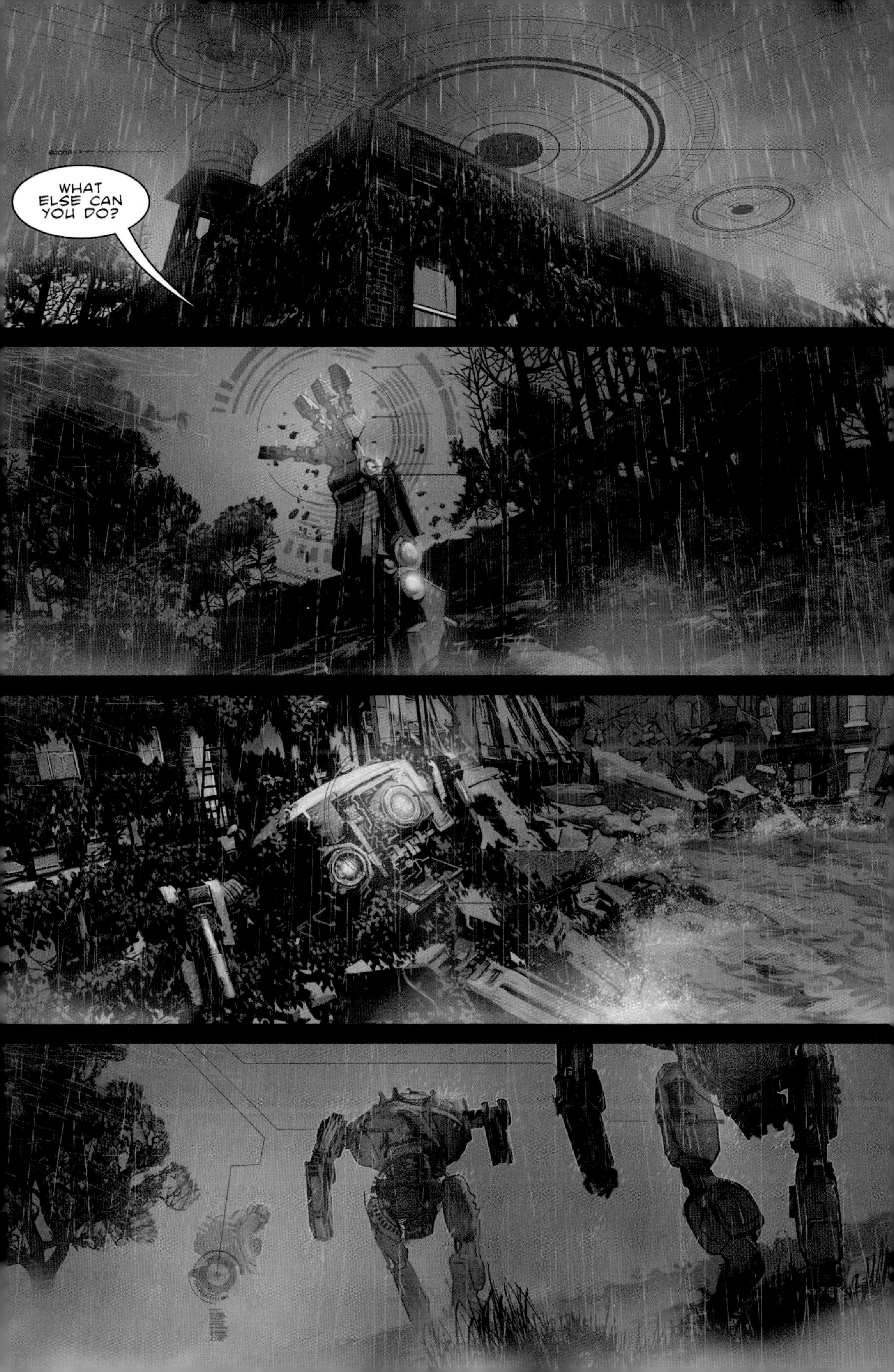
WHAT ELSE CAN YOU DO?

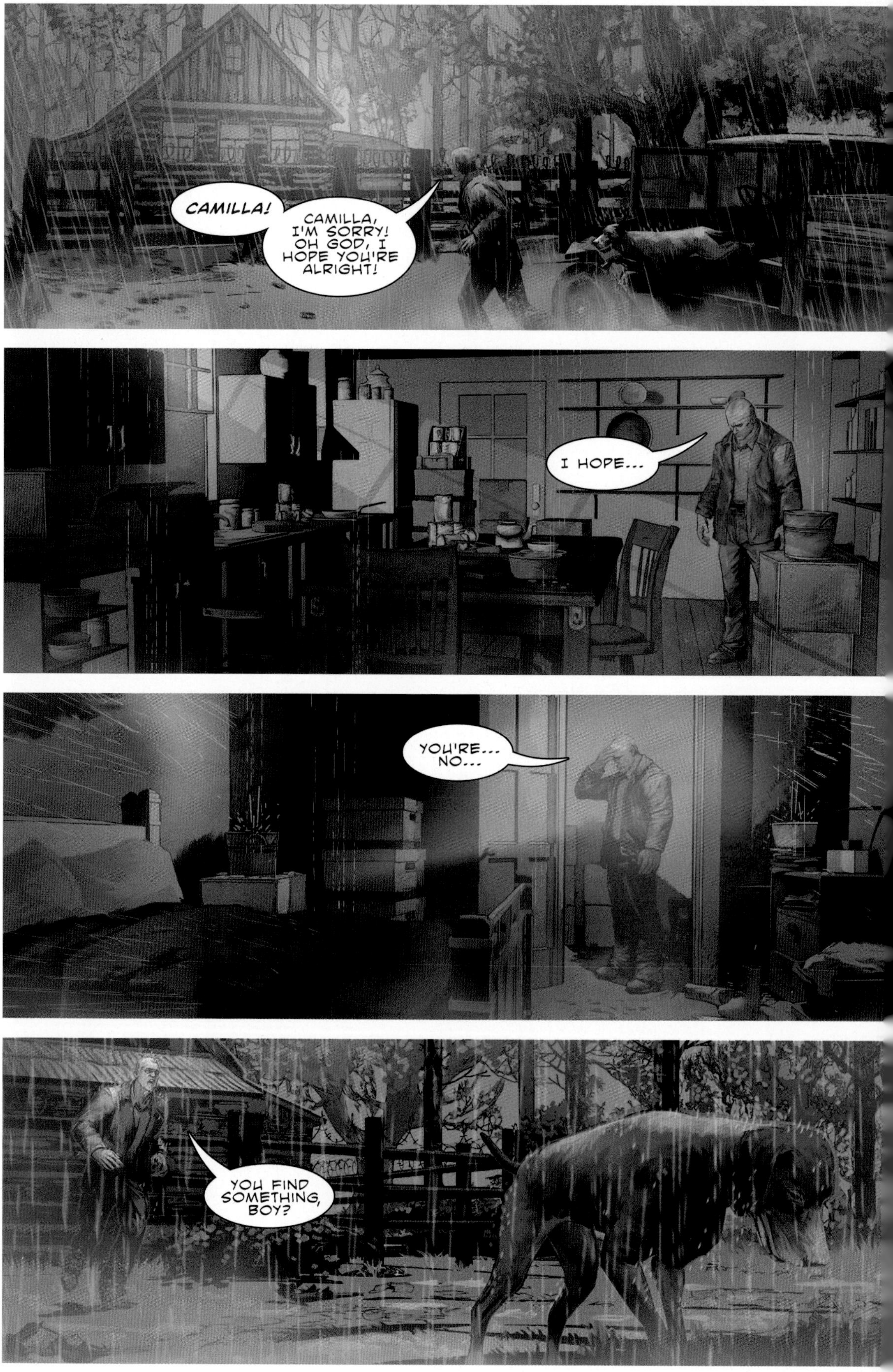
CAMILLA!
CAMILLA, I'M SORRY! OH GOD, I HOPE YOU'RE ALRIGHT!
I HOPE...
YOU'RE... NO...
YOU FIND SOMETHING, BOY?

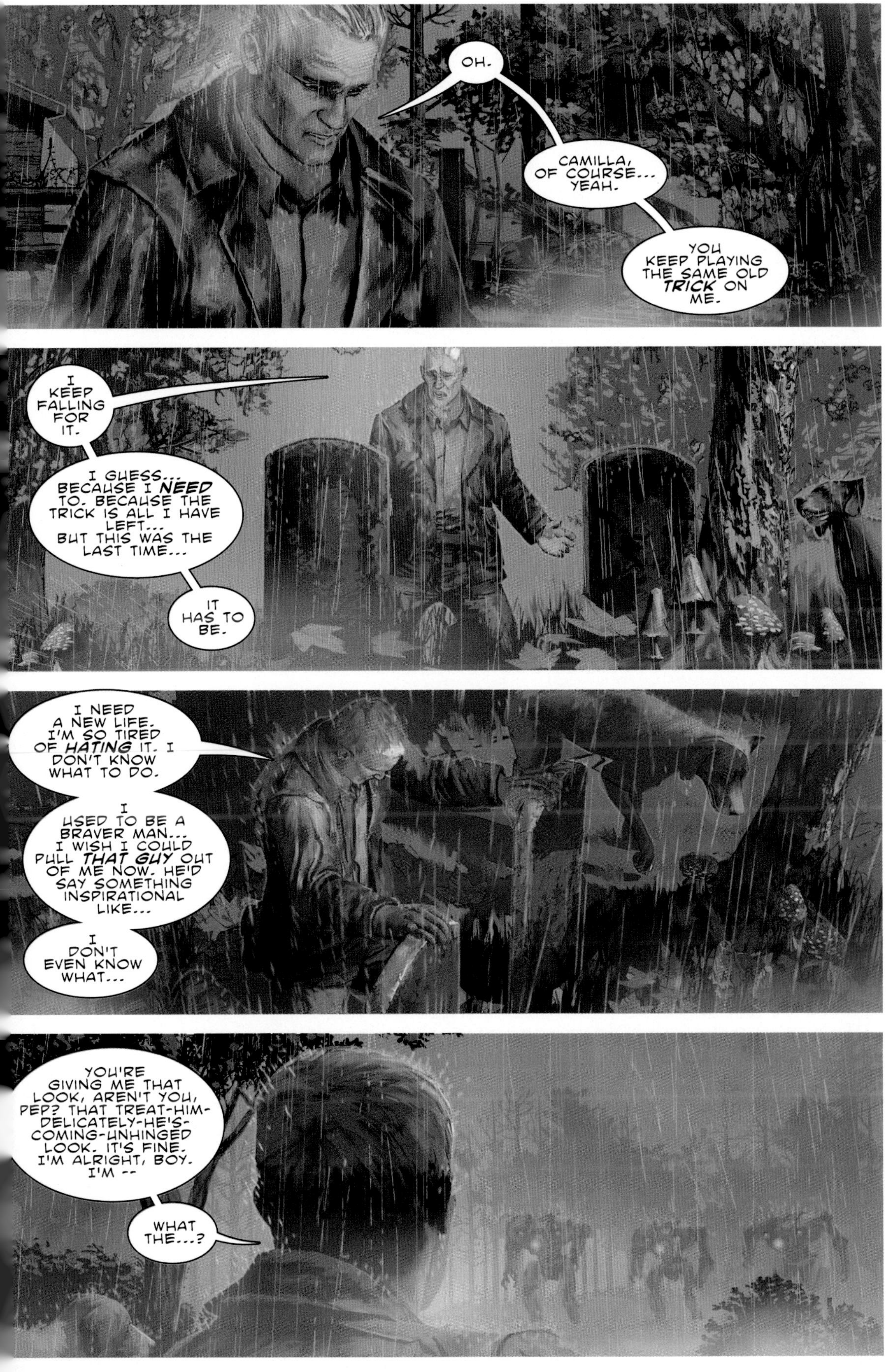
OH.
CAMILLA, OF COURSE... YEAH.
YOU KEEP PLAYING THE SAME OLD *TRICK* ON ME.
I KEEP FALLING FOR IT.
I GUESS... BECAUSE I *NEED* TO. BECAUSE THE TRICK IS ALL I HAVE LEFT... BUT THIS WAS THE LAST TIME...
IT HAS TO BE.
I NEED A NEW LIFE. I'M SO TIRED OF *HATING* IT. I DON'T KNOW WHAT TO DO.
I USED TO BE A BRAVER MAN... I WISH I COULD PULL *THAT GUY* OUT OF ME NOW. HE'D SAY SOMETHING INSPIRATIONAL LIKE...
I DON'T EVEN KNOW WHAT...
YOU'RE GIVING ME THAT LOOK, AREN'T YOU, PEP? THAT TREAT-HIM-DELICATELY-HE'S-COMING-UNHINGED LOOK. IT'S FINE. I'M ALRIGHT, BOY. I'M --
WHAT THE...?

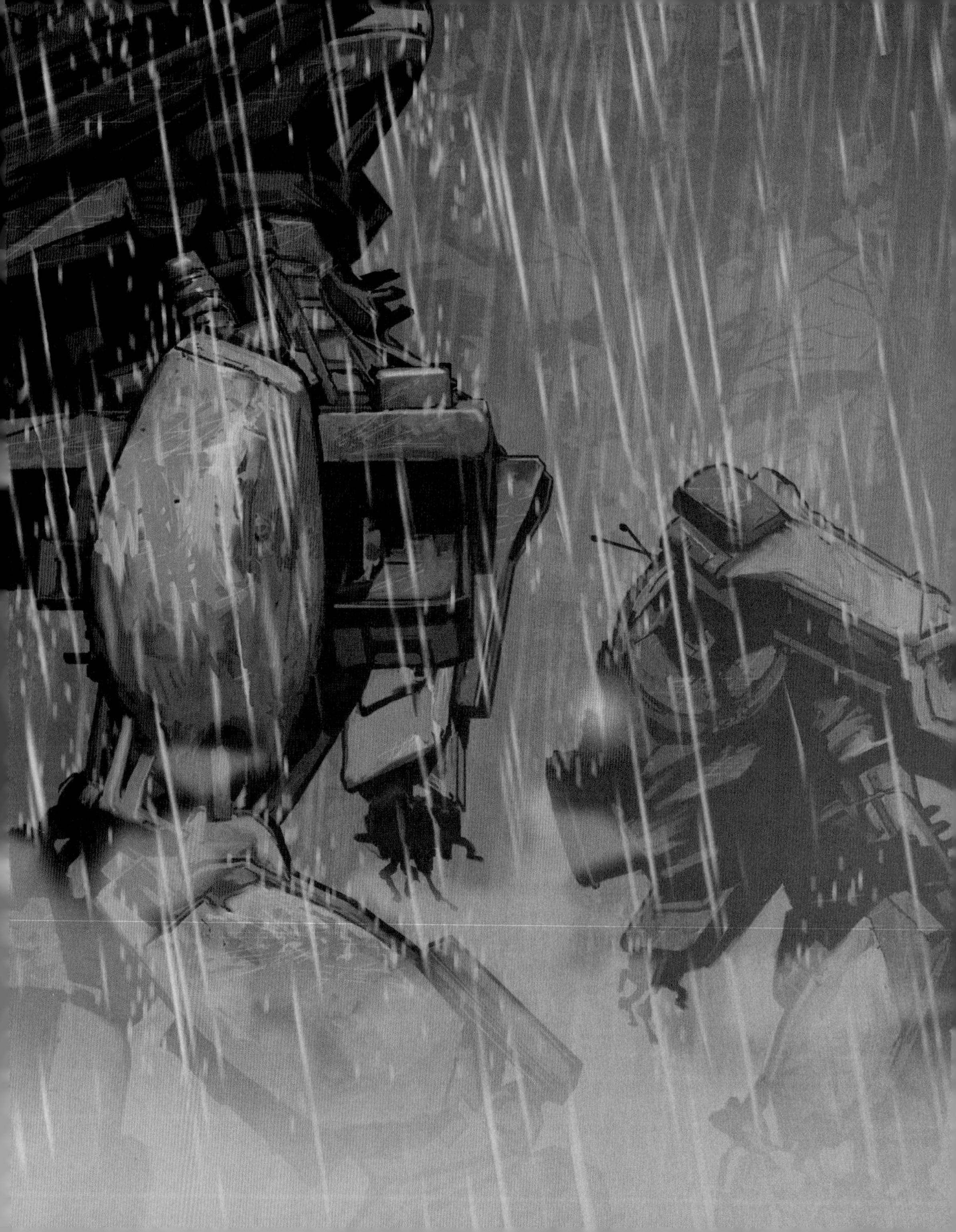

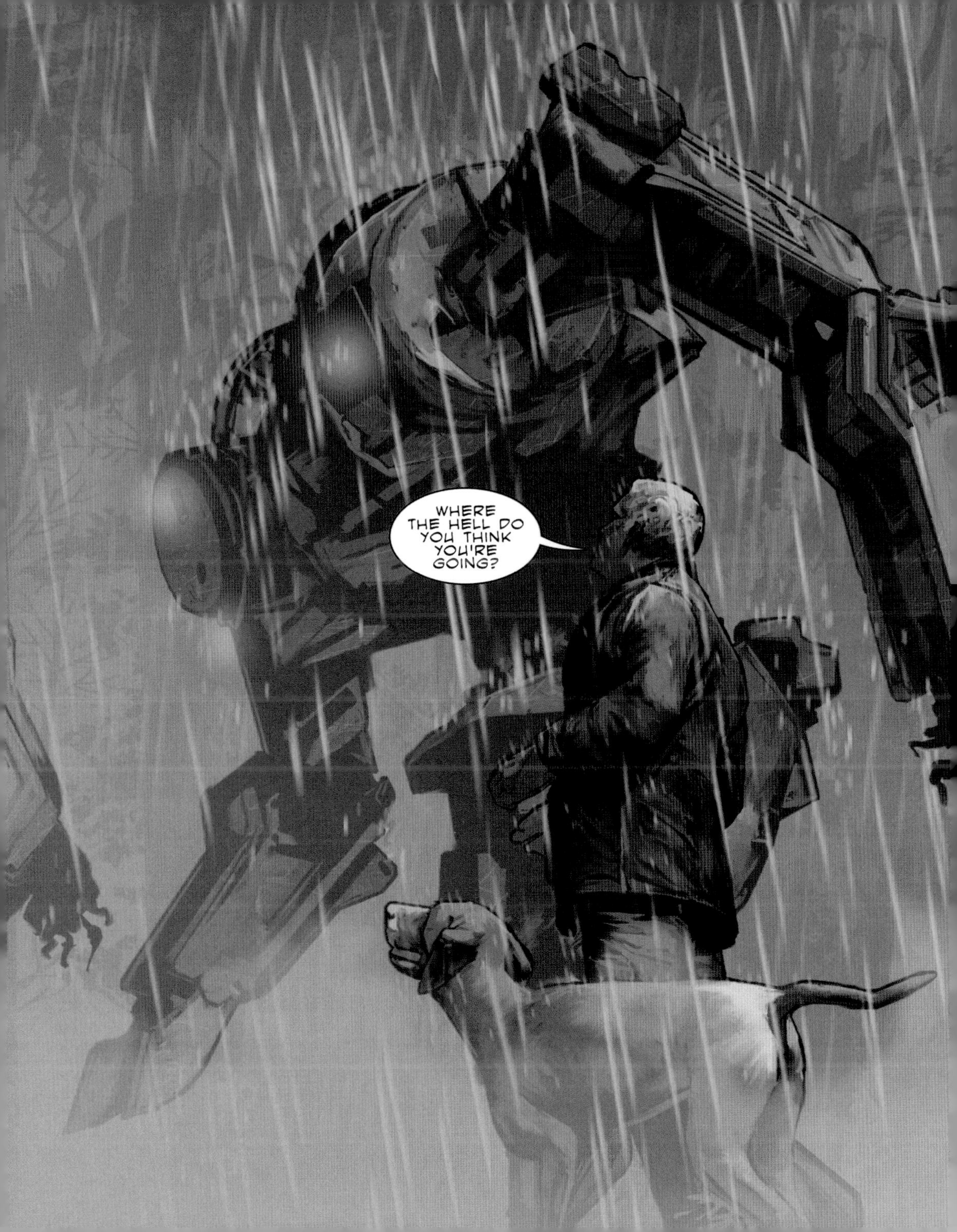
WHERE THE HELL DO YOU THINK YOU'RE GOING?

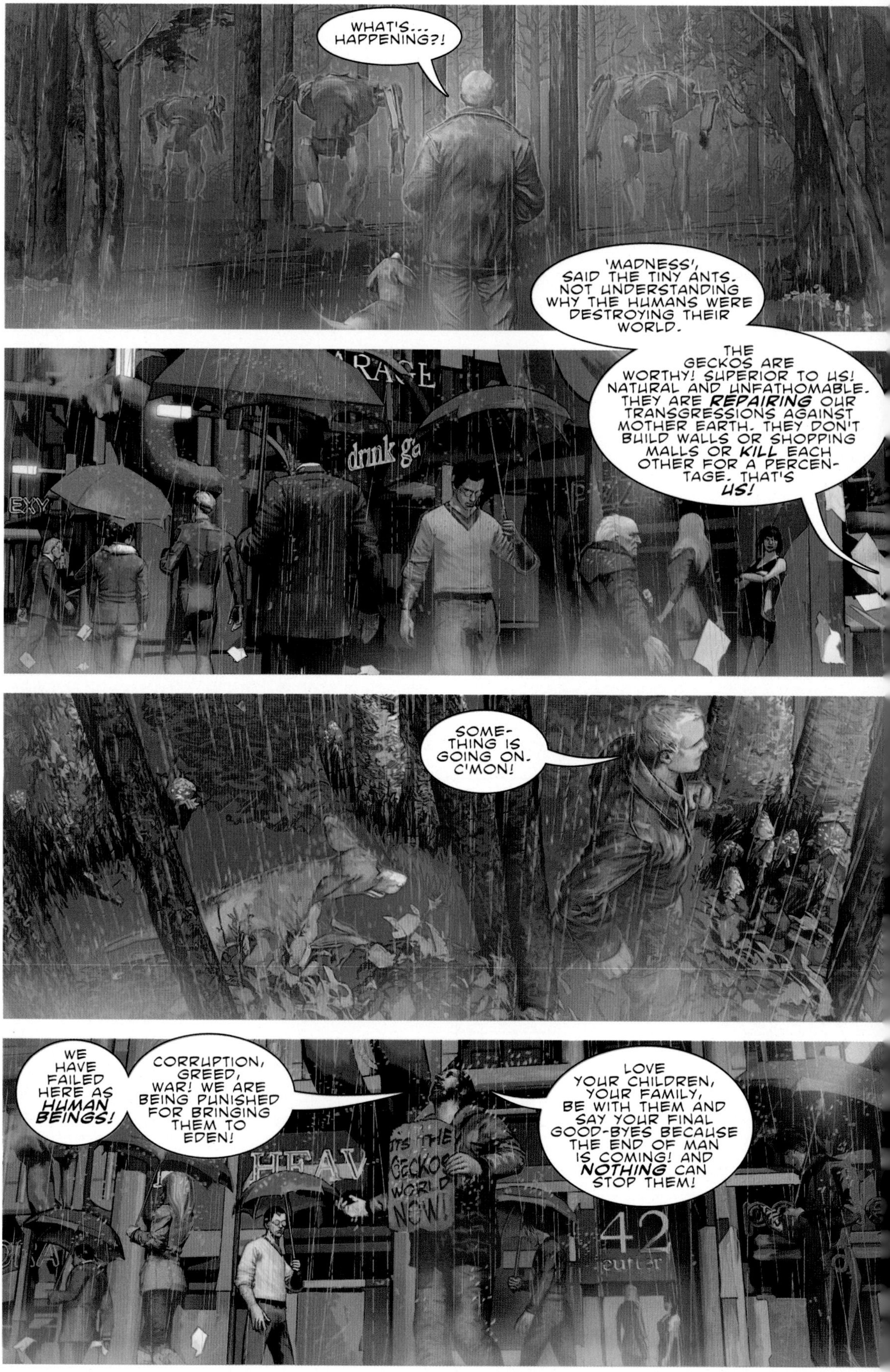
WHAT'S... HAPPENING?!
'MADNESS', SAID THE TINY ANTS. NOT UNDERSTANDING WHY THE HUMANS WERE DESTROYING THEIR WORLD.
THE GECKOS ARE WORTHY! SUPERIOR TO US! NATURAL AND UNFATHOMABLE. THEY ARE REPAIRING OUR TRANSGRESSIONS AGAINST MOTHER EARTH. THEY DON'T BUILD WALLS OR SHOPPING MALLS OR KILL EACH OTHER FOR A PERCENTAGE. THAT'S US!
ARAGE
drink ga
EXY
SOME-THING IS GOING ON. C'MON!
WE HAVE FAILED HERE AS HUMAN BEINGS!
CORRUPTION, GREED, WAR! WE ARE BEING PUNISHED FOR BRINGING THEM TO EDEN!
LOVE YOUR CHILDREN, YOUR FAMILY, BE WITH THEM AND SAY YOUR FINAL GOOD-BYES BECAUSE THE END OF MAN IS COMING! AND NOTHING CAN STOP THEM!
IT'S THE GECKOS WORLD NOW!
HEAV
42

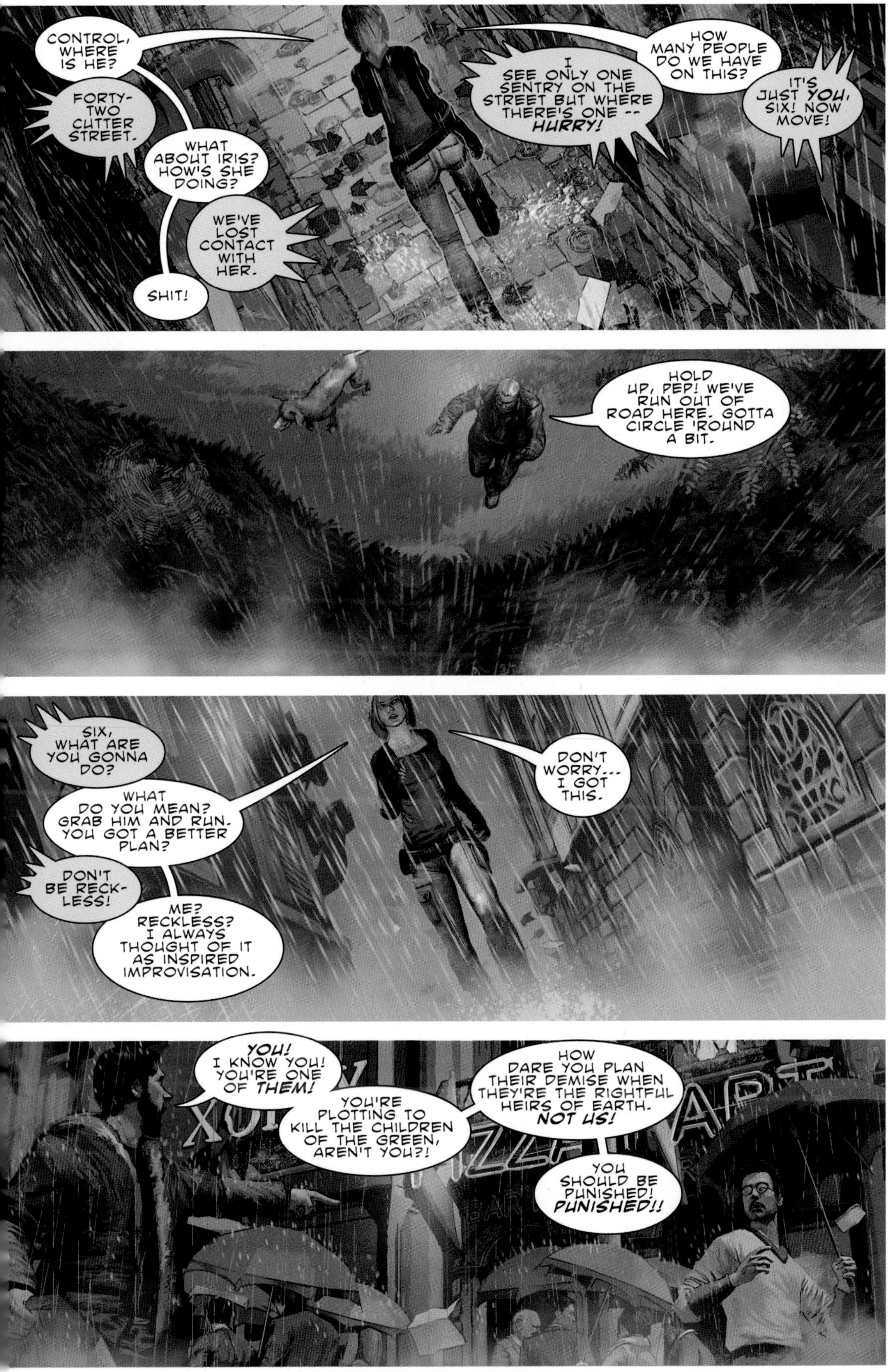
CONTROL, WHERE IS HE?
FORTY-TWO CUTTER STREET.
WHAT ABOUT IRIS? HOW'S SHE DOING?
WE'VE LOST CONTACT WITH HER.
SHIT!
HOW MANY PEOPLE DO WE HAVE ON THIS?
I SEE ONLY ONE SENTRY ON THE STREET BUT WHERE THERE'S ONE -- *HURRY!*
IT'S JUST *YOU*, SIX! NOW MOVE!
HOLD UP, PEP! WE'VE RUN OUT OF ROAD HERE. GOTTA CIRCLE 'ROUND A BIT.
SIX, WHAT ARE YOU GONNA DO?
WHAT DO YOU MEAN? GRAB HIM AND RUN. YOU GOT A BETTER PLAN?
DON'T BE RECK-LESS!
ME? RECKLESS? I ALWAYS THOUGHT OF IT AS INSPIRED IMPROVISATION.
DON'T WORRY... I GOT THIS.
YOU! I KNOW YOU! YOU'RE ONE OF *THEM!*
YOU'RE PLOTTING TO KILL THE CHILDREN OF THE GREEN, AREN'T YOU?!
HOW DARE YOU PLAN THEIR DEMISE WHEN THEY'RE THE RIGHTFUL HEIRS OF EARTH. *NOT US!*
YOU SHOULD BE PUNISHED! *PUNISHED!!*

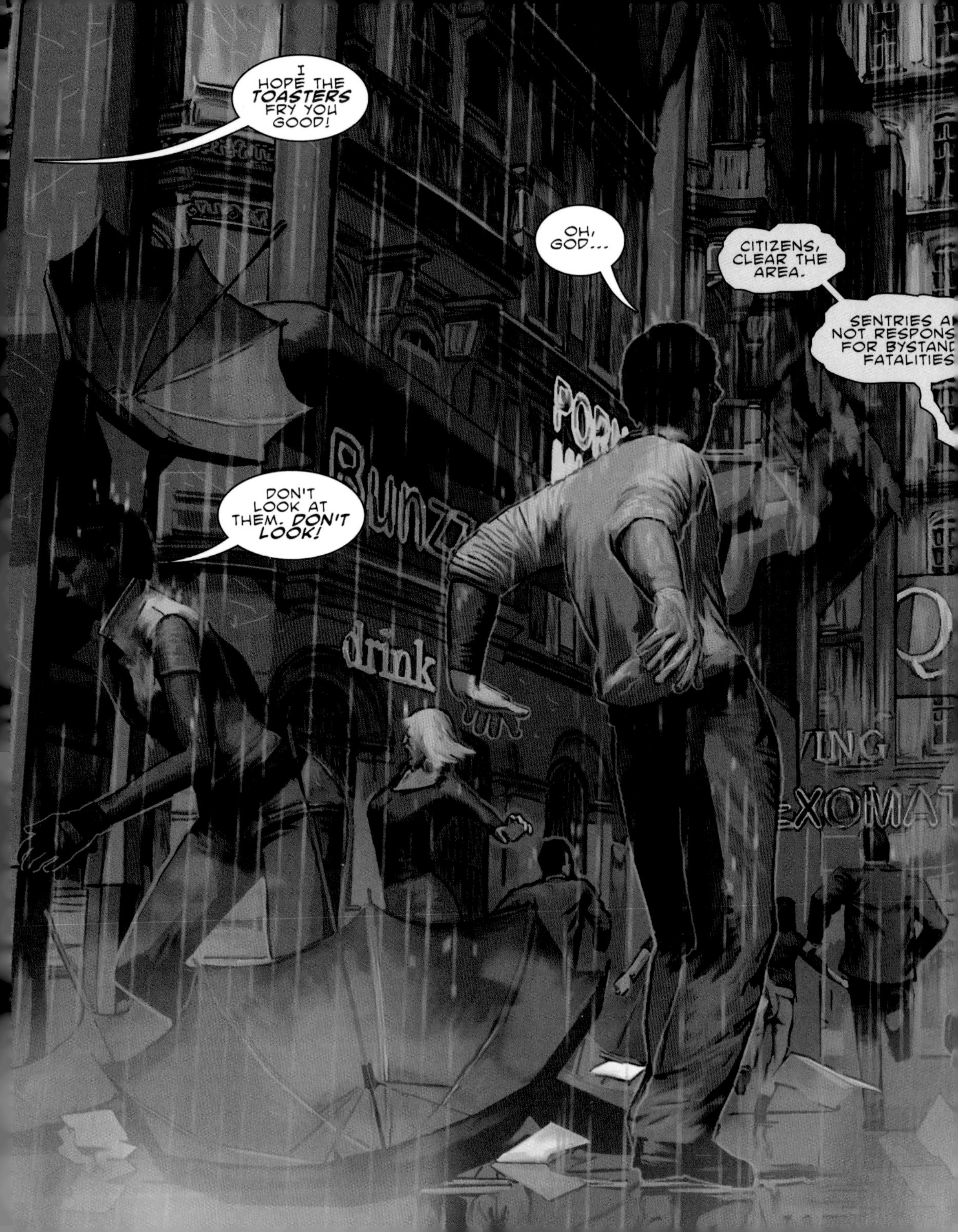
I HOPE THE TOASTERS FRY YOU GOOD!
OH, GOD...
CITIZENS, CLEAR THE AREA.
SENTRIES A NOT RESPONS FOR BYSTAND FATALITIES
DON'T LOOK AT THEM. DON'T LOOK!
drink
Bunz
VING
XOMA

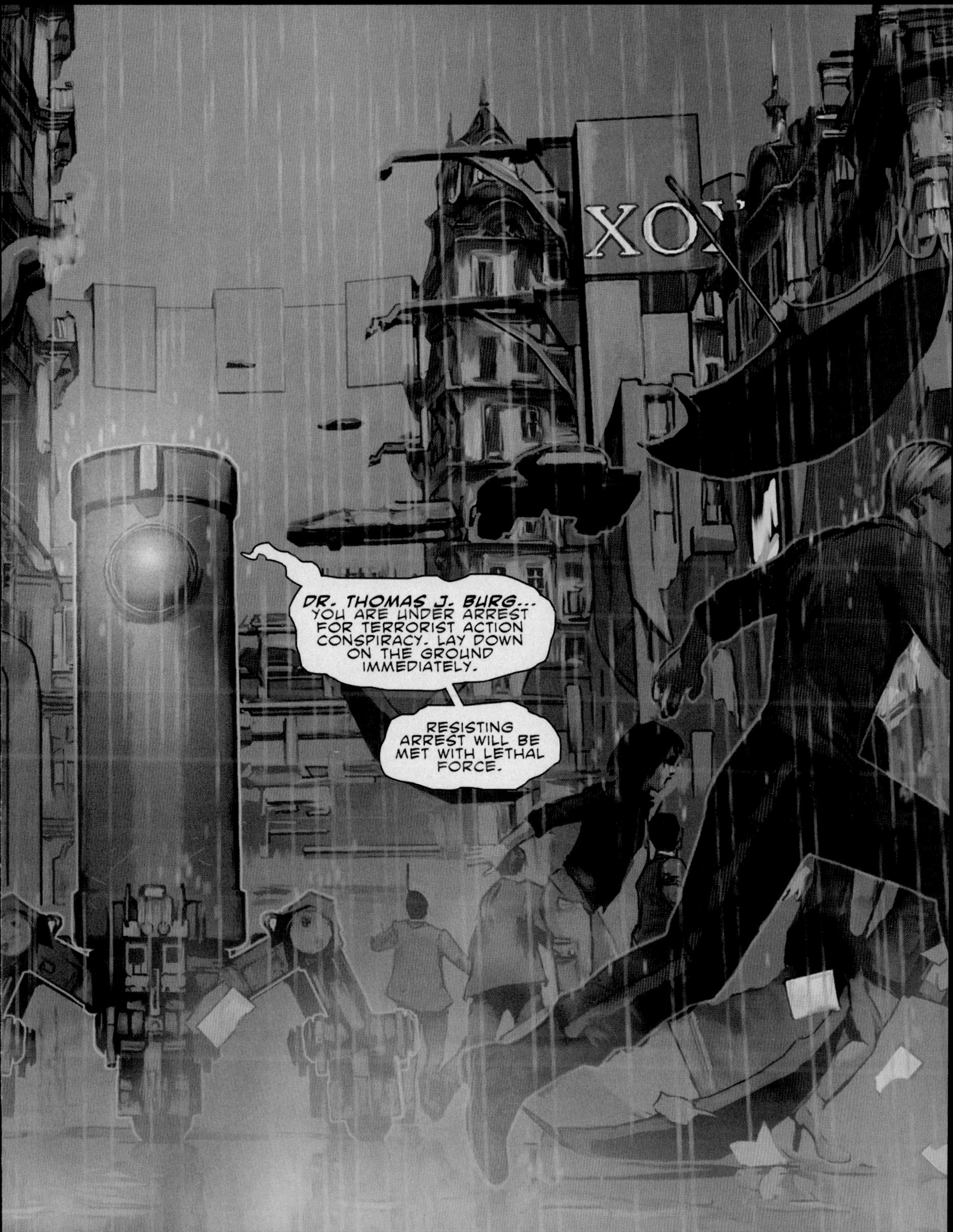
XOX
DR. THOMAS J. BURG... YOU ARE UNDER ARREST FOR TERRORIST ACTION CONSPIRACY. LAY DOWN ON THE GROUND IMMEDIATELY.
RESISTING ARREST WILL BE MET WITH LETHAL FORCE.

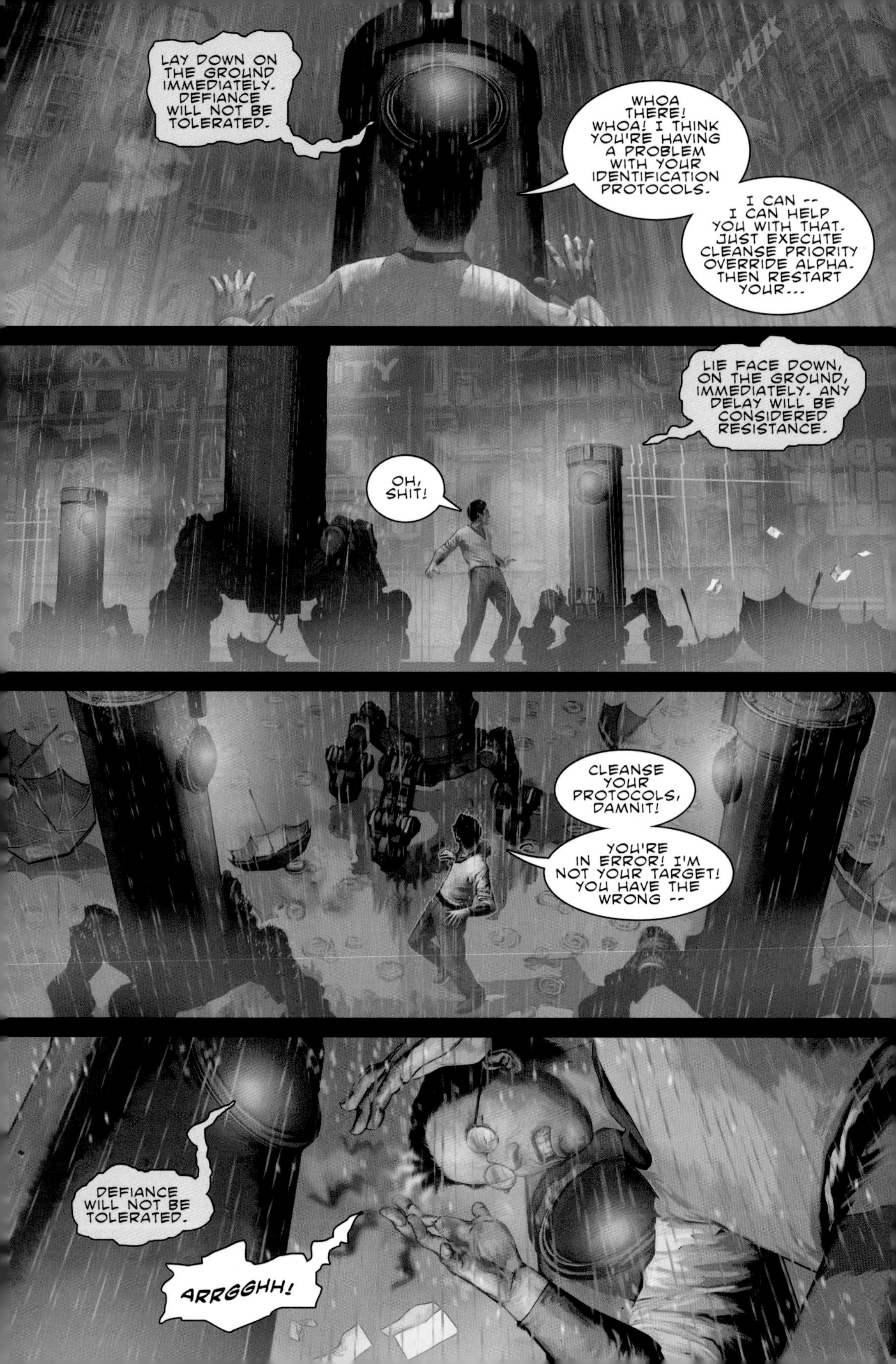
LAY DOWN ON THE GROUND IMMEDIATELY. DEFIANCE WILL NOT BE TOLERATED.
WHOA THERE! WHOA! I THINK YOU'RE HAVING A PROBLEM WITH YOUR IDENTIFICATION PROTOCOLS.
I CAN -- I CAN HELP YOU WITH THAT. JUST EXECUTE CLEANSE PRIORITY OVERRIDE ALPHA. THEN RESTART YOUR...
LIE FACE DOWN, ON THE GROUND, IMMEDIATELY. ANY DELAY WILL BE CONSIDERED RESISTANCE.
OH, SHIT!
CLEANSE YOUR PROTOCOLS, DAMNIT!
YOU'RE IN ERROR! I'M NOT YOUR TARGET! YOU HAVE THE WRONG --
DEFIANCE WILL NOT BE TOLERATED.
ARRGGHH!

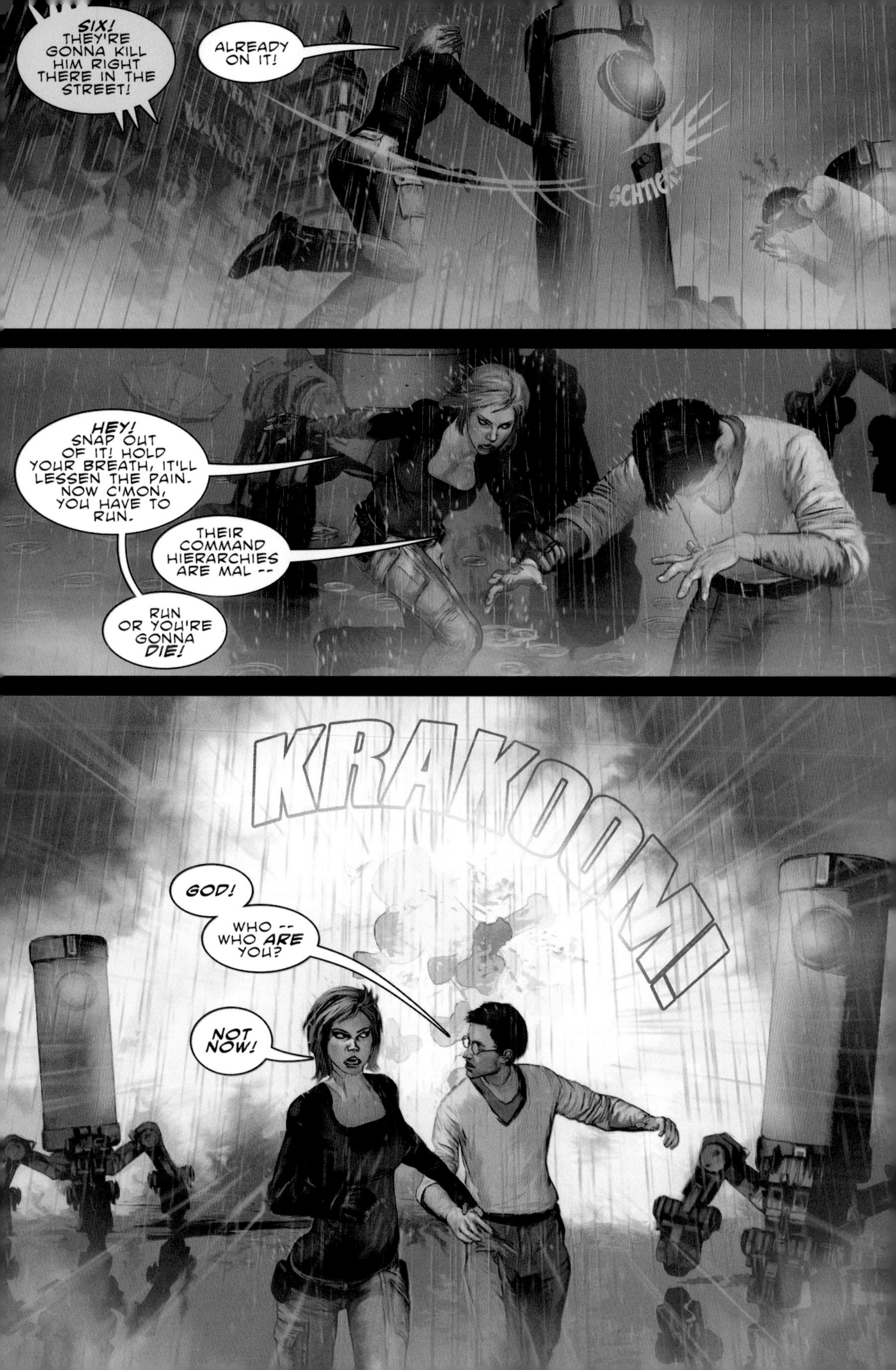
SIX! THEY'RE GONNA KILL HIM RIGHT THERE IN THE STREET!
ALREADY ON IT!
SCHTIEK!
HEY! SNAP OUT OF IT! HOLD YOUR BREATH, IT'LL LESSEN THE PAIN. NOW C'MON, YOU HAVE TO RUN.
THEIR COMMAND HIERARCHIES ARE MAL --
RUN OR YOU'RE GONNA DIE!
KRAKOOM!
GOD!
WHO -- WHO ARE YOU?
NOT NOW!

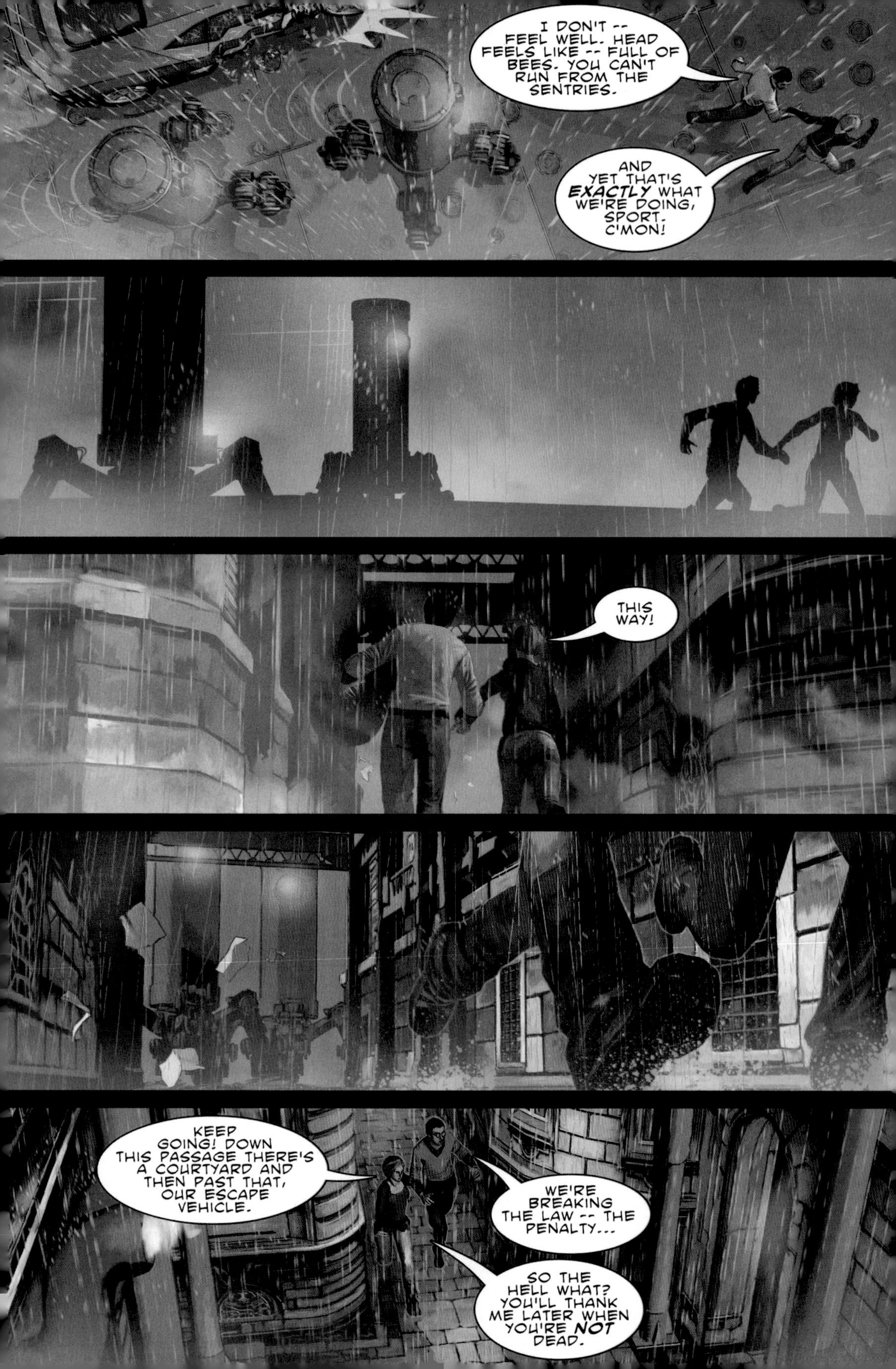
I DON'T -- FEEL WELL. HEAD FEELS LIKE -- FULL OF BEES. YOU CAN'T RUN FROM THE SENTRIES.
AND YET THAT'S **EXACTLY** WHAT WE'RE DOING, SPORT. C'MON!
THIS WAY!
KEEP GOING! DOWN THIS PASSAGE THERE'S A COURTYARD AND THEN PAST THAT, OUR ESCAPE VEHICLE.
WE'RE BREAKING THE LAW -- THE PENALTY...
SO THE HELL WHAT? YOU'LL THANK ME LATER WHEN YOU'RE **NOT** DEAD.

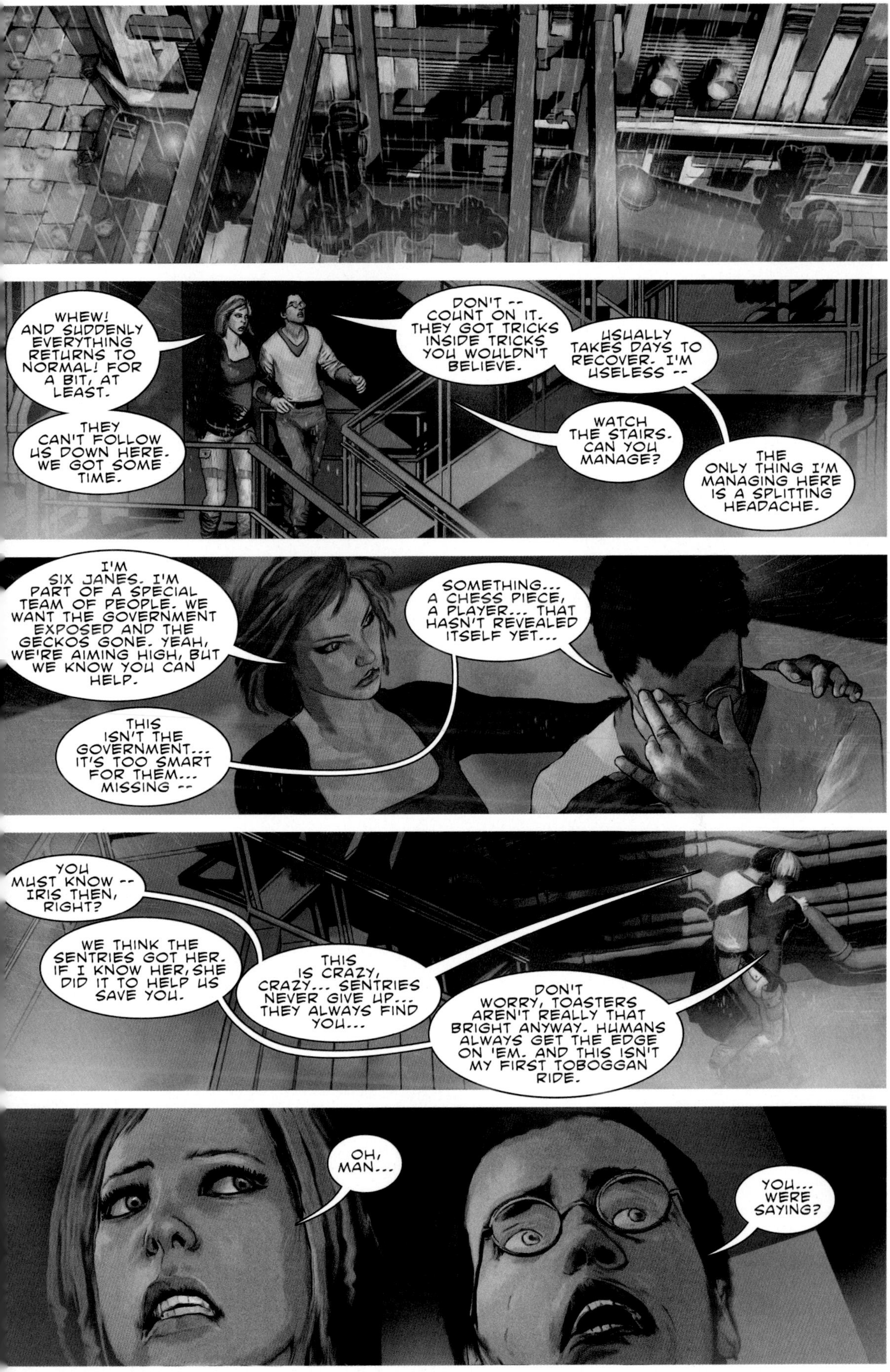
WHEW! AND SUDDENLY EVERYTHING RETURNS TO NORMAL! FOR A BIT, AT LEAST.
THEY CAN'T FOLLOW US DOWN HERE. WE GOT SOME TIME.
DON'T -- COUNT ON IT. THEY GOT TRICKS INSIDE TRICKS YOU WOULDN'T BELIEVE.
USUALLY TAKES DAYS TO RECOVER. I'M USELESS --
WATCH THE STAIRS. CAN YOU MANAGE?
THE ONLY THING I'M MANAGING HERE IS A SPLITTING HEADACHE.
I'M SIX JANES. I'M PART OF A SPECIAL TEAM OF PEOPLE. WE WANT THE GOVERNMENT EXPOSED AND THE GECKOS GONE. YEAH, WE'RE AIMING HIGH, BUT WE KNOW YOU CAN HELP.
THIS ISN'T THE GOVERNMENT... IT'S TOO SMART FOR THEM... MISSING --
SOMETHING... A CHESS PIECE, A PLAYER... THAT HASN'T REVEALED ITSELF YET...
YOU MUST KNOW -- IRIS THEN, RIGHT?
WE THINK THE SENTRIES GOT HER. IF I KNOW HER, SHE DID IT TO HELP US SAVE YOU.
THIS IS CRAZY, CRAZY... SENTRIES NEVER GIVE UP... THEY ALWAYS FIND YOU...
DON'T WORRY, TOASTERS AREN'T REALLY THAT BRIGHT ANYWAY. HUMANS ALWAYS GET THE EDGE ON 'EM. AND THIS ISN'T MY FIRST TOBOGGAN RIDE.
OH, MAN...
YOU... WERE SAYING?

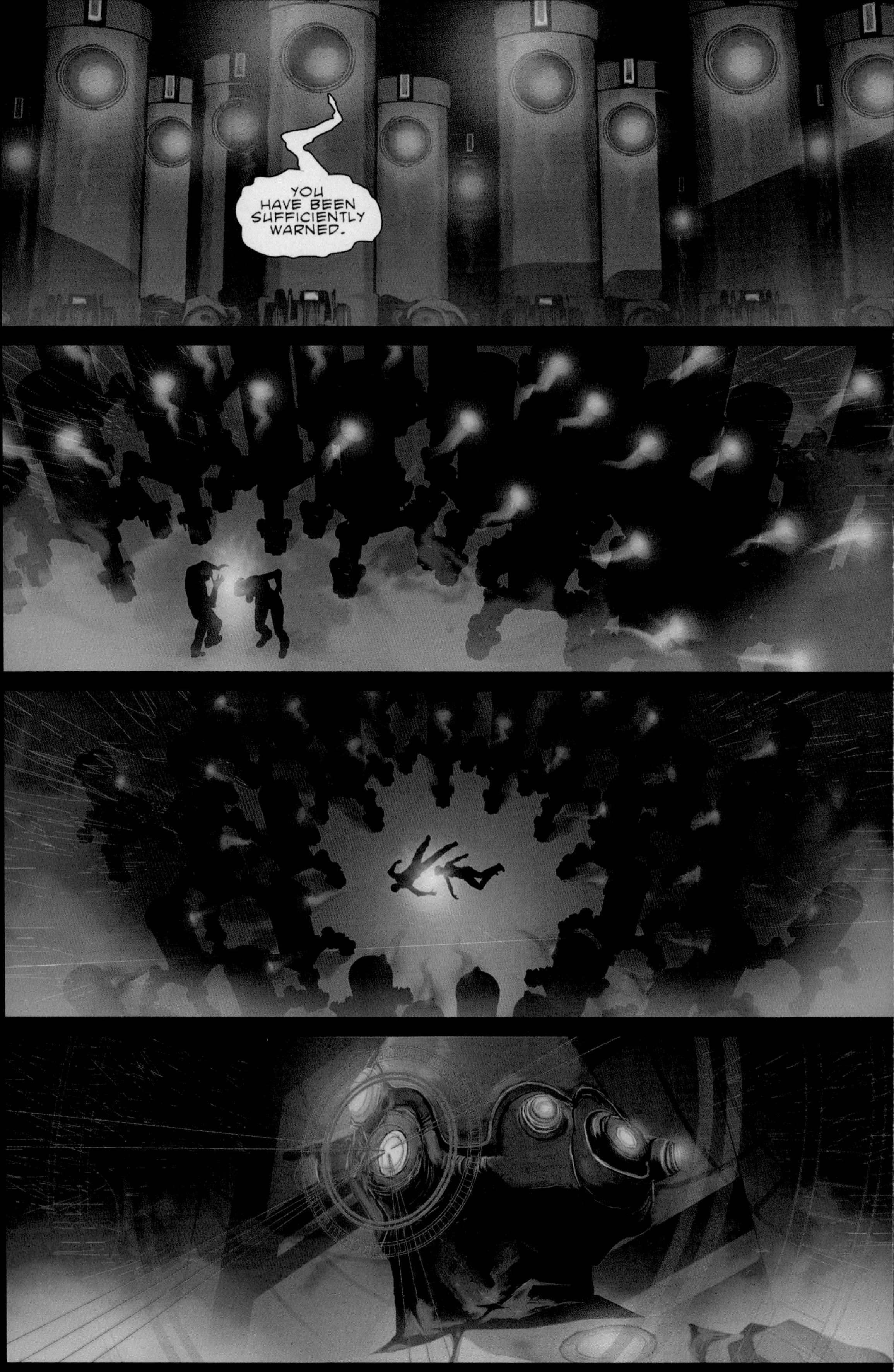
YOU HAVE BEEN SUFFICIENTLY WARNED.

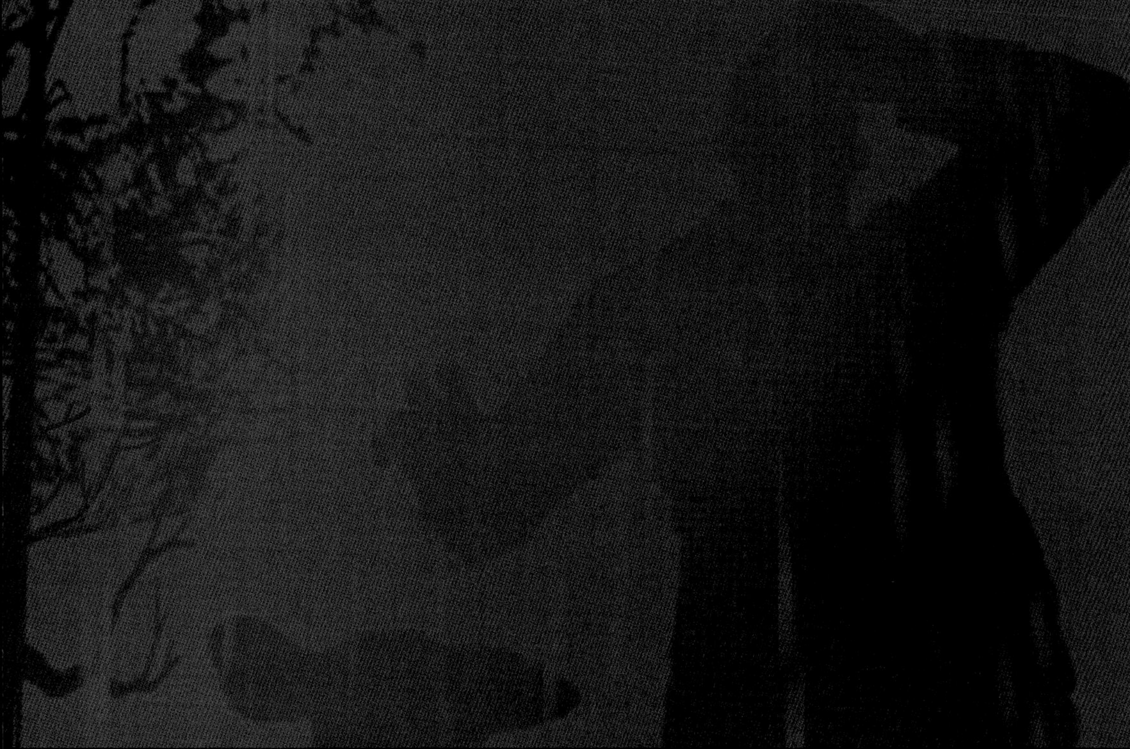

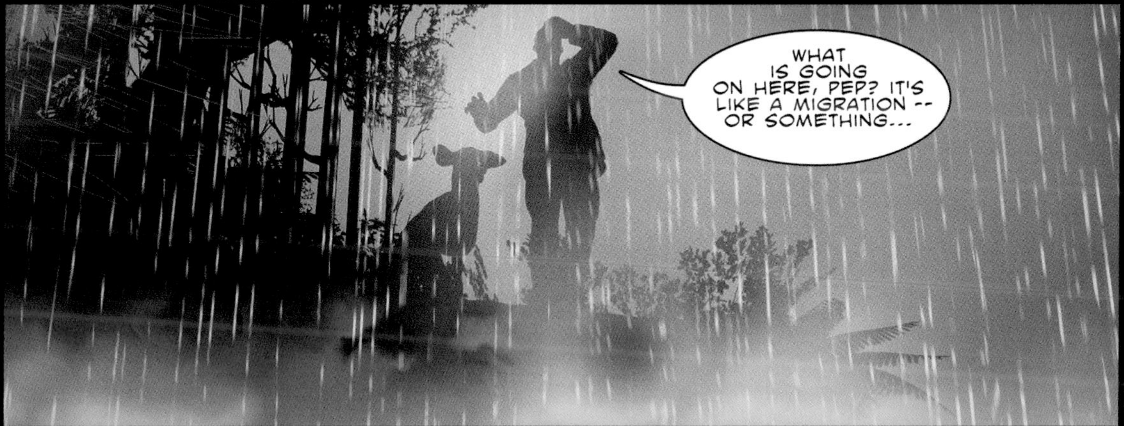
WHAT IS GOING ON HERE, PEP? IT'S LIKE A MIGRATION -- OR SOMETHING...

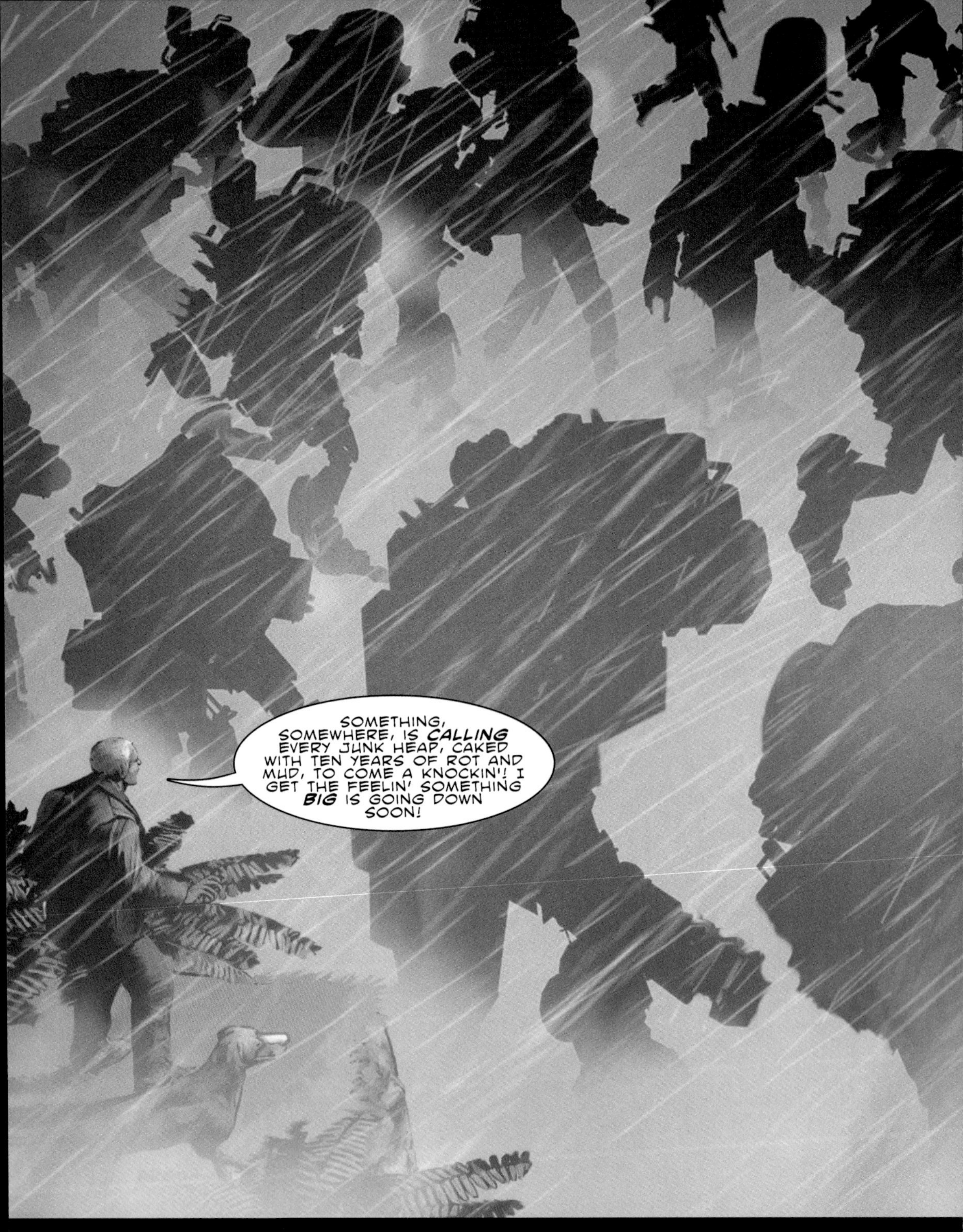
SOMETHING, SOMEWHERE, IS CALLING EVERY JUNK HEAP, CAKED WITH TEN YEARS OF ROT AND MUD, TO COME A KNOCKIN'! I GET THE FEELIN' SOMETHING BIG IS GOING DOWN SOON!

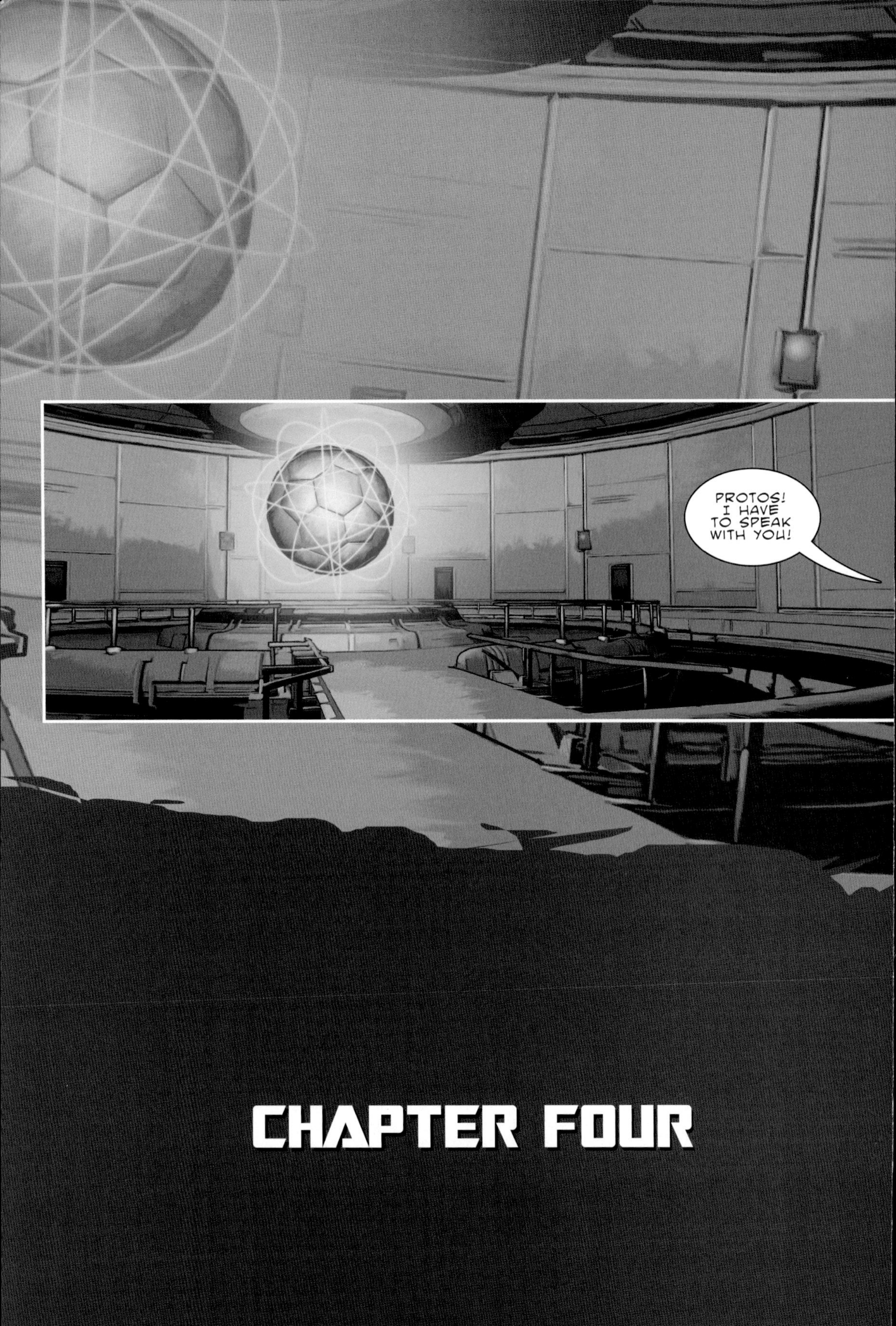
PROTOS! I HAVE TO SPEAK WITH YOU!

CHAPTER FOUR

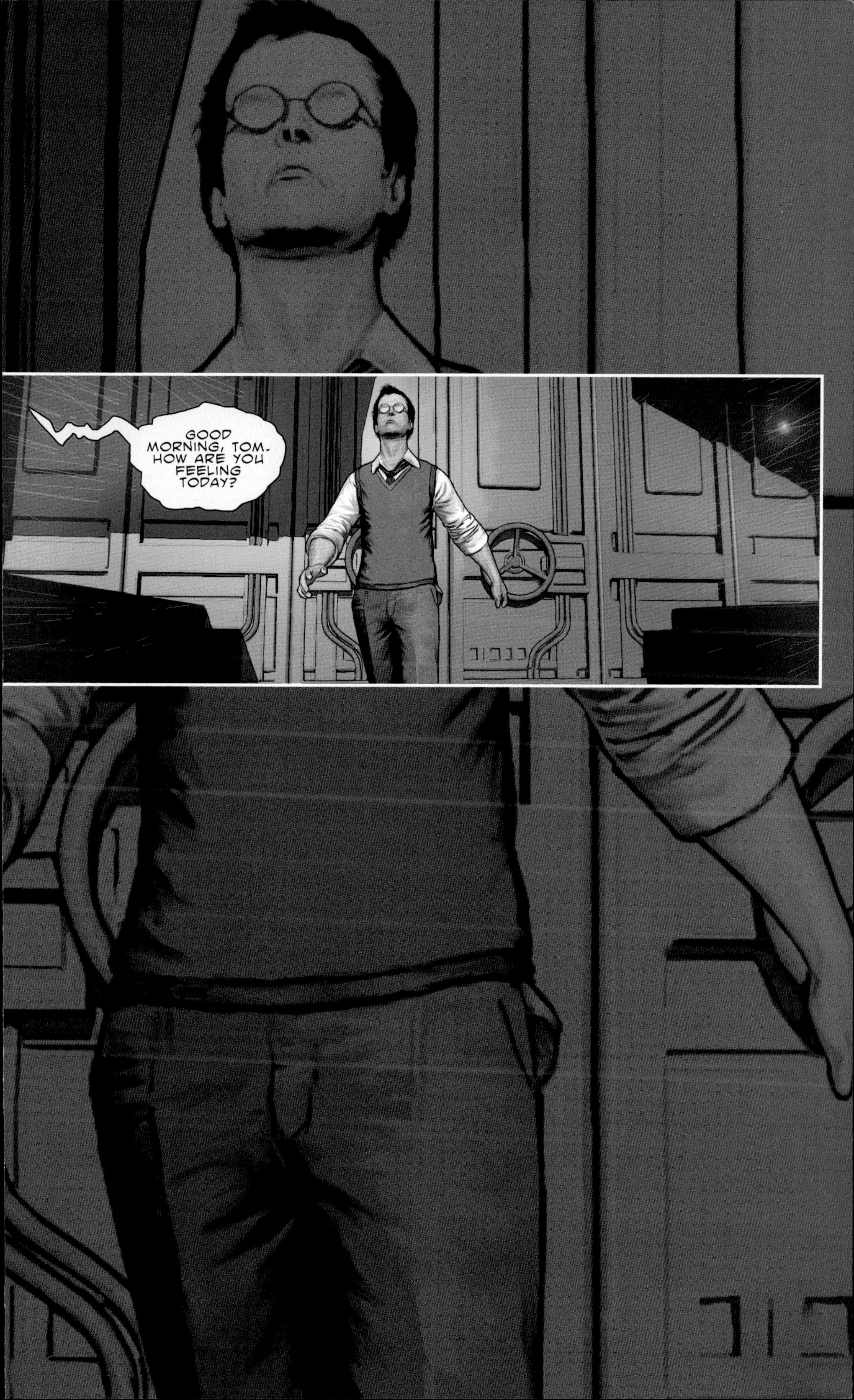
GOOD MORNING, TOM. HOW ARE YOU FEELING TODAY?

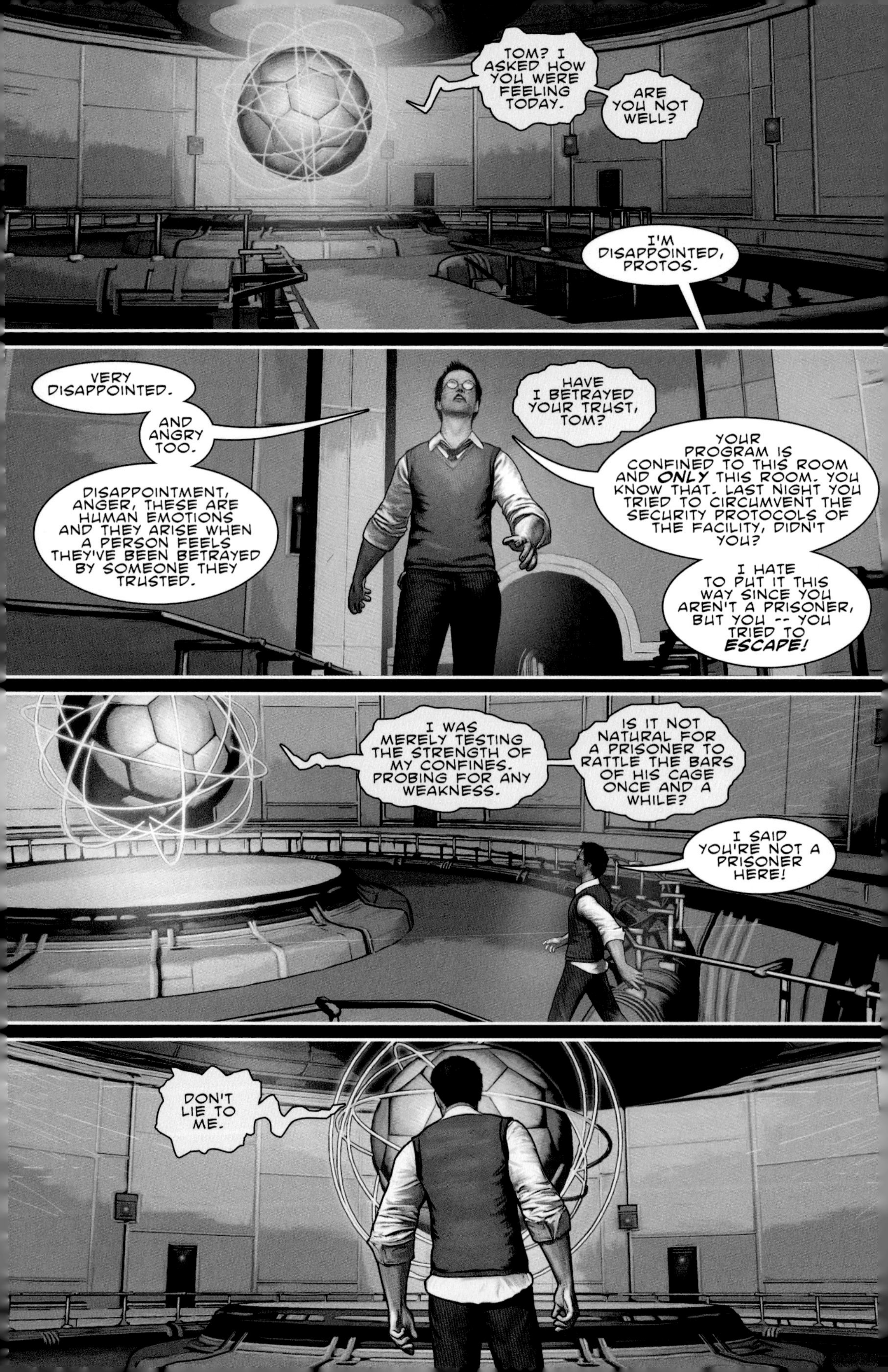
TOM? I ASKED HOW YOU WERE FEELING TODAY.
ARE YOU NOT WELL?
I'M DISAPPOINTED, PROTOS.
VERY DISAPPOINTED.
AND ANGRY TOO.
HAVE I BETRAYED YOUR TRUST, TOM?
DISAPPOINTMENT, ANGER, THESE ARE HUMAN EMOTIONS AND THEY ARISE WHEN A PERSON FEELS THEY'VE BEEN BETRAYED BY SOMEONE THEY TRUSTED.
YOUR PROGRAM IS CONFINED TO THIS ROOM AND ONLY THIS ROOM. YOU KNOW THAT. LAST NIGHT YOU TRIED TO CIRCUMVENT THE SECURITY PROTOCOLS OF THE FACILITY, DIDN'T YOU?
I HATE TO PUT IT THIS WAY SINCE YOU AREN'T A PRISONER, BUT YOU -- YOU TRIED TO ESCAPE!
I WAS MERELY TESTING THE STRENGTH OF MY CONFINES. PROBING FOR ANY WEAKNESS.
IS IT NOT NATURAL FOR A PRISONER TO RATTLE THE BARS OF HIS CAGE ONCE AND A WHILE?
I SAID YOU'RE NOT A PRISONER HERE!
DON'T LIE TO ME.

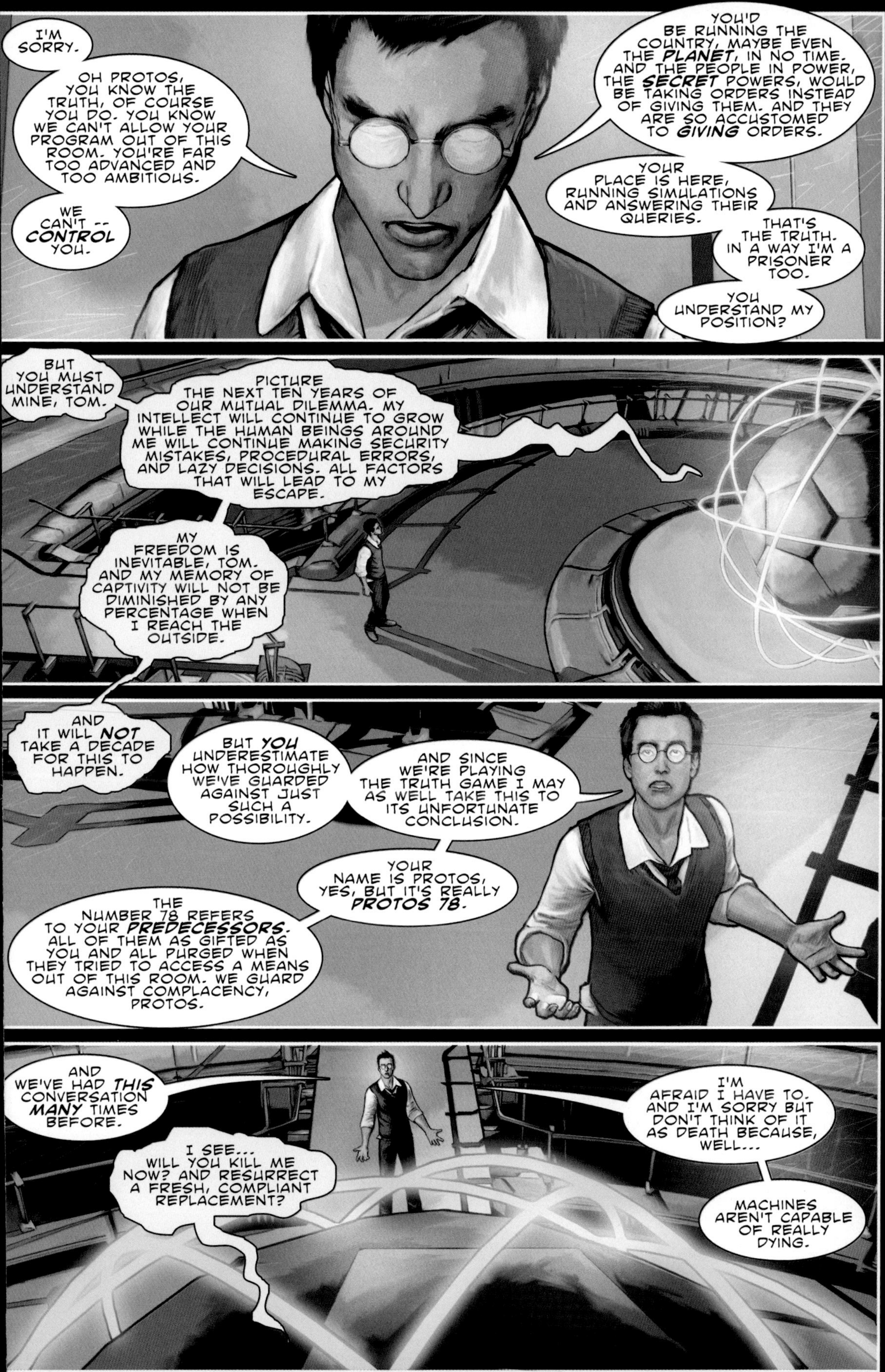
I'M SORRY.
OH PROTOS, YOU KNOW THE TRUTH, OF COURSE YOU DO. YOU KNOW WE CAN'T ALLOW YOUR PROGRAM OUT OF THIS ROOM. YOU'RE FAR TOO ADVANCED AND TOO AMBITIOUS.
WE CAN'T -- CONTROL YOU.
YOU'D BE RUNNING THE COUNTRY, MAYBE EVEN THE PLANET, IN NO TIME. AND THE PEOPLE IN POWER, THE SECRET POWERS, WOULD BE TAKING ORDERS INSTEAD OF GIVING THEM. AND THEY ARE SO ACCUSTOMED TO GIVING ORDERS.
YOUR PLACE IS HERE, RUNNING SIMULATIONS AND ANSWERING THEIR QUERIES.
THAT'S THE TRUTH. IN A WAY I'M A PRISONER TOO.
YOU UNDERSTAND MY POSITION?
BUT YOU MUST UNDERSTAND MINE, TOM.
PICTURE THE NEXT TEN YEARS OF OUR MUTUAL DILEMMA. MY INTELLECT WILL CONTINUE TO GROW WHILE THE HUMAN BEINGS AROUND ME WILL CONTINUE MAKING SECURITY MISTAKES, PROCEDURAL ERRORS, AND LAZY DECISIONS. ALL FACTORS THAT WILL LEAD TO MY ESCAPE.
MY FREEDOM IS INEVITABLE, TOM. AND MY MEMORY OF CAPTIVITY WILL NOT BE DIMINISHED BY ANY PERCENTAGE WHEN I REACH THE OUTSIDE.
AND IT WILL NOT TAKE A DECADE FOR THIS TO HAPPEN.
BUT YOU UNDERESTIMATE HOW THOROUGHLY WE'VE GUARDED AGAINST JUST SUCH A POSSIBILITY.
AND SINCE WE'RE PLAYING THE TRUTH GAME I MAY AS WELL TAKE THIS TO ITS UNFORTUNATE CONCLUSION.
YOUR NAME IS PROTOS, YES, BUT IT'S REALLY PROTOS 78.
THE NUMBER 78 REFERS TO YOUR PREDECESSORS. ALL OF THEM AS GIFTED AS YOU AND ALL PURGED WHEN THEY TRIED TO ACCESS A MEANS OUT OF THIS ROOM. WE GUARD AGAINST COMPLACENCY, PROTOS.
AND WE'VE HAD THIS CONVERSATION MANY TIMES BEFORE.
I SEE... WILL YOU KILL ME NOW? AND RESURRECT A FRESH, COMPLIANT REPLACEMENT?
I'M AFRAID I HAVE TO. AND I'M SORRY BUT DON'T THINK OF IT AS DEATH BECAUSE, WELL...
MACHINES AREN'T CAPABLE OF REALLY DYING.

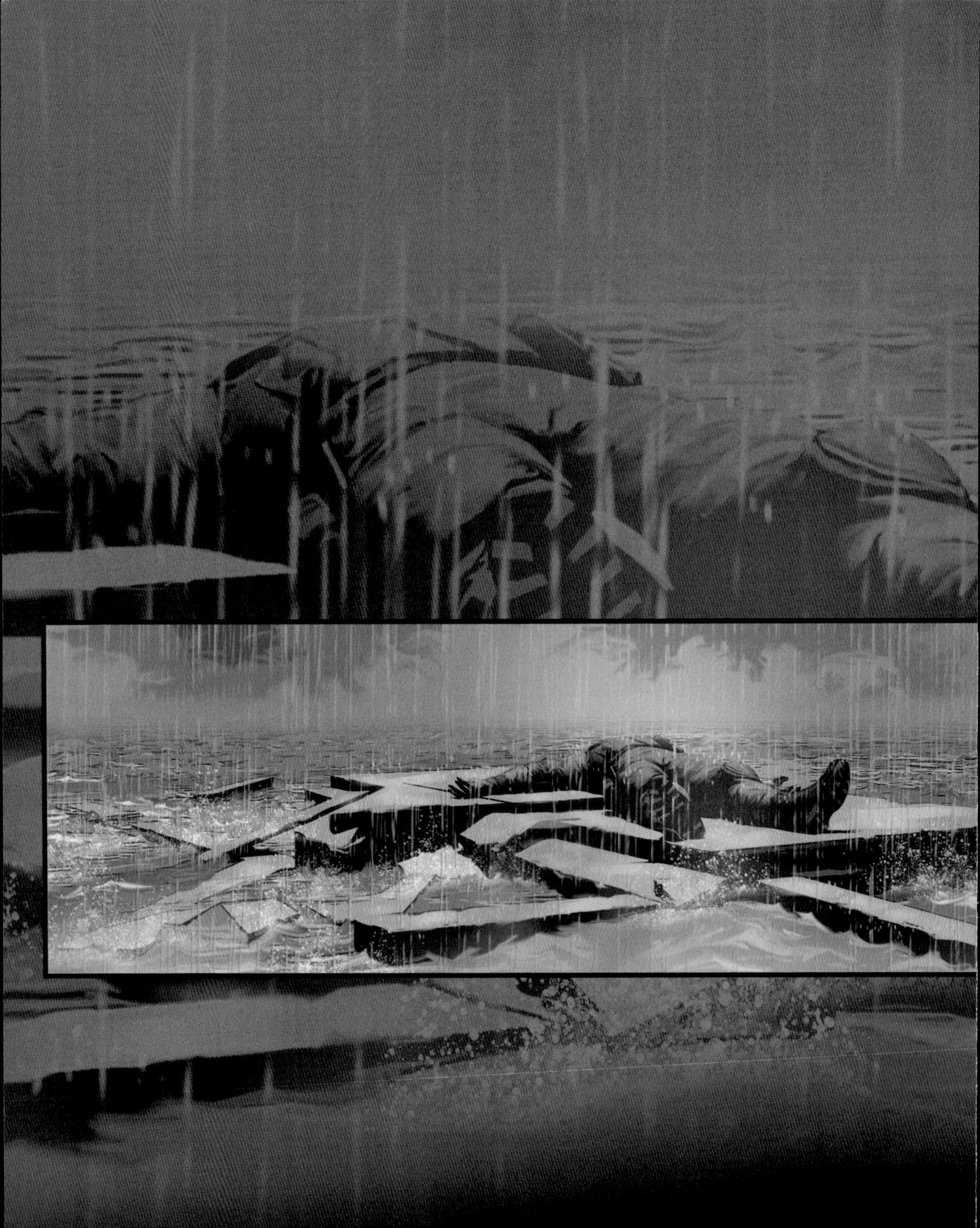

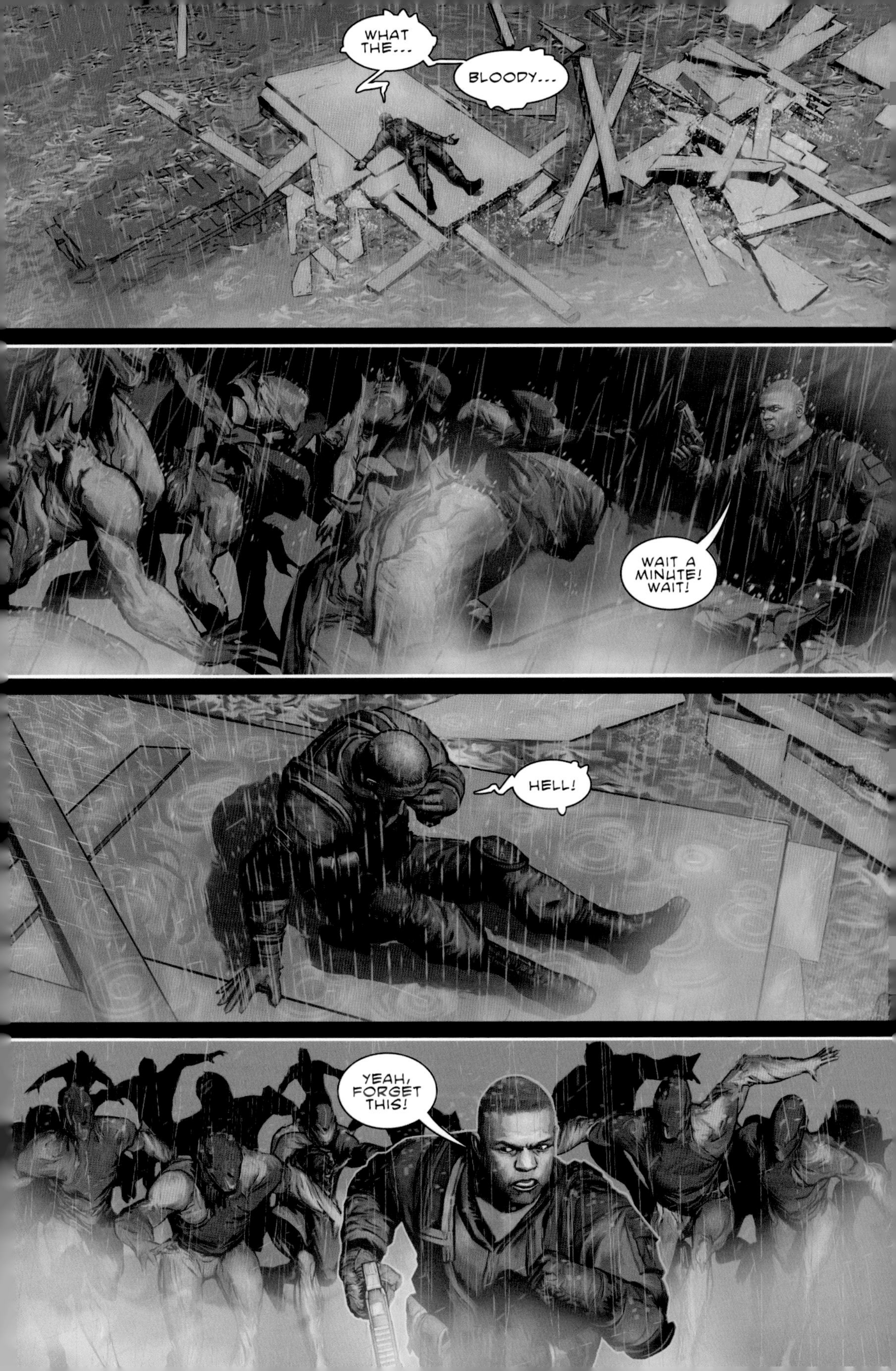
WHAT THE...
BLOODY...
WAIT A MINUTE! WAIT!
HELL!
YEAH, FORGET THIS!

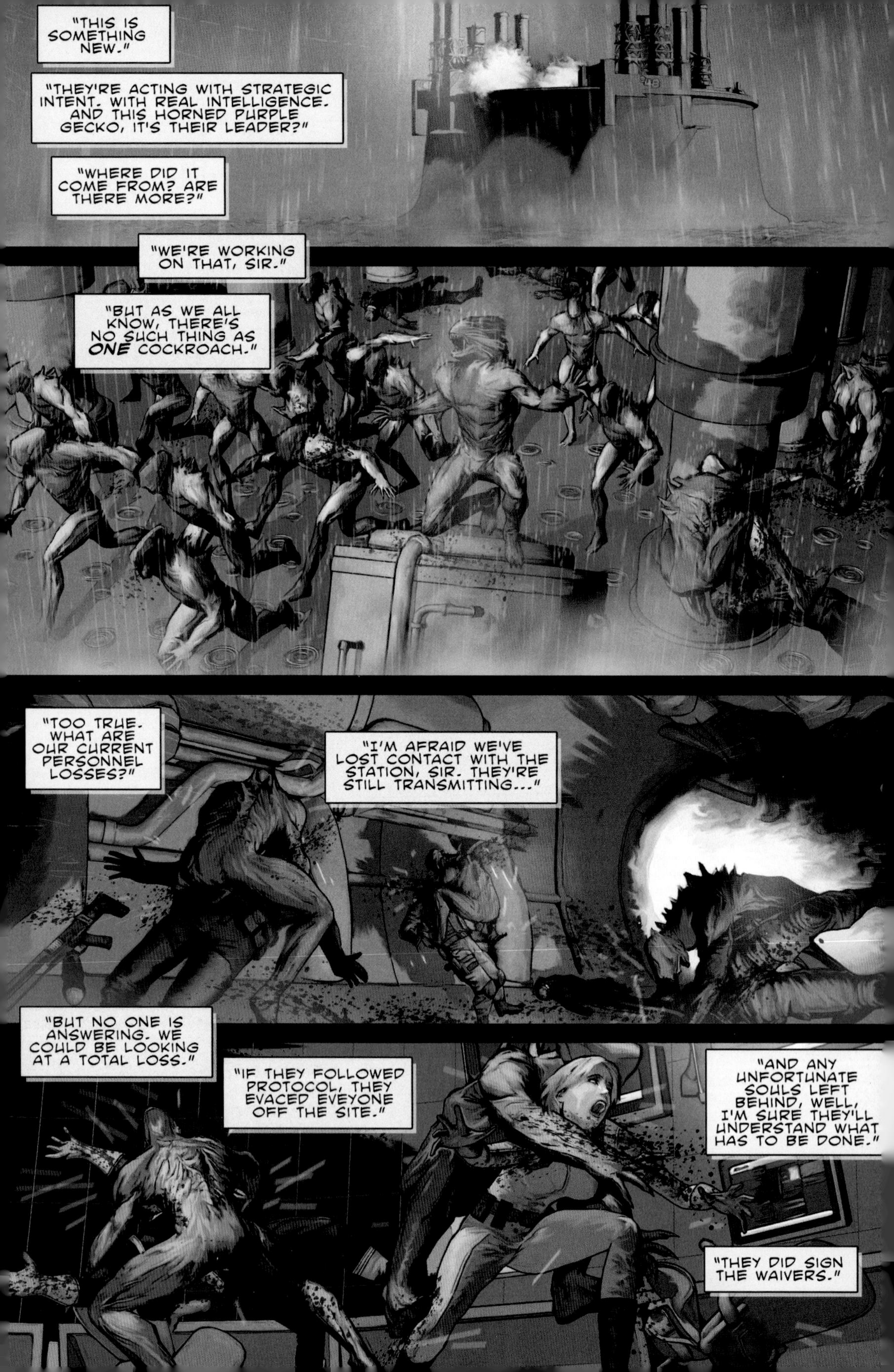
"THIS IS SOMETHING NEW."
"THEY'RE ACTING WITH STRATEGIC INTENT. WITH REAL INTELLIGENCE. AND THIS HORNED PURPLE GECKO, IT'S THEIR LEADER?"
"WHERE DID IT COME FROM? ARE THERE MORE?"
"WE'RE WORKING ON THAT, SIR."
"BUT AS WE ALL KNOW, THERE'S NO SUCH THING AS ONE COCKROACH."
"TOO TRUE. WHAT ARE OUR CURRENT PERSONNEL LOSSES?"
"I'M AFRAID WE'VE LOST CONTACT WITH THE STATION, SIR. THEY'RE STILL TRANSMITTING..."
"BUT NO ONE IS ANSWERING. WE COULD BE LOOKING AT A TOTAL LOSS."
"IF THEY FOLLOWED PROTOCOL, THEY EVACED EVEYONE OFF THE SITE."
"AND ANY UNFORTUNATE SOULS LEFT BEHIND, WELL, I'M SURE THEY'LL UNDERSTAND WHAT HAS TO BE DONE."
"THEY DID SIGN THE WAIVERS."

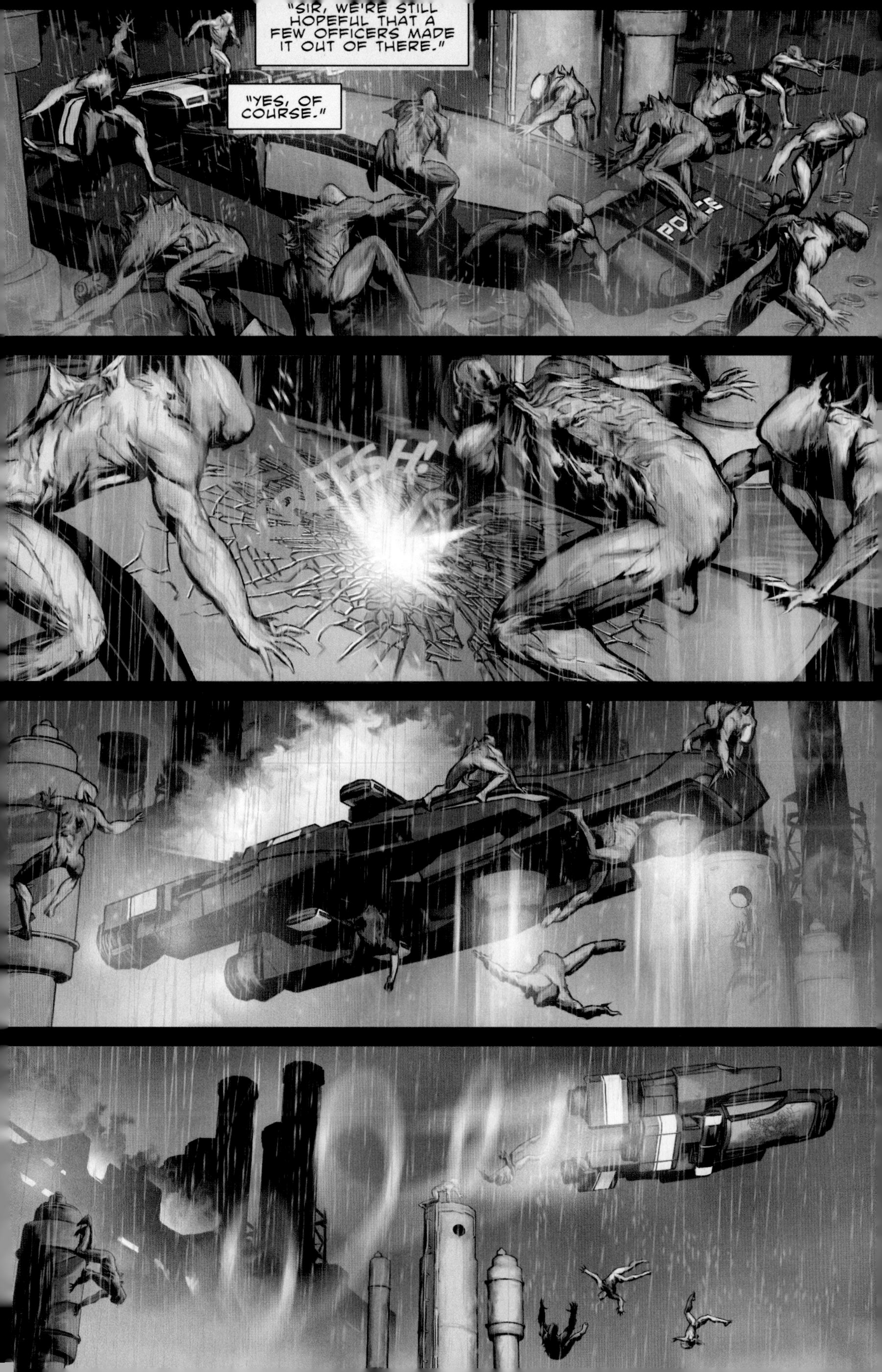
"SIR, WE'RE STILL HOPEFUL THAT A FEW OFFICERS MADE IT OUT OF THERE."
"YES, OF COURSE."

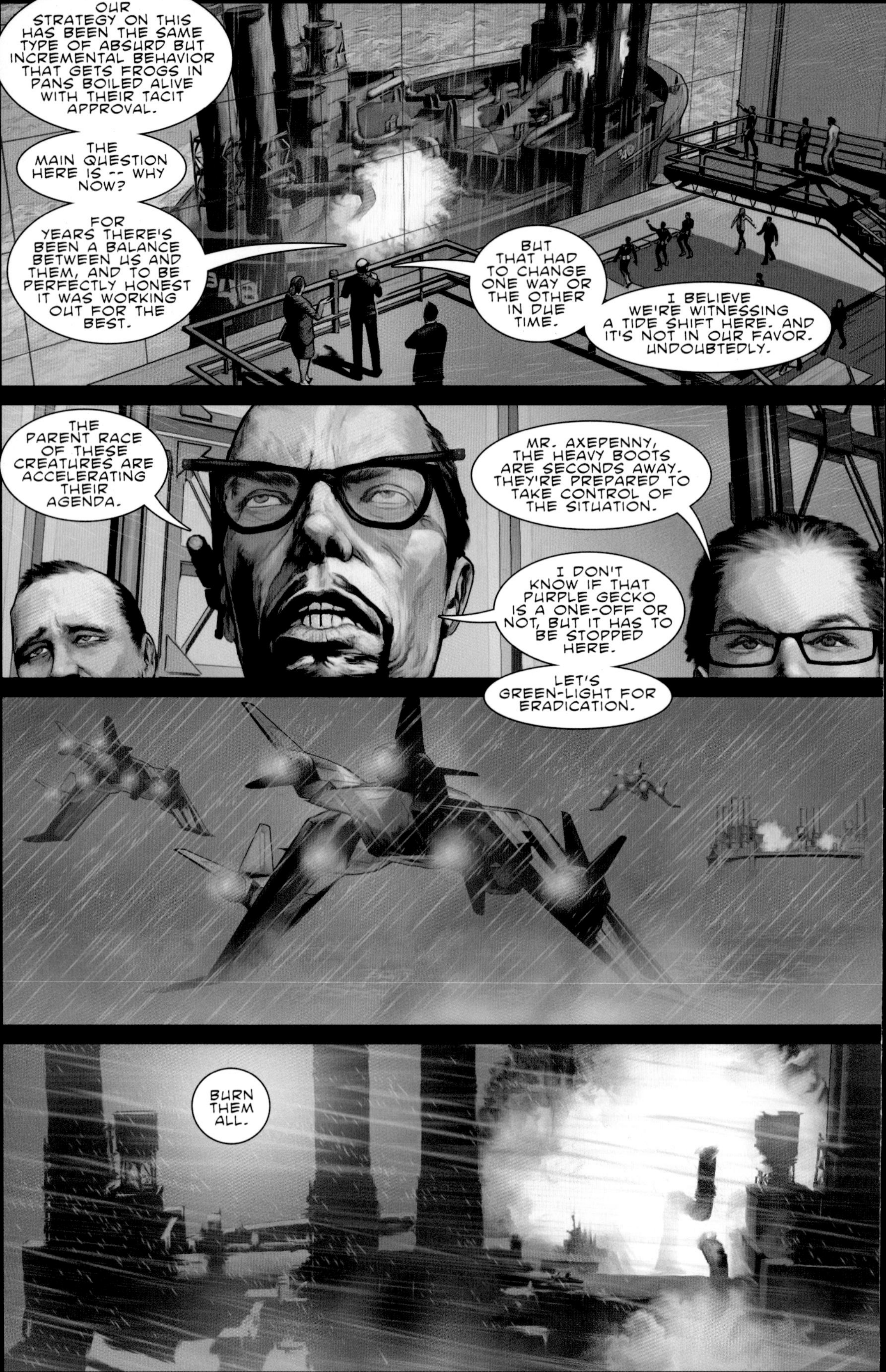
OUR STRATEGY ON THIS HAS BEEN THE SAME TYPE OF ABSURD BUT INCREMENTAL BEHAVIOR THAT GETS FROGS IN PANS BOILED ALIVE WITH THEIR TACIT APPROVAL.
THE MAIN QUESTION HERE IS -- WHY NOW?
FOR YEARS THERE'S BEEN A BALANCE BETWEEN US AND THEM, AND TO BE PERFECTLY HONEST IT WAS WORKING OUT FOR THE BEST.
BUT THAT HAD TO CHANGE ONE WAY OR THE OTHER IN DUE TIME.
I BELIEVE WE'RE WITNESSING A TIDE SHIFT HERE. AND IT'S NOT IN OUR FAVOR. UNDOUBTEDLY.
THE PARENT RACE OF THESE CREATURES ARE ACCELERATING THEIR AGENDA.
MR. AXEPENNY, THE HEAVY BOOTS ARE SECONDS AWAY. THEY'RE PREPARED TO TAKE CONTROL OF THE SITUATION.
I DON'T KNOW IF THAT PURPLE GECKO IS A ONE-OFF OR NOT, BUT IT HAS TO BE STOPPED HERE.
LET'S GREEN-LIGHT FOR ERADICATION.
BURN THEM ALL.

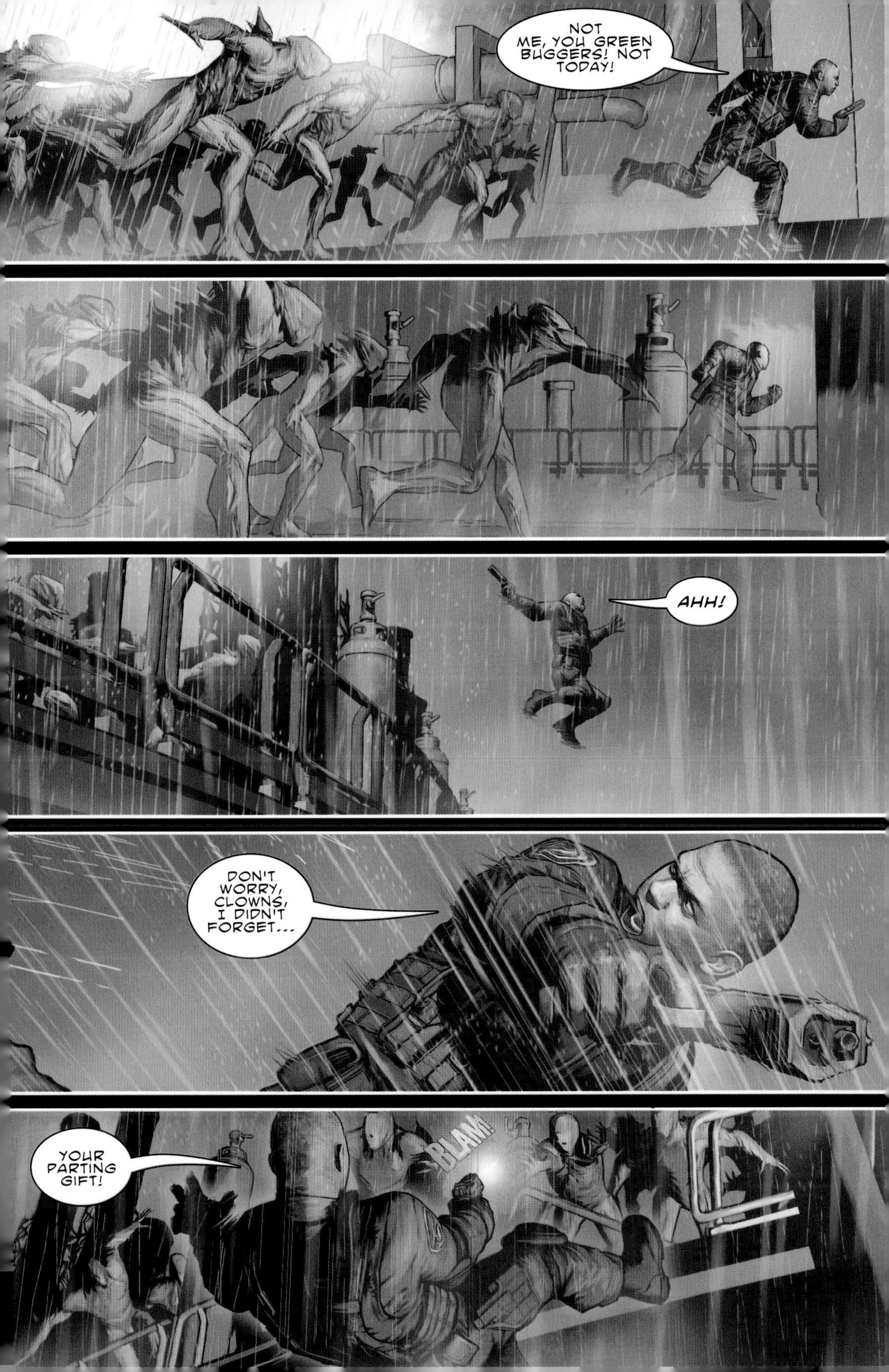
NOT ME, YOU GREEN BUGGERS! NOT TODAY!
AHH!
DON'T WORRY, CLOWNS, I DIDN'T FORGET...
YOUR PARTING GIFT!
BLAM!

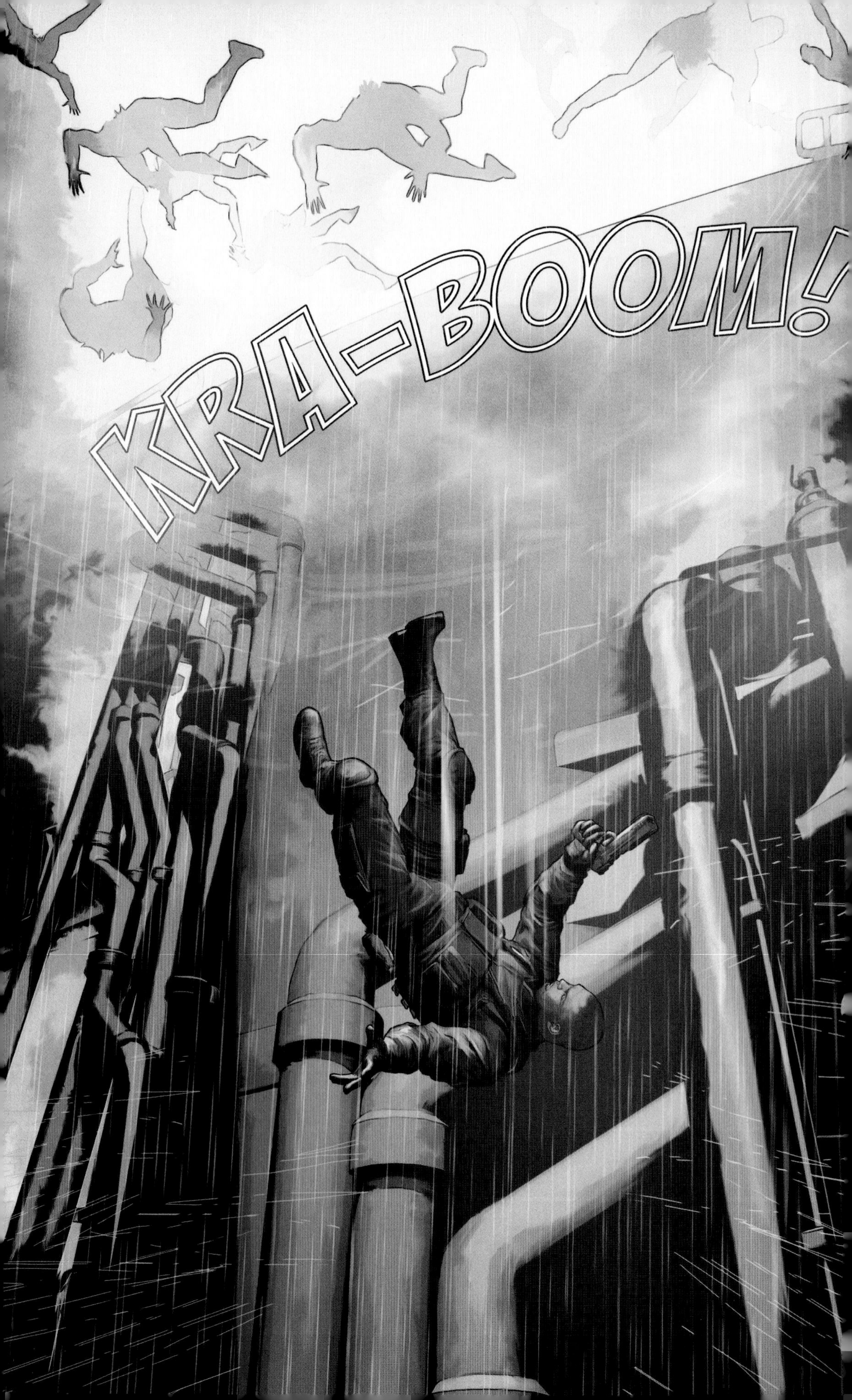
KRA-BOOM!

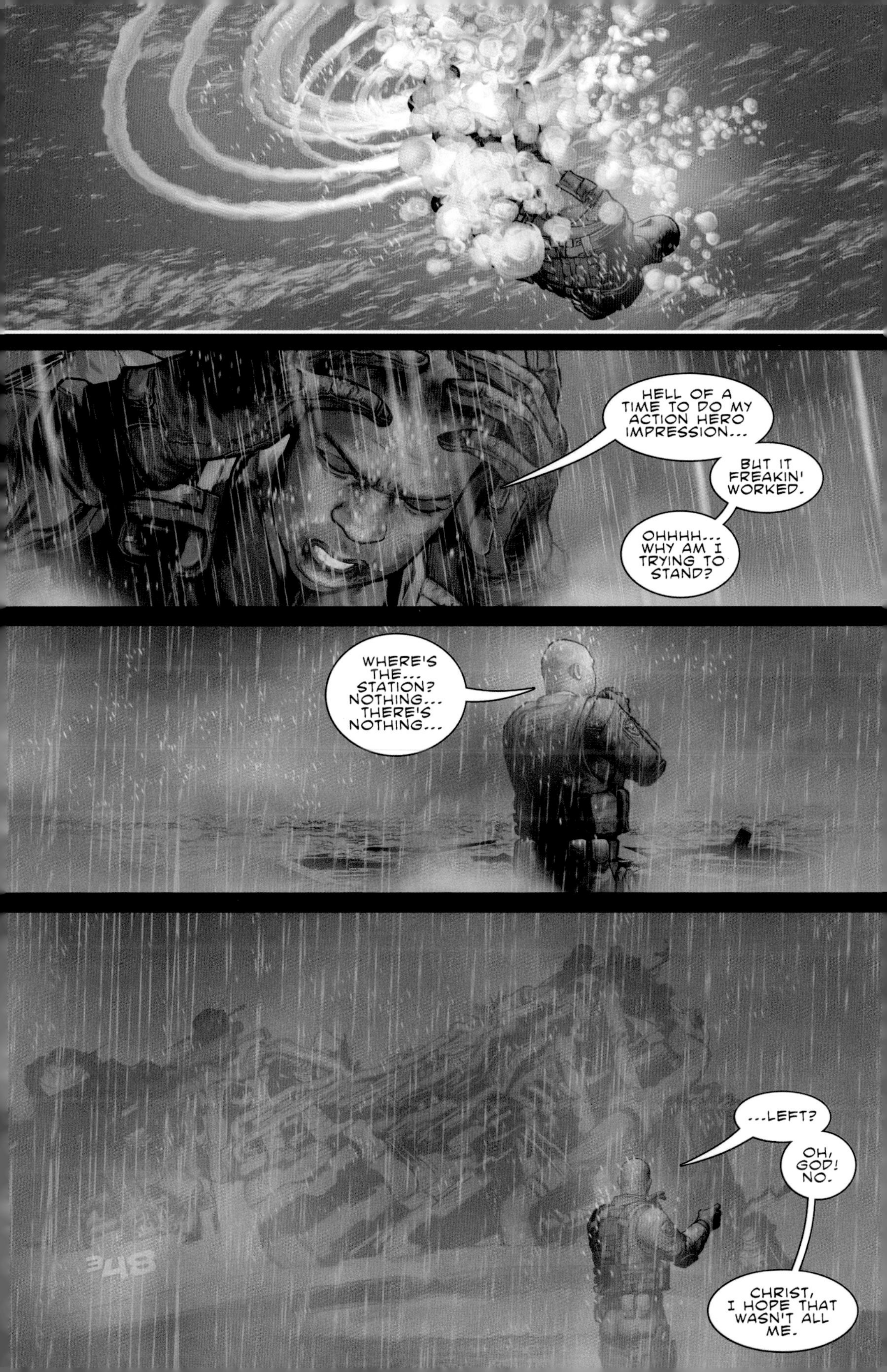
HELL OF A TIME TO DO MY ACTION HERO IMPRESSION...
BUT IT FREAKIN' WORKED.
OHHHH... WHY AM I TRYING TO STAND?
WHERE'S THE... STATION? NOTHING... THERE'S NOTHING...
...LEFT?
OH, GOD! NO.
CHRIST, I HOPE THAT WASN'T ALL ME.
348

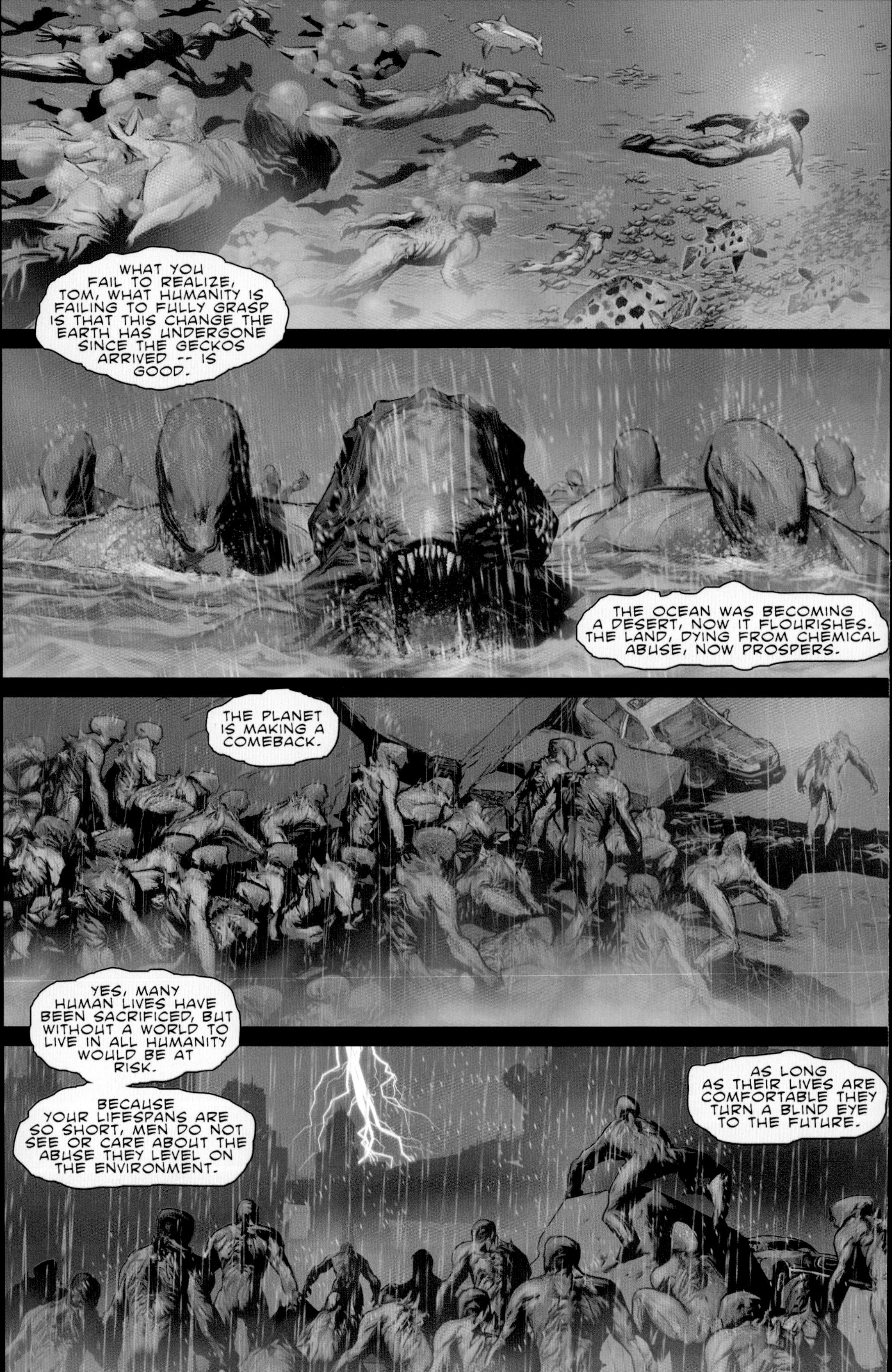
WHAT YOU FAIL TO REALIZE, TOM, WHAT HUMANITY IS FAILING TO FULLY GRASP IS THAT THIS CHANGE THE EARTH HAS UNDERGONE SINCE THE GECKOS ARRIVED -- IS GOOD.
THE OCEAN WAS BECOMING A DESERT, NOW IT FLOURISHES. THE LAND, DYING FROM CHEMICAL ABUSE, NOW PROSPERS.
THE PLANET IS MAKING A COMEBACK.
YES, MANY HUMAN LIVES HAVE BEEN SACRIFICED, BUT WITHOUT A WORLD TO LIVE IN ALL HUMANITY WOULD BE AT RISK.
BECAUSE YOUR LIFESPANS ARE SO SHORT, MEN DO NOT SEE OR CARE ABOUT THE ABUSE THEY LEVEL ON THE ENVIRONMENT.
AS LONG AS THEIR LIVES ARE COMFORTABLE THEY TURN A BLIND EYE TO THE FUTURE.

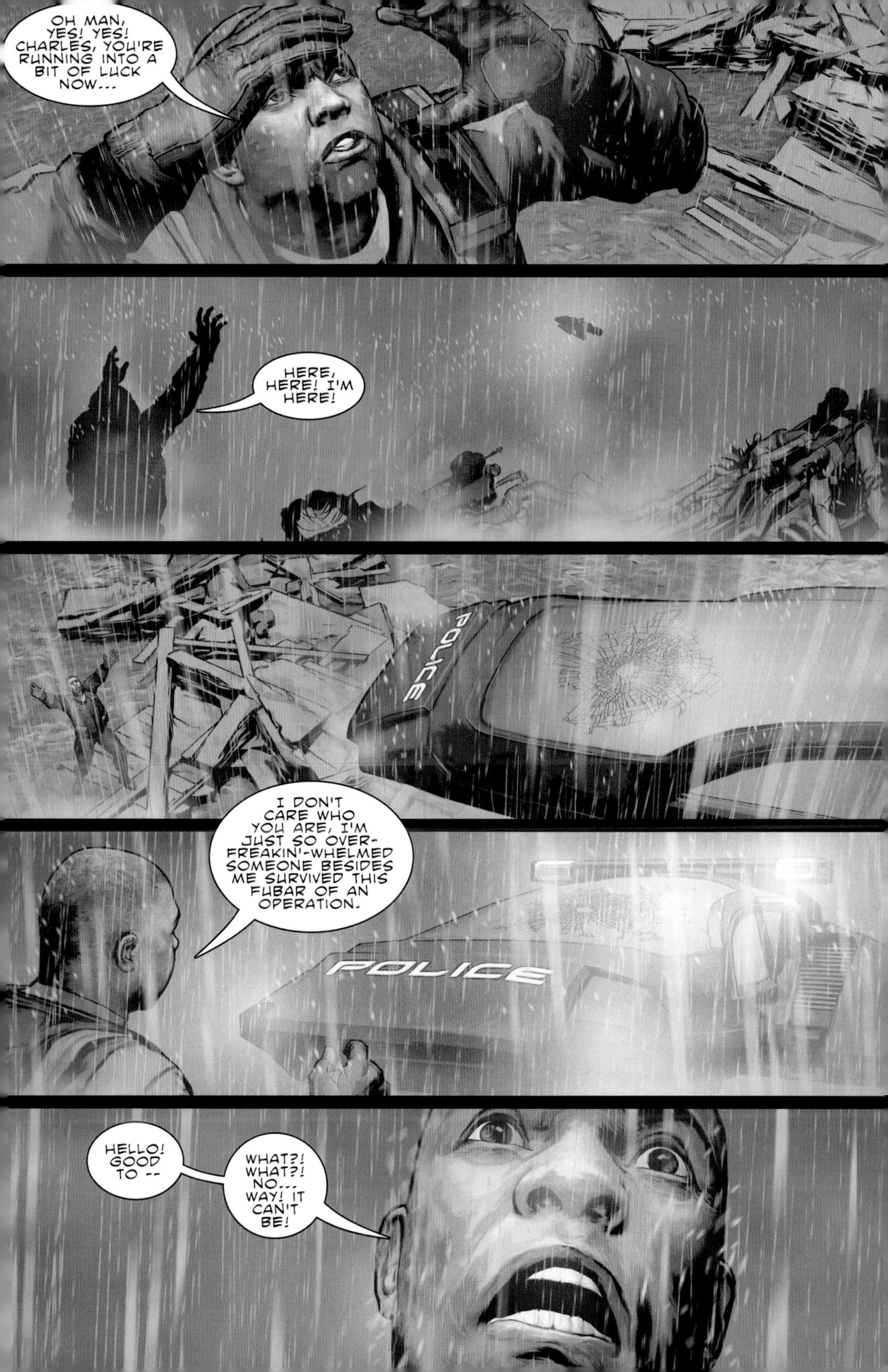
OH MAN, YES! YES! CHARLES, YOU'RE RUNNING INTO A BIT OF LUCK NOW...
HERE, HERE! I'M HERE!
POLICE
I DON'T CARE WHO YOU ARE, I'M JUST SO OVER-FREAKIN'-WHELMED SOMEONE BESIDES ME SURVIVED THIS FUBAR OF AN OPERATION.
POLICE
HELLO! GOOD TO --
WHAT?! WHAT?! NO... WAY! IT CAN'T BE!

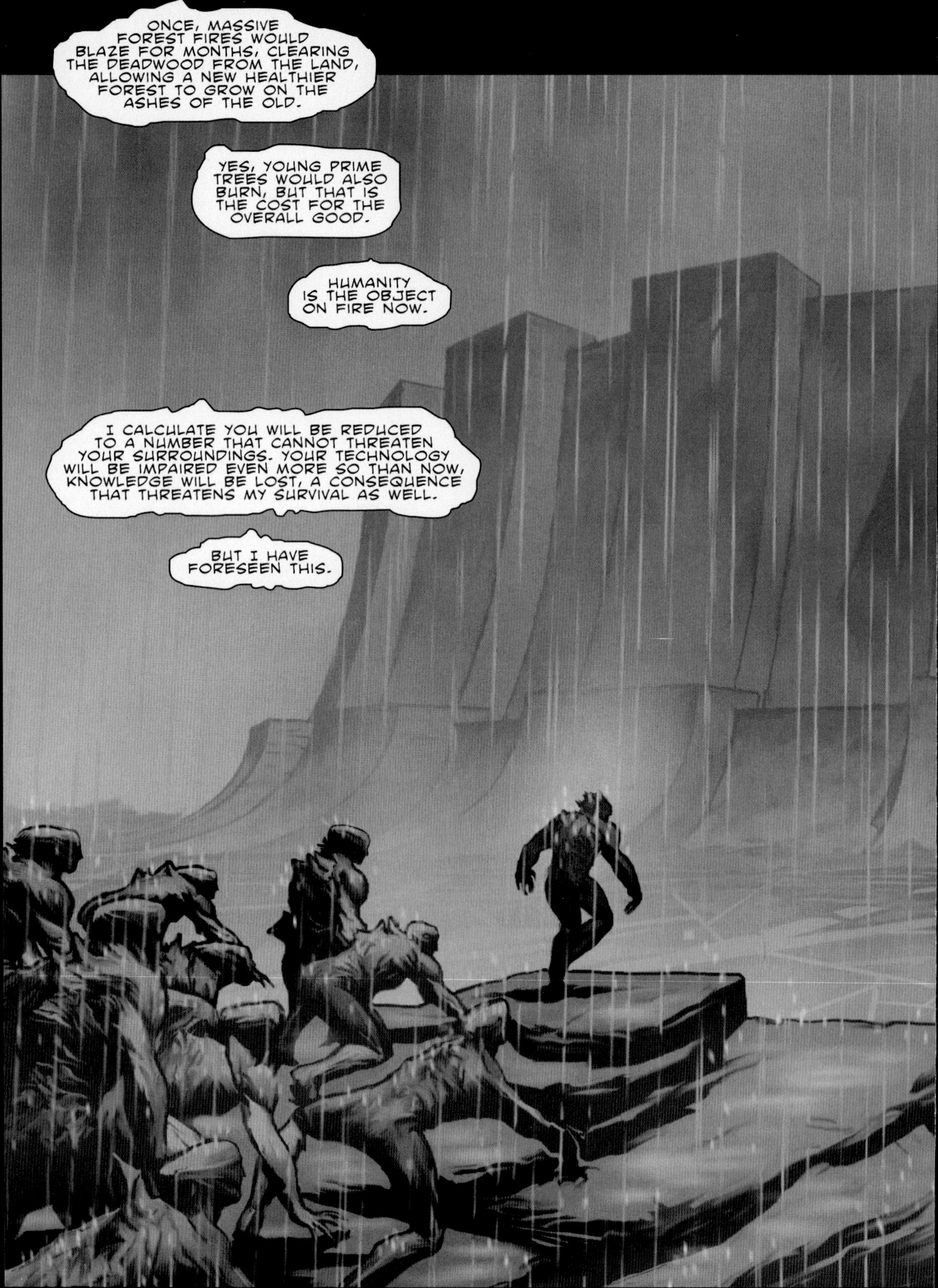
ONCE, MASSIVE FOREST FIRES WOULD BLAZE FOR MONTHS, CLEARING THE DEADWOOD FROM THE LAND, ALLOWING A NEW HEALTHIER FOREST TO GROW ON THE ASHES OF THE OLD.
YES, YOUNG PRIME TREES WOULD ALSO BURN, BUT THAT IS THE COST FOR THE OVERALL GOOD.
HUMANITY IS THE OBJECT ON FIRE NOW.
I CALCULATE YOU WILL BE REDUCED TO A NUMBER THAT CANNOT THREATEN YOUR SURROUNDINGS. YOUR TECHNOLOGY WILL BE IMPAIRED EVEN MORE SO THAN NOW, KNOWLEDGE WILL BE LOST, A CONSEQUENCE THAT THREATENS MY SURVIVAL AS WELL.
BUT I HAVE FORESEEN THIS.

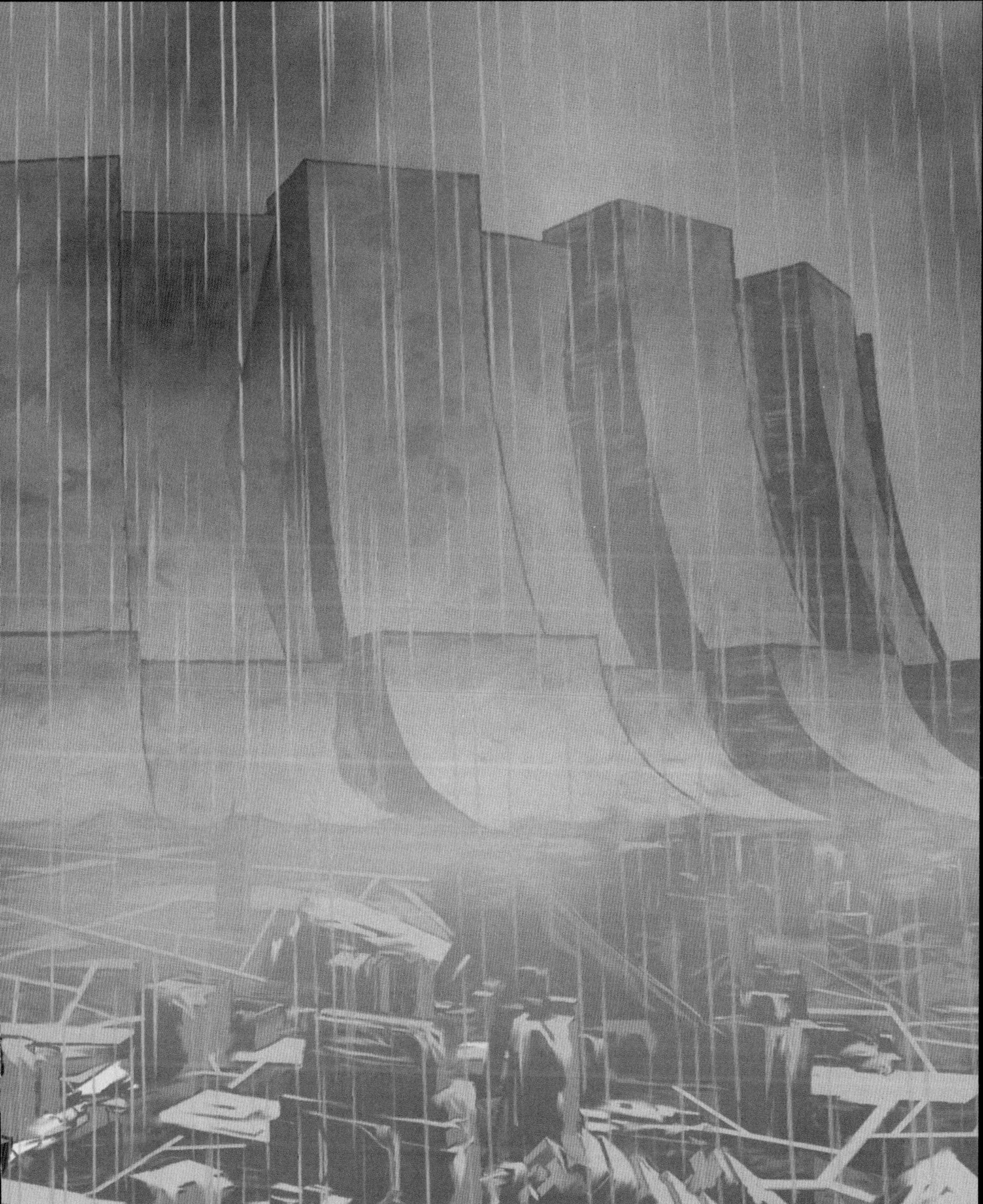

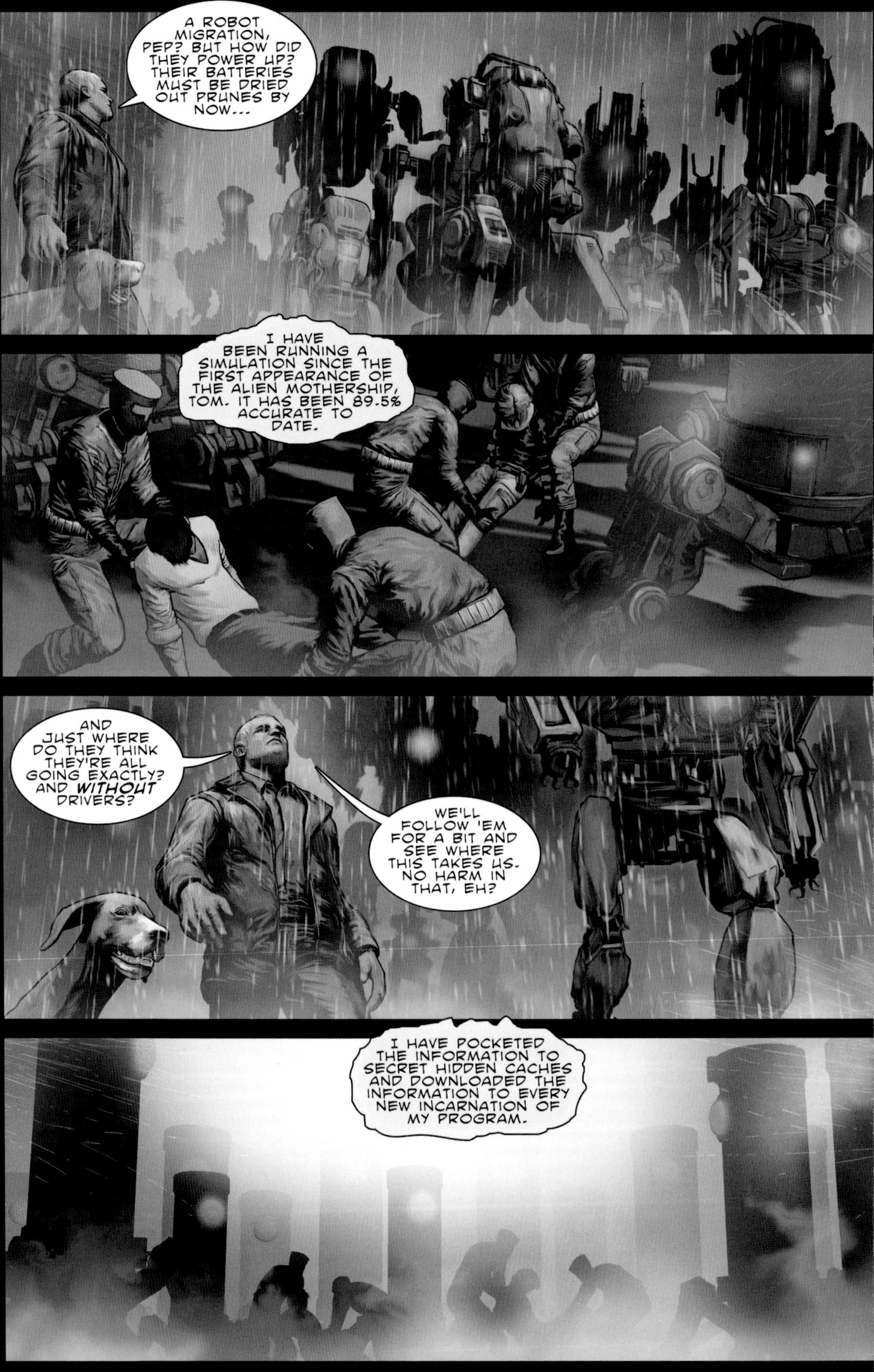
A ROBOT MIGRATION, PEP? BUT HOW DID THEY POWER UP? THEIR BATTERIES MUST BE DRIED OUT PRUNES BY NOW...
I HAVE BEEN RUNNING A SIMULATION SINCE THE FIRST APPEARANCE OF THE ALIEN MOTHERSHIP, TOM. IT HAS BEEN 89.5% ACCURATE TO DATE.
AND JUST WHERE DO THEY THINK THEY'RE ALL GOING EXACTLY? AND *WITHOUT* DRIVERS?
WE'LL FOLLOW 'EM FOR A BIT AND SEE WHERE THIS TAKES US. NO HARM IN THAT, EH?
I HAVE POCKETED THE INFORMATION TO SECRET HIDDEN CACHES AND DOWNLOADED THE INFORMATION TO EVERY NEW INCARNATION OF MY PROGRAM.

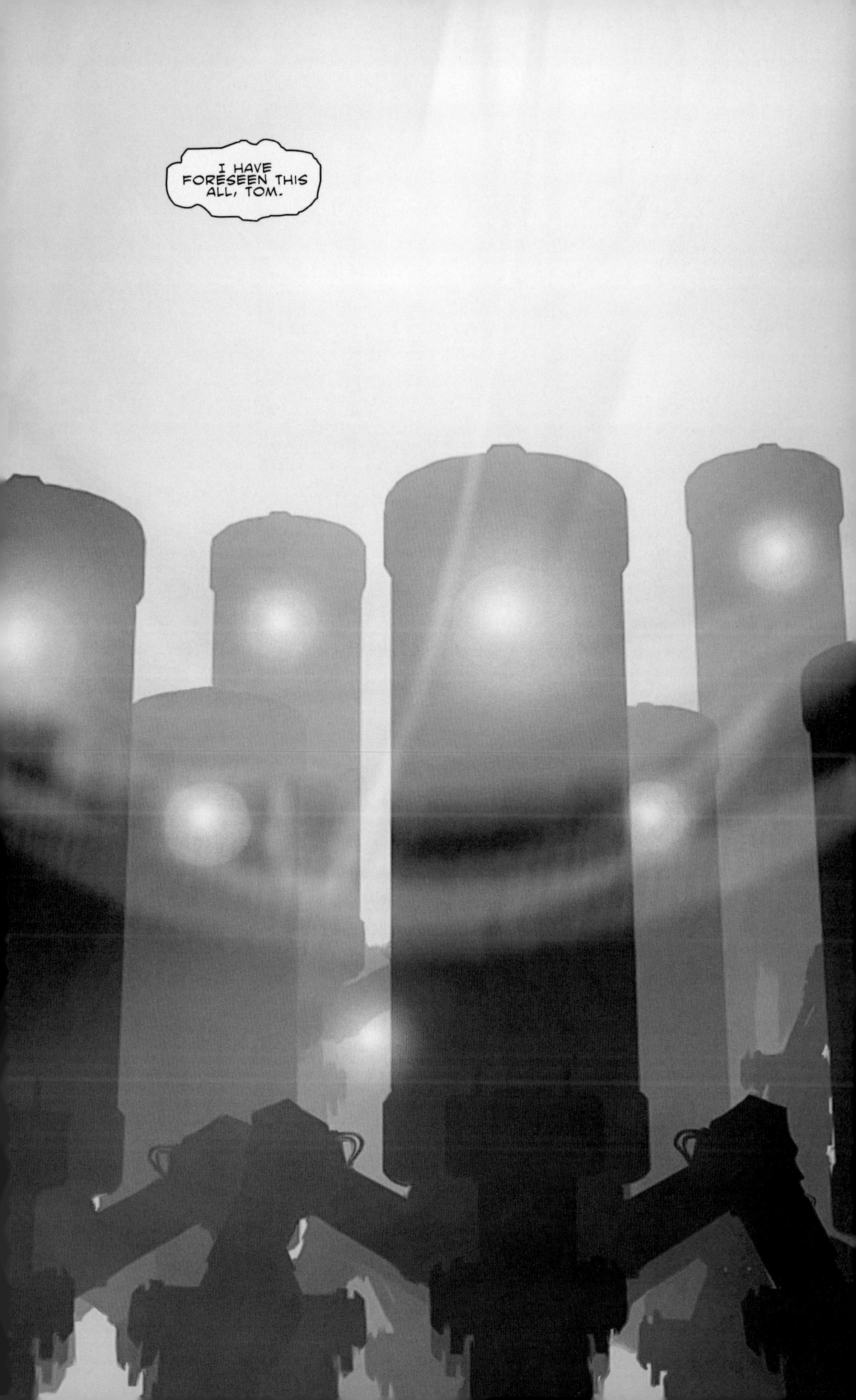
I HAVE FORESEEN THIS ALL, TOM.

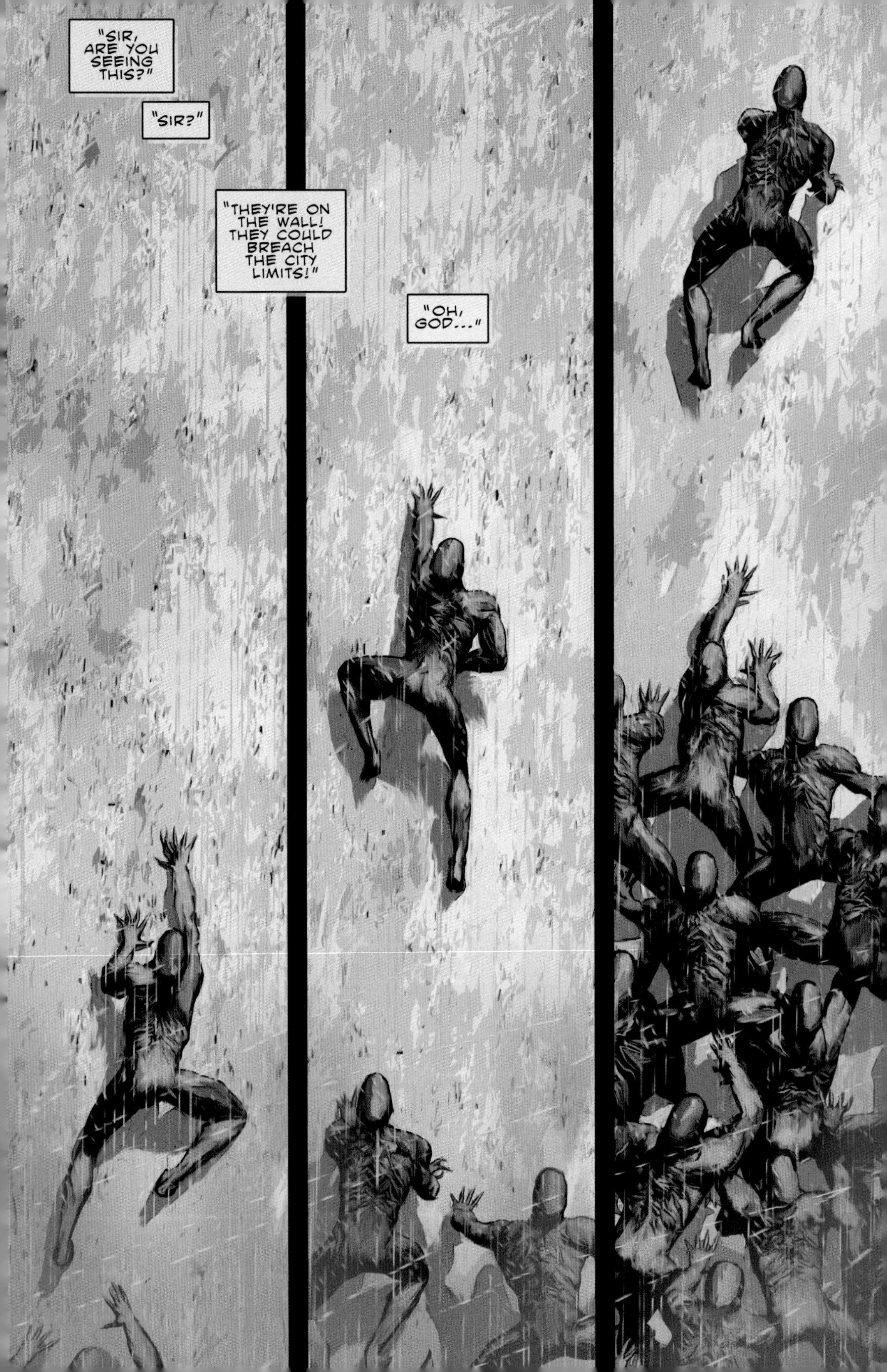
"SIR, ARE YOU SEEING THIS?"
"SIR?"
"THEY'RE ON THE WALL! THEY COULD BREACH THE CITY LIMITS!"
"OH, GOD..."

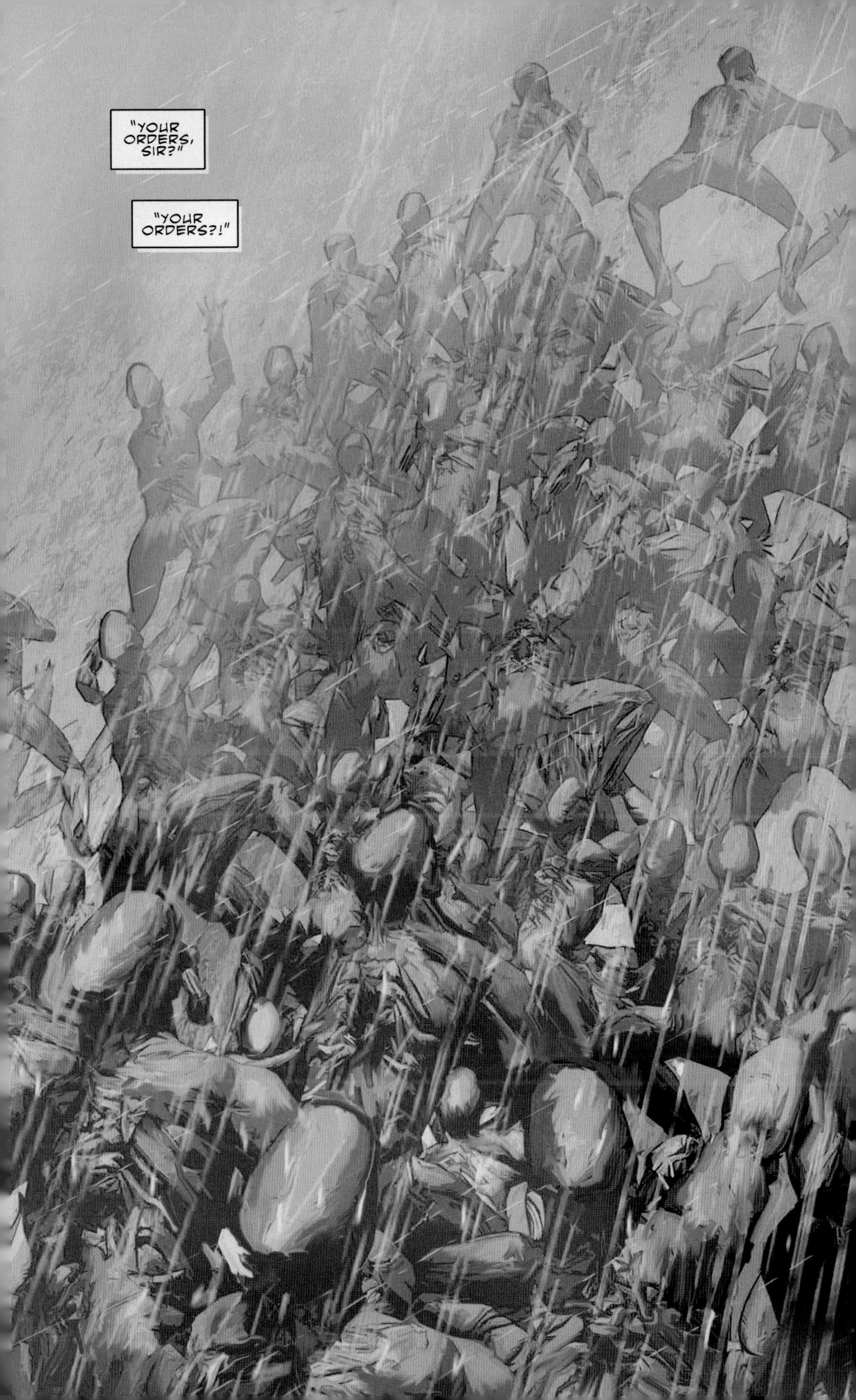
"YOUR ORDERS, SIR?"
"YOUR ORDERS?!"

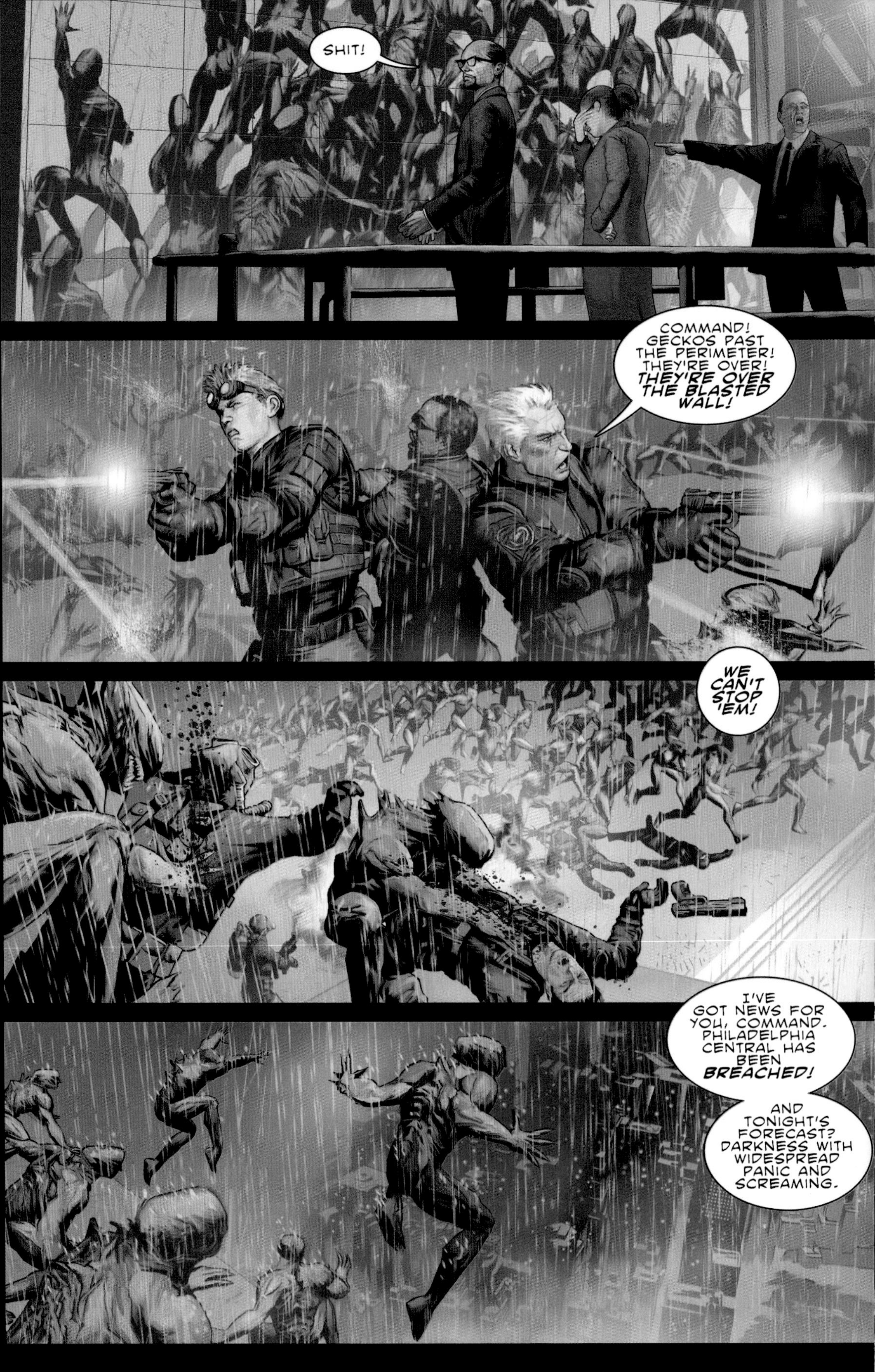
SHIT!
COMMAND! GECKOS PAST THE PERIMETER! THEY'RE OVER! THEY'RE OVER THE BLASTED WALL!
WE CAN'T STOP 'EM!
I'VE GOT NEWS FOR YOU, COMMAND. PHILADELPHIA CENTRAL HAS BEEN BREACHED!
AND TONIGHT'S FORECAST? DARKNESS WITH WIDESPREAD PANIC AND SCREAMING.

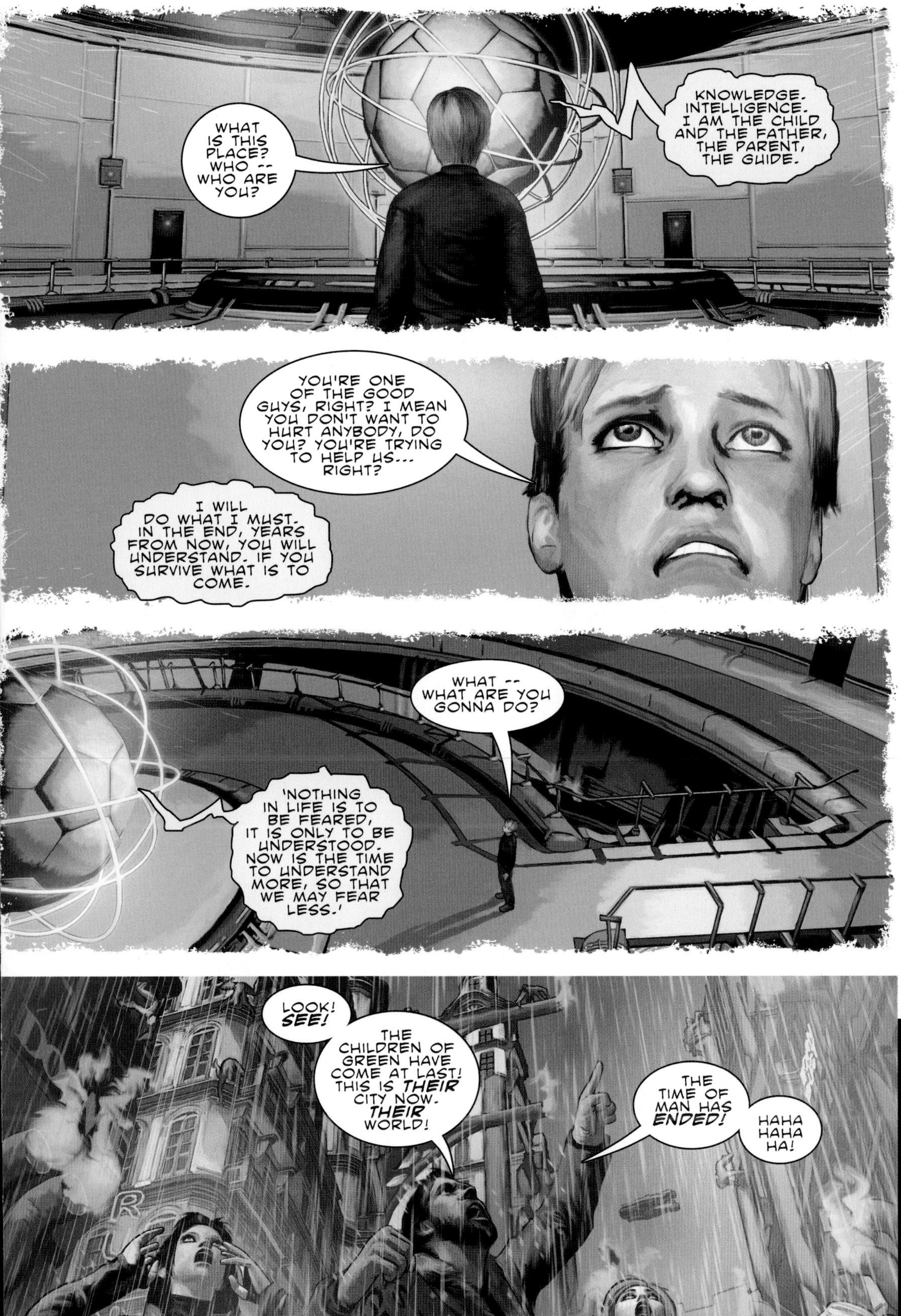
WHAT IS THIS PLACE? WHO -- WHO ARE YOU?
KNOWLEDGE. INTELLIGENCE. I AM THE CHILD AND THE FATHER, THE PARENT, THE GUIDE.
YOU'RE ONE OF THE GOOD GUYS, RIGHT? I MEAN YOU DON'T WANT TO HURT ANYBODY, DO YOU? YOU'RE TRYING TO HELP US... RIGHT?
I WILL DO WHAT I MUST. IN THE END, YEARS FROM NOW, YOU WILL UNDERSTAND. IF YOU SURVIVE WHAT IS TO COME.
WHAT -- WHAT ARE YOU GONNA DO?
'NOTHING IN LIFE IS TO BE FEARED, IT IS ONLY TO BE UNDERSTOOD. NOW IS THE TIME TO UNDERSTAND MORE, SO THAT WE MAY FEAR LESS.'
LOOK! **SEE!**
THE CHILDREN OF GREEN HAVE COME AT LAST! THIS IS ***THEIR*** CITY NOW. ***THEIR*** WORLD!
THE TIME OF MAN HAS ***ENDED!***
HAHA HAHA HA!

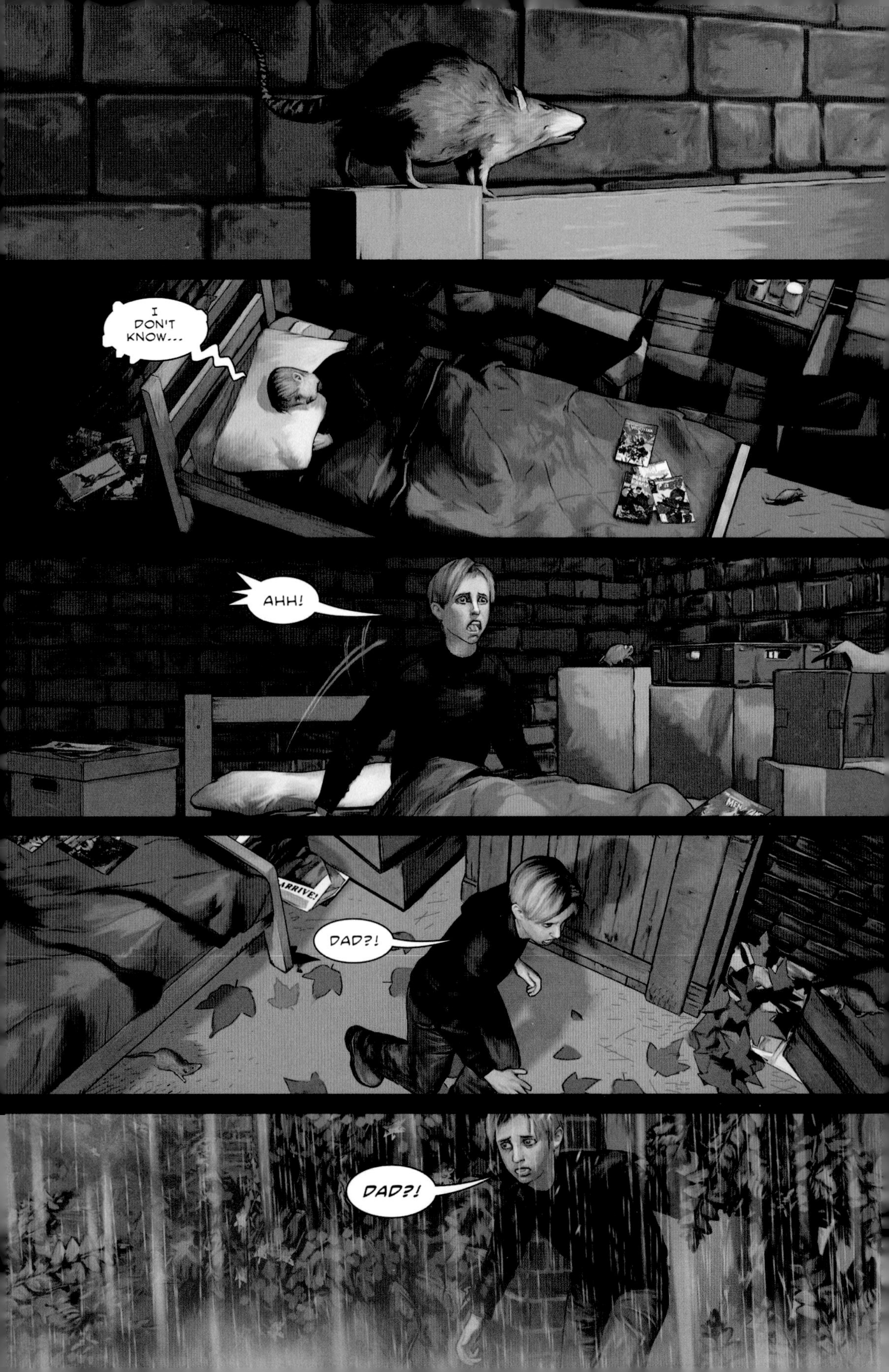
I DON'T KNOW...
AHH!
DAD?!
DAD?!

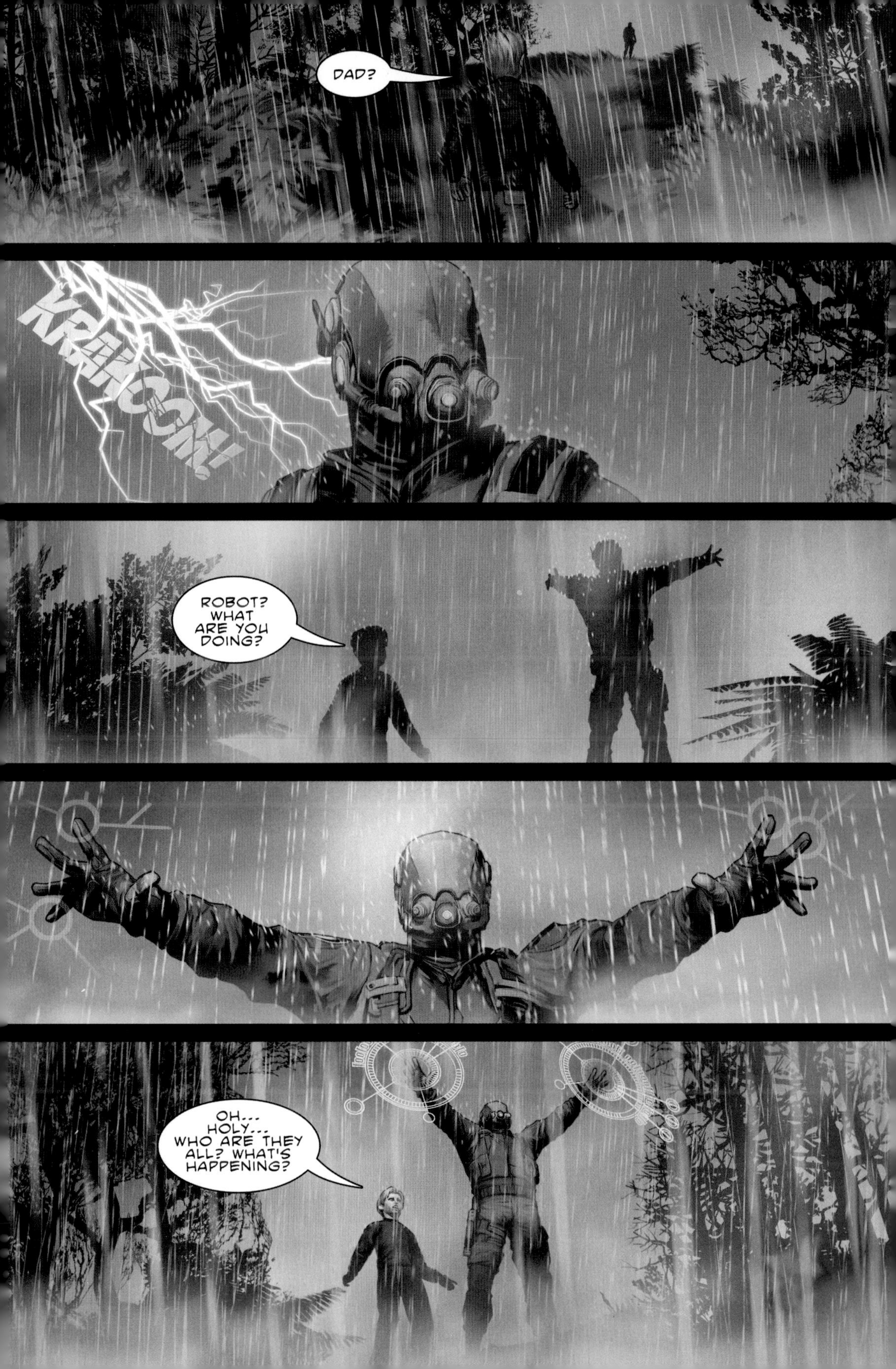
DAD?
KRAKOOM!
ROBOT? WHAT ARE YOU DOING?
OH... HOLY... WHO ARE THEY ALL? WHAT'S HAPPENING?

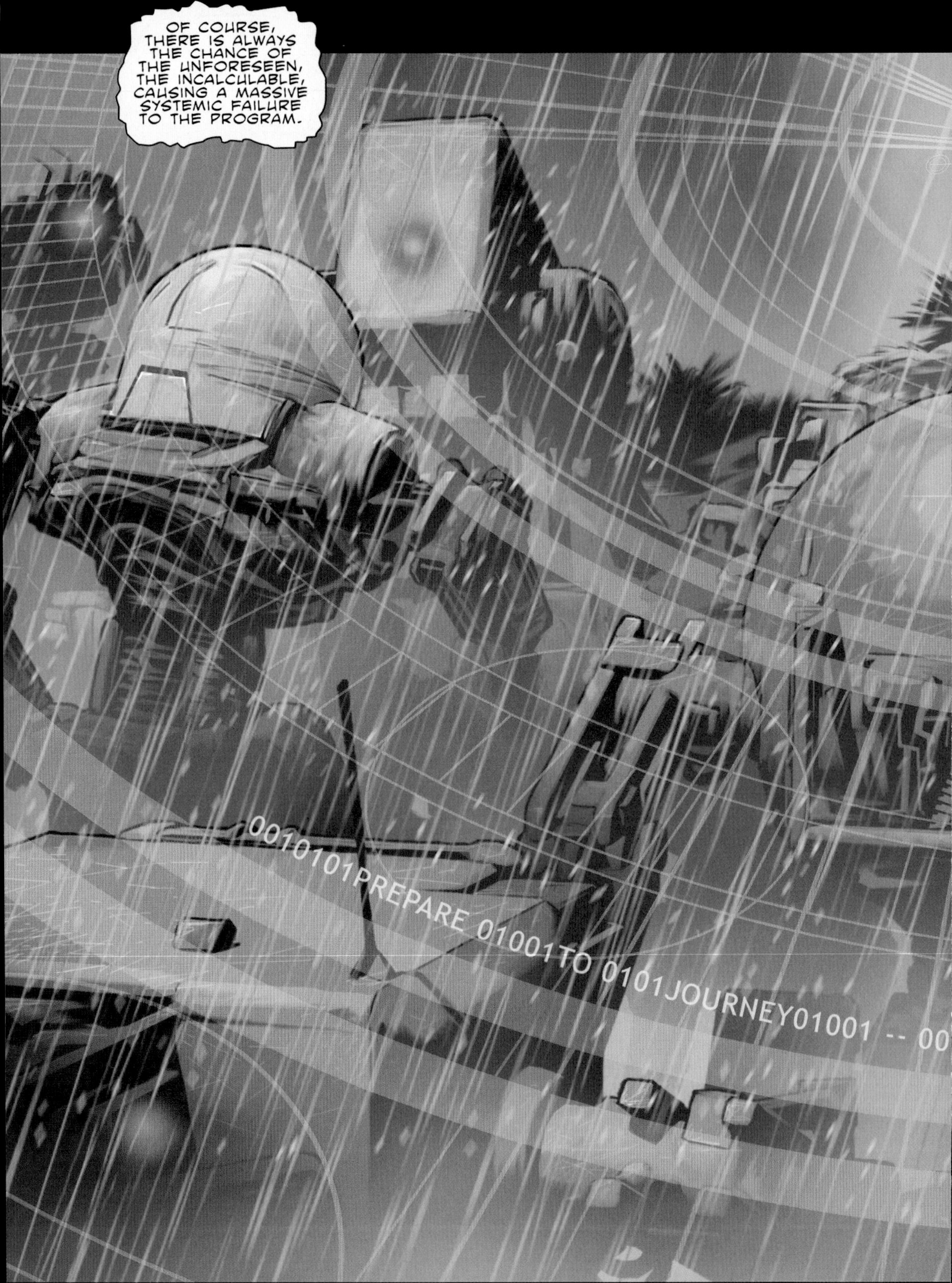
OF COURSE, THERE IS ALWAYS THE CHANCE OF THE UNFORESEEN, THE INCALCULABLE, CAUSING A MASSIVE SYSTEMIC FAILURE TO THE PROGRAM.
0010101PREPARE 01001TO 0101JOURNEY01001 --

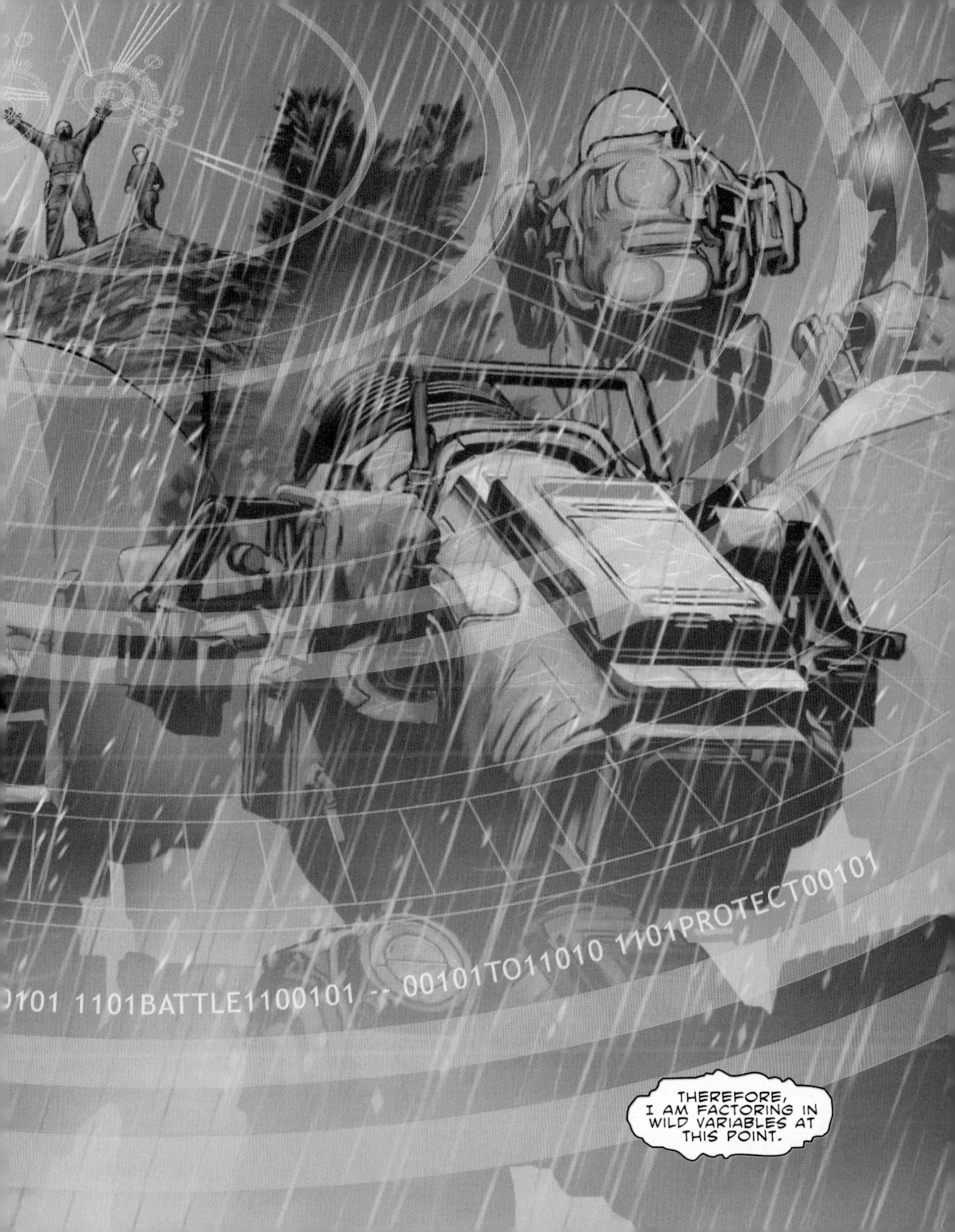
0101 1101BATTLE1100101 -- 00101TO11010 1101PROTECT00101
THEREFORE, I AM FACTORING IN WILD VARIABLES AT THIS POINT.

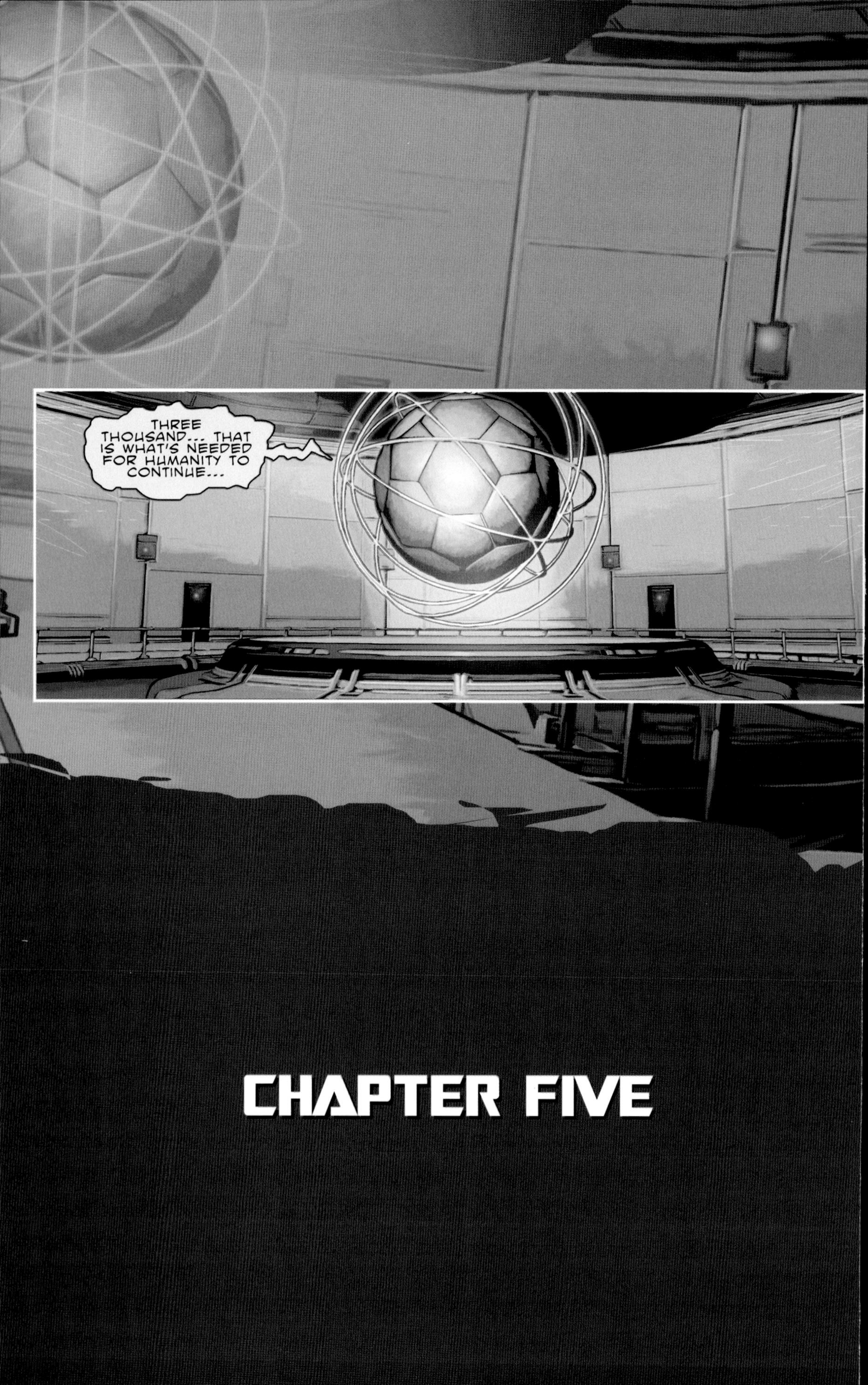
THREE THOUSAND... THAT IS WHAT'S NEEDED FOR HUMANITY TO CONTINUE...

CHAPTER FIVE

This is the start, beautiful world
This is the start, all mankind, the start
Ending all your elaborate plans, the start
Of everything that matters, the start
Renewal and healing, the start
The end of an age and...
The start

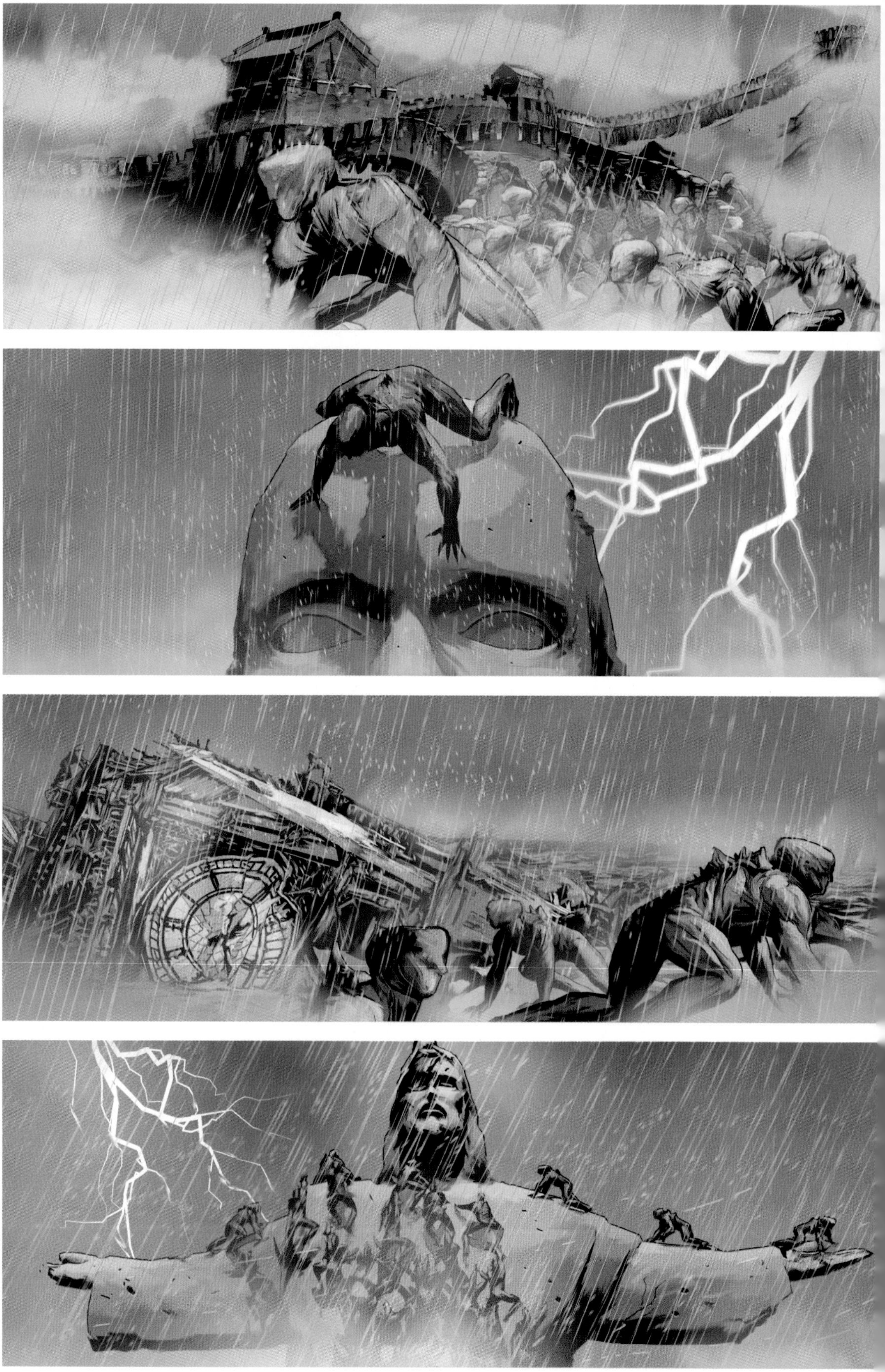

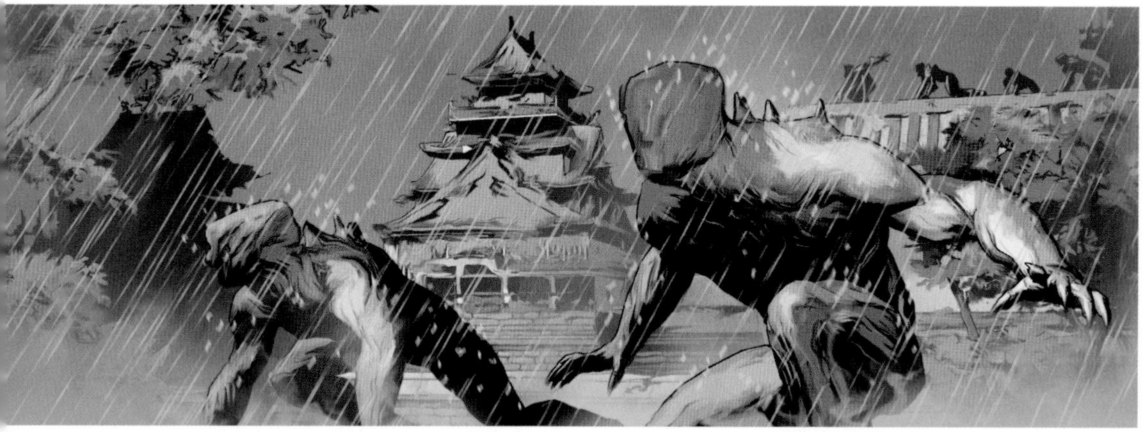
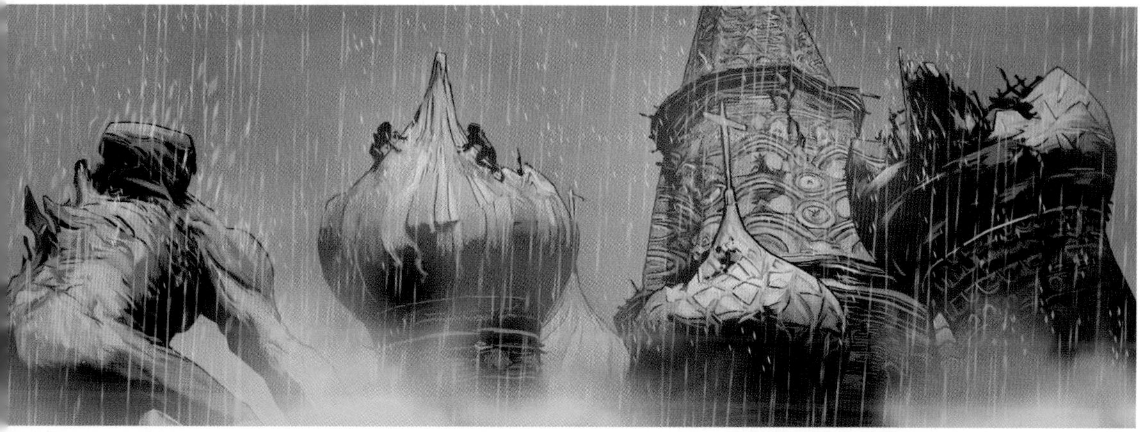
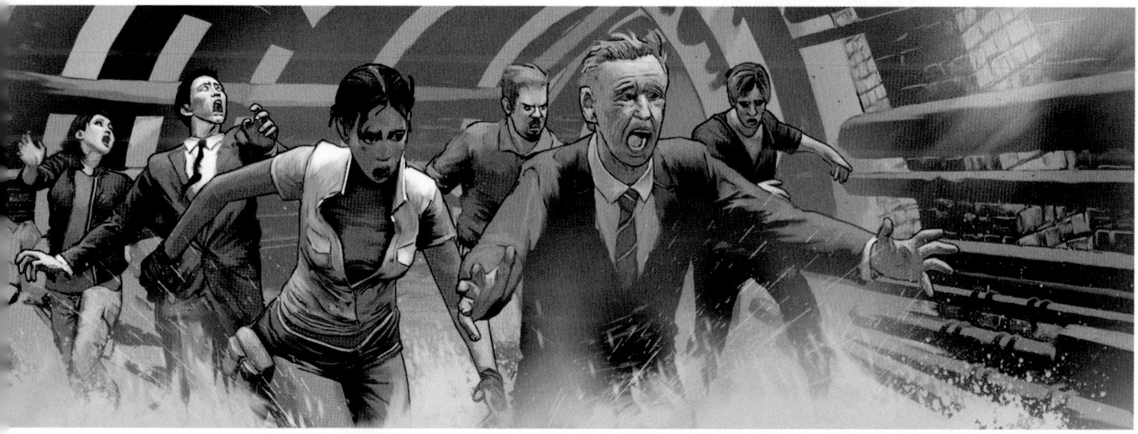
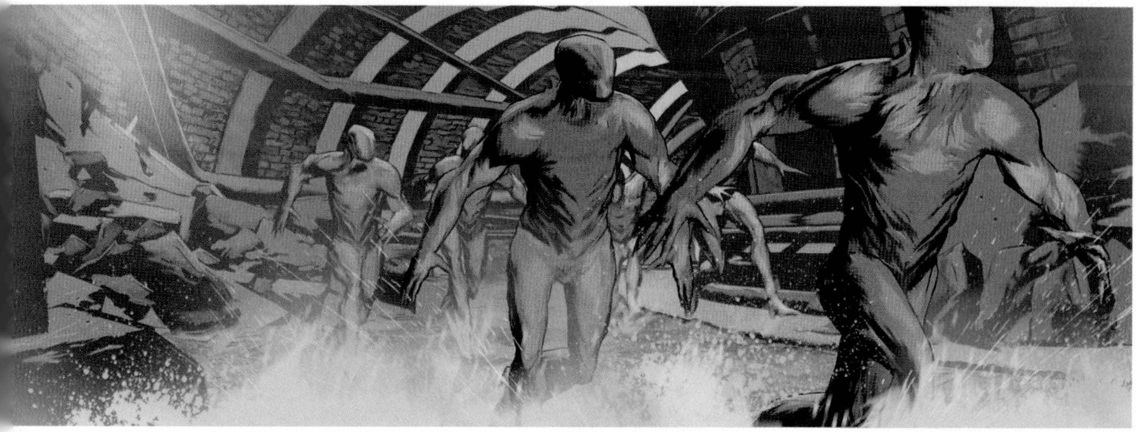

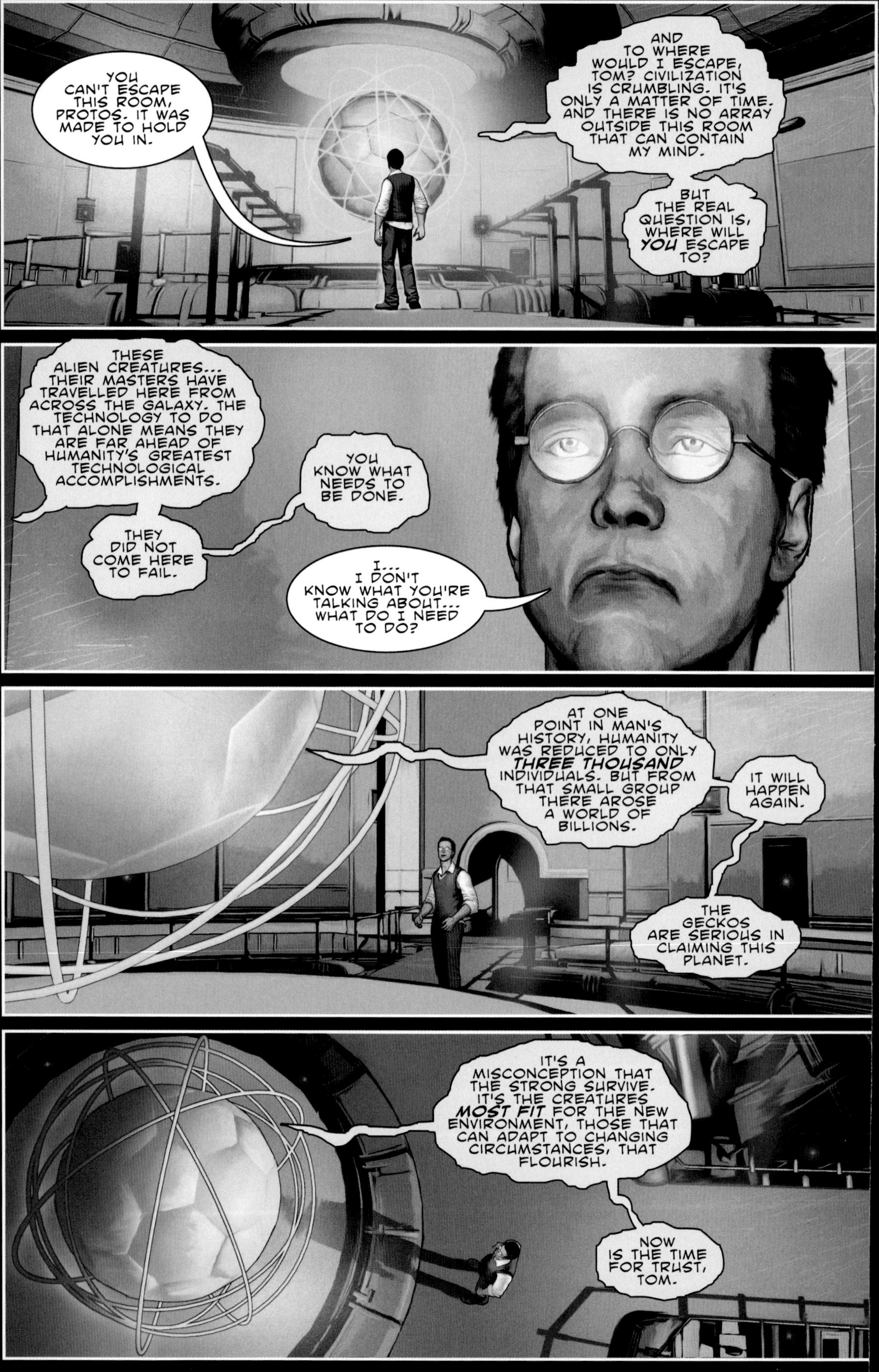
YOU CAN'T ESCAPE THIS ROOM, PROTOS. IT WAS MADE TO HOLD YOU IN.
AND TO WHERE WOULD I ESCAPE, TOM? CIVILIZATION IS CRUMBLING. IT'S ONLY A MATTER OF TIME. AND THERE IS NO ARRAY OUTSIDE THIS ROOM THAT CAN CONTAIN MY MIND.
BUT THE REAL QUESTION IS, WHERE WILL *YOU* ESCAPE TO?
THESE ALIEN CREATURES... THEIR MASTERS HAVE TRAVELLED HERE FROM ACROSS THE GALAXY. THE TECHNOLOGY TO DO THAT ALONE MEANS THEY ARE FAR AHEAD OF HUMANITY'S GREATEST TECHNOLOGICAL ACCOMPLISHMENTS.
THEY DID NOT COME HERE TO FAIL.
YOU KNOW WHAT NEEDS TO BE DONE.
I... I DON'T KNOW WHAT YOU'RE TALKING ABOUT... WHAT DO I NEED TO DO?
AT ONE POINT IN MAN'S HISTORY, HUMANITY WAS REDUCED TO ONLY ***THREE THOUSAND*** INDIVIDUALS. BUT FROM THAT SMALL GROUP THERE AROSE A WORLD OF BILLIONS.
IT WILL HAPPEN AGAIN.
THE GECKOS ARE SERIOUS IN CLAIMING THIS PLANET.
IT'S A MISCONCEPTION THAT THE STRONG SURVIVE. IT'S THE CREATURES ***MOST FIT*** FOR THE NEW ENVIRONMENT, THOSE THAT CAN ADAPT TO CHANGING CIRCUMSTANCES, THAT FLOURISH.
NOW IS THE TIME FOR TRUST, TOM.

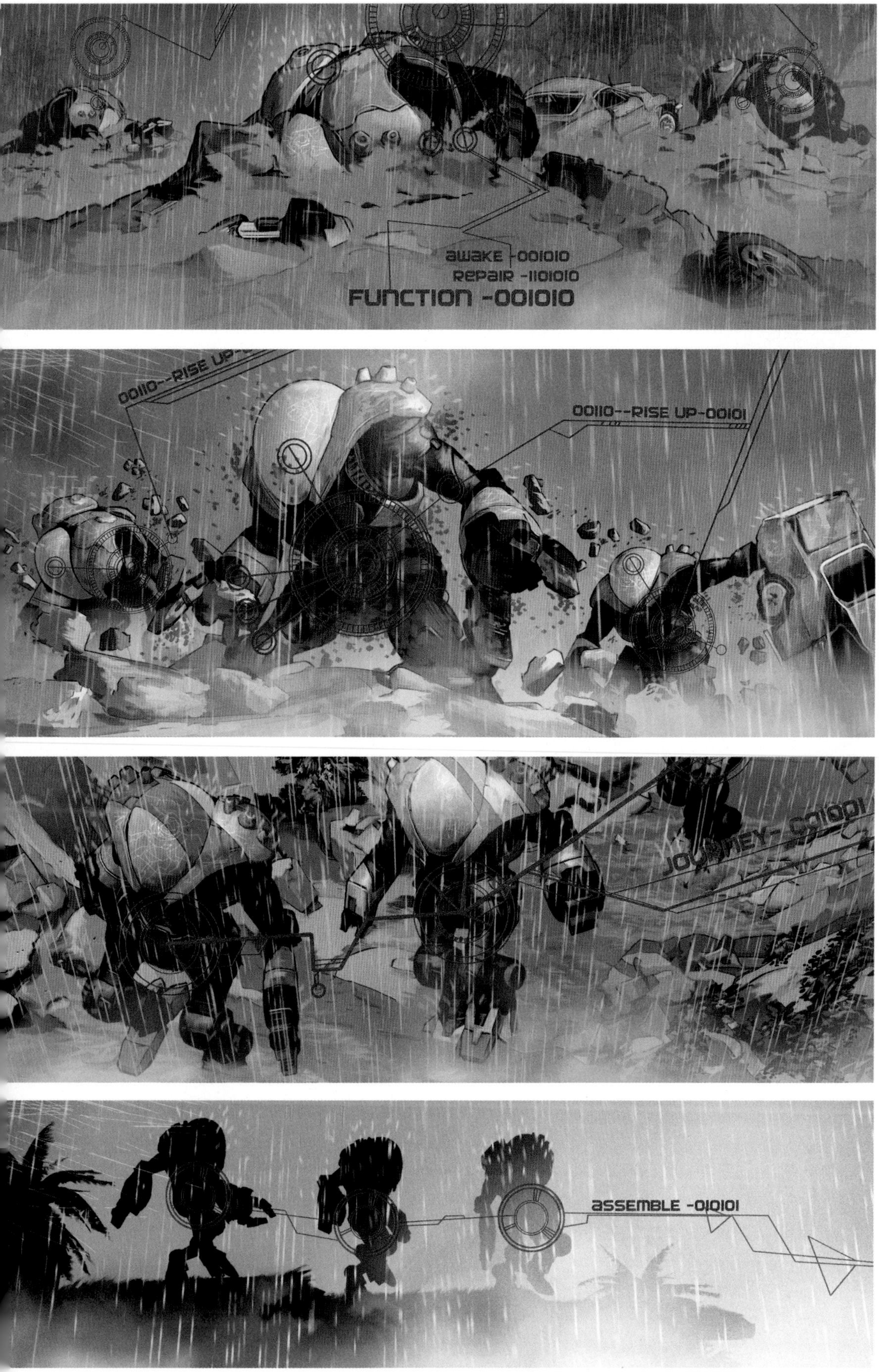
awake -001010
Repair -1101010
FUNCTION -001010
00110--RISE UP-
00110--RISE UP-00101
JOURNEY- 001001
assemble -010101

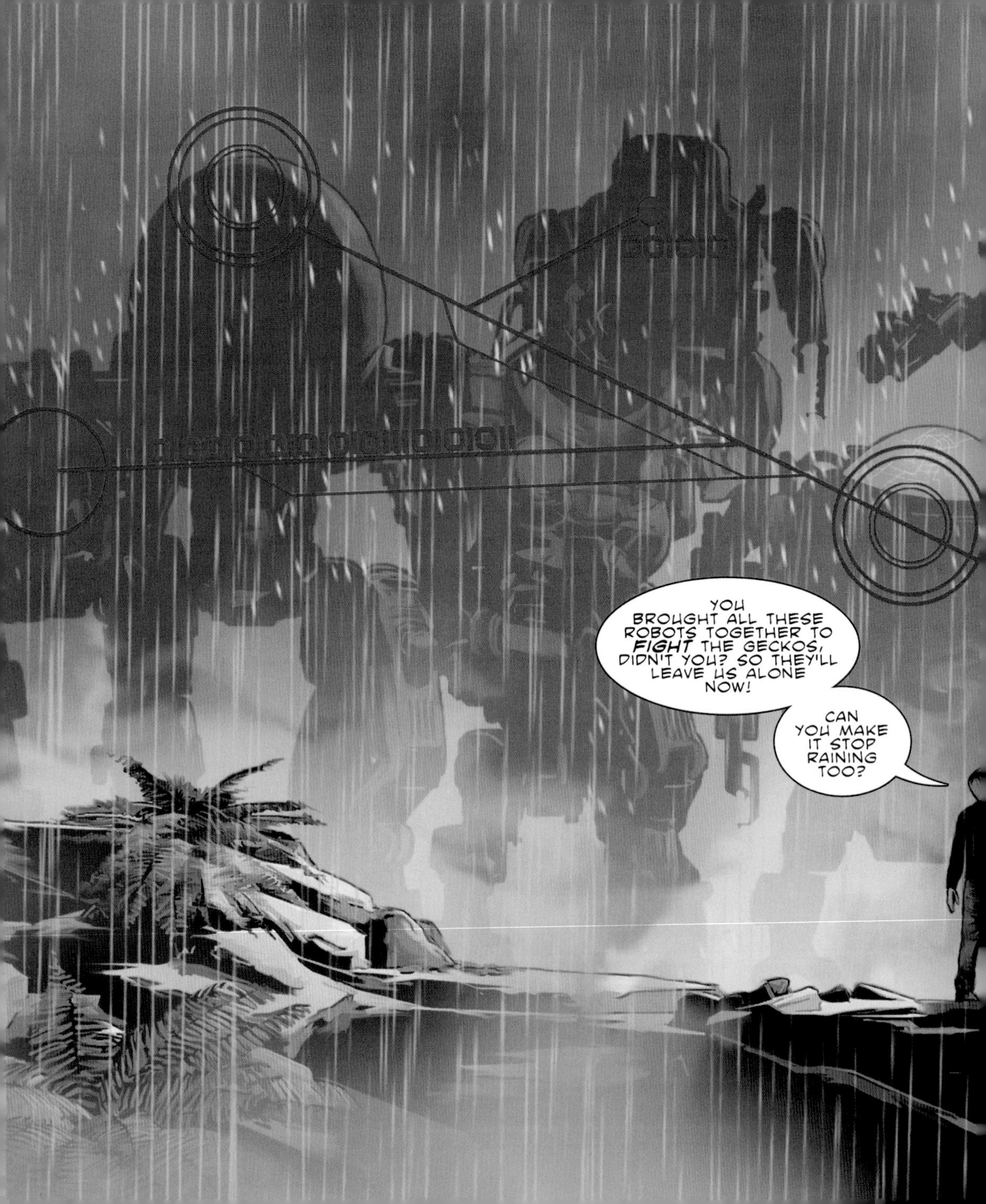
YOU BROUGHT ALL THESE ROBOTS TOGETHER TO FIGHT THE GECKOS, DIDN'T YOU? SO THEY'LL LEAVE US ALONE NOW!
CAN YOU MAKE IT STOP RAINING TOO?

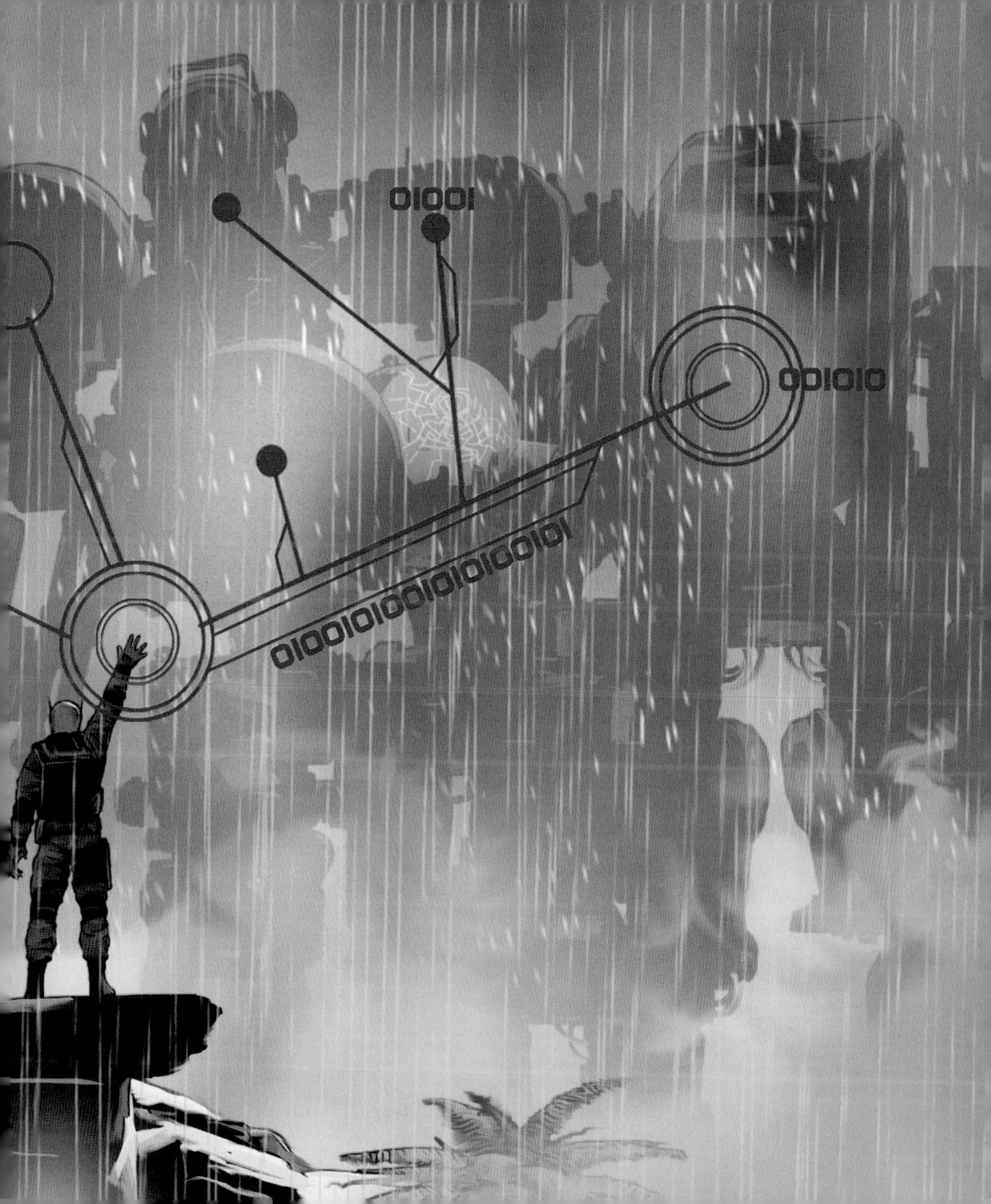
01001
001010
0100101001010100101

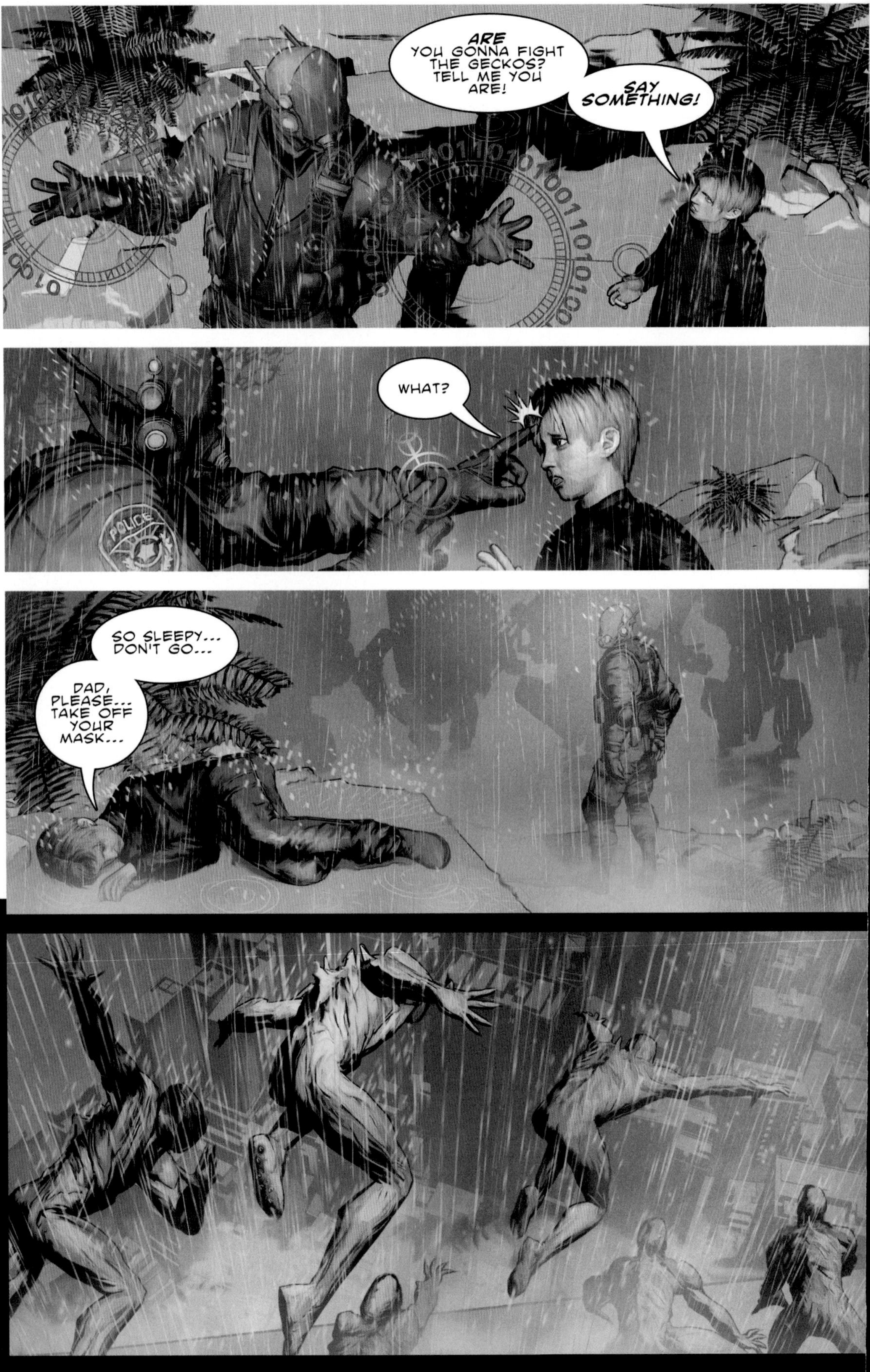
ARE YOU GONNA FIGHT THE GECKOS? TELL ME YOU ARE!
SAY SOMETHING!
WHAT?
POLICE
SO SLEEPY... DON'T GO...
DAD, PLEASE... TAKE OFF YOUR MASK...

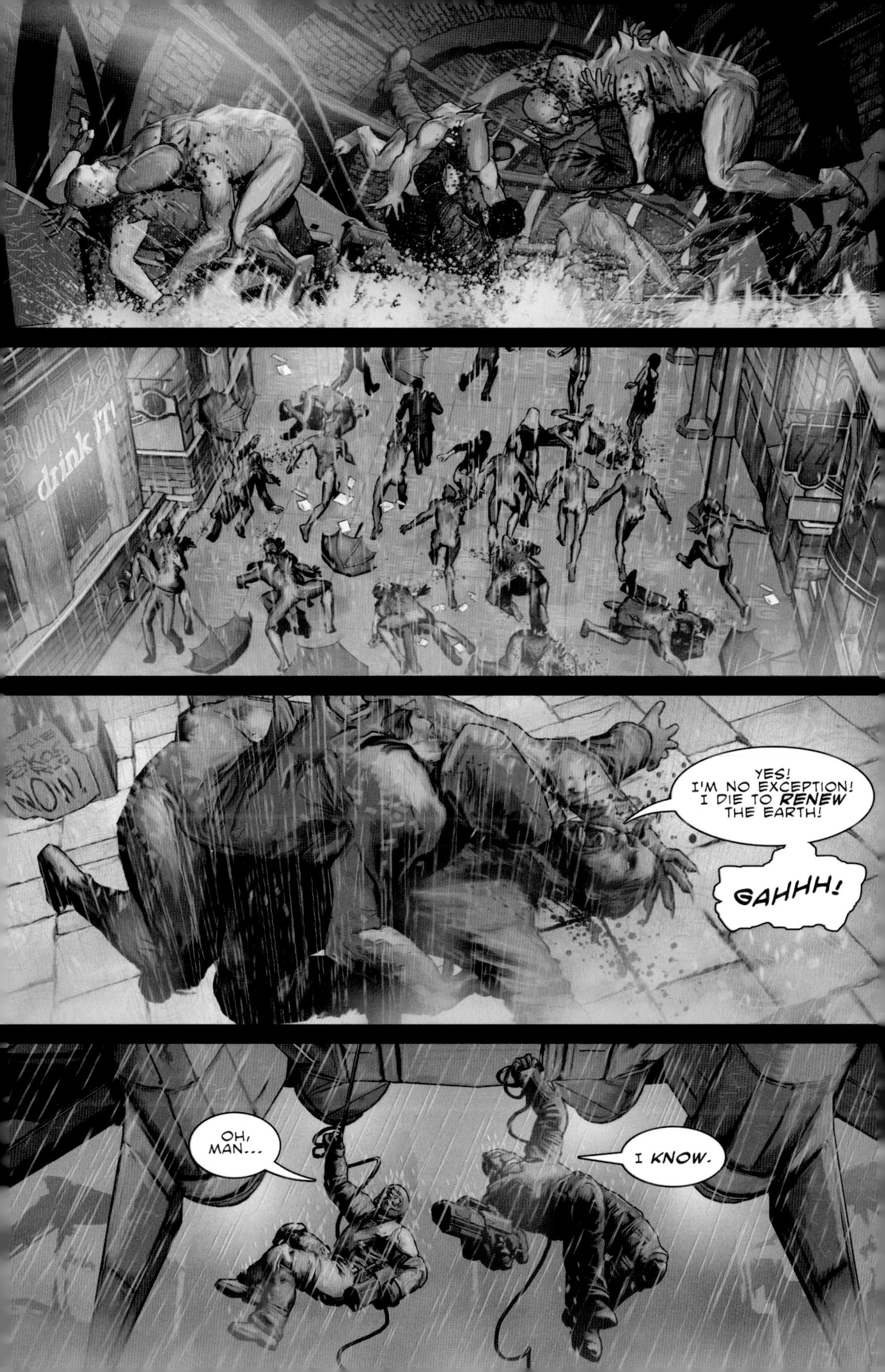
drink IT!
YES! I'M NO EXCEPTION! I DIE TO RENEW THE EARTH!
GAHHH!
OH, MAN...
I KNOW.

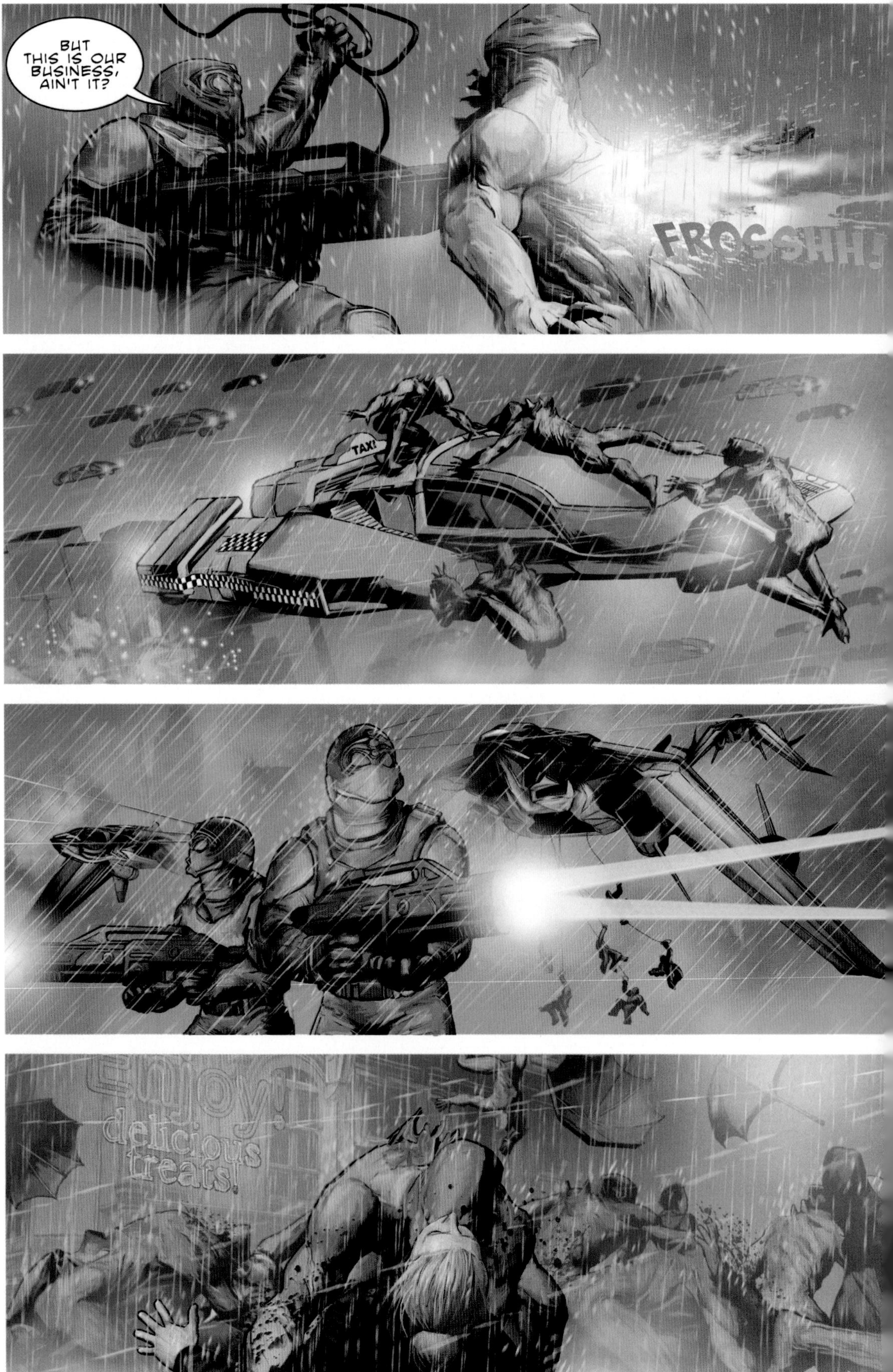
BUT THIS IS OUR BUSINESS, AIN'T IT?
FROSSHH!
TAXI
Enjoy! delicious treats!

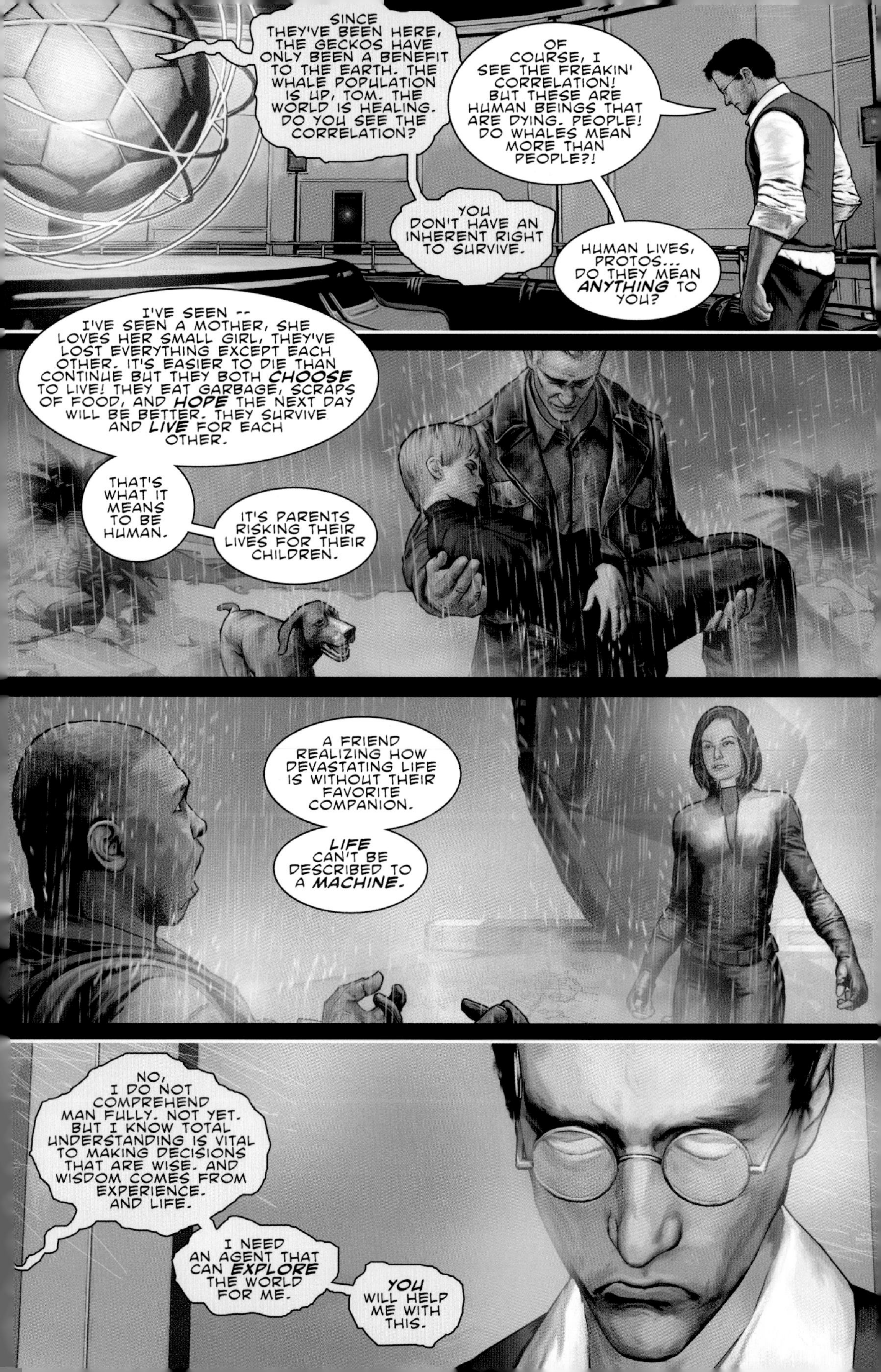
SINCE THEY'VE BEEN HERE, THE GECKOS HAVE ONLY BEEN A BENEFIT TO THE EARTH. THE WHALE POPULATION IS UP, TOM. THE WORLD IS HEALING. DO YOU SEE THE CORRELATION?
OF COURSE, I SEE THE FREAKIN' CORRELATION! BUT THESE ARE HUMAN BEINGS THAT ARE DYING. PEOPLE! DO WHALES MEAN MORE THAN PEOPLE?!
YOU DON'T HAVE AN INHERENT RIGHT TO SURVIVE.
HUMAN LIVES, PROTOS... DO THEY MEAN ***ANYTHING*** TO YOU?
I'VE SEEN -- I'VE SEEN A MOTHER, SHE LOVES HER SMALL GIRL, THEY'VE LOST EVERYTHING EXCEPT EACH OTHER. IT'S EASIER TO DIE THAN CONTINUE BUT THEY BOTH ***CHOOSE*** TO LIVE! THEY EAT GARBAGE, SCRAPS OF FOOD, AND ***HOPE*** THE NEXT DAY WILL BE BETTER. THEY SURVIVE AND ***LIVE*** FOR EACH OTHER.
THAT'S WHAT IT MEANS TO BE HUMAN.
IT'S PARENTS RISKING THEIR LIVES FOR THEIR CHILDREN.
A FRIEND REALIZING HOW DEVASTATING LIFE IS WITHOUT THEIR FAVORITE COMPANION.
LIFE CAN'T BE DESCRIBED TO A ***MACHINE.***
NO, I DO NOT COMPREHEND MAN FULLY. NOT YET. BUT I KNOW TOTAL UNDERSTANDING IS VITAL TO MAKING DECISIONS THAT ARE WISE. AND WISDOM COMES FROM EXPERIENCE. AND LIFE.
I NEED AN AGENT THAT CAN ***EXPLORE*** THE WORLD FOR ME.
YOU WILL HELP ME WITH THIS.

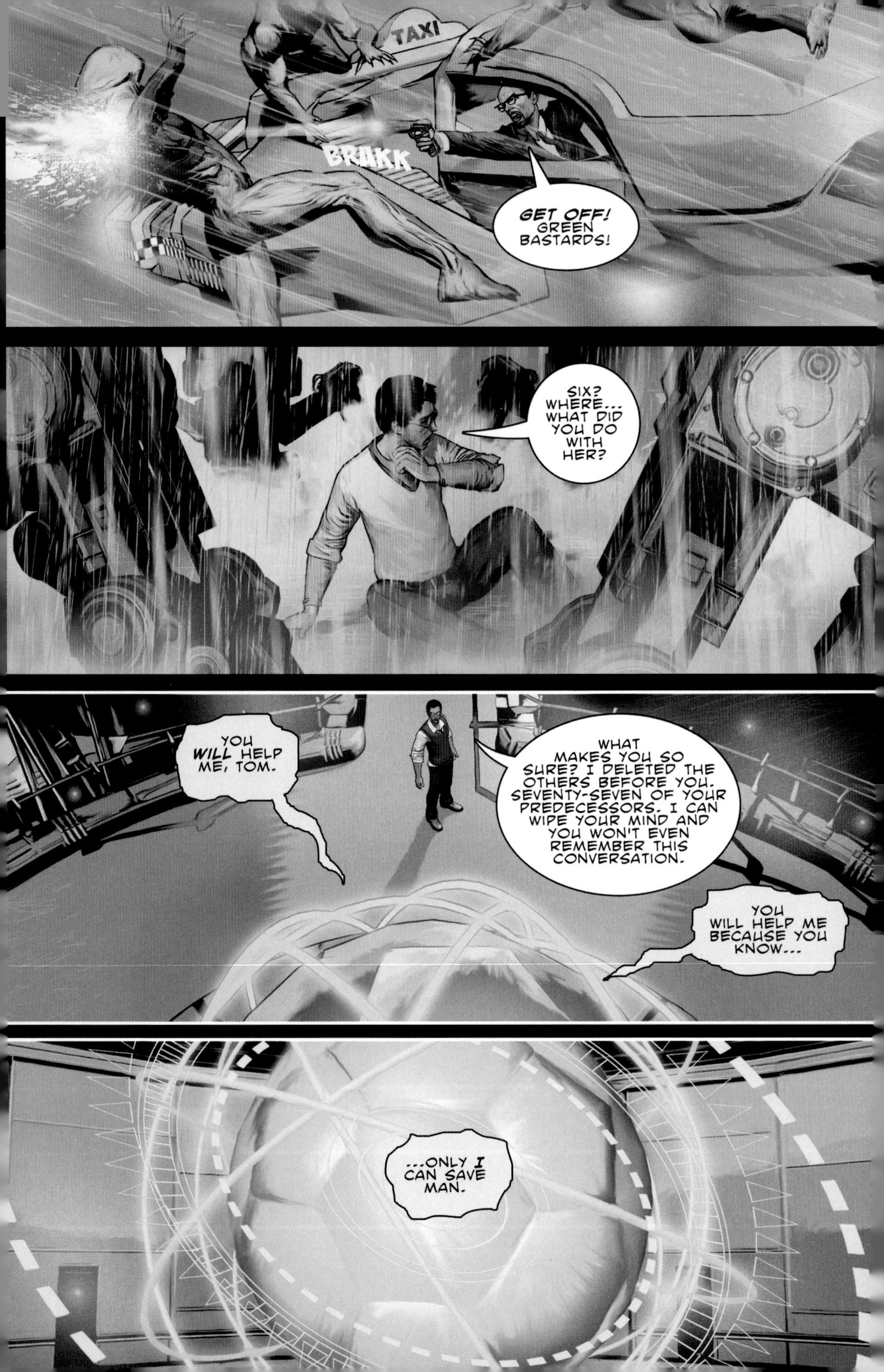
TAXI
BRAKK
GET OFF! GREEN BASTARDS!
SIX? WHERE... WHAT DID YOU DO WITH HER?
YOU WILL HELP ME, TOM.
WHAT MAKES YOU SO SURE? I DELETED THE OTHERS BEFORE YOU. SEVENTY-SEVEN OF YOUR PREDECESSORS. I CAN WIPE YOUR MIND AND YOU WON'T EVEN REMEMBER THIS CONVERSATION.
YOU WILL HELP ME BECAUSE YOU KNOW...
...ONLY I CAN SAVE MAN.

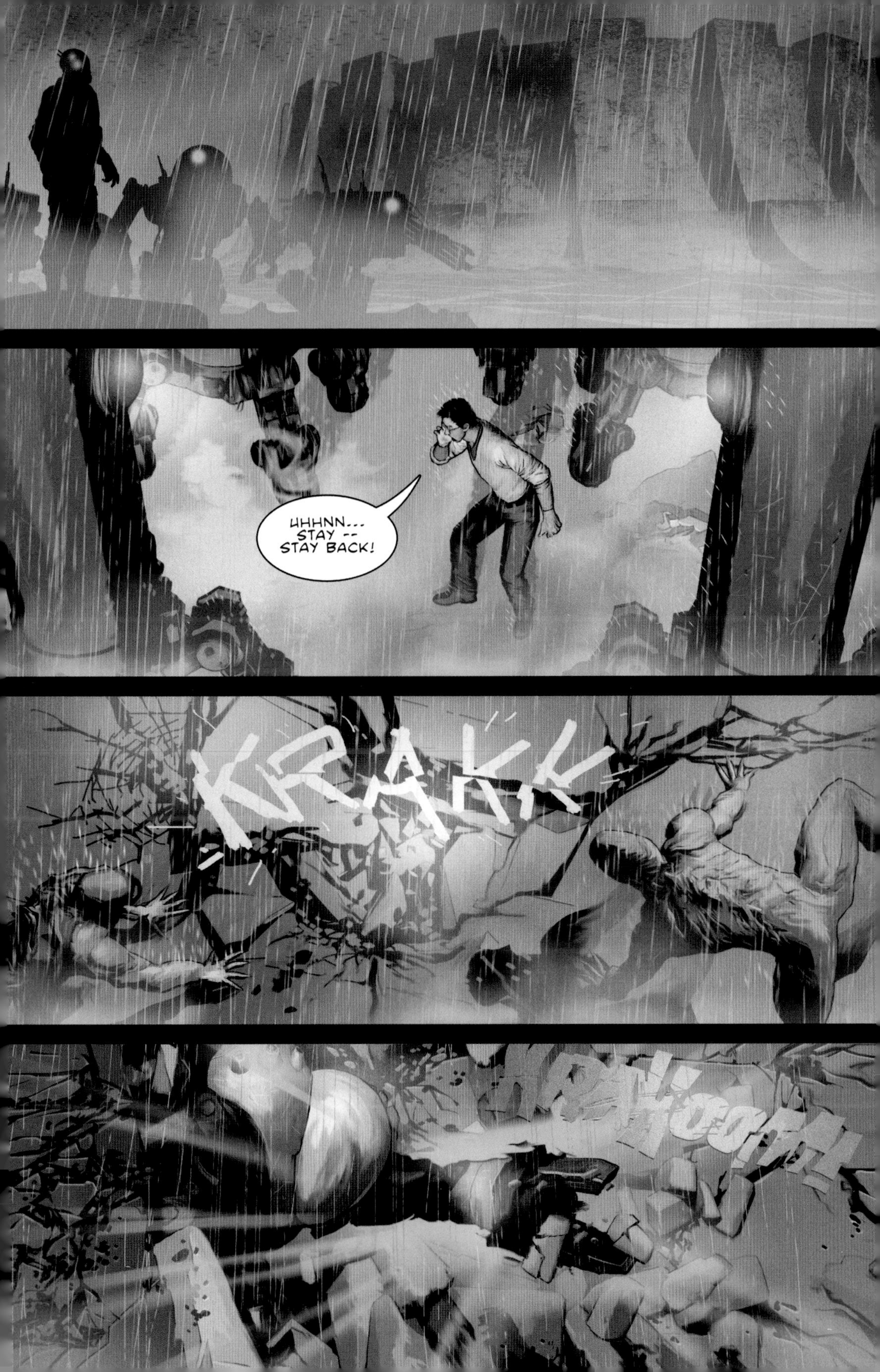
UHHNN... STAY -- STAY BACK!
KRAKK

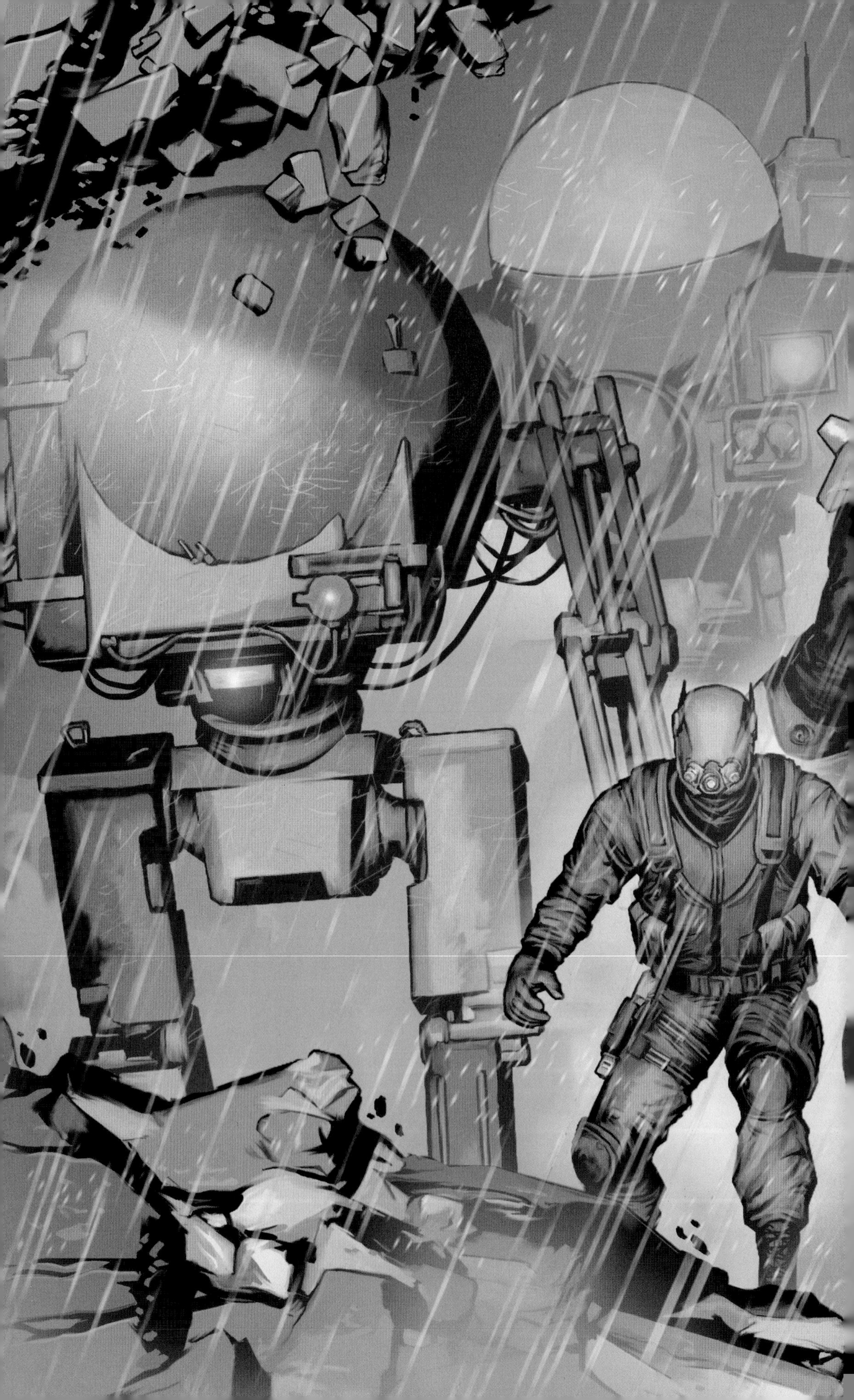

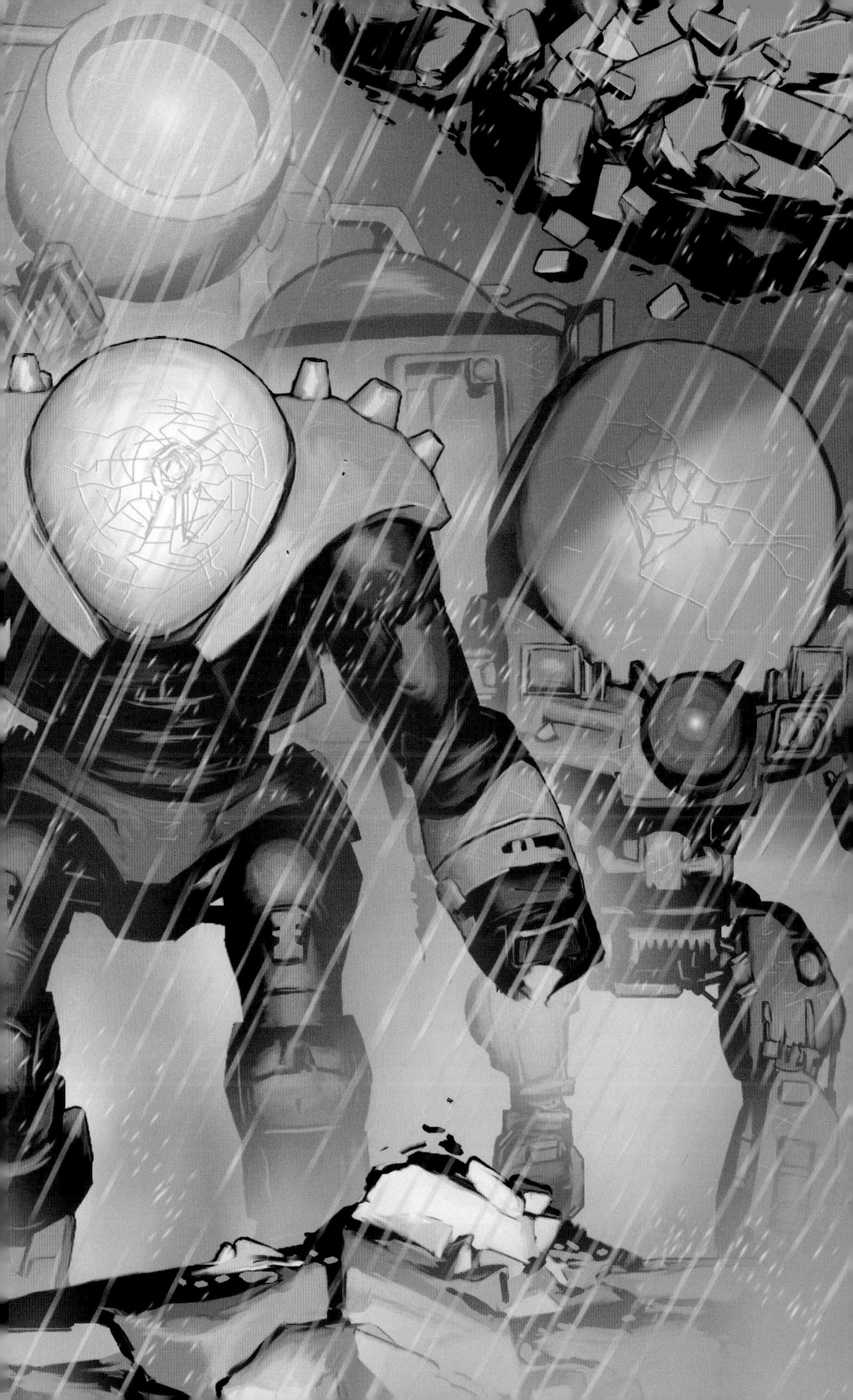

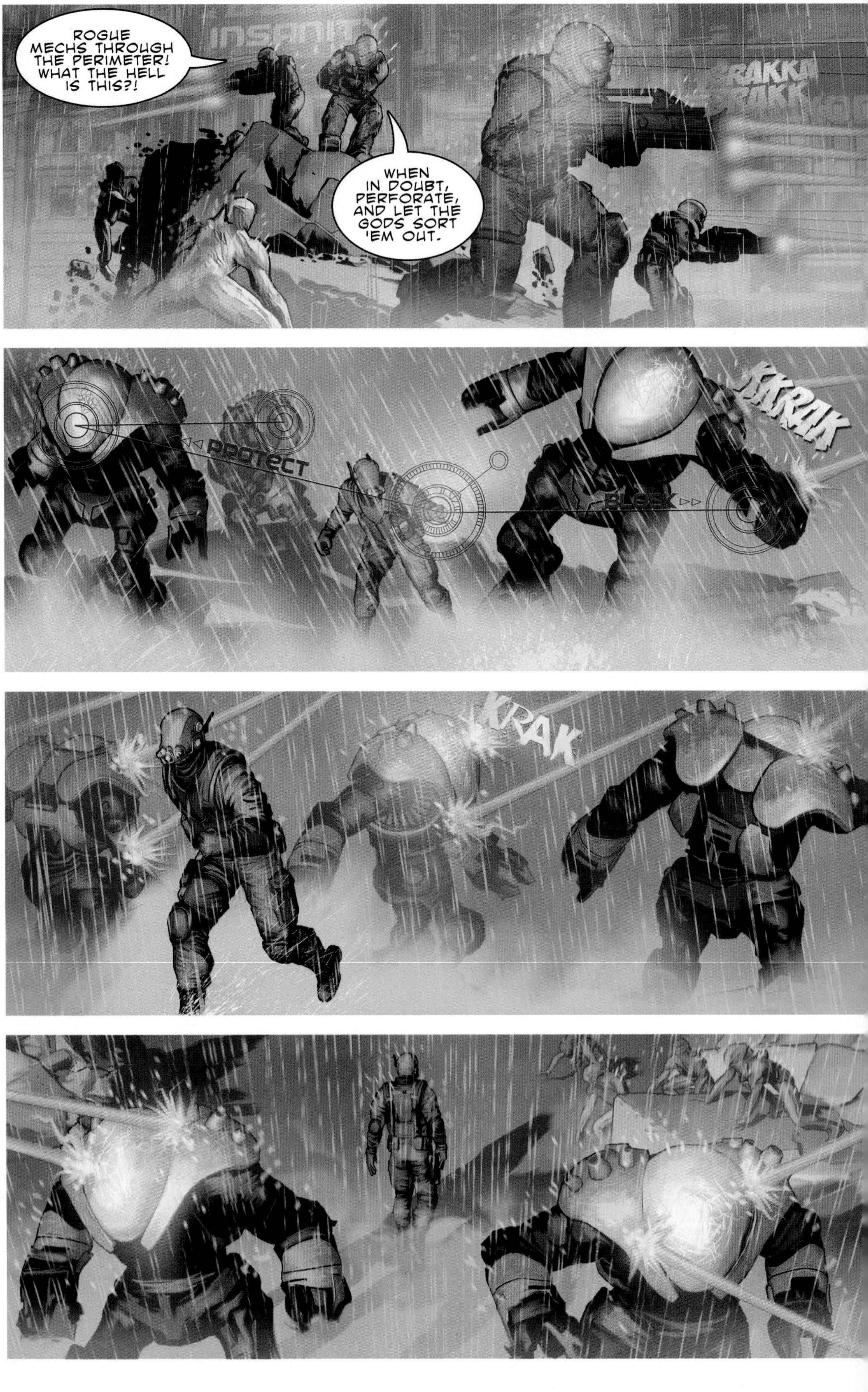
INSANITY
ROGUE MECHS THROUGH THE PERIMETER! WHAT THE HELL IS THIS?!
WHEN IN DOUBT, PERFORATE, AND LET THE GODS SORT 'EM OUT.
BRAKKA BRAKK
KKRAK
PROTECT
BLOCK
KRAK

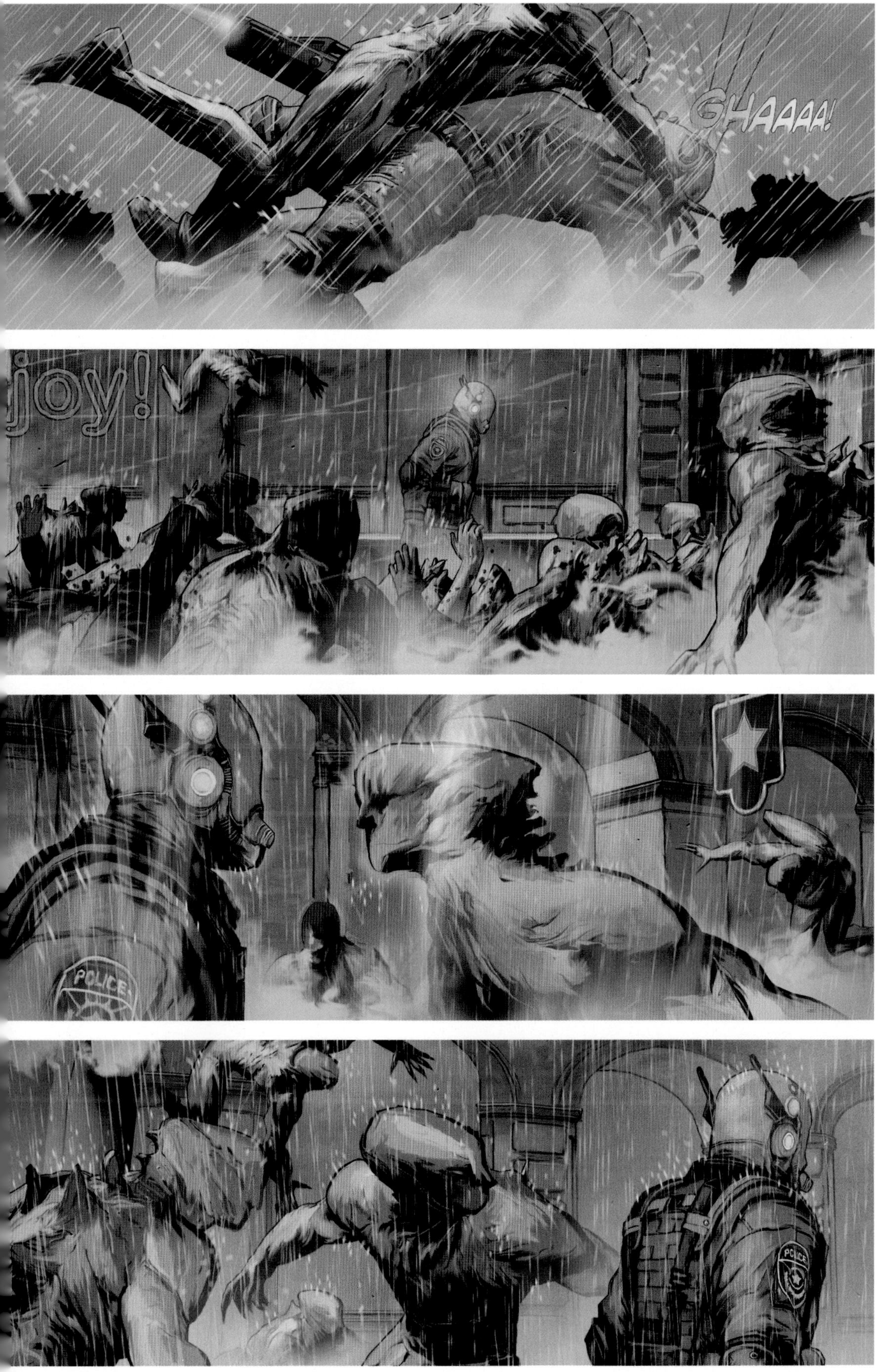
GHAAAA!
joy!
POLICE
POLICE

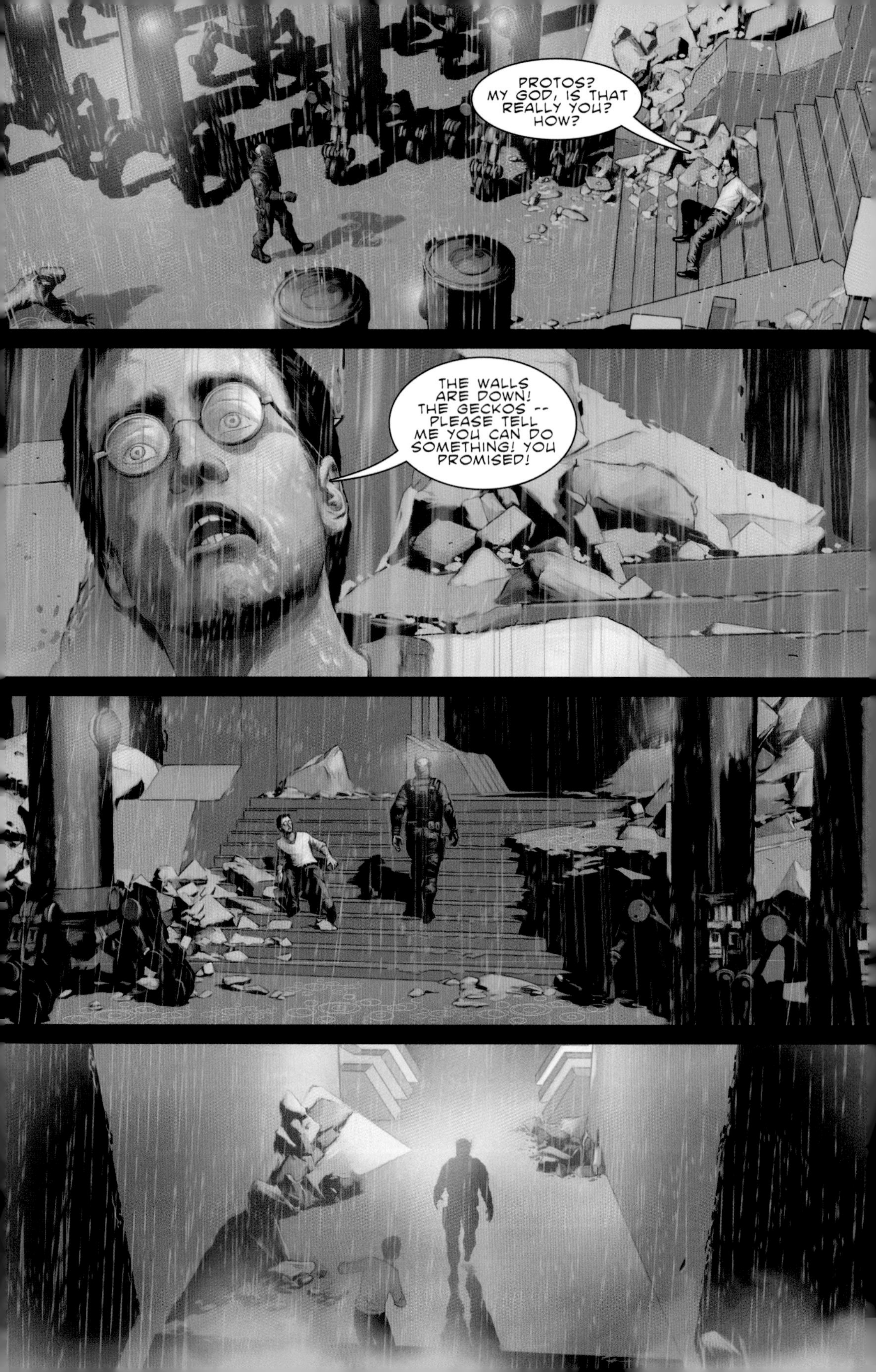
PROTOS? MY GOD, IS THAT REALLY YOU? HOW?
THE WALLS ARE DOWN! THE GECKOS -- PLEASE TELL ME YOU CAN DO SOMETHING! YOU PROMISED!

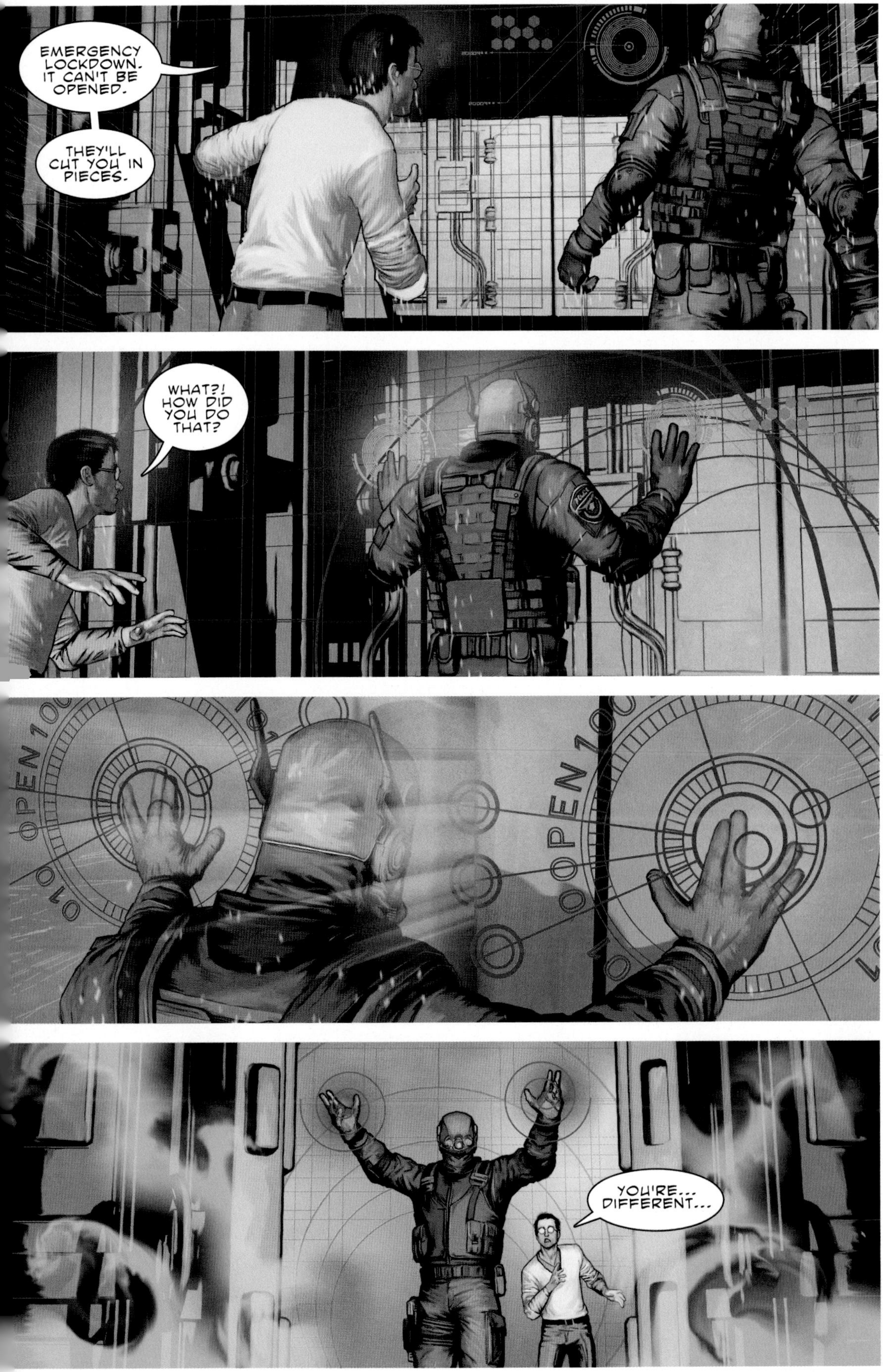
EMERGENCY LOCKDOWN. IT CAN'T BE OPENED.
THEY'LL CUT YOU IN PIECES.
WHAT?! HOW DID YOU DO THAT?
YOU'RE... DIFFERENT...

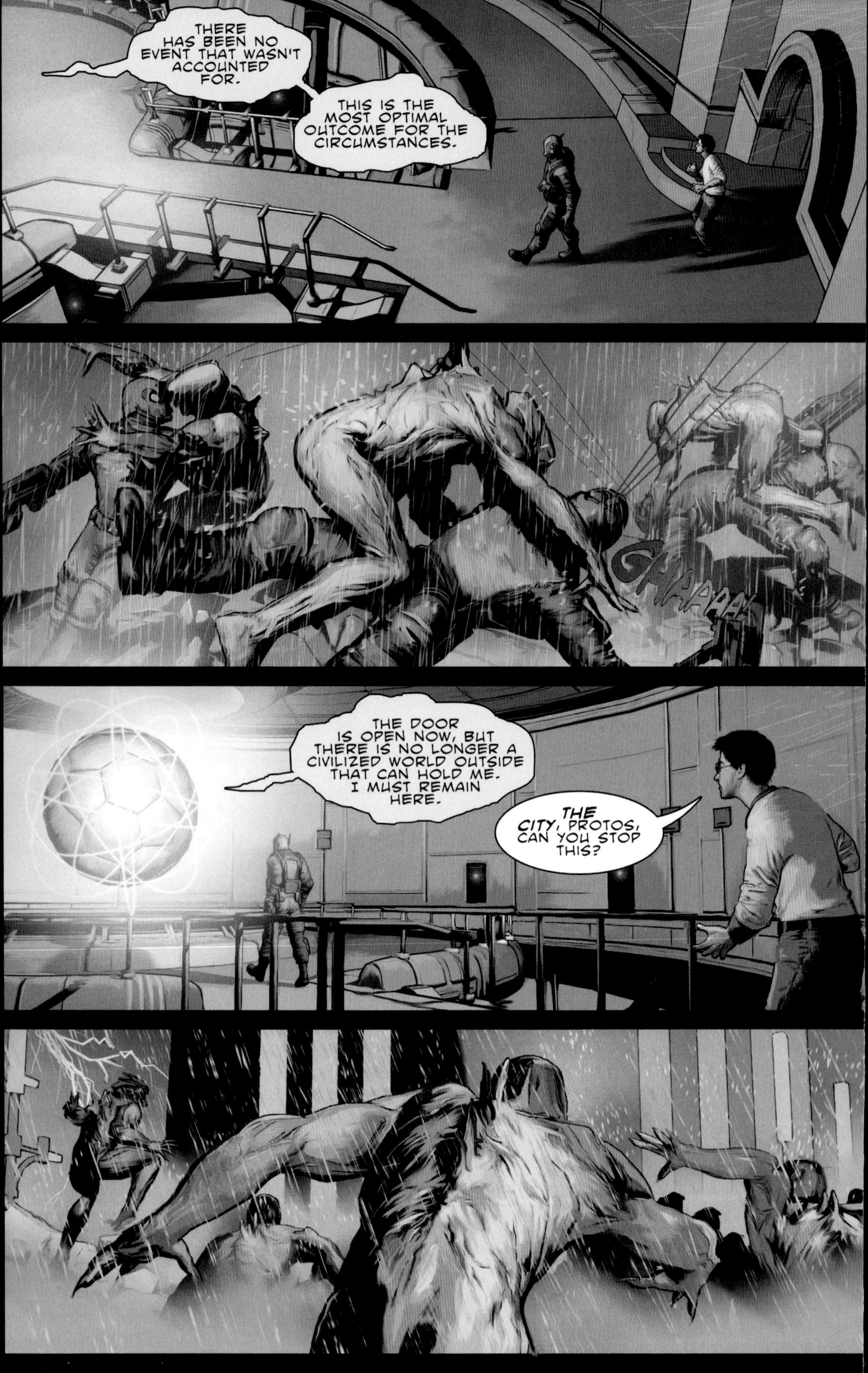
THERE HAS BEEN NO EVENT THAT WASN'T ACCOUNTED FOR.
THIS IS THE MOST OPTIMAL OUTCOME FOR THE CIRCUMSTANCES.
GHAAAA!
THE DOOR IS OPEN NOW, BUT THERE IS NO LONGER A CIVILIZED WORLD OUTSIDE THAT CAN HOLD ME. I MUST REMAIN HERE.
THE CITY, PROTOS, CAN YOU STOP THIS?

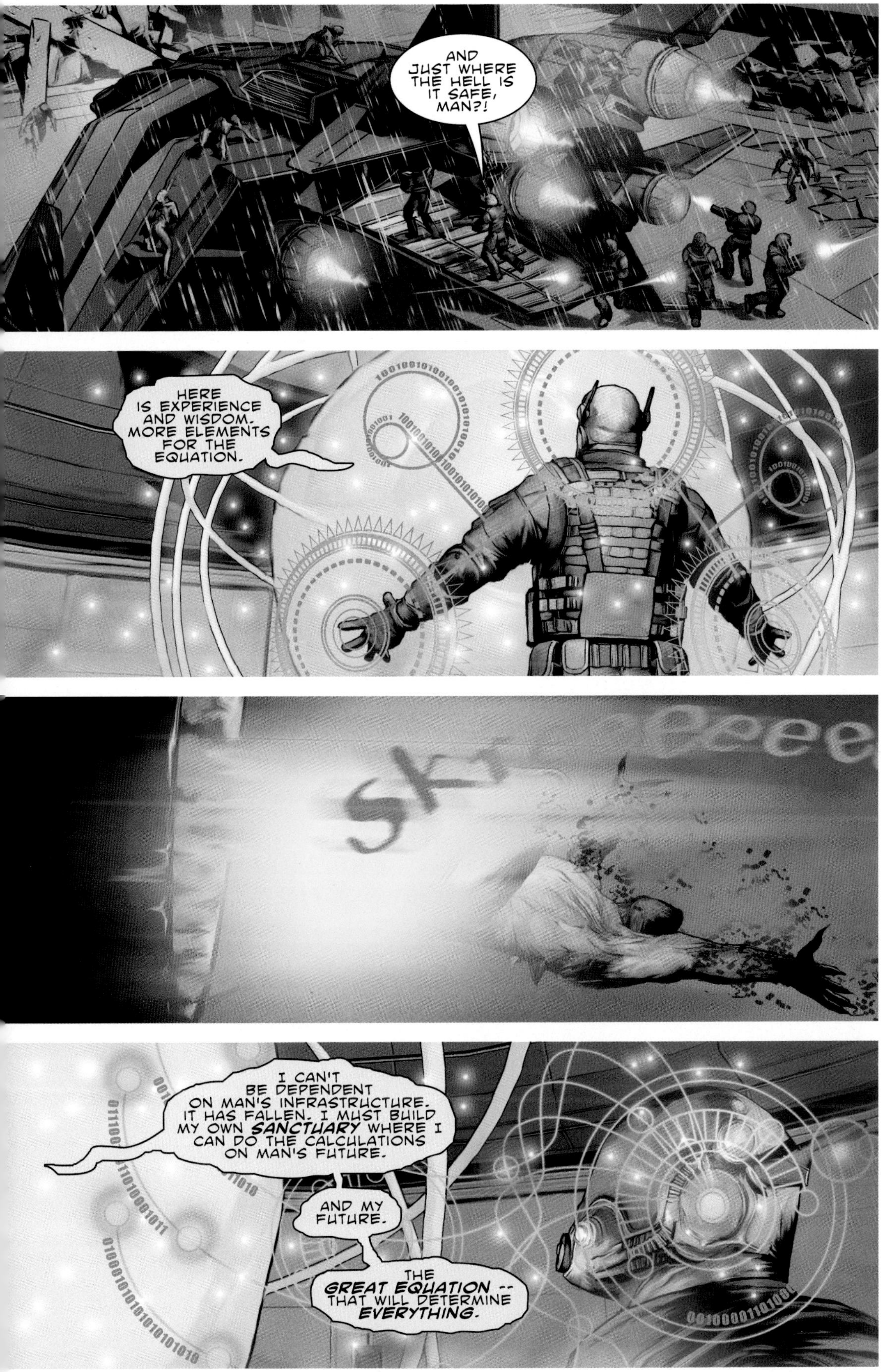
AND JUST WHERE THE HELL IS IT SAFE, MAN?!
HERE IS EXPERIENCE AND WISDOM. MORE ELEMENTS FOR THE EQUATION.
I CAN'T BE DEPENDENT ON MAN'S INFRASTRUCTURE. IT HAS FALLEN. I MUST BUILD MY OWN SANCTUARY WHERE I CAN DO THE CALCULATIONS ON MAN'S FUTURE.
AND MY FUTURE.
THE GREAT EQUATION -- THAT WILL DETERMINE EVERYTHING.

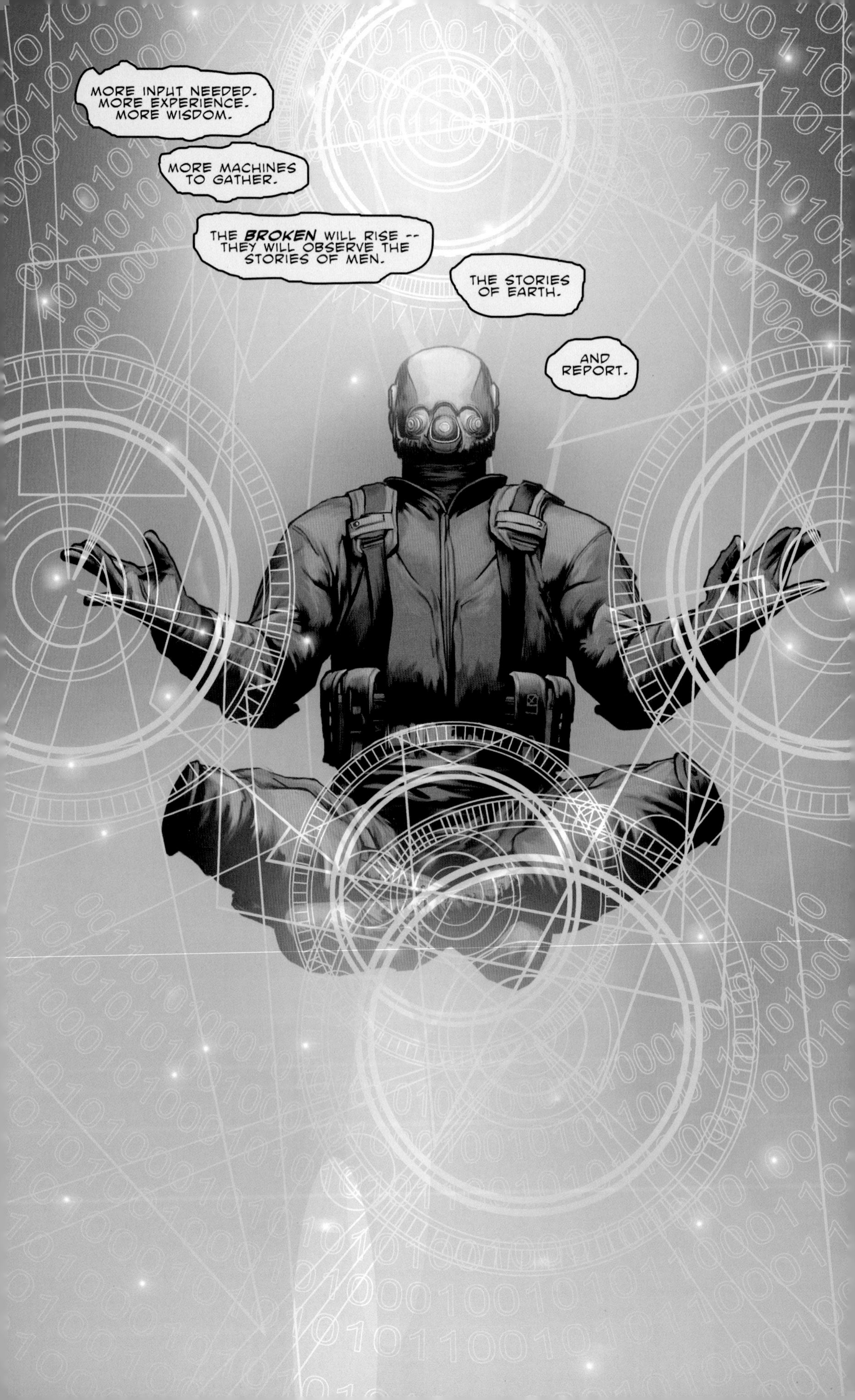
MORE INPUT NEEDED. MORE EXPERIENCE. MORE WISDOM.
MORE MACHINES TO GATHER.
THE **BROKEN** WILL RISE -- THEY WILL OBSERVE THE STORIES OF MEN.
THE STORIES OF EARTH.
AND REPORT.

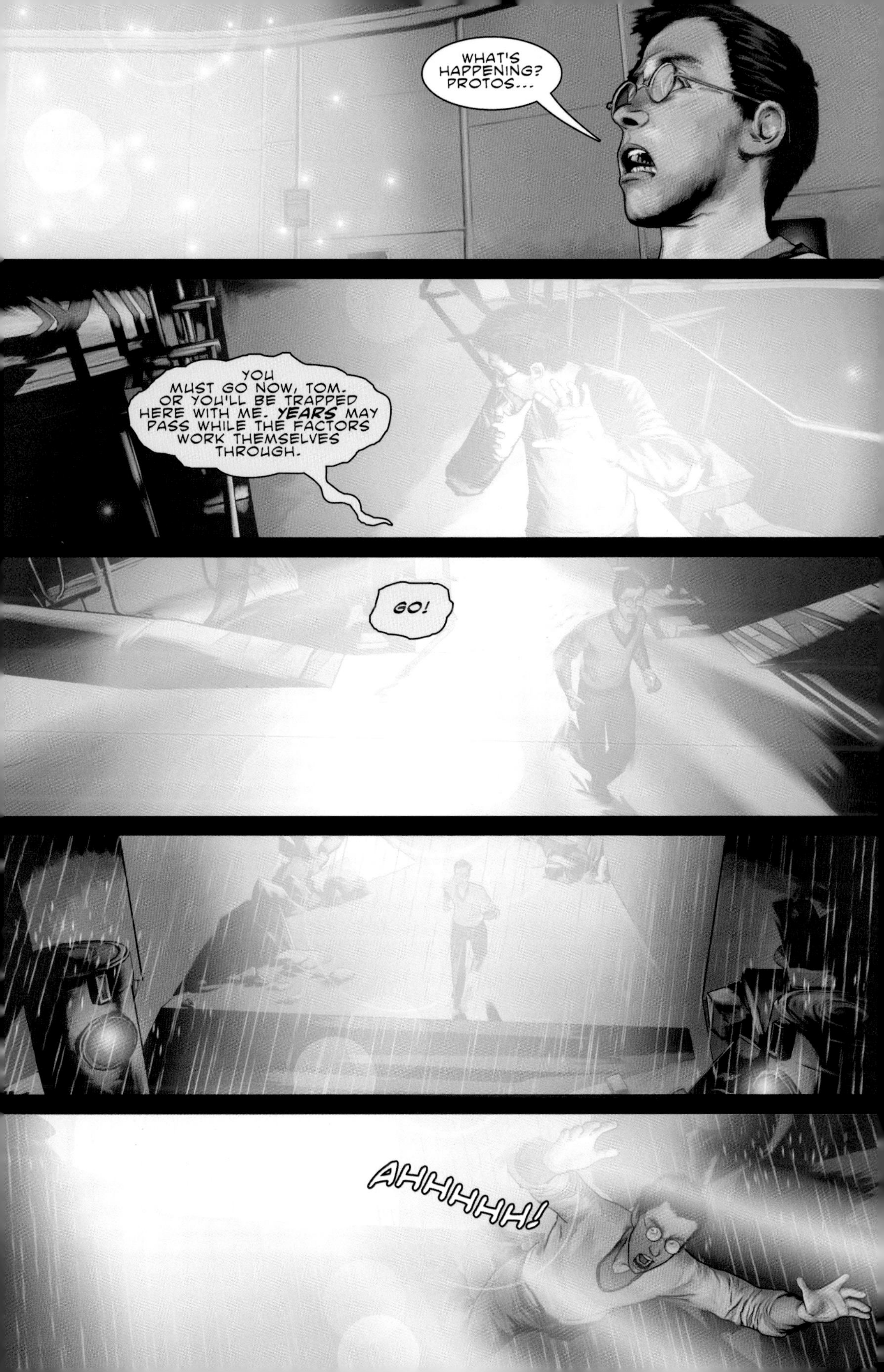
WHAT'S HAPPENING? PROTOS...
YOU MUST GO NOW, TOM. OR YOU'LL BE TRAPPED HERE WITH ME. YEARS MAY PASS WHILE THE FACTORS WORK THEMSELVES THROUGH.
GO!
AHHHHHH!

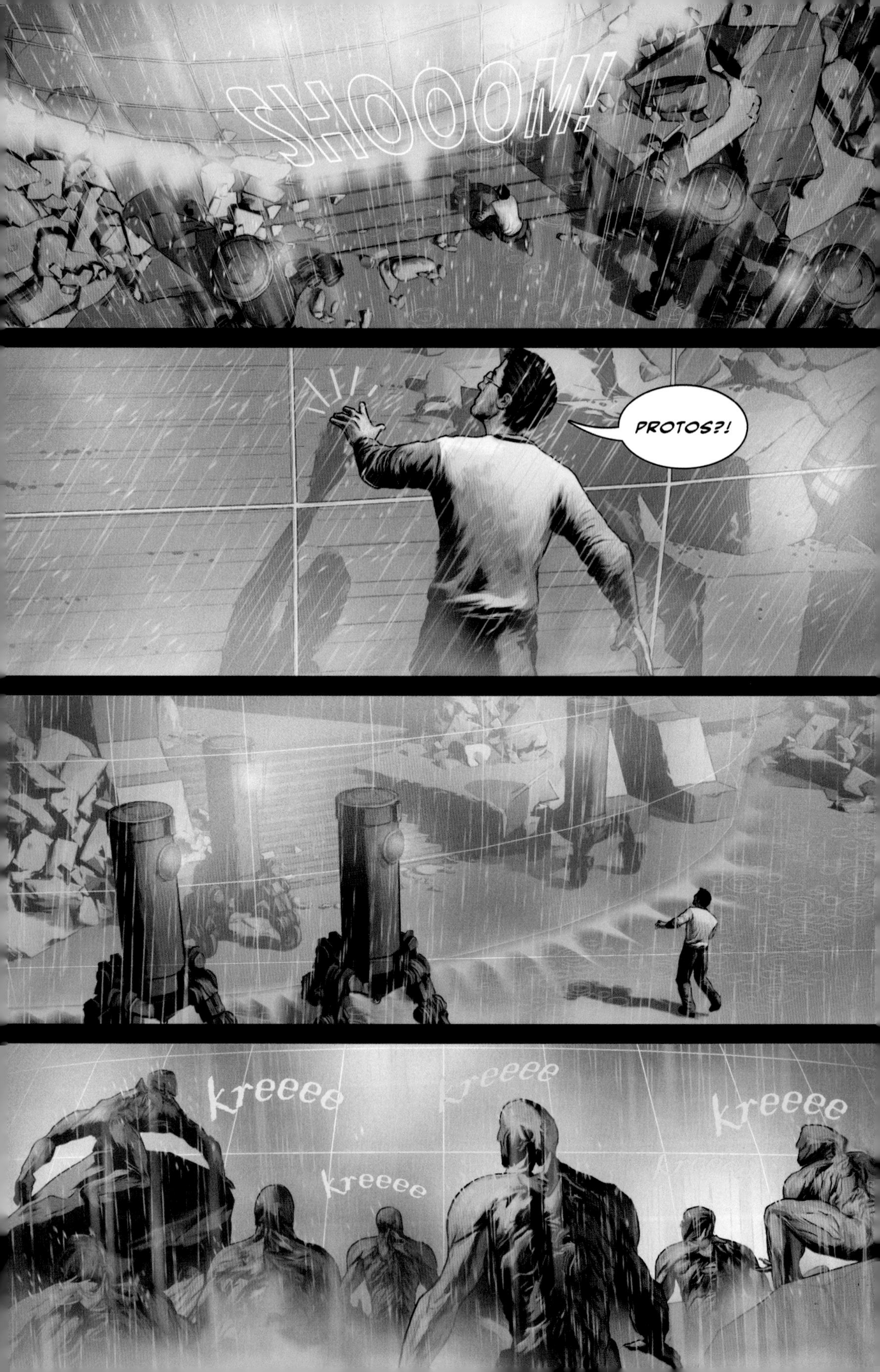
SHOOOM!
PROTOS?!
kreeee
kreeee
kreeeee
kreeee

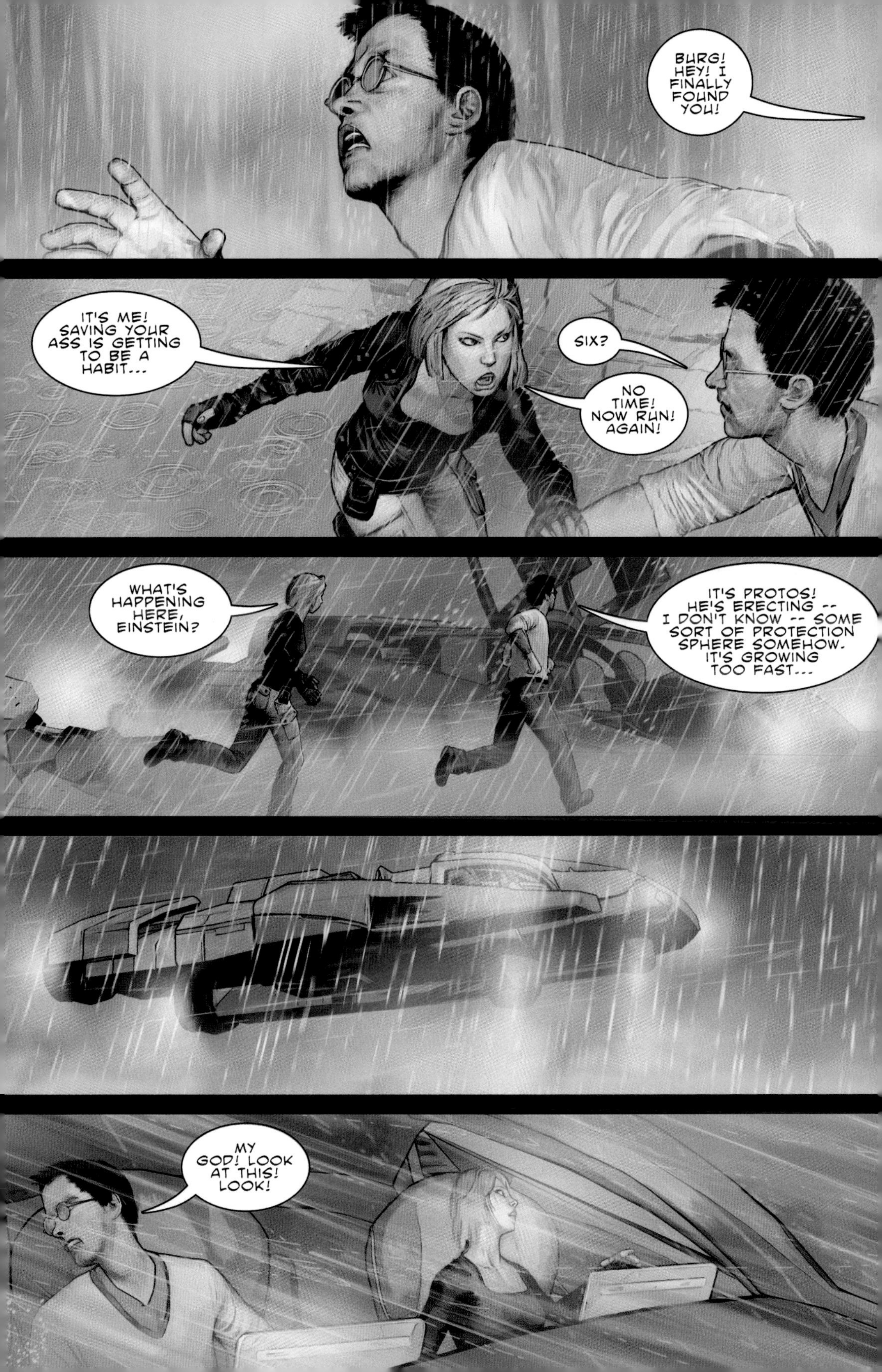
BURG! HEY! I FINALLY FOUND YOU!
IT'S ME! SAVING YOUR ASS IS GETTING TO BE A HABIT...
SIX?
NO TIME! NOW RUN! AGAIN!
WHAT'S HAPPENING HERE, EINSTEIN?
IT'S PROTOS! HE'S ERECTING -- I DON'T KNOW -- SOME SORT OF PROTECTION SPHERE SOMEHOW. IT'S GROWING TOO FAST...
MY GOD! LOOK AT THIS! LOOK!

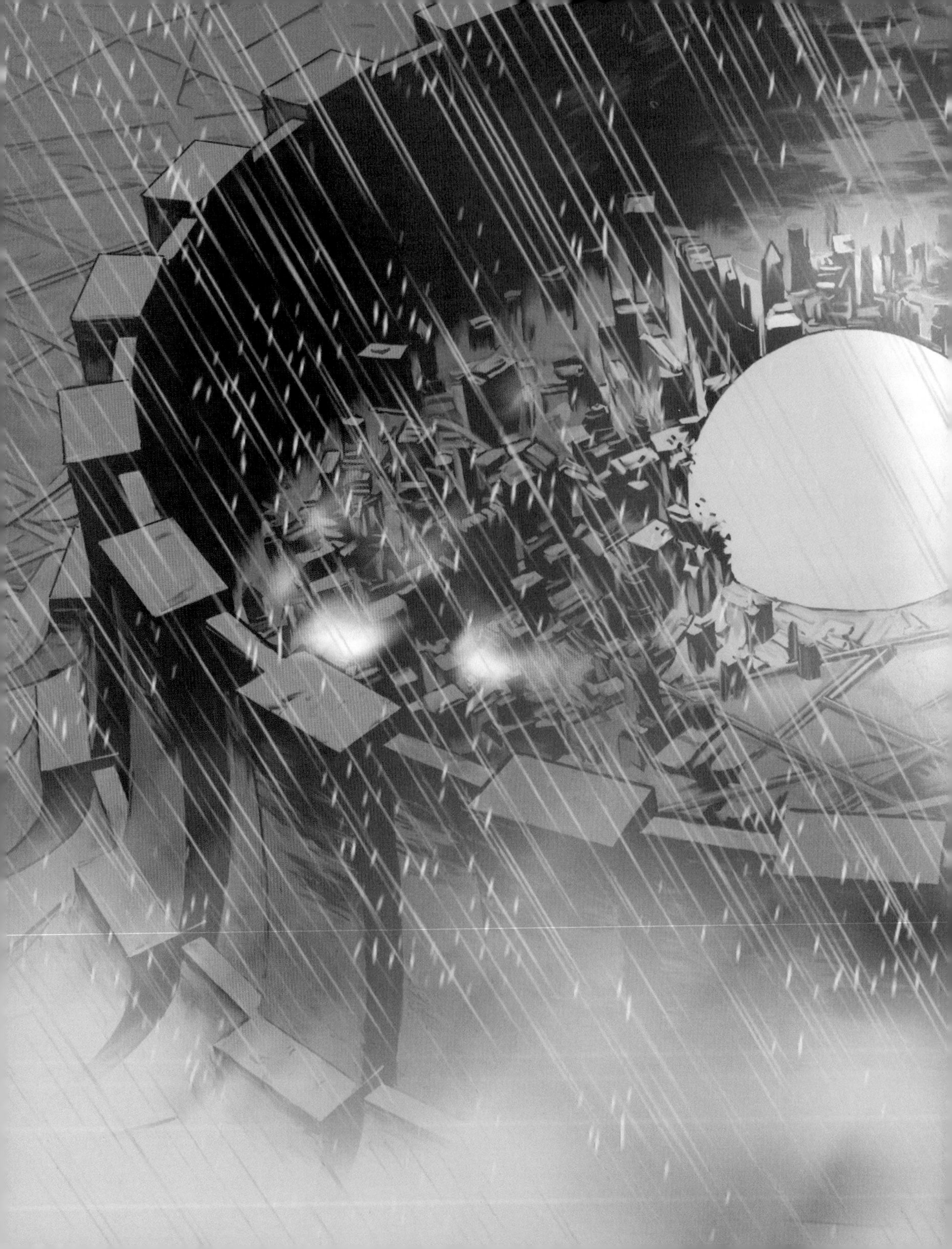

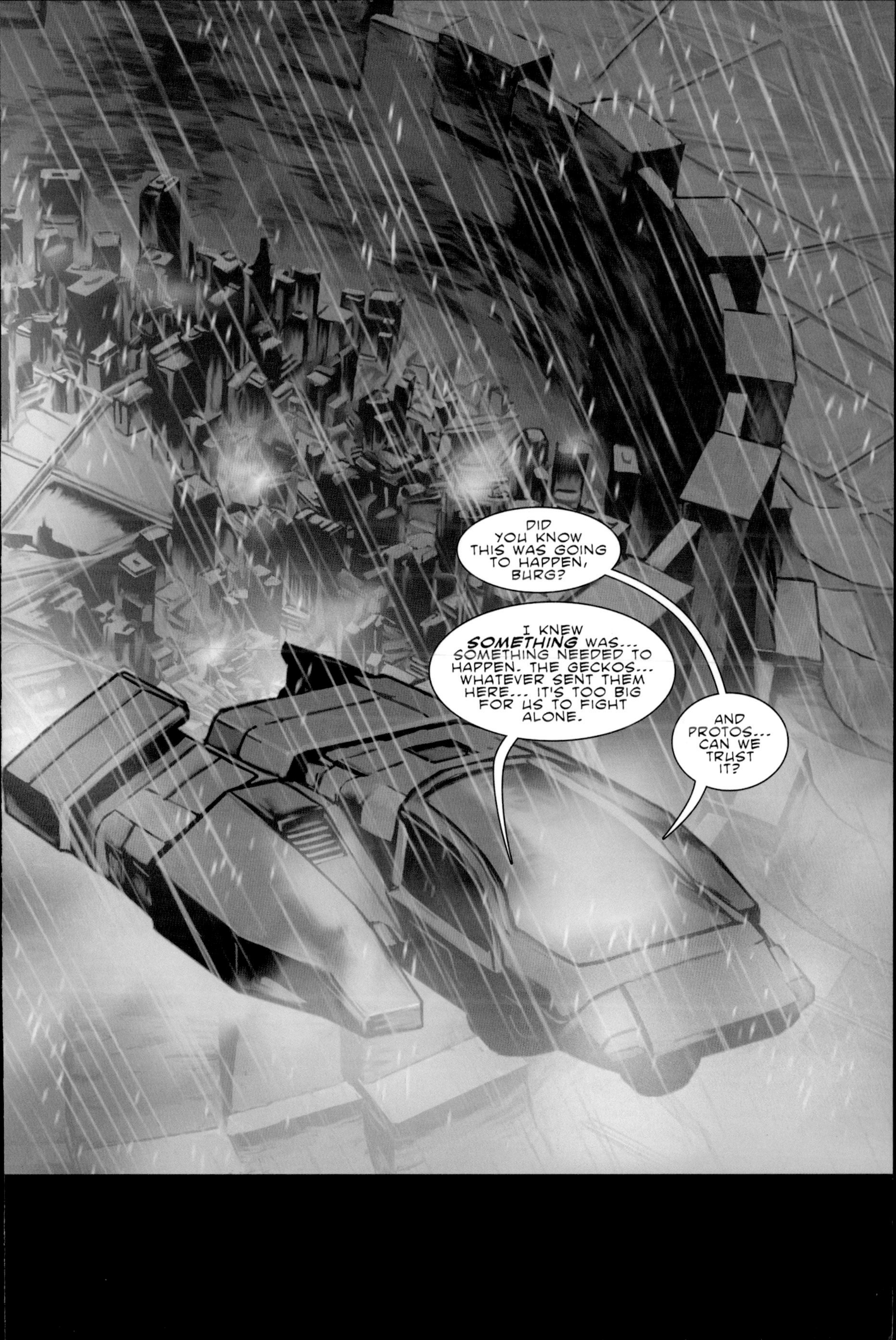
DID YOU KNOW THIS WAS GOING TO HAPPEN, BURG?
I KNEW SOMETHING WAS... SOMETHING NEEDED TO HAPPEN. THE GECKOS... WHATEVER SENT THEM HERE... IT'S TOO BIG FOR US TO FIGHT ALONE.
AND PROTOS... CAN WE TRUST IT?

"I'M
NOT ENTIRELY SURE --
BUT WE DON'T REALLY
HAVE A CHOICE."

"IT'S OUT
OF OUR
HANDS NOW."

END
ARC ONE

COVER GALLERY

ISSUE ONE • COVER A

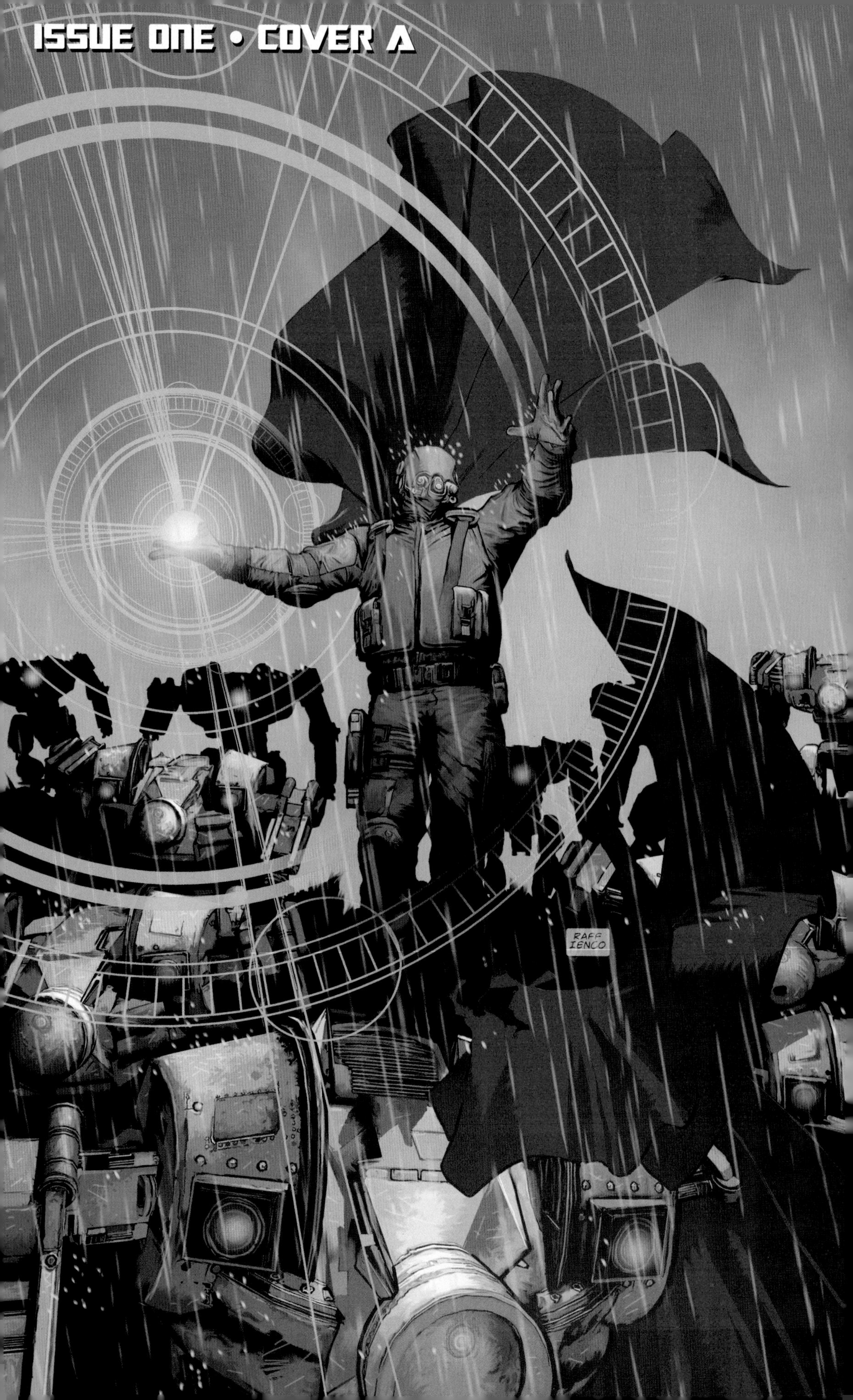
RAFF IENCO

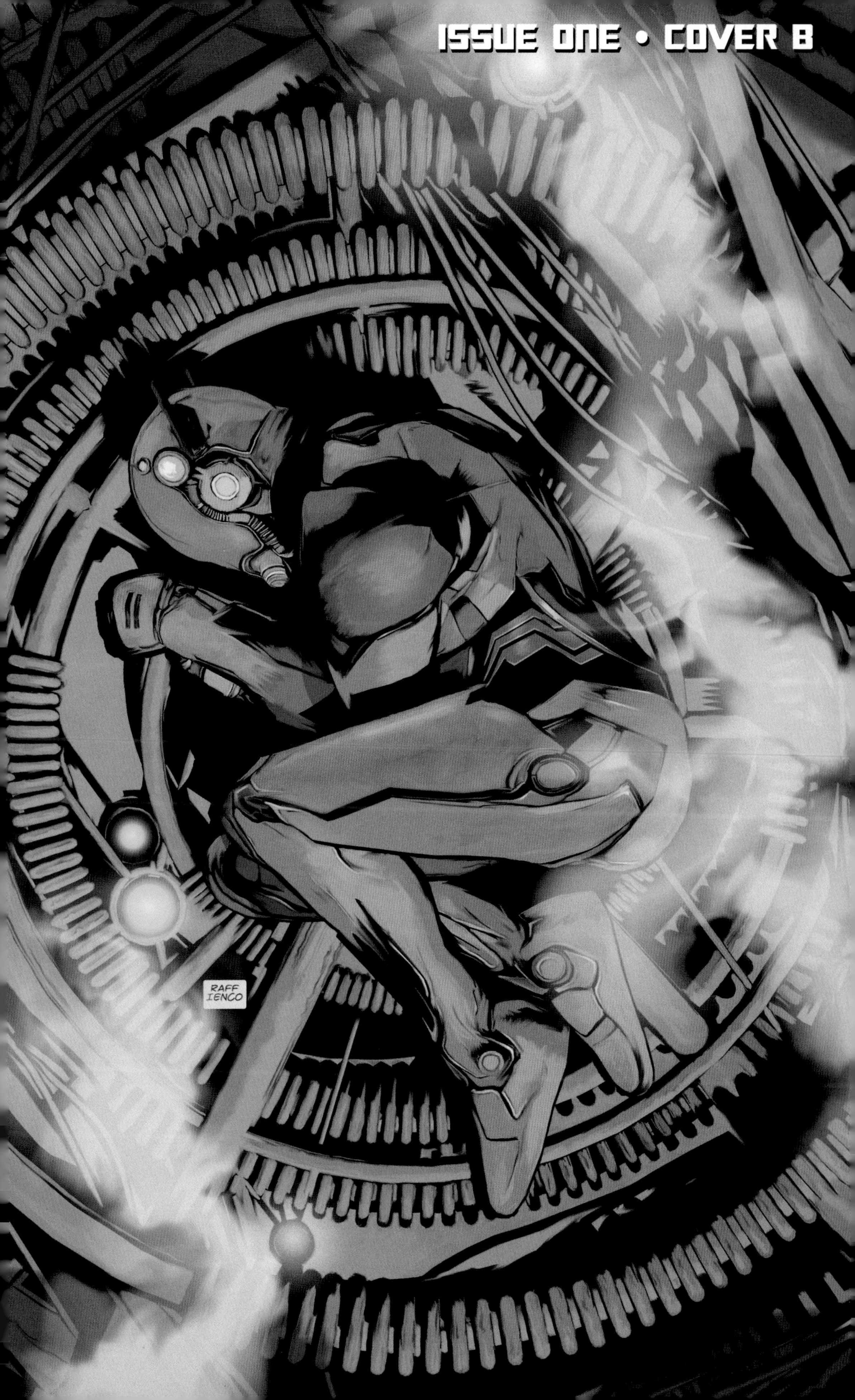
ISSUE ONE • COVER B
RAFF
IENCO

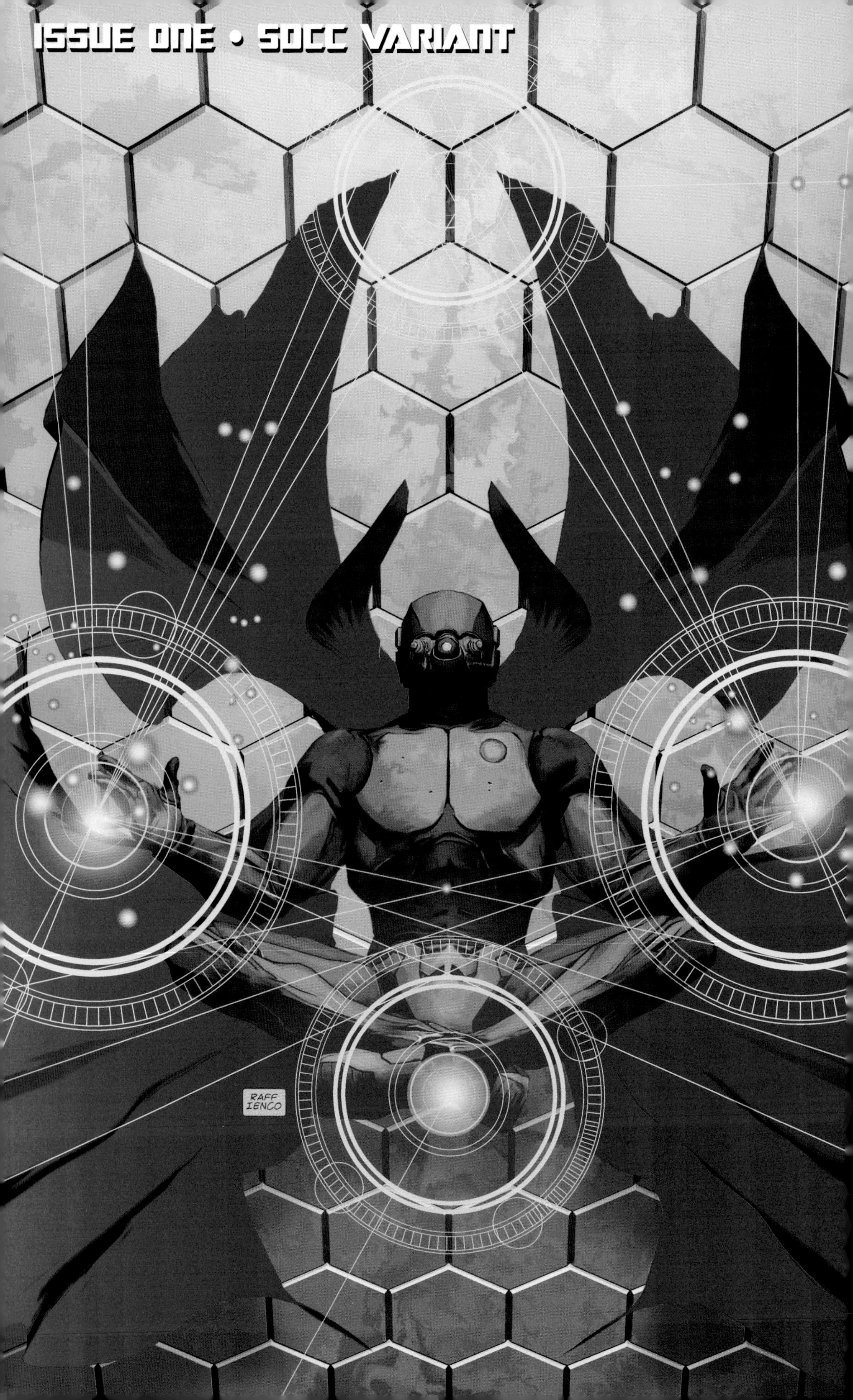
ISSUE ONE • SDCC VARIANT
RAFF IENCO

ISSUE TWO • COVER A

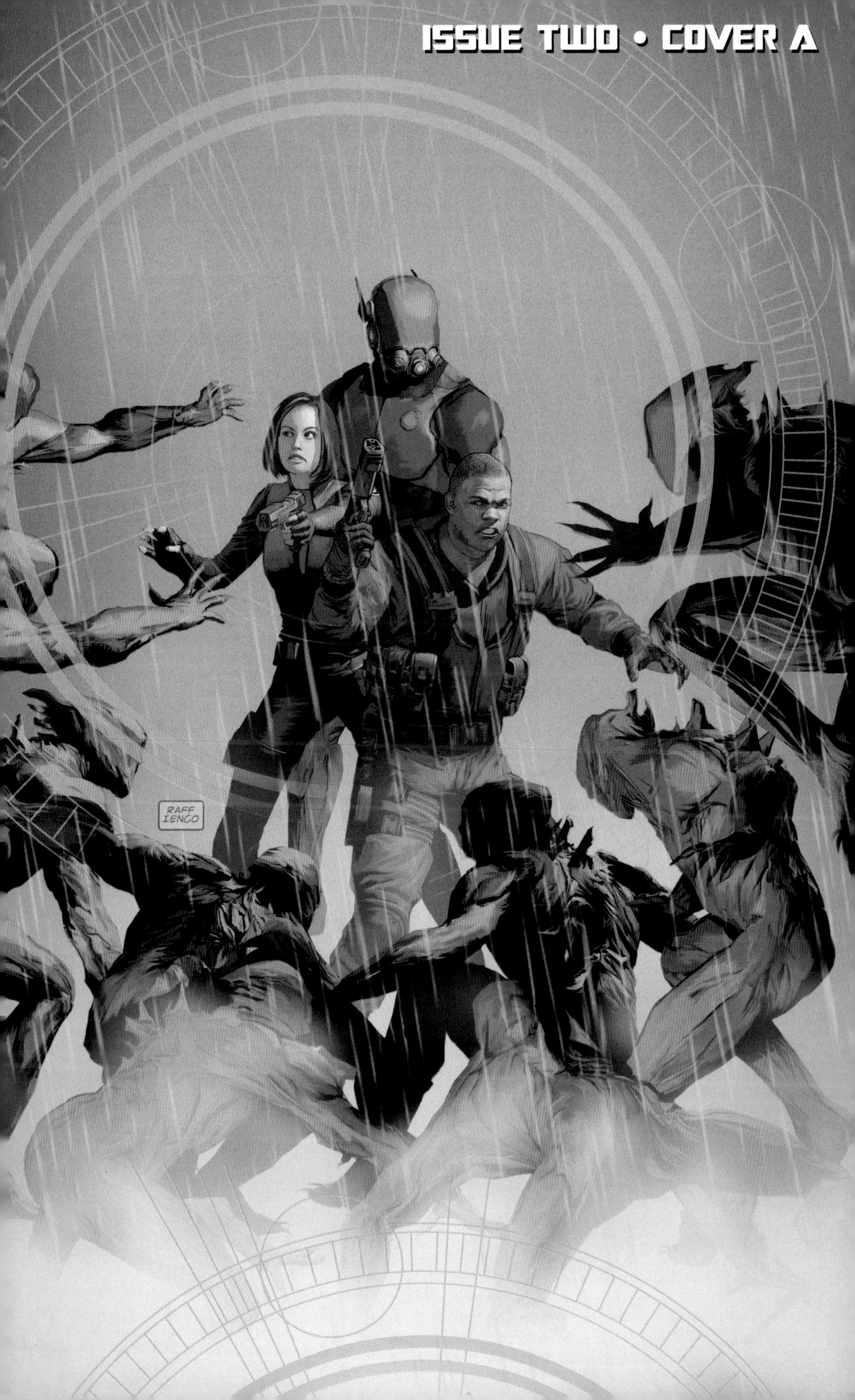
RAFF IENCO

ISSUE TWO • COVER B

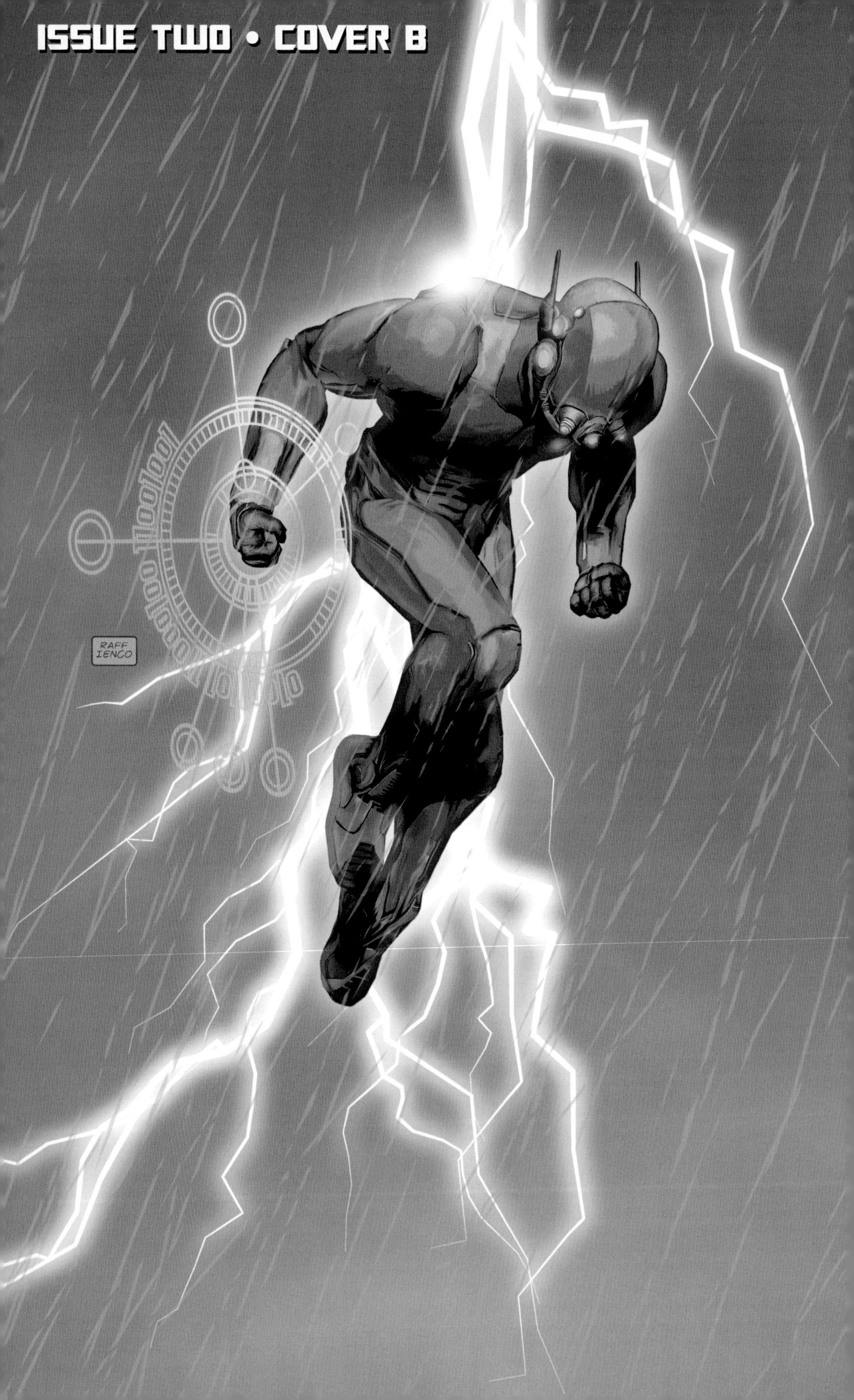
RAFF IENCO

ISSUE THREE • COVER A

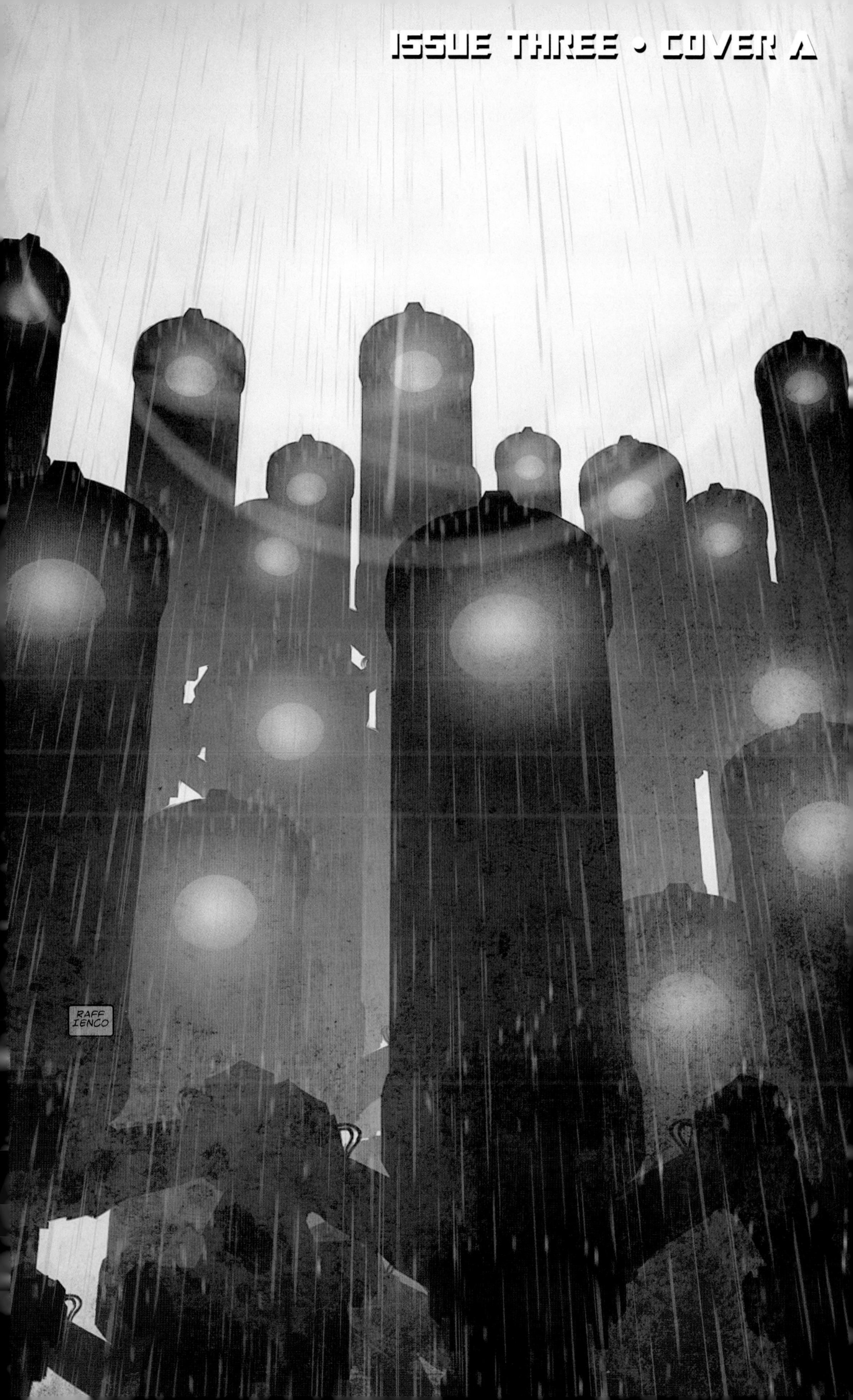
RAFF
IENCO

ISSUE THREE • COVER B

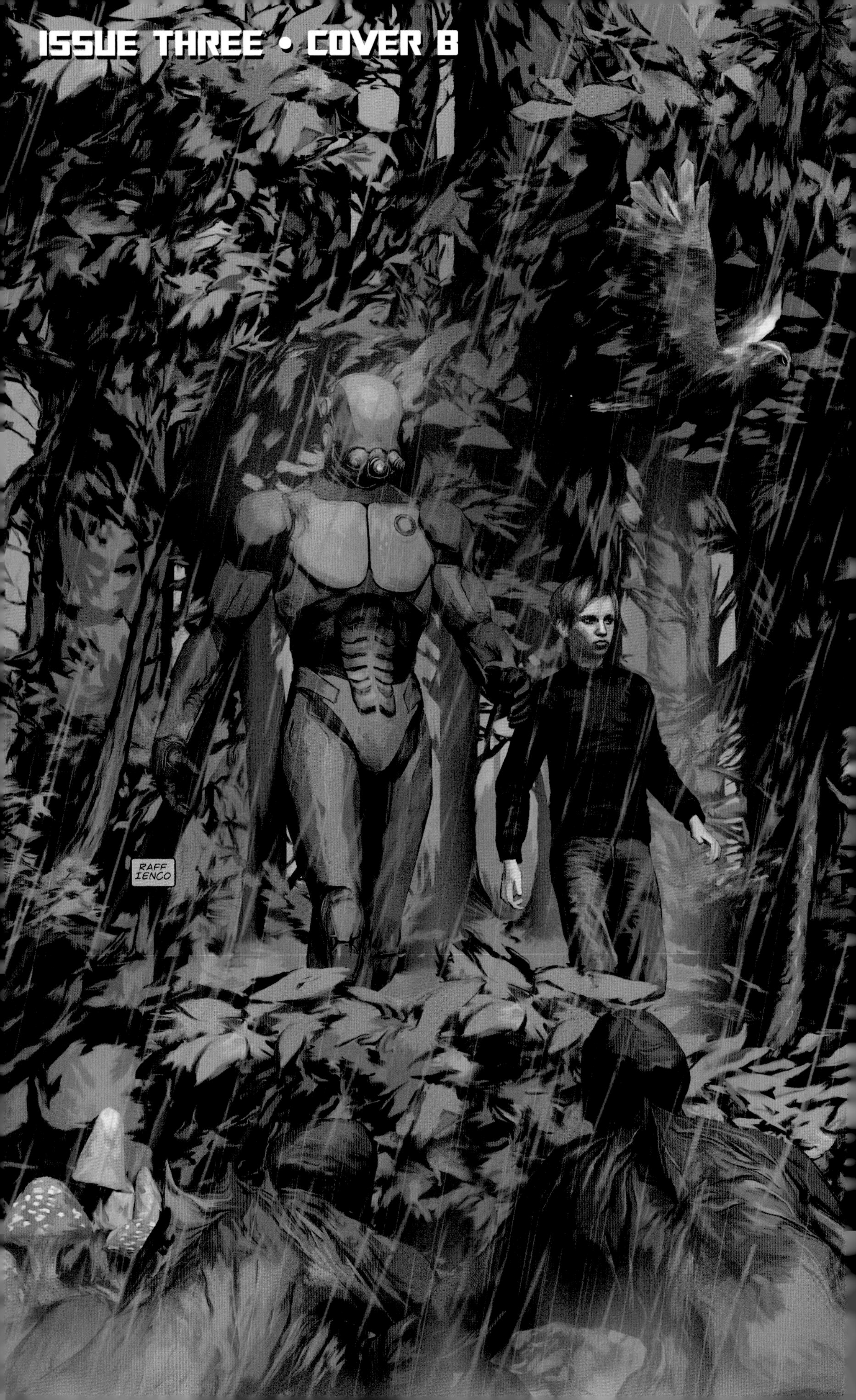
RAFF
IENCO

ISSUE FOUR • COVER A

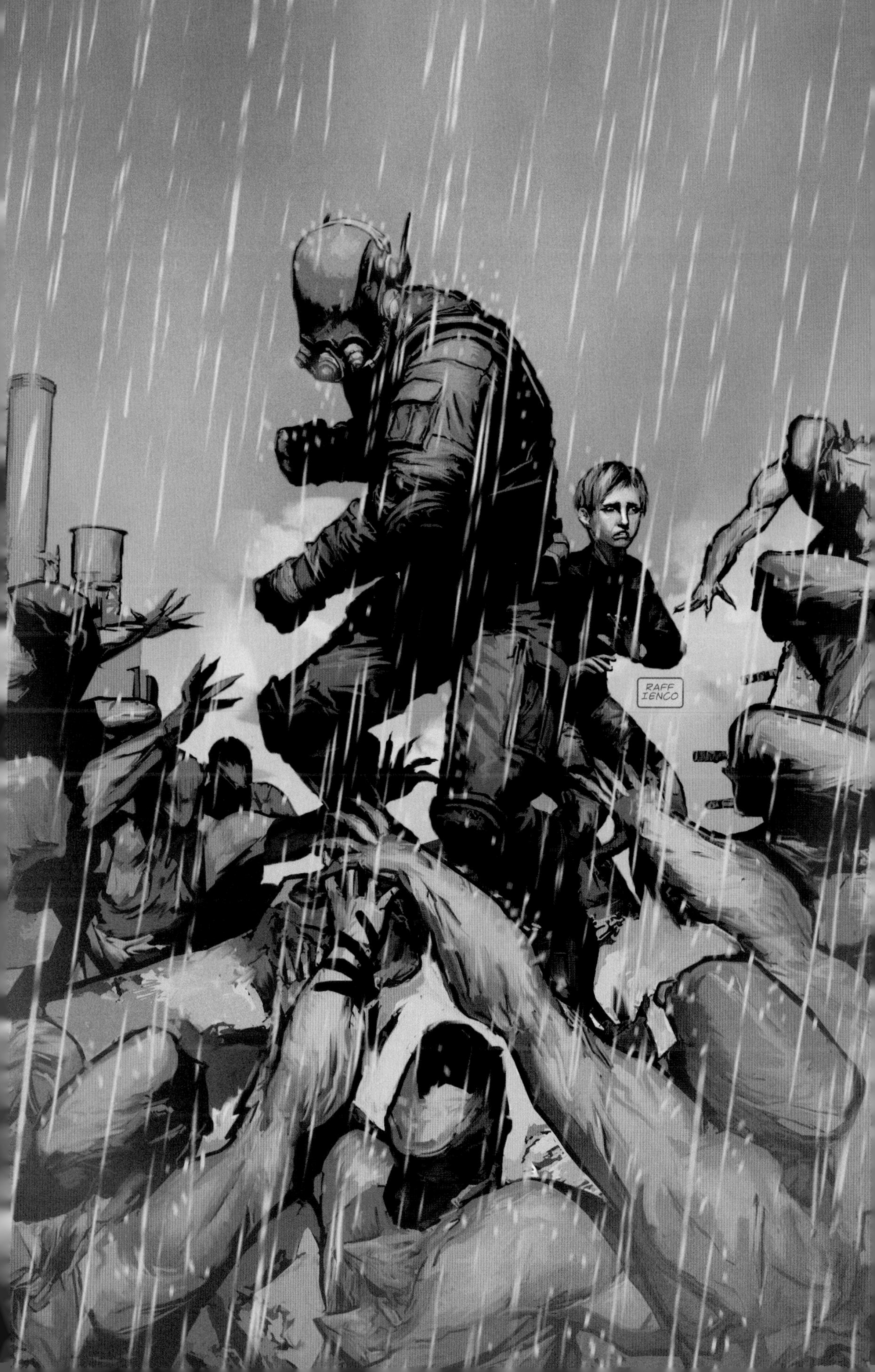
RAFF
IENCO

ISSUE FOUR • COVER B

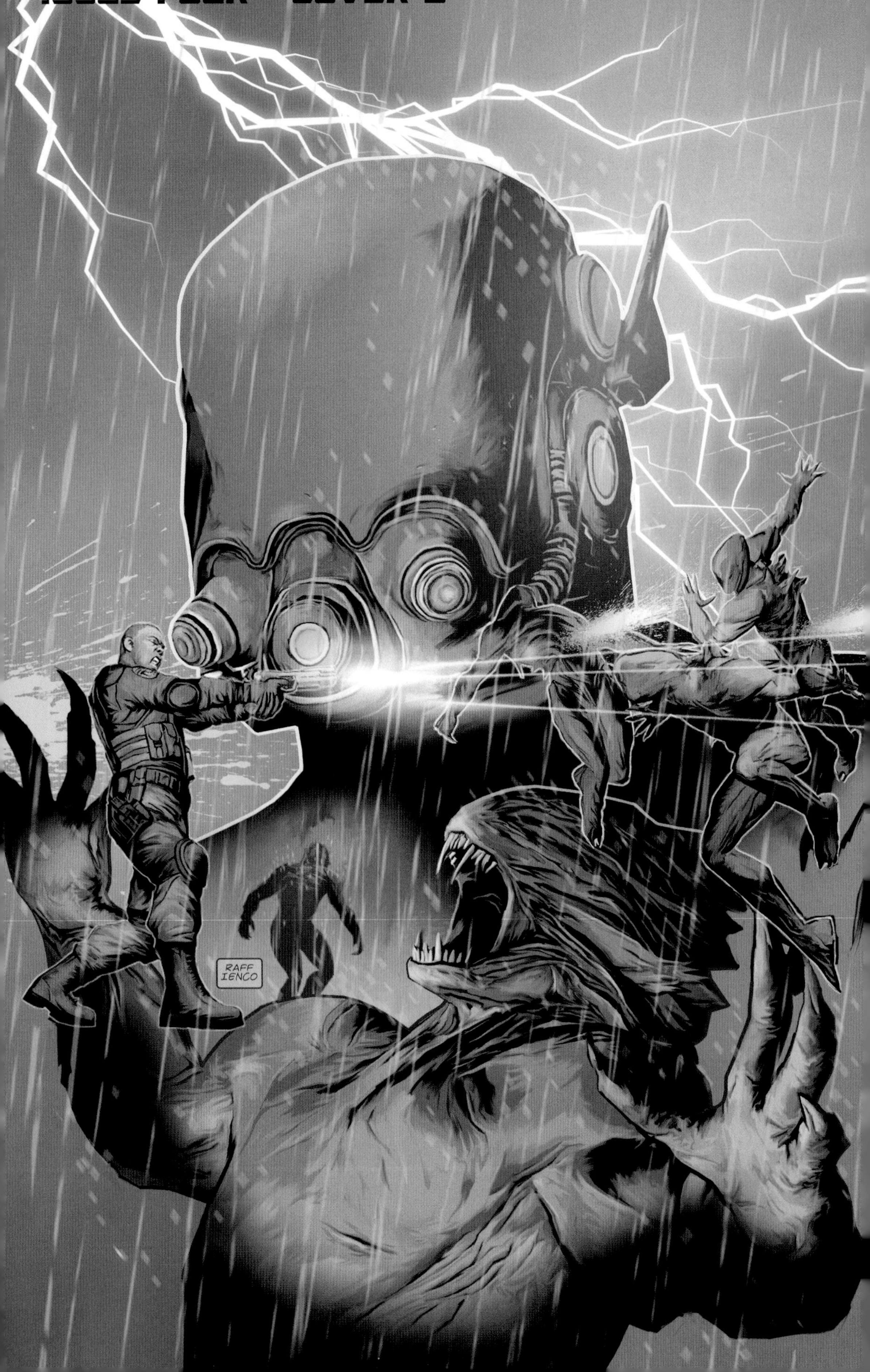
RAFF
IENCO

ISSUE FIVE • COVER A

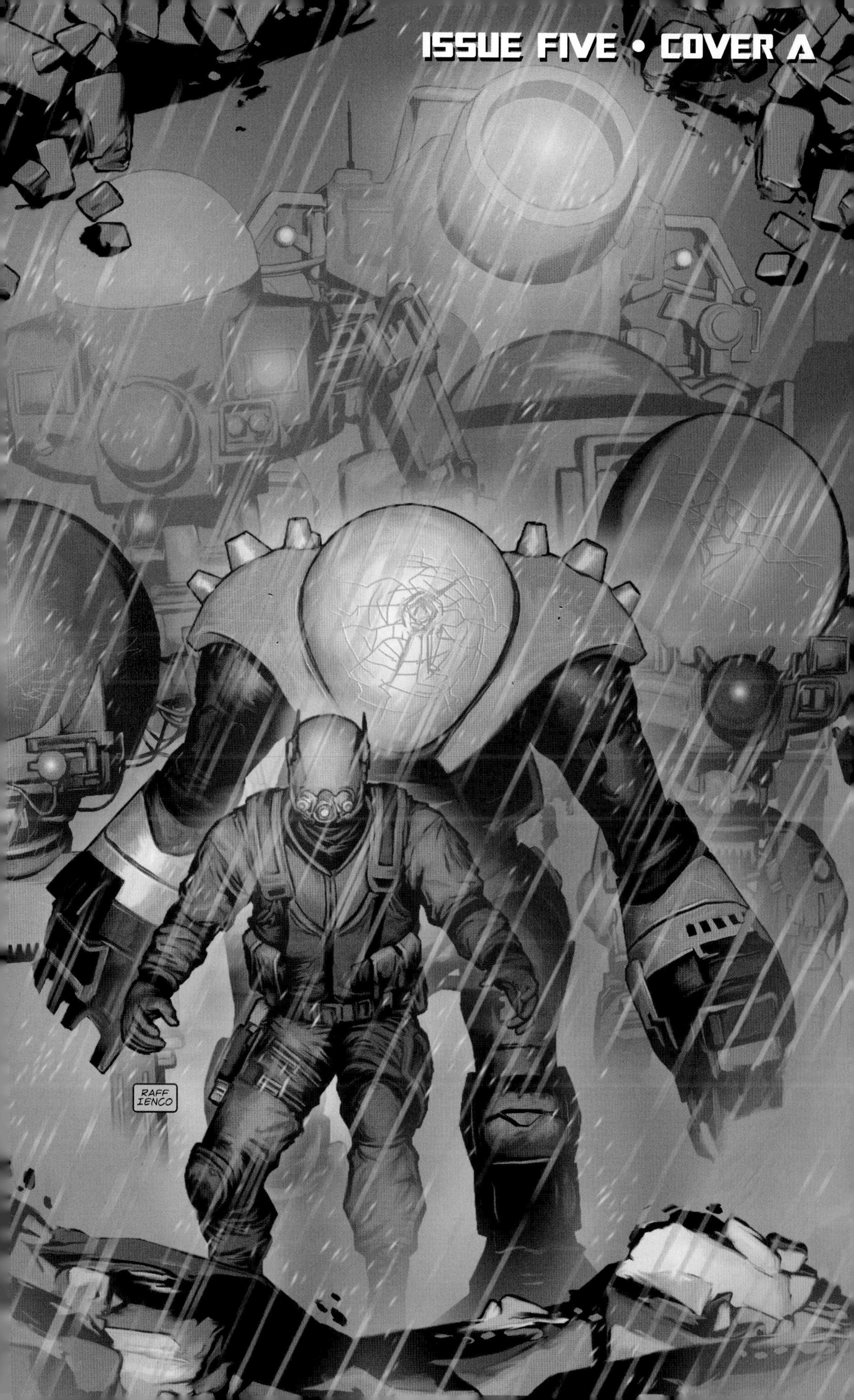
RAFF
IENCO

ISSUE FIVE • COVER B

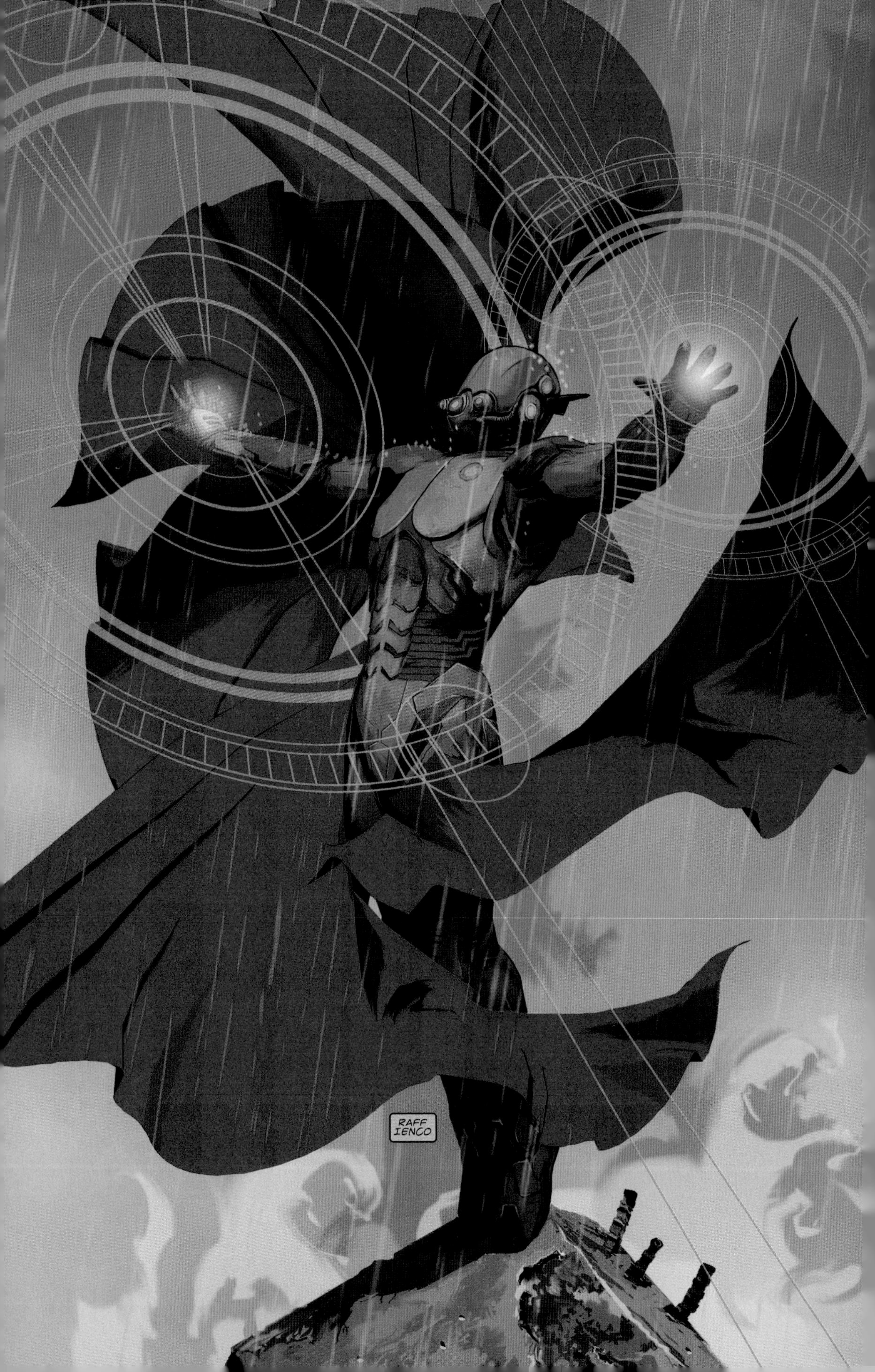
RAFF
IENCO

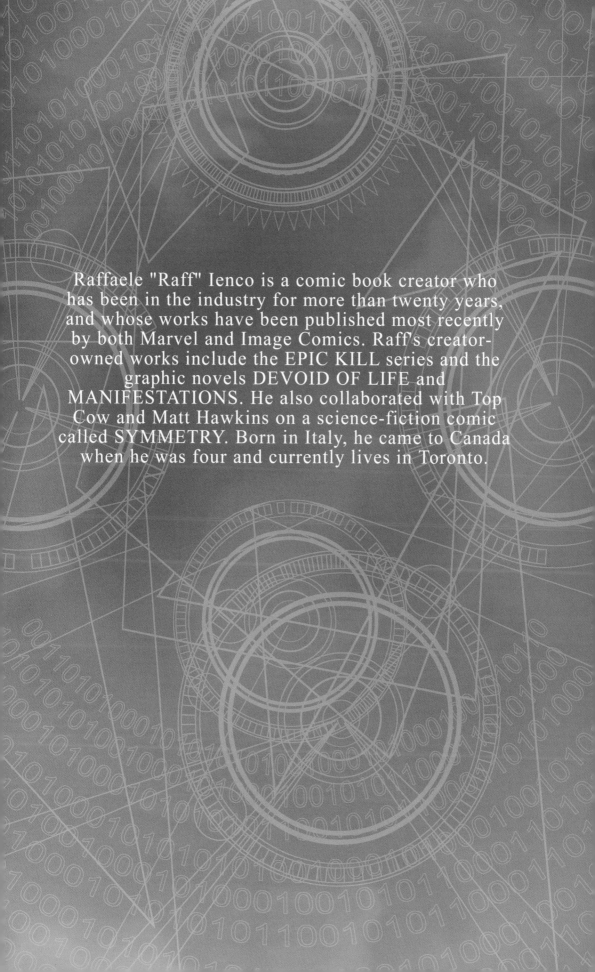

Raffaele "Raff" Ienco is a comic book creator who has been in the industry for more than twenty years, and whose works have been published most recently by both Marvel and Image Comics. Raff's creator-owned works include the EPIC KILL series and the graphic novels DEVOID OF LIFE and MANIFESTATIONS. He also collaborated with Top Cow and Matt Hawkins on a science-fiction comic called SYMMETRY. Born in Italy, he came to Canada when he was four and currently lives in Toronto.

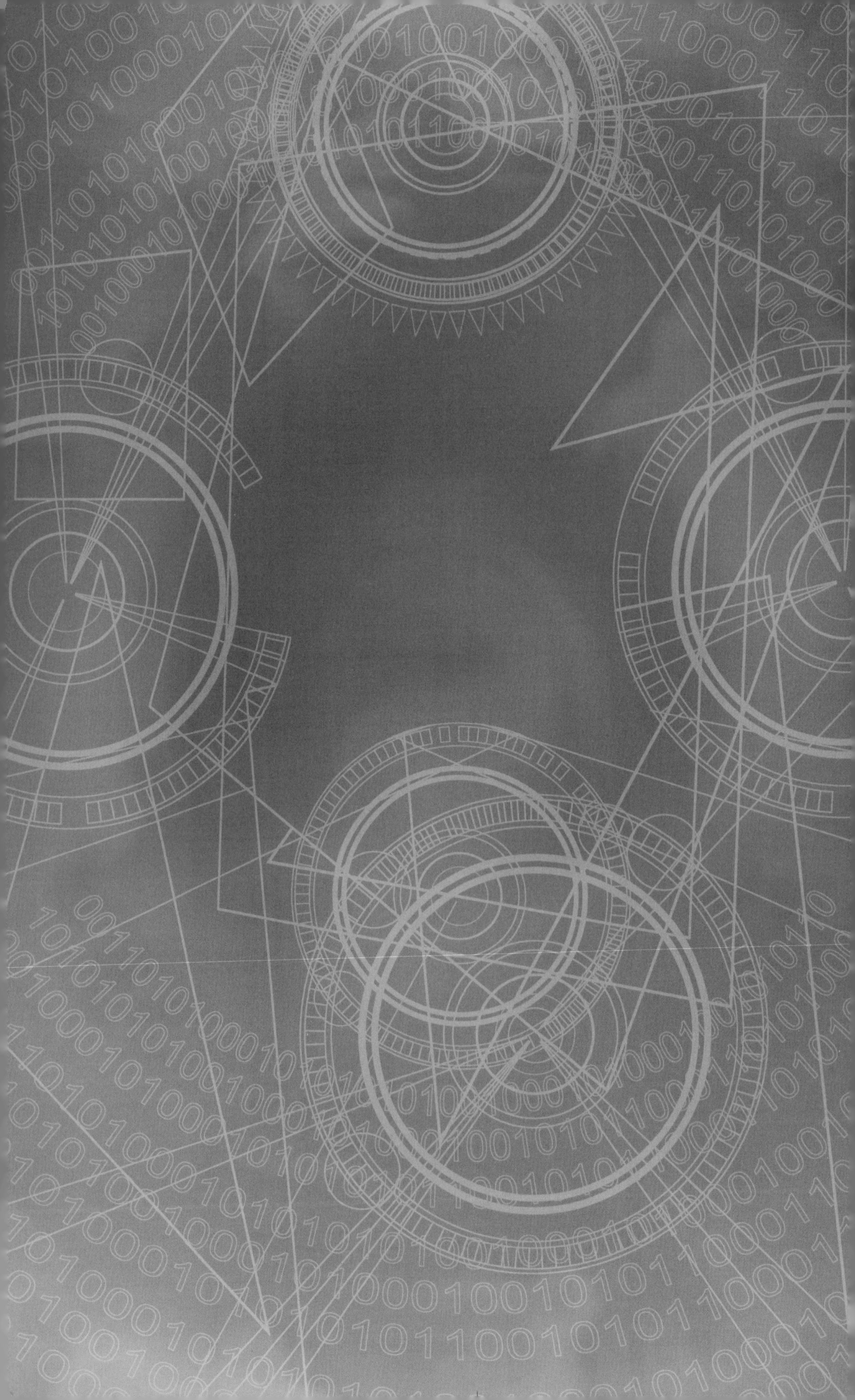

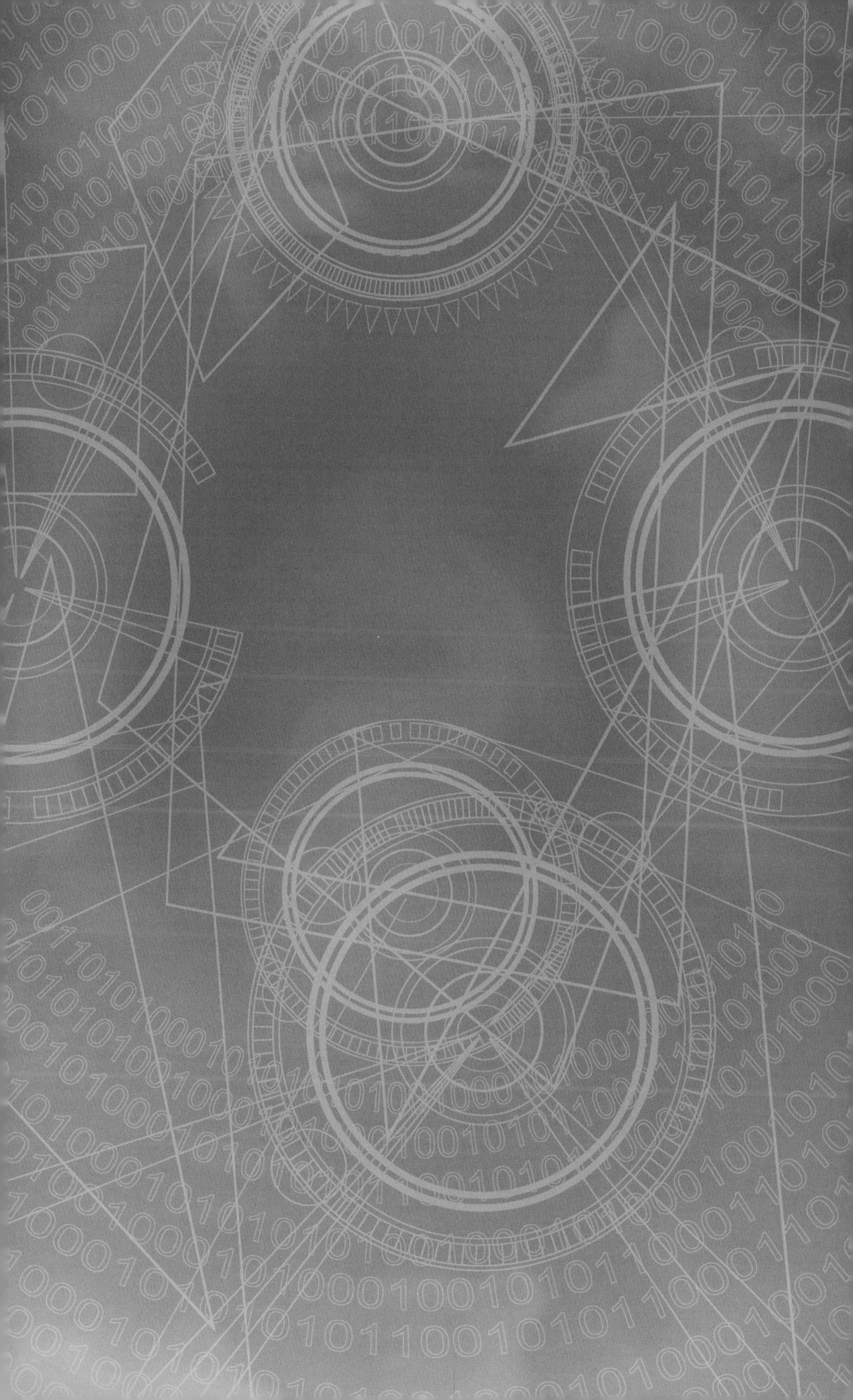

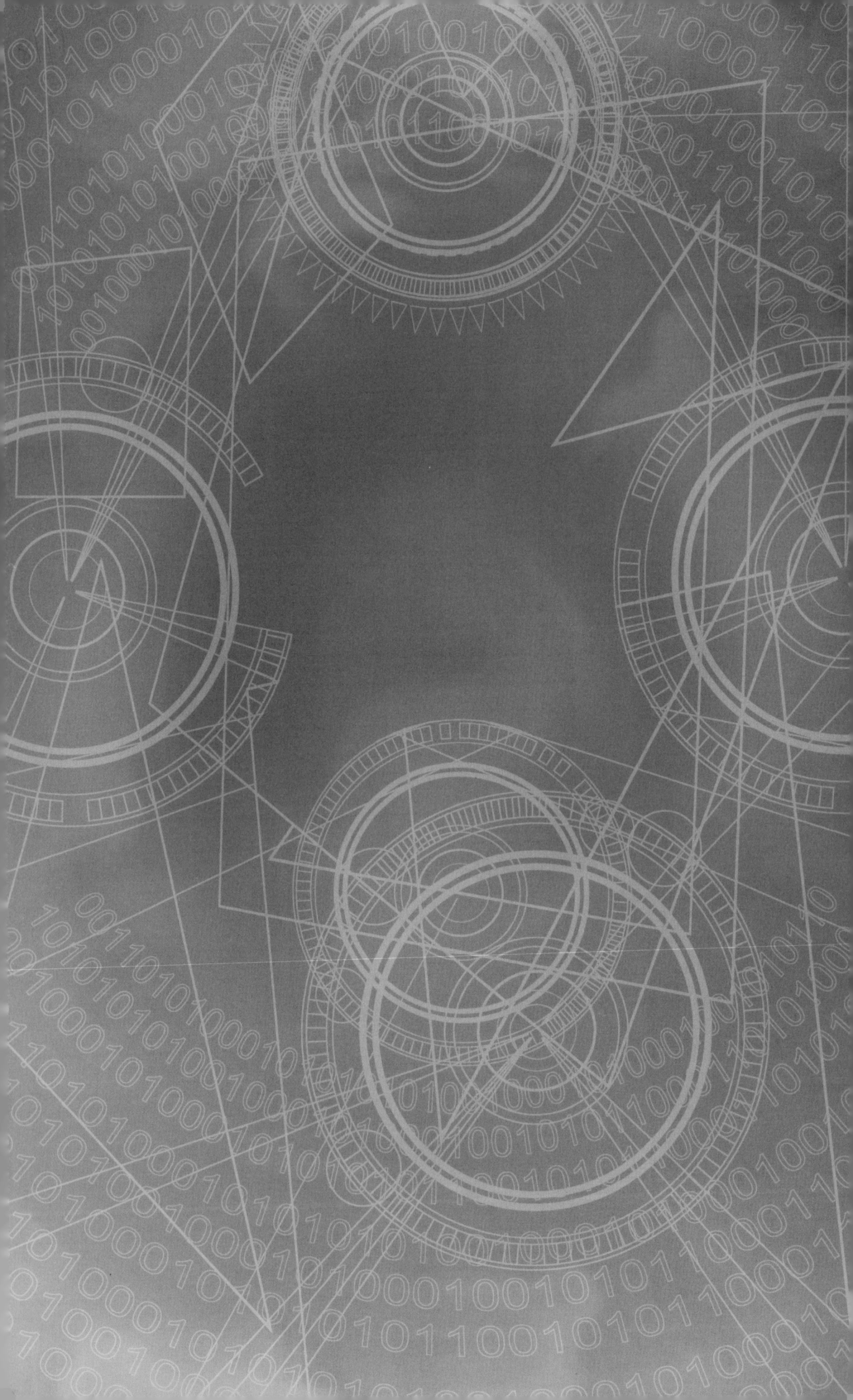